"BREATHTAKING . . . THE SEASON'S PAGE TURNER"
Winter Haven News Chief

MAGNOLIA DREAMS

"Are you ever afraid, Laurie?"

"Afraid? Of what?"

"Oh, I don't know. Of what lies ahead . . . the unknown. Whatever will be your destiny." Charlee's voice slowed as she drifted off. "I fear my life won't be serene, Laurie. Whenever I try to picture my future, it seems dark and cloudy . . ."

Long after Charlotte had fallen asleep, Lauren lay awake brooding over her cousin's words. Would she ever know who Charlee really was, she wondered. Whatever had happened to her warm, funny, wild and impetuous cousin—the one who knew just where she was heading? Who was this timorous girl who worried about dark holes and hats on the bed? And which one of them was the real Charlee?

"A SUPERB STORYTELLER WHO SUCCEEDS IN HOLDING HER READERS GLUED TO THE PAGE"
West Co

"REMINISCENT O
REC
L

"WITH S
THIS NOVEL IS SURE TO BE SEEN ON MANY A PATIO OR BEACH"
Booklist

MAGNOLIA DREAMS

HARRIET SEGAL

(Published in Hardcover As
Shadow Mountain)

All of the characters in this book are fictitious and any resemblance to actual persons living or dead is purely coincidental. All places and events are fictitious, or are used in a fictional manner. Randolph Springs and Oakland Hills are imaginary, as are Strickland Hospital, the Russell Clinic, Booker T. Washington Hospital, and Mission Hospital. None of these is based on or meant to represent any actual place or institution.

AVON BOOKS
A division of
The Hearst Corporation
1350 Avenue of the Americas
New York, New York 10019

Published by arrangement with Donald I. Fine, Inc.
Library of Congress Catalog Card Number: 89-46038
ISBN: 0-380-71457-4

First Avon Books Printing: May 1992

Printed in the U.S.A.

RA 10 9 8 7 6 5 4 3 2 1

For Sheldon
with all my love
and
In loving memory of my mother
Madeline Schas Feinberg

Author's Note

I gratefully acknowledge the assistance of these generous people:

In Asheville, N.C.—Bob Terrell, Asheville *Citizen-Times;* Douglas Swaim, The Historic Resources Commission of Asheville and Buncombe County; Edward Epstein, Asheville Public Library; Catherine Cecil, Carolina Day School; and especially my cousin, the late Mildred G. Gordon, whose interest and helpfulness meant so much.

At the University of North Carolina at Chapel Hill—H.G. Jones, Wilson Library; David Williamson, UNC News Bureau; Martha Thomas, School of Medicine, Division of Orthopaedic Surgery; and particularly, R. Beverly Raney, M.D., former chairman of the Division of Orthopaedic Surgery, whose long career as a leader in orthopedic practice proved fascinating and inspirational.

At Duke University Medical Center in Durham—Professor James Gifford, Historian; and particular thanks to Lenox D. Baker, M.D., former chairman of the Division of Orthopaedics, a pioneer in his field, whose reflections on his career and essays on the early days of orthopedic surgery at Duke were extremely valuable.

Also, Valerie Johnson, National Medical Association; Robert Fort, Norfolk Southern Corporation; Louise Janelle, Rocky Mount Historical Society; and Jane Peterson, Cape Fear Coast Convention & Visitors Bureau.

And special thanks to these friends for sharing their knowledge with me: Craig Smith, Charles A. Cooper, George M. Langford, Sylvia Langford, and Allan G. Rosenfield, M.D.

As always, my greatest support and inspiration came from my husband, Sheldon, and my daughters, Amy, Jennifer, and Laura.

Harriet Segal
December 1989

Prologue

August 1943

LAUREN AWAKENED THAT morning, instinctively reaching out for David. As always, the realization that he was not lying in bed next to her filled her with an aching loneliness.

The night before, she had tried in vain to contact him at Camp Shanks, the embarkation point on the Hudson River. For a military post, the personnel were unbelievably disorganized, first claiming he had transferred to Massachusetts with his hospital unit, then, that he had left for another staging area. Finally, long after midnight, she had convinced a bored desk sergeant that her husband was still at the base, but David had not answered the page.

Surely he would be in his quarters this morning, she told herself, picking up the telephone. Her hands trembled as she grasped the receiver. *Please let him be there. Please!*

Waiting for the connection, a terrible possibility occurred to her. *What if there had been a change in his orders—What if he had already shipped out!* She banished the thought from her mind, convinced that David would have found a way to let her know.

''Captain Bernard has signed out of the base on furlough,'' the military switchboard attendant reported.

Furlough! Did that mean he was on his way home? But—he had said it would not be until the beginning of next week . . . When the long distance operator came back on the line, Lauren hesitated only a second before asking to be connected to an unlisted private number in New York City.

She tried to quell her anxiety as she heard the phone ringing in Charlotte's Park Avenue apartment.

"Good morning, Fields residence." It was the new Irish girl. In the days before the war, Lauren knew the inexperienced maid would never have been employed in that household; but shortly after Pearl Harbor, the butler and most of the staff had departed for better-paying defense jobs. It probably would not have occurred to Charlee to do without servants.

"Is Mrs. Fields at home, Mairie? It's her cousin calling from Chapel Hill."

"She said I'm not to disturb her, ma'am," Mairie answered in her timid brogue. "Can she call you later?"

"No! I must speak to her *now,* it's important," Lauren snapped, directing all her frustration toward the hapless young woman.

While she waited for Charlotte to come to the telephone, Lauren questioned again why she had not heard from David. Even if he was due home on leave before he went overseas, he should have kept in touch with her meantime. If only he were arriving in Chapel Hill today . . . She *needed* him! The new pediatrician had not returned her call. They said he was at the hospital, yet she hesitated to phone him there. When you were a doctor's wife, you learned not to bother a busy physician on the weekend.

Lauren was exhausted. Her blond hair hung in limp disorder and there were faint half-moons of fatigue under her violet-blue eyes. One sleepless night with a sick child could really take a toll. Mark had fallen asleep at last, after she had sat up for hours sponging him and giving him aspirin, but his temperature would not come down and he was complaining of pains in his joints. All she had to rely on was a mother's instinct, and something in her young son's face told her this was not a simple childhood fever.

She closed her eyes, wondering exactly what she expected to accomplish with this call. She was painfully aware that it was the second time lately she had telephoned her cousin with anxious questions, and although she hoped Charlee might know David's plans, she hated to ask. Somehow it dragged up all their old adolescent rivalries for Lauren to admit she was unable to reach her own husband. To reveal just how distant she had grown from him over the past seven months. As the weariness washed over her, she realized she had been on edge ever since David had been stationed in New York.

It certainly was taking Charlee long enough! Whatever could she be doing?

At that moment Charlotte's low, melodious voice came over the wire, a breathy blend of cultivated vowel sounds and muted Southern warmth, as unique as everything else about her. "Laurie, honey, is that really you? Heavens, it's practically the crack of dawn!"

Despite her agitation, Lauren was instantly soothed by the indefinable charm that had always been part of Charlotte Lee. "You're usually such an early riser, Charlee, I thought you'd be up and around by now. Sorry if I woke you."

"You didn't," her cousin replied, with an amused laugh. "I'm feeling a little sniffle coming on, so I was being lazy. The weather is positively *atrocious,* raining cats and dogs."

Lauren purposely kept her tone casual. "I was just wondering whether you might have spoken to David. They say he's not at the base."

There was a brief silence, then Charlotte said, "No, honey, I haven't heard from him in *ages.* I thought you told me he was coming home. When is it he's supposed to be leaving the country?"

"You know he can't discuss his orders, but he should be here by Monday. I suppose it can wait until then—Mark's been running a temp and I can't get the pediatrician to make a house call. With our regular man away in the service, I'd just feel better if I could talk to David."

Lauren's voice trailed off uncertainly. She could picture her tall, elegant cousin smiling tolerantly as she leaned back on a chaise longue in the luxurious penthouse. Looking at it from Charlotte's point of view, she did sound rather like a hysterical mother. Or a wife who was unable to cope without her husband.

Suddenly her fears appeared foolish. What could David possibly do from that distance, anyway, other than call the doctor at the hospital? She could do that herself! And if necessary, she would simply bundle Mark up and take him over to the clinic.

"I can try to track David down for you, Laurie," Charlotte was saying.

"No thanks, Char. That seems a bit extreme. I'm sure I'll hear from the doctor any minute. I've kept this phone tied up so long, he's probably been trying to reach me."

"Well then, Laurie, if you're absolutely certain . . ."

"Yes, I'm positive," she assured her cousin, assuming the brisk manner that had always been her cover. "Say! I'm surprised you aren't in Connecticut for the weekend."

"I haven't been using the house much lately. In fact, I've closed it—it's too expensive to keep going."

"Really?" That certainly didn't sound like Charlee, trying to save a few dollars.

"If I'm up to it later this afternoon, I may go out to visit some friends in Southampton," yawned Charlotte. "Well 'bye, Laurie. Tell Mark that Cousin Charlee sends him a big hug. And I do hope he's recovered by tomorrow."

"I'm sure he'll be fine, but I'm glad David's coming home soon. It's always worrisome when children get sick during polio season."

After she hung up, Lauren called the hospital and left another message for the pediatrician. Fighting back tears, she vowed to remain calm, but she had a sickening feeling that everything was coming apart. Her son was ill, her husband was about to go overseas . . . and there was something else.

Something too terrible to contemplate.

In the upstairs sitting room of the sumptuous duplex apartment, Charlotte's luminous hazel eyes clouded as she mulled over the conversation with Lauren. Was Mark really sick, she wondered uneasily. Laurie tended to be a worrier, but she hadn't seemed all that upset . . .

With a dismissive gesture, Charlotte stood up, wrapping the silk kimono around her slender form. Her glossy chestnut hair caught the pale morning light from the windows, as she languidly walked into the connecting bedroom.

A handsome, dark-haired man reclined on the bed with his eyes closed. She gazed appreciatively at his long, muscular body, naked under the embroidered linens. He turned as she threw off her robe and slipped in beside him.

''What took you so long?'' he murmured.

''Nothing important, darling. Just one of my committee ladies. She prattled on so, I could hardly get her off the phone.'' Charlotte nuzzled his neck. ''I have a perfectly *inspired* idea!''

''What's that?''

''Let's go up to the house in Westport for one last weekend.''

''In this weather? I thought you were catching cold.''

''It will be *marvelous,* with the storm raging around us. We'll light a fire, and be all cozy and undisturbed. Besides, I'll have my own doctor in the house, won't I?''

He smiled lazily, kissing her. ''Your very own.''

''But before we leave, I think we have time for . . .'' her lips curved tantalizingly as she whispered against his ear.

Charlee grinned with delight at the mixture of shock and excitement on his face. ''Darling David,'' she purred, arching herself against him. ''How *terribly* sweet you are. Really. The perfect Southern gentleman.''

Book I

Randolph Springs

1932—1936

Chapter 1

Randolph Springs, North Carolina, 1932

THE WHITE-COLUMNED MANSION stood halfway up Shadow Mountain Drive in a compound guarded by twin stone pillars. Timeless and serene, behind a screen of cypress and loblolly pines, its sun-mellowed bricks gleamed softly against the rise of rolling meadow.

Lauren loved the house, almost with the pride of ownership. As a child, she had delighted in exploring its many parlors, its annexes and hidden alcoves. From every room there was a commanding view of the surrounding Blue Ridge Mountains. The shelves of the library were jammed with books it would take her a lifetime to read. There were two pianos—a baby grand in the living room and a full concert grand, painted antique white, in the music room.

Uncle Max had bought the house in 1910, when he discovered the spectacular scenery and healthful mountain air of western North Carolina. Impressed with the great homes built by men of wealth from the North—men like George W. Vanderbilt and Hayes Randolph, for whose family Randolph Springs was named—Max Mortimer had intended to use the estate as a summer place. Even now, after all these years, he was attached to his native Georgia. His family was a distinguished clan of German Jews from Atlanta—part of the bedrock of that city, having lived there since it was a railroad stop named Marthasville. But when he married Aunt Reba, she never felt at ease living in Atlanta, and so they had returned to settle in Randolph Springs.

It was a house for dreaming.

Lauren liked nothing better than to go off by herself on one of the vine-shaded verandas crammed with gaily cushioned wicker lounges. In the rear, extending between the wings, a large flagstone terrace overlooked the gardens, where family and friends often gathered for one of the *al fresco* entertainments her aunt and uncle were forever giving. Inside, the broad front hall was dominated by a graceful circular staircase. She and Charlee used to dress up in Aunt Reba's cast-off finery and practice gliding down the stairs, pretending to be royal princesses.

Some of Lauren's happiest moments had been spent in this house. In later years, she would need only to breathe the richness of highland soil, the pungence of juniper, or the air of a Southern night, to find herself immediately transported to the place that had dominated her childhood.

Afternoon sunlight streamed through a front bedroom window, flaming Lauren's hair in a blaze of molten gold, as she helped ease the deep pink organza ballgown over Charlotte Lee's head. She stood with folded arms, grinning at her cousin's impatience, while Miss Odile adjusted and pinned the bouffant skirt with tiny sprigs of mulberry-rose ribbon.

Charlee held herself with a boyish, athletic grace, tossing the long fall of her rich chestnut-colored hair over one shoulder. "Well, Laurie, what do you think?"

"I think it might look a lot better if you took off the riding boots!"

"She's right, Miz Charlotte," murmured the dressmaker, a thin, pale-skinned black woman with aquiline features. "I can't measure the hem unless you wear the right shoes."

Charlotte made a face. "Oh, all right." Leaning against the canopied four-poster, she raised one foot. "Here, Laurie—pull."

"And perhaps the breeches, too," suggested Miss Odile with a patient smile, when the boots had been removed.

Throwing the riding habit aside and slipping her feet

into a pair of rose silk dancing pumps, Charlotte turned in a circle. *"Now* . . . How do I look?"

Standing back to study her tall, willowy cousin, Lauren clasped her hands and nodded approvingly. "Wow, Charlee! Wait till the stagline at the horse show ball set their eyes on you."

Charlotte gave a satisfied little laugh, the corners of her smoky-ringed hazel eyes crinkling. "I do wish Aunt Mimi and Uncle Samuel would let you go to Pinehurst with me. It would be ever so much more fun if you came along."

"I know," sighed Lauren. "I'm a whole year older than you. It's hardly fair."

"My parents are really much more modern than yours, aren't they? You'd think since our mothers are sisters, they'd bring up their daughters in the same way."

Lauren felt a prick of resentment at Charlotte's implied criticism. "Mama's fifteen years older than Aunt Reba. She was really like a mother to her, raising her after our grandmother died," she reminded her cousin. "Anyway, Papa's the one who won't allow me to go. He says horse show balls are for gentiles—and besides, he thinks I'm too young to attend formal dances. I can only go to the silly old Juniors until I turn seventeen."

"Well, Lauren Jacobson, it's only two weeks until your seventeenth birthday . . ."

"I can't *wait!"*

In a family known for its good looks, Lauren's loveliness was often taken for granted. Her luxuriant blond hair, a mass of shining waves, framed a delicate, heart-shaped face and was her most outstanding feature. That, and her extraordinary violet eyes, along with a quiet demeanor and petite stature, were in sharp contrast to her tall, striking cousin, whose dark beauty and capricious energy were a source of great charm to others. And of constant concern to her doting parents.

"We're all finished with the fitting, Miz Charlotte," said the dressmaker, helping her step out of the gown and carefully carrying it away.

Charlee ran a brush through her hair and scrambled into her breeches. Pulling on the boots, she glanced at the clock. "Good Lord, I have to hurry! I promised Perry Nathan I'd go riding with him at four o'clock, and it's ten past."

Lauren followed her cousin as she clattered down the stairs and out across the veranda. With an exultant cry, Charlotte swung around, throwing her head back and spreading her arms wide. "What a glorious afternoon! Just *look* at that sky, Laurie—not a cloud in sight. This is *my* kind of day!"

"It's a 'Charlee day,' all right." Lauren smiled at their old childhood joke, thinking there were times when her cousin did indeed seem to command the elements.

"Where *is* Bertram with that car?" Charlotte demanded imperiously. "He can drive you home after he drops me at the stables."

"No thanks, Charlee. Phil should be coming for me any minute." No sooner had Lauren spoken than she caught sight of her brother steering their father's Packard up the long winding driveway. "Here he is now."

Charlotte immediately ran down the front steps where the automobile stopped under a porte cochere. She leaned her elbows on the rim of the open window, giving the handsome tawny-haired young man at the wheel a sidelong glance. "Hel-lo, Philip. And how did you manage to get away from the Liberty Department Store before closing time?" Charlee wriggled her aristocratic nose as she brushed her lips against his cheek.

"Had some errands to run, and a sister to retrieve," said Philip, winking at Lauren while ruffling Charlotte's hair. "Going riding, youngster?"

"Uh-huh." Charlotte favored him with a coquettish grin. "I have a date."

"Lucky boy, whoever he is. Whattaya say, Laurie, shall we get going?" Lauren climbed into the passenger seat.

" 'Bye, Laurie. Don't forget the Juniors tomorrow night. I'm counting on you to distract Perry. I have my eye on that boy from Tulane who's visiting the Majorses."

"I thought he was going out with Marcia."

Her cousin's merry laughter lit the air. "All's fair in love, Laurie!"

"Charlee—you're hopeless."

With a good-bye wave, they were off. As soon as they were out of earshot, Philip said, "That is the most precocious girl I've ever known! I could swear she was flirting with me, and I'm her cousin."

"She *was* flirting with you. Charlee's always had a crush on you, Phil. When she was ten and you were sixteen, she told me she was going to marry you."

Philip snorted. "Are you kidding?"

"No, really. When I explained that you two couldn't be married because you were cousins, she said that Mama and Papa were cousins and *they* got married, so that meant she could marry you."

Philip laughed. "Leave it to Charlee. Never at a loss for an answer, even when she was ten." His greenish blue eyes softened with sympathy as he glanced over at his sister. "So. She's off to the dance at Pinehurst next weekend and Pa won't let you go."

Lauren plucked at her skirt. "Yes, but it doesn't matter. I wouldn't have enjoyed tagging along. Ever since Charlee started showing horses, I've felt like an extra foot."

"I understand," he said kindly. "You probably won't believe me, Laurie, but I know that you're going to turn into a more fantastic woman than Charlotte Lee Mortimer can ever hope to become." He noted her glum expression. "It's not just those fabulous golden curls of yours, or the huge pools of your lavender blue eyes I'm talking about, either—" Lauren giggled at his overblown prose. "That's better. I was afraid you'd forgotten how to smile."

"Oh, Phil," she sighed, "sometimes I feel like I'm second-best. Whenever Charlee's around, the boys don't look at anyone else. I never thought I was the type to care about those things, but that's what everyone seems to think is important."

"You have nothing to worry about, Laurie," said Phil as he pulled into the driveway of their parents' gray gabled frame house on Lenoir Avenue. "Just as soon as Pa lets you go out on dates, you'll have plenty of beaux. You're a much more interesting person than Charlee is, and I'm not saying that because I'm your brother. Hell, I can never find anything to talk about with her."

"Philip . . . I suspect that the boys aren't really interested in *talking* to Charlee."

The delicious aroma of baking bread greeted them as they entered the kitchen door. There was a comforting feeling about the Jacobson house, as if everyone in it was well loved. It had been their grandfather's until he died and Mama had lived here all her life. Of course, it couldn't begin to compare with the Mortimer estate, thought Lauren. No more than she could compare to Charlotte Lee!

In Lauren's opinion, her own blond prettiness appeared insipid next to her cousin's compelling dark looks. At times she longed to be more like Charlee, to attract men the way she did. And to live in the beautiful house on Shadow Mountain Drive. But if there was one quality Lauren most admired about Charlotte, it was her *sureness*—that absolute conviction about who she was and what she wanted. In contrast, Lauren felt herself to be tentative and uncertain.

How she envied the way her cousin could stand up for her rights. She would give anything to possess that kind of spirit. Charlee, whose current fascination was with college men, thought nothing of defying her father. Just the other day, she had stormed onto the veranda where Lauren was reading. "You won't believe what Daddy did! I met this boy from Duke at the Shadow Mountain Club picnic, and he called to ask me out. Daddy answered the phone and spoiled it by telling him I was only fifteen!"

"Well . . . you *are* fifteen."

Fitfully, she had thrown herself into a swing, giving Lauren a look of annoyance. "I'm *almost* sixteen, Laurie—and most people think I'm a lot older."

Lauren tried to cajole her out of her bad mood. "So, will you be able to go out with the boy from Duke?"

Charlee's smile was mischievous as she scrunched her shoulders. "I already sneaked out with him after the last Juniors dance."

"You didn't! Did Uncle Max find out?"

"Of course not. Daddy thinks nothing could possibly go wrong at the Juniors." Glancing at Lauren out of the corner of her eye, Charlotte's smile had been full of intrigue. "Do you want to know what happened?"

This was the Charlee she could never resist. "Yes, tell me!"

Eyes crinkling, Charlotte bent forward and whispered, "He soul-kissed me."

"You're kidding! You mean he—"

"Put his tongue right in my mouth!"

"Oh, I don't believe it! What was it *like?*"

"It felt nice actually . . . not at all the way you would think. At first, he just did it a little bit. And then, when he saw I wasn't getting mad or anything, he put it all the way in."

Lauren gasped, clapping her hands over her mouth. "Oh, Charlee!"

Charlotte giggled. "I always thought it sounded kind of icky—I mean, the idea of someone else's tongue. But, I tell you, Laurie, I *liked* it. I really did."

"Well, I guess if you enjoyed it," said Lauren dubiously.

"That's not all he did . . ."

"What do you mean?" Lauren stared at her, round-eyed.

Charlotte quickly glanced over her shoulder, but no one was in sight. "He put his hand on me. Here—" She pointed to her breast. "He tried to undo my bra, but of course, I wouldn't let him." She leaned back, chortling. "Lord, you should have seen how worked up he got! I thought he was going to blow a gasket."

"Charlee!"

Charlotte gave one of her delicious laughs. "If you could see how shocked you look, Laurie!"

"Mama says boys lose their respect for girls who let them 'take liberties.' "

"Yes," Charlotte replied negligently. "So does my mama." She looked at Lauren through lowered lashes. "I tell you, Laurie, I think it's a conspiracy. They just want to keep us from knowing how good it feels."

* * *

Lauren had to prevent herself from taking the lead from Perry Nathan on Saturday evening, as they two-stepped to the slow waltz rhythm of "Somewhere I'll Find You." Charlee's rejects always seemed to end up dancing with her . . . half the time, she suspected they hung around just to be near her cousin. If there was a circle of fawning young men at a Juniors dance, you could be sure that dazzling, fun-loving Charlotte Lee Mortimer with her low, throaty drawl was at its center.

As Lauren circled the dance floor with Perry, she wondered what Uncle Max would have to say if he knew Charlee had gone necking with some of the boys she met at these carefully arranged gatherings. By now the Juniors were an institution, a series of tea dances and evening parties for the purpose of "getting the young people to know one another." Under the watchful eyes of Aunt Reba and the other mothers, Jewish boys and girls from the mountain-locked towns in the Carolinas came together once a month to socialize. This year's dances were unpretentious little affairs because nearly everyone in Swannanoa County had lost their money in the land bust.

Over Perry's shoulder, Lauren observed Charlotte dancing with the visitor from Tulane. She was giving him what Lauren called the "sparkling Charlee treatment"—a way she had of leaning back while slanting her hips and shoulders, then doing something absolutely marvelous with her eyes. It never failed to captivate a young man. Lauren had tried practicing this mannerism in the mirror, but she had looked perfectly ridiculous. Anyone would, except Charlee.

"Your cousin sure is the life of the party, isn't she?" whined Perry, in his hopeless mountain-boy twang.

Two boys were closing in on Mr. Tulane, and the three of them formed a little semicircle around Charlotte, who stood laughing and sparkling at them, shrugging her shoulders and swaying her slim hips while the interlopers made a joke of tossing a coin to see who would get to cut in. With a sportsmanlike smile, the loser walked away, while the one from Tulane surveyed the dance floor and—Lauren caught her breath—headed directly toward them.

He tapped her partner on the shoulder. "May I?" He was a much better dancer than Perry, expertly guiding her into a foxtrot. "My name is Alex Kessel."

She smiled at him shyly. "I'm Lauren Jacobson."

"Yes, I know. I've been wanting to meet you all evening."

Charlee would have known exactly what to say, but all Lauren could do was smile and wonder why, if that was true, it had taken him so long to ask her to dance.

"I hear you like New Orleans jazz."

Now, who could have told him that? "Yes, I love it!" Actually, she preferred classical music.

"And I understand you play the piano."

"How do you know so much about me, Alex? We've never met."

"I'm Sandy Majors's cousin. I asked him about you."

"Oh, I see." Sandy had invited her to his high school junior prom last May, but when her father wouldn't allow her to go, he had never called again.

"I like to fool around with the banjo," Alex was saying. "How would you like to get together sometime this week and, uh, make some music?"

"Well, maybe . . ." Papa probably wouldn't let her do that, either.

"I'll give you a call," he promised. And then he danced with her until the party was over.

On the way home, Charlotte seemed peculiarly silent in the rear of the big silver Marmon sedan, driven by Bertram, the dignified black man who served as the Mortimers' butler and chauffeur. "It was a good dance, wasn't it, Charlee?" said Lauren, who was sleeping over at her cousin's house, as she often did on Saturday nights after the Juniors.

"It was all right." Charlotte irritably kicked her foot against the seat in front of her. "I'm getting rather *bored* with the Juniors, the same old faces."

Lauren didn't answer. She sensed one of Charlee's moods coming on.

After a silence, Charlotte said, "I saw you dancing with Alex Kessel."

"Yes, Charlee, we danced a little."

"What did you talk about?"

"Music mostly. Sandy told him I liked Dixieland."

"Oh. Did he say he would call you?"

"No," she lied. How strange, she thought; if she didn't know better, she would suspect Charlee was acting almost jealous. But that was silly! What possible reason had Charlee to be jealous of *her?* "Even if he should ask me out, you know Papa won't let me go."

"Well, it would certainly make no difference to me if he did." Suddenly in better humor, Charlotte tossed her head and laughed—that wonderful, infectious chuckle. "I'll tell you a secret, Laurie. There's nothing so special about college boys, except they're a little older."

The following Friday afternoon, Lauren smiled to herself as she measured the pencil marks on the inside of her closet door. That made three inches in a year! In only one more week she would be seventeen, and she was growing at last.

Turning sideways she studied her reflection in the mirror with an appraising eye. Her breasts were a bit small. Wouldn't you know, just as bosoms were coming back into style. She did have a good complexion, though, and people were always remarking about her hair.

Outside the bedroom window, she could hear her mother talking to the vegetable man, reminding her that it was much too nice a day to be dawdling indoors. Snatching a blue cloth-bound notebook from the nightstand, Lauren ran downstairs to the porch swing and opened her journal.

Engrossed in her writing, she suddenly became aware of a feminine voice fluttering across the front lawn, "Hey, you-all!"

Looking up, she waved to Nancy Miller who was walking hand-in-hand with her latest admirer. Lauren pretended to be absorbed in her journal until they passed, and then lifted her head to watch the pair swing down the hill. She could imagine Samuel Jacobson's disapproval if his daughter ever went walking with a boy like that, holding hands for all the neighbors to see. I've never even had a beau, she thought indignantly. Charlee has tons more experience with boys than I do.

Lauren stifled her irritation. She didn't know why exactly, but she was often fractious lately. Her parents were intolerant of moods, so she had to be careful when she was cross. Yesterday, for example, after seeing Charlee off, she had felt out of sorts at the dinner table. "If you can't be civil, young lady, you may go to your room," Samuel had declared in that tone no one dared disobey. Practically seventeen, and ordered to go to her room! Somehow, writing in her journal helped to vent her feelings.

Randolph Springs was dull as doornails with Charlee away in Pinehurst competing in the horse show. They used to ride together until her cousin had taken up jumping, which Lauren quit after a bad fall. Nothing seemed to daunt the intrepid Charlotte, however, whose daredevil antics on horseback or the high diving board drew all sorts of attention.

As long as Lauren could remember, she and Charlee had been as close as sisters. They spent so much time together, it was probably healthy that they were developing different interests and new friends lately. After all, they were almost adults and it was time for them to learn to stand alone.

She loved her cousin more than anyone in the world—well, aside from her parents and Philip, of course. Charlee was certainly the most important person in her life. And yet, there were times when she felt . . . not exactly angry, but just the slightest bit resentful of her.

Lauren knew that she was smarter than Charlee, who disliked studying, rarely read a book, and cared only for popular music, but it had become her habit to place herself in the background. Long ago, she had learned to defer to her cousin and to play down her own accomplishments. They seemed to get along better that way. It always surprised her that Charlotte should mind when she outshined her at school or took the lead in the class play, because in almost every realm of endeavor that mattered, Charlee clearly led the field.

The girls at school, some of them anyway, were jealous, envying not only Charlee's beauty, but her family's wealth. Lauren had overheard one of the Parkinson twins, known for her acid tongue, saying "Just because she looks like a blueblood, Charlotte Mortimer thinks she's such hot stuff. Her father may be rich, but he's still a Jew!"

The Mortimers were, in fact, the town's richest family, aside from the Randolphs. Uncle Max's fortune had amply increased over the years. Scarcely touched by the stock market crash, he owned vast tracts of forest, a lumber mill, a furniture factory, and his paper empire had become the largest supplier of newsprint in the South. Charlee had inherited her competitive nature from her father, who was a civic leader and served on every important board in the county. Max worked hard at being an outstanding member of the community at large. Of course, he supported Jewish causes, as well—the more conspicuous, the better. As Papa had once remarked, "Hayes Randolph gave the town an Episcopal church, so naturally, Max felt compelled to build us a temple."

Although Lauren's parents had never known anything near the wealth of the Mortimers, they had been comfortable enough until the depression. If only her father had followed Uncle Max's advice! "Get out of real estate, Samuel, while you can," Max had urged his brother-in-law at the height of the boom. "These prices won't hold much longer." But Papa, who was stubborn, would say, "Max is still a Georgia boy at heart. He doesn't understand the mountains, doesn't have faith in our economy."

Samuel had held on too long and ended up like everyone else in the bust, with worthless paper—options and deeds to useless properties. Luckily, the mortgages on their house and The Liberty Store had been paid off, but when the local banks failed in 1930, the Jacobsons had lost most of their life's savings.

Miriam and Samuel weren't even bitter about their losses, especially since so many of their friends had been completely ruined. They had known far more serious tragedies in their lifetime . . . losing two children in infancy . . . their eldest son killed in France in the battle of the Meuse-Argonne. Joel, whom Lauren couldn't remember, was supposed to have been the handsomest and brightest of all the Jacobson children. *If only Joel had lived . . .* How many times had she heard that throughout her childhood?

Everyone in her family seemed to have some sort of problem! Poor Phil—his hopes for studying law had gone out the window with the crash. After graduating from Randolph College last year, he had planned to leave for Chapel Hill this fall. Even though she had not looked forward to his departure, Lauren shared her brother's disappointment. She knew how much Philip hated living at home and working in the family business—

"Laurie," Miriam Jacobson called from the kitchen, interrupting her thoughts. "The men will be home soon, dear. Please come help me get supper."

"In a minute, Mama," she answered, running up to her room to put her journal away.

Her mother was setting out cold meat and salads when Lauren came downstairs. Pansy had taken the day off and no one felt like eating a heavy meal in this warm weather. "Your father called to say Uncle Abe and Aunt Jean are coming for dinner," said Miriam, hardly pausing as she removed platters from the ice box. "Slice some rye bread, dear, and see if there's enough cake and fruit compote for dessert."

They hurried back and forth between pantry and dining room, adding extra place settings to the table, slicing more meat and salad vegetables for the platters, and making another pitcher of iced tea. Miriam appeared crisp and cool, wearing an apron over her blue and white cotton house dress. She was a handsomely attractive woman and had kept her trim figure, despite seven pregnancies. Her gray-streaked brown hair was pinned back in a neat bun and her blue eyes held their usual serenity. In the heat of the kitchen, she appeared unruffled, in fact delighted at the prospect of last-minute company.

"Mama, do you think I'll ever be contented like you?" Lauren asked impetuously.

Miriam gave her a look of surprise. "Why, of course you will, dear. After you graduate high school and find the man you're going to marry."

Something about the way her mother said it, as if her entire future was foreordained, caused a chill to run through Lauren. I *don't want* to spend my life this way, she thought—planning meals, waiting all day for my husband, and living vicariously through my children. But what else was a woman supposed to do?

The men arrived home from the store, parking the car in the driveway and coming in through the kitchen entrance. Philip immediately went up to bathe and change into fresh clothing before supper, as if he wanted to wash away everything to do with The Liberty and its vulgar clientele.

When Lauren and Charlee were children, it had been a treat for them to visit the store. They would play hide and seek between the racks of flannel shirts and overalls, try on open-toed sandals from the square counters, and climb the stairs to the balcony to talk to the cashier in her iron mesh cage, with its humming pneumatic tubes. Leaning over the railing, they used to spy on the weathered, tobacco-chewing farmers buying work clothes and boots. In those days, Lauren thought it would be thrilling to help out in the store like her brothers, Lionel and Philip, but her parents would not hear of it. "It's no place for a little lady," her father would say. Uncle Abe had been less delicate. "You don't want to be around all those yokels and *shvahtsas,* honey."

After washing his hands at the pantry sink, Samuel sat in the kitchen, talking to the women. He was a large, square-shouldered man with ash blond hair and fair skin, ruggedly handsome, especially when he smiled. He had fallen in love with Miriam on the day he had arrived in Randolph Springs forty years ago, a young greenhorn fresh from Russia, still mourning his parents. Trudging up the stone walk behind Miriam's father—who was his own father's first cousin—he had seen a tall, dark-haired girl waiting for them on the front porch. Almost five years later to the day, they had been married.

"What did you do today, Laurie?" he asked, kissing his youngest child on the cheek and embracing her, then pulling away and patting her shoulder.

When she was little, she used to hold up her arms and beg, "Make a lap, Papa," and he would sit down to take her on his knee, hugging and kissing her again and again. But he was awkward with her now. Once his daughters began to mature physically, blooming Venuses with breasts and hips and secrets of the flesh, Samuel became intimidated by them. The boys presented no such threat, and he had developed a man-to-man closeness to both Lionel and Philip.

Out in the hall, the telephone rang. Philip raced down the stairs to answer it. "It's for you, Laurie," he said, coming into the kitchen and giving her a knowing smile. "Someone by the name of Alex Kessel."

Lauren could feel herself blush. "That's Sandy Majors's cousin from New Orleans who's visiting in town. I met him at the dance last week." She looked at her mother beseechingly. "He's going to ask me out, Mama. What shall I tell him?"

Samuel began to speak, but his wife put her hand on his shoulder. "She'll be seventeen in a week, Samuel. Don't you think she's old enough to go out with a nice young man?"

Lauren held her breath. Her father was looking so serious; but then he smiled. "I hate to see the baby of the family grow up, but Mama is right. You may go, Laurie."

"Ohh—thank you, Papa!" She hugged her father and ran to get the phone.

After a few minutes of chatting, Alex said, "Tomorrow's my last night in Randolph Springs, Lauren. If you're not already busy, will you come to the JCC supper dance at the Shadow Mountain Club?"

"I just happen to be free, Alex . . ." If he only knew—*all* of her Saturday nights were "free." When they hung up, she floated to the dinner table. Tomorrow night she would be going out on her first date!

Before they sat down, Miriam lit the Sabbath candles. All through the meal, it was impossible for Lauren to keep from smiling. Philip gave her funny, meaningful glances, but he didn't tease, thank goodness. She found herself laughing at every little amusing comment anyone made, and she realized she was "sparkling" in her own way. Maybe that was Charlee's secret; just being happy and knowing you had something to look forward to.

When dinner was over, they sat out on the porch talking until it was time to go to bed. All the old homes on Lenoir Avenue were set back from the street, framed in wide porches that served as gathering places for families. Children scampered on lawns, catching fireflies and playing tag. The young people clustered on steps or strolled along the tree-lined boulevard, stopping to chat with neighbors, while the older folks gossiped in porch swings and rockers.

To Lauren, summer evenings in Randolph seemed to embrace the romance of the mountains, and she found something reassuring in the sameness of the nightly routine. There was strength and peace in the circle of kinfolk and friends. The night chorus of crickets and katydids filled the darkness, as the orange sunset, framed by the rim of surrounding peaks, quickly turned to purple dusk, soon giving way to indigo skies of star-filled clarity.

At midnight when everyone slept, the mountains became shrouded in silvery mist. Sitting at her window in the silent house, Lauren gazed out at the ghostly veiled summits, dreaming about the world beyond Randolph Springs.

Chapter 2

PANSY KNOCKED, ENTERING the bedroom with grave dignity. "You have a caller, Miz Laurie."

"Thank you, Pansy." Their eyes met and Pansy quickly shut the door as they clasped each other, dissolving in peals of laughter.

"I declare," said Pansy, wiping her eyes, "I can't believe my baby is goin' dancin' with a gentleman. He's mighty fine lookin', all slicked up."

"I'm so nervous, Pansy. Do I look all right?" Lauren inquired anxiously of the sweet-faced black woman who had once been her nursemaid and had stayed on with them as housekeeper.

"Just beautiful, honey. You've always been pretty as a picture, ever since you was born." Pansy adjusted the collar of Lauren's new blue dress, purchased that afternoon at the Paris Shop on Randolph Square. "I'll tell your young man you'll be down directly. He's talkin' with your parents in the livin' room."

"Poor boy, Papa's probably putting him through the third degree."'

Lauren felt perfectly ridiculous sitting there watching the second hand go around on the clock, when she had been ready for half an hour. Charlee always said you should keep a boy waiting at least five minutes; otherwise, he'd think you were too eager to go out with him. Alex sprang to his feet when she walked downstairs to the living room, and so did her father. Samuel, dressed in a three-piece suit, was an austere and impressive figure. Miriam had been sitting next to Alex on the sofa, putting him at ease.

Papa walked them to the front door. "Of course, you will see that Lauren is home by midnight."

Suddenly Alex looked more like a schoolboy than a college man. "Of—of course, sir." They were terribly silent driving to the Shadow Mountain Club in his uncle's car.

The first people they saw there were her brother Lionel and his wife Fay. "Well, if it isn't Laurie! Don't you look pretty, honey . . . And who is this fellow here with you?" Lionel shook Alex's hand heartily, "I'm Lionel Jacobson." Slapping him on the back, he said, "Come on, let me take y'all around to meet these folks."

Lionel was very hail-fellow-well-met, a great favorite of everyone, and he steered them through the room, amid curious glances and whispers that Alex would have been blind not to notice. Lauren was cringing as he was given the once-over by her married sister Joanna and her women friends. It took forever to escape and reach their table, and then they had to go through the whole process again, with Alex's aunt and uncle and their party. She sighed, thinking this wasn't exactly how she had envisioned her first date.

When they were dancing, Alex said, "I thought *I* had a lot of relatives. Is there anyone in this room you're not related to?" But he said it with good humor.

Philip arrived later on, alone. Nancy Miller was there with her beau, and Lauren noticed her making a play for Phil. Lauren wondered why he didn't have a girl. Philip was so attractive and eligible, it would seem any female in town would want to go out with him.

Phil walked over to them. "Am I permitted to dance with my sister?"

"Why didn't you bring a date tonight?" she asked when they were on the dance floor.

"Who would you suggest? There's not a soul around here I want to go out with," he said with bitterness. Lauren wondered at the fleeting expression of unhappiness on his handsome face, and then it passed.

Because of Lauren's curfew, they had to leave the dance

before it ended. As they drove home, she wondered whether Alex would kiss her good night. Charlee said boys always tried, but you shouldn't let them on a first date, unless it was someone you really liked. She couldn't say whether or not she liked Alex, at least in that way. She knew him no better at the end of this evening than she had last week when they'd first met. Surrounded as they were with other people all night, they'd scarcely had a conversation.

When they reached Lenoir Avenue, her house was lit up like City Hall. Lamps were shining from every window, and all the porch lights were on. Fat chance he'd try to kiss her. It was so bright, it could have been high noon!

Alex parked the car under a big elm tree that gave them a little shadow. "Well, I hope you had a good time, Laurie."

"It was a lot of fun, Alex." Her eyes sparkled with humor. "I'm sorry so many of my relatives were there."

He laughed easily. "I've been through worse. They were all nice, and they certainly do think a lot of you."

"We're a close family, but sometimes it gets a little overpowering."

He looked at his watch. "I'll be in trouble if I don't take you in now. It's five minutes past twelve."

He came around to help her out of the car and walked her to the door. "Do you think maybe you'll get to New Orleans sometime?"

"I've never been there, but I'd like to go."

"We never did get together to play jazz, did we?"

"No. We didn't."

"Well . . . I might come back to Randolph next summer . . ."

"That would be nice."

And then he did something she wasn't quite sure how to interpret. He reached out and patted her on the head. Like you would a child. But then, his hand lingered, and he ran it through her hair wonderingly. "It's so beautiful," he whispered. They looked into each other's eyes and he slowly bent down until his lips were touching hers . . . and she was actually being kissed.

They sprang apart as the door opened behind them. Her mother was standing there, completely dressed, as if it were the shank of the evening instead of after midnight. "Oh, it's *you*, Laurie. I thought I heard something."

Who *else* would it be, for heaven's sake! "Yes, Mama, we've been here for a few minutes. We were just talking."

"Won't you come in for a cup of coffee, Mr. Kessel?"

"No, thank you, Mrs. Jacobson." Alex had quickly recovered his equilibrium. "I'd better get along home. I leave first thing in the morning. Well, good night, Lauren . . . ma'am." He hurried down the steps. As Lauren closed the door and turned out the porch lights, she heard him drive away.

She took a deep breath. "Mama, was that necessary? For you to open the front door? I was on my way in."

Miriam's tone was mild as she picked up her knitting basket and prepared to go upstairs. "I knew you were out there, dear. I was aware when the car drove up. What I feared was that your father might also have heard it. As you know, he doesn't approve of girls lingering in automobiles with young men." She smiled at Lauren and pulled her close in a warm embrace. "I didn't mean to spoil your evening, Laurie. I hope you had a good time."

She smiled brightly, suppressing her annoyance. "Oh, yes, Mama. I had a lovely time."

On her seventeenth birthday, they were supposed to go over to Aunt Reba's after dinner for the usual Saturday-night get-together.

"Why don't you wear your new blue frock, Laurie?" her mother suggested.

"I don't feel like changing, Mama. Maybe I won't go with you tonight. I'll just stay home and read."

She should have caught a clue from Miriam's reaction. "You *have* to come along, dear! We don't want to leave you alone on your birthday. Charlotte would be disappointed and you'll hurt Aunt Reba's feelings."

"Oh, all right. But please don't make me wear the blue dress." She went to freshen up and comb her hair, then joined Miriam and Samuel who were waiting in the car.

"Why are you-all so dressed up? It's just family."

"They might have other company drop by on a Saturday night," said Miriam.

"Where's Phil?"

"He went out with some of his friends."

"I don't see why *he* can get away with that and I have to go along with you," grumbled Lauren, hurt that Philip hadn't taken her with him on her birthday.

"Now, dear, don't be disagreeable," said her mother, reaching back to pat her hand, as Samuel drove down the hill through Lenoir Park to the exclusive enclave where Max and Reba lived.

The Mortimers were the only Jewish family to own a home on Shadow Mountain. The minute the car turned into the park-like approach to the drive, a particular aroma of juniper and magnolias wafted through the open windows. Winding up the road, they passed the great houses hidden from view among cultivated gardens and shrubs. Through thick stands of evergreens came a glimpse of lights shining, and the drift of laughter and party conversation floated across well-tended lawns.

When they walked into the big parlor and everyone shouted *"Surprise!"* Lauren was at first dumbfounded, and then embarrassed.

"I almost let the cat out of the bag a dozen times, but you didn't even suspect," cried Charlee.

All their friends were there, and the cousins. Phil, that rascal, was grinning at her from the corner behind the baby grand piano. She felt foolish in her old cotton skirt and barefoot sandals while everyone was dressed-up for a party. And she had been so bitchy to her mother.

"Happy Birthday, Laurie," Miriam whispered a few minutes later, when she broke away from the circle of well-wishers.

"Thank you, Mama." Lauren hugged her. "I'm sorry I was nasty before."

"That's all right, dear. I put your blue dress and high heels upstairs, if you want to change."

When she came down, they were playing records on the phonograph in the great hall. Perry Nathan was the first to ask her to dance and Sandy Majors cut in on him. "My cousin Alex won a bet with me," said Sandy.

"What kind of bet?" she asked, feeling the color rise in her cheeks.

"I bet him he couldn't get a date with you. Or is it just me you won't go out with?"

"Sandy, I explained to you about my father."

"You mean that was the truth?"

"Well, of course it was! I couldn't go on dates until I turned seventeen."

"In that case, Miss Jacobson, will you do me the honor of attending the Fall Formal with me?"

"I'd love to, Sandy!" Realizing she would never have to make phony excuses again, Lauren could hardly wait to tell Charlee. Although she wondered whether her cousin would be entirely happy at the news.

"I hear you went out on a date with Alex Kessel, after all," Charlotte had said when she returned from the horse show.

"Well—he called at the last minute, Char, and Papa allowed me to go," she replied, feeling a strange need to make excuses. "You don't mind, do you?"

"Heavens, no! Quite frankly, I found him a bore." And suddenly, going out with Alex had seemed not nearly as exciting as Lauren had thought.

After Lady, the family cook, had served a tremendous chocolate-layer birthday cake, everyone adjourned to the big sun parlor, where Lauren opened her gifts. She untied the pink satin ribbon from a huge gift-wrapped box labeled *Bon Marché, Asheville,* and folded back the layers of tissue paper. Inside was the most heavenly blue tulle off-the-shoulder evening dress she had ever seen.

"Ohh! Thank you, Aunt Reba . . . Uncle Max." Lauren threw her arms around them. "My first long gown, and it's my favorite color, too."

Max flushed with pleasure at his niece's affection. He was a fine-looking man, with a full head of thick chestnut hair and shaggy eyebrows above commanding hazel eyes. He had quite swept Reba off her feet twenty-one years ago, when he had arrived in Randolph Springs. In those days,

Reba had been a beauty, but over the years, she had put on weight and her russet curls were fading. She still had a glowing complexion and a vivacious manner, however, and now she beamed at Lauren, her blue eyes dancing.

"Why, Laurie, darling, you *know* you've always been just like a daughter to us . . . Hasn't she, Max?"

Lauren had been brought to the house on Shadow Mountain Drive on the first day of her life.

After the difficult, premature delivery, the doctor was more concerned about Miriam than the tiny new baby girl. Lauren may have been born without eyelashes or fingernails, but her wail rose above the scolding of blue jays outside the open window, her heartbeat was strong, and she was perfectly formed, with a fuzz of gold covering her scalp.

"In fact, she's quite beautiful," pronounced Reba, peering into the cradle, her eyes narrowed and calculating as she pushed the blanket aside to get a better view of the infant's features. Miriam sank into a deep slumber, satisfied that her fastidious sister considered their new daughter comely. For, no greater calamity could befall a Jewish girl in the South than to be born without looks.

Samuel knew his wife needed rest, and yet, that afternoon when Reba suggested taking Lauren home with her until Miriam convalesced, he was reluctant to agree. Even though their house was stretched to the limit with four older children, Samuel did not care for the peremptory manner in which Reba was taking charge of his new daughter. A child should live with her own parents, he thought angrily. Just as soon as Miriam was out of bed—two weeks at the most—he vowed they would bring the baby home.

As it turned out, Lauren stayed with the Mortimers for well over a year.

At home on Shadow Mountain, Reba set about furnishing a nursery for Lauren, ordering cherry wood colonial furniture from Hickory, employing a seamstress to run up curtains and skirting for the wicker bassinet from yards and yards of imported eyelet-embroidered Swiss cotton. She even hired Pansy, a niece of her cook Lady, as a nursemaid, and after a few days of nervous experimentation, the household settled down. Reba soon regarded Lauren as her own, secretly harboring the hope that having an infant in the house would cause her to become pregnant.

"Nonsense, that's folklore," chided Max. Nevertheless, he was only too happy to cooperate to the full extent of his capabilities, which were considerable.

Lauren might have been sent home to her parents within a month or two, but one after the other, the Jacobson children came down with mumps. Before anyone gave it much thought, Lauren was five months old, perfectly content and thriving under Pansy's care. And Reba was pregnant!

"She's brought us good luck, Mimi," exclaimed Reba, when Miriam said it was time for Lauren to come home with them. "Please let me keep her a little while longer. I want to look at her so I'll have a girl and she'll be as pretty as Lauren."

Miriam exchanged glances with her husband, but even Samuel had a hard time denying such a request, and Reba *did* love Lauren so and gave her everything an infant could possibly require. And so, for the moment, Lauren remained with her aunt. During the first year of her life she spent an occasional night at home with her own family, but she was always fretful in the strange surroundings, crying and keeping everyone in the house awake. It became ever easier to leave her with the Mortimers.

On Lauren's first birthday, Reba invited the family for dinner. There were twenty-eight of them seated around the huge banquet table in the formal dining room where Lady, assisted by Bertram, Pansy, and the maids, served the dessert of homemade peach ice cream and a lemony layer cake with white and pink frosting. Heavily pregnant, Reba preened as Max raised his glass to toast Lauren, the impending birth, and everyone's good health.

Two months later, Charlotte Lee Mortimer made her first grand entrance.

On the day following Charlotte Lee's birth, Reba was sitting up in her big double bed against a pile of lace-covered pillows, having her hair brushed and eating everything on the tray Lady had prepared. But as soon as she heard Max's voice in the hall that evening, she lay back, pale and weak under creamy, lace-edged sheets and a rose satin comforter.

"How's my brave, darlin' wife?" Max bent to kiss her, his heart squeezing with love and pity at the eternal mystery of womanhood.

Reba smiled wanly. "I'm still in pain, dear, and I feel *so* tired out."

"Well, of *course* you do, sweetheart, after what you went through." Reba's labor had not been especially prolonged and the delivery perfectly uncomplicated. "That baby's the cutest little thing in the world, goin' to look just like her beautiful mama."

"Have you seen her tonight?"

"Sure did! I just watched Mathilda give her the bottle."

Reba stifled her irritation that Max had not come directly to her room before going to view their new daughter. "Lauren is *thrilled* with Charlotte Lee, isn't she, Max?"

"I know she *appears* to be, Reba, but I told Mathilda to keep a sharp eye on her whenever she's in the nursery. Sometimes children hide jealousy by pretendin' to love a new baby."

"Ohh, I don't think Lauren would ever *hurt* Charlotte Lee."

"But we want to play safe, don't we, darlin'?"

"I suppose so, dear." She stroked his cheek, drawing her lips into a kiss.

It soon became evident that Charlotte would prove a challenge for the entire Mortimer household. Accustomed to Lauren, a sweet-tempered, obedient child who had slept through the night from the time she was three months old, Charlotte's lively temperament kept them off-balance. Unusually alert, she lifted her head to follow Reba around the room at a stage when other babies stared at their fingers. She smiled at Max when only a few days old, compelling him to spend inordinate hours hanging over the bassinet making sounds never before heard emanating from a Mortimer.

"You'll spoil her, sure 'nough," said Pansy, when she encountered Max in his dressing gown, walking the halls with Charlotte in the middle of the night.

From the very first, Charlee was Max's pet.

When Charlotte Lee was four months old, Samuel said it was time that Lauren came home to live.

"If you take her now, she'll think it's because of the baby," protested Reba.

"She has to leave sometime, Reba. The sooner the better. It's gone on too long."

"Please let her stay a little longer, Samuel. She and Charlotte Lee are so sweet together. They're just like sisters."

"That's exactly the point, Reba. They *aren't* sisters."

Finally, he agreed they would wean Lauren away from her aunt and uncle's house gradually, until she became accustomed to living with her own family. But several more months passed and Lauren was still spending most of the time at Reba's.

One Sunday, as usual, the family was gathered at the Mortimer house for dinner, when Lauren called Reba "*Mama.*" Without further delay, her clothes and toys were packed, and the bewildered child taken home to the Jacobson house—this time to stay.

Lauren attached herself to her brothers and sisters, who doted on her. In those first frightening weeks, she failed to understand why she was sleeping there instead of in her room at Aunt Reba's. Everyone agreed that Lauren should not go back to the house on Shadow Mountain for a month, and then only for a short visit. When the month passed, the little girl was shy, clinging to her mother's hand when they arrived at the Mortimers'.

The minute Charlotte Lee saw her cousin, she began

jumping up and down in her bouncing chair, squealing with joy. Lauren ran to the baby, throwing her arms around her with a cry of delight. "Char-lee . . . Char-lee!"

"Aren't they simply *adorable* together!" exclaimed Reba. "Isn't it *wonderful* that they'll always have each other?"

Chapter 3

"ONLY TWO MONTHS until graduation!" Charlee gloated, flinging out her arms and twirling around. Her eyes were dancing and her hair caught the wind on a sunny afternoon in March 1933, as they came down the hill in front of Randolph Academy, the town's only private school.

"I wish I were as happy about graduating as you are," said Lauren, laughing at her cousin's exuberance. "Our senior year is passing so quickly, I hate to see it come to an end."

"You've always liked school more than me, Laurie. I wouldn't have gotten through half my courses if you hadn't studied with me."

You mean practically written all your papers, Lauren thought wryly, but why say something to spoil the day. "Don't forget, you skipped a grade, Charlee, and you're the youngest one in our class."

"I may be the youngest, but I'm the tallest."

"Oh look! What's going on?"

They joined several of their classmates who were standing in the rear of a crowd gathered on Swannanoa Avenue where a county politician was extolling the new Democratic administration in Washington. The girls' fathers were constantly arguing about Roosevelt's New Deal and what it might mean for the country. Max said it was bad for business, which would ensure its failure, but Samuel believed in FDR's ideas for helping "the forgotten man."

A number of sun-baked farmers from the countryside, dressed in tattered denims, were among the throng that lined the road. It had been a quiet, orderly crowd, but suddenly a man yelled, *"Commie bastard!"* Then someone told him to shut up, and soon they were scuffling.

There was an eruption as the dense pack of spectators began to sway and press backward against the uniformed schoolgirls. A woman screamed and male curses resounded, as arms flailed. "Careful, young ladies, give 'em room." The girls from Randolph Academy scattered as two men traded punches.

"It's Jack Weaver," snickered Elsie Jean Morley, who was their class president. "Drunk as usual."

The men rolled over and over on the ground until their friends managed to separate and haul them to their feet. One had a bloody nose and his eye was starting to turn color, while the man called Jack Weaver remained unscathed, with a cocky grin on his handsome, dissipated face.

"White trash!" muttered his assailant, wiping his bleeding nose.

Taller, but older, Weaver growled, "I dare you to say that again, you pig." The bleeding man made a lunge for him, but was held back by two companions.

The girls watched Weaver move up the street on unsteady legs. Some of the seniors began to walk away. "Hey, Charlee . . . come get a soda with us!" called Elsie Jean. "You too, Laurie." The animated group of girls, all dressed alike in maroon and gray plaid skirts and gray blazers monogrammed with the school crest, headed for the ice cream parlor.

Jack Weaver and the fist fight were soon forgotten.

"What are your plans for next year, Laurie?" asked Elsie Jean on graduation day, as the seniors formed a line for the processional.

"I guess I'll continue with music lessons, and—well, I'm not really sure." Lately, Lauren had tried not to think about what would happen after graduation. Her parents believed the only desirable future for their daughter was to get married and start to raise a family. But there was absolutely no one among the boys she knew whom she wanted to marry.

Reba and Max had invited the entire graduating class with their parents to a reception at their home that evening. Except for a few business and professional men who had attended Max's numerous civic committee meetings, none of the parents had ever entered the house before. With undisguised curiosity, they examined the Persian rugs and fine antique furnishings. The Mortimer mansion seemed to overwhelm them, for they appeared stiff and ill-at-ease. But that didn't stop them from enjoying the lavish buffet Reba had planned—a variety of chafing dish gumbos, molded salads, and a pastry table filled with Lady's specialties. They ate as if they'd never seen food before.

When the other guests had left, only the relatives remained. Charlotte and Lauren, arms around each other, were clowning with Philip while he took snapshots with his Kodak Brownie. "Come on, Daddy, get in the picture with us," called Charlee, holding out her hand.

Max went to stand between his daughter and his niece, putting an arm around each of them. Charlotte fondly ruffled his hair and kissed him. "We do this same pose every year, don't we?" she laughed.

As always, the evening ended with Lauren playing the piano while everyone gathered around to sing. Charlee, unusually subdued, slipped away to sit in a wing chair. She was experiencing an agitation, a feeling she sometimes had, almost like panic. It came on all of a sudden, with no explanation.

Noticing her cousin alone in the corner, Lauren brought the musical interlude to an end, and everyone prepared to leave. "Stay over with me tonight, Laurie," urged Charlotte, just as she had when they were little girls. Lauren kissed her parents good-bye and followed her cousin upstairs.

When they reached the bedroom, she flung her straw hat on the bed. Charlee snatched it away. "Don't you know that's bad luck?"

"You don't really believe that silly stuff, do you?"

Charlotte shrugged self-consciously. "I see no point in tempting fate."

When they were in bed, they lay awake discussing their

classmates until long into the night. "I doubt we'll see much of them from now on; our paths will take different turns," said Charlee, in her low voice. "You know, Laurie, I was so anxious for graduation to come, and now that it's over, I'm wondering why. I feel like I'm standing on the edge of a deep dark hole, and sooner or later, I have to jump."

"You have nothing to worry about, Charlee. No matter what happens, you always land on your feet."

"Thus far. But what if my luck has run out?"

Charlotte was so quiet that Lauren thought she was asleep, when she suddenly asked, "Are you ever afraid, Laurie?"

"Afraid? Of what?"

"Oh, I don't know. Of what lies ahead . . . the unknown. Whatever will be your destiny."

"Sometimes," she answered slowly, realizing that her cousin had articulated what she had been denying. "I often wonder what I'll make of my life. I don't believe I should just marry someone, like Joanna did. Of course, I'd like to have a husband and children someday, but I don't want that to be the *only* thing."

"Mmmmm . . . marriage would be the easy way out, wouldn't it?" murmured Charlee, her voice slowing as she drifted off. "I fear my life won't be serene, Laurie. Whenever I try to picture my future, it seems dark and cloudy . . ."

Long after Charlotte had fallen asleep, Lauren lay awake brooding over her cousin's words. Would she ever know who Charlotte really was, she wondered. Whatever had happened to her warm, funny, wild and impetuous cousin—the one who knew just where she was heading? Who was this timorous girl who worried about dark holes and hats on the bed? And which of them was the real Charlee?

Chapter 4

"Now that you girls are all grown up and graduated, it's time we made some plans," announced Reba, the following morning at breakfast. After exchanging conspiratorial smiles with Max, she set about laying the groundwork for what Charlee would later refer to as "the Great Road Show."

It began with an old-fashioned Southern ball at home. Within the week, invitations had been hand-addressed by a social secretary:

Mr. and Mrs. J. Maxwell Mortimer
request the pleasure of your company at a small
dance in honor of their daughter
Charlotte Lee
at eight o'clock in the evening
on Saturday, the fifteenth of July
nineteen hundred thirty-three
Shadow Mountain Drive
Randolph Springs

"You'd think Charlee was making her bow at the Court of St. James, the way Aunt Reba is fussing," remarked Philip, examining the invitation.

"Reba's been so busy planning this party, she's terrified something will spoil it."

"Mama, the dance is ridiculous. Jewish girls do not come out in Randolph Springs," groused Phil. "Besides, Charlee's already been 'out' for three years!"

"It's not really a debut, Philip," his mother defended

her younger sister. "They just wanted to have a little party to celebrate her—her coming of age." Miriam didn't mention that Reba and Max had wanted to give the dance in honor of both Charlotte and Lauren, but Samuel had refused.

On the evening of her dance, Charlotte received with her parents in the great hall of their imposing residence. Looking like a plantation belle of the Old South, she was a vision in a frothy blush-colored tulle gown with an immense hoop skirt caught up with silk roses.

"Isn't Philip out-of-this-world handsome tonight?" she whispered to Lauren as she whirled away on the arm of a ZBT from Chapel Hill. "I swear, every girl at the dance is falling in love with him!"

Watching her brother waltz with a pretty brunette from Greenville, whose name she had forgotten, Lauren agreed. Tall, slim, and poised in tails, in the romantic lighting his hair was the color of butterscotch and when he smiled, she knew just what Charlee meant.

Lauren's eyes sparkled as she tapped her foot to the music. She was having a wonderful time tonight. Her dance card was filled and she had met some dashing young men—

"I believe this is my dance, Miss Jacobson."

"Ben! It couldn't be—I've already danced with you twice."

"If you check your card, you'll see. There! Doesn't that say Benson Miller?"

Benson was Philip's friend, one of the neighborhood boys who had gone to school with him. He had never viewed Lauren as anything other than Phil's kid sister, but tonight, here she was at the dance, all grown up and pretty as a picture.

"Are you enjoying the ball?" Lauren asked, surprised that he was such a good dancer. As long as she'd known Ben Miller, he had never struck her as someone you would want to date. He was positively good-looking tonight, without his glasses, his dark hair neatly combed with that nice wave in front. Tails certainly did bring out the best in a man.

She knew her father did not think much of the Miller family. Samuel put a great deal of stock in background. Not the way Max did, judging everyone by which club they belonged to, how much money they had, or how long their family had been in America. With Papa it was subtle, something less specific. You could call it breeding. It had to do with a family's entire character, their ideals, sense of values, and their tradition of learning.

"You're awfully serious tonight, Laurie. This is supposed to be fun!" Ben was gazing at her in a way that was new.

She smiled, glad he hadn't been able to read her thoughts. "I *am* having fun, Ben. I was just enjoying the music and the rhythm. Don't you love to dance?"

"Yes." He pulled her closer in his arms and pressed his cheek against her hair. "I surely do."

The set ended with a ruffle and a flourish, and everyone turned expectantly toward the bandstand as the musicians broke into "Dixie." Couples stopped dancing, conversation halted, those who were seated around the ballroom's periphery rose. *"I wish I was in the land of cotton . . ."* they sang.

Max had wanted to hang his grandfather's Confederate flag tonight, but Reba objected, saying it just wasn't done in Randolph Springs and would subject them to ridicule. "It's *tradition,* Reba! It's done at all the cotillions. You can't wipe out our history. Why, the Confederacy ended only fifteen years before I was born!" Reba had prevailed and the Stars and Bars remained packed in camphor in the attic. But eyes misted, faces became animated, hearts beat in unison, as all voices joined in a rousing chorus of the song that had become a Southern anthem. *". . . Away . . . away . . . away down So-o-outh in Dixie!"*

A few of the more rambunctious young men let loose with Rebel yells, and they all trooped out to the terrace for a midnight supper.

The rest of that summer was filled with dances and luncheons and picnics and supper-parties. By August, Lauren and Charlotte were busily assembling new fall wardrobes, and with the first scarlet leaves in the Smokies, there began a series of visits to the vast network of relatives that traversed the South like a railroad map.

As soon as Yom Kippur had passed, they were off to formal balls in Charlotte, Winston-Salem, Raleigh, and Greensboro where, through their mothers' third cousin, Ruth Felder, and her husband Jay, they met scores of young men from the University of North Carolina and Duke, many of whom took down their addresses and said they would write.

Two weeks later in Gastonia, they visited Florence Young, a first cousin once removed to the Jacobsons. Then, on to Chattanooga, Memphis, Columbia, and Augusta—and soon they began to lose count of the dances and the new faces.

"Get ready for the big time!" announced Charlee gleefully one day, just as things were beginning to settle down. "Mama thinks we're at last ready for Charleston . . . and *Atlanta!*"

Everything up to now had been in preparation for Atlanta. Lauren sensed the tension before they left Randolph Springs. Not only Aunt Reba, but Uncle Max went along. There was a barely contained excitement and anxiety in Max's heartiness. He was bringing his little girl home and he could not wait to show her off to the folks in his native city.

On their first night in Atlanta, Max's Cousin Edith and her husband gave a supper dance in the girls' honor. That was the beginning of ten days of constant social activity—luncheons, teas, dinners, balls, and musicales. Halfway through the week, Lauren and Charlotte were in the ladies' room of Atlanta's elite Standard Club, when they overheard a conversation between two matrons.

"Max Mortimer's daughter is here tonight. Have you met her?"

"Not yet, Sylvia. I caught a glimpse at the dinner table. Lovely looking, isn't she?"

"Yes, she's a real 'type.' I imagine she could use some time in Atlanta, though, to get the mountains out of her system."

''Well, of course Randolph Springs *is* a hick town, no question, but if I know Max, he'll see that his daughter gets properly finished. Who's the other little girl, the pretty blonde?''

''No one special—a poor relation.''

Lauren didn't have time to examine her own feelings because she recognized the gleam in Charlotte's eye. Chin jutting in her most aggressive manner, Charlee strode into the dressing area. The two women were rattled. One fled the room while the other remained trapped in her seat, a wan smile on her face.

''Good evening, girls. We were just saying what *lovely* young ladies you two are and how wonderful it is to have you-all here in Atlanta with us.'' She extended her hand.

Lauren, who was standing closer to the woman, shook hands. ''I'm Lauren Jacobson, ma'am. And this is my cousin, Charlotte Lee Mortimer.'' She threw Charlee a look that said *Be nice!*

''We are absolutely *delighted* to be visitin' Atlanta, ma'am,'' replied Charlotte sweetly. Too sweetly, observed Lauren. ''Such a *refreshin'* change after the hectic life we've been leadin' lately. Everything here seems kind of slow and gracious . . . quite restful, really.''

''Hectic life?'' inquired the woman uncertainly.

''Oh, yes. At this time of year, with all the seasonal residents comin' down for the horse shows and golf tournaments and all—Why, there's more goin' on in Randolph Springs than—*Paris, France!''* With that, Charlotte swept out of the dressing room, Lauren in her wake.

''Charlee! How *could* you?''

''Serves her right, the old biddy! Calling you a poor relation.'' She tossed her head, *''Hick* town? What in the world does she think Atlanta is? I'll tell you the truth, Laurie—there's only one place in this whole country that isn't a hick town, and that's New York City. I am just *longing* to see it, aren't you?''

''Mmm, I don't know, Charlee. I'm getting kind of tired of traveling around.''

They managed to get through the remainder of their stay in Atlanta with no unpleasant repercussions. Max was more than satisfied with the splash the girls had made. "You-all cut quite a swath in my home town," he said triumphantly, kissing them both when they were settled in their compartment on the train. "I was real proud of my daughter and my little niece."

"This Great Road Show needs an efficiency expert," announced Charlee as they journeyed north over the Piedmont toward the mountains. "We are criss-crossing and backtracking, and going every which-way, with a considerable waste of time and motion. Mama, why don't you just hire a hall at a central location and announce a general auction to the highest bidder?"

"Charlotte Lee!" Reba was scandalized to think her daughter would be so tactless as to reveal her motives.

"Well, what else is it for, if not to find us husbands?"

Reba's face flushed. A Southern girl was supposed to act like it was just natural to travel two hundred miles or more to go to a dance, ho hum. It had not a thing to do with catching a husband. "Darling, you're *years* from marriage," she assured her daughter. "This is the way young people meet in the South. It's *always* been this way. Jewish families, especially, like to know one another."

"Oh, good Lord! Then why not have one big convention and get it over with!"

Back in Randolph Springs, while Lauren unpacked, Philip lay across her bed listening eagerly as she regaled him with their adventures. "Sounds like you two had a lot of fun, Laurie."

"It was fun all right, but I'm glad it's over. I'm not sure I'm cut out for that kind of life, Phil. I am absolutely fed up with being on my best, most ladylike behavior. My face aches from smiling and I could *gag* from all the inane and banal conversations." An evil little smile crossed her lips. "I think I'd like you to take me out somewhere tonight to get drunk on moonshine."

"That's a date, sis!" Phil winked at her, as Miriam entered the room.

Lauren had to repeat all the stories, of course, slightly edited for her mother's ears. When she had finished, Philip said, "Well, it sure sounds like the purpose was accomplished, doesn't it?"

"And what is that supposed to mean, Philip Jacobson?" Miriam asked her son reprovingly.

"The purpose, Mama, was to see Charlee meets every eligible man in the South. But if I know Uncle Max, it'll take a lot more than that to satisfy him!"

Chapter 5

MAX HAD BEEN watching Philip for years, observing his development, admiring his quiet elegance and grace. He thought he was the kind of young man he would like to have had for a son. If only Reba had been willing to bear more children, he might be playing golf right now with his own boy. But Philip was a good substitute.

"Nice shot," murmured Max's customer, a publisher from Charlotte, as Phil sent a long drive down the third fairway. "Do you play at Asheville?"

"I've played there a few times, sir. I prefer Shadow Mountain."

"Sometime when you're in Charlotte, you'll have to let me take you out to my club."

"That's very kind of you, sir. I'd be honored."

The boy did have innate good manners. Max was proud to show off his handsome nephew. He felt as if the Jacobson offspring were his blood relatives, not merely his wife's kin. He'd been mighty lucky in his marriage, when you considered everything. Well, aside from the physical part—but even there, he had to admit Reba was a lovely looking woman and when he got her in the right mood, there was still a bit of fire between them.

Philip often shot eighteen holes with Max and his friends. They liked playing with him because his handicap was four and he set them a good pace. Shadow Mountain wasn't restricted like many of the golf clubs, but Jewish people in Randolph Springs weren't exactly breaking down the doors to become members. A Jew could join the Asheville Country Club these days, now that it needed the money, but Shadow Mountain never had been restricted. Max was a founder of the Shadow Mountain Club, and he had been wanting to put Philip up for a junior membership. Just this afternoon Phil had told him to go ahead.

"The initiation fee is a birthday present from your Aunt Reba and me," said Max. Phil knew his father would object to Max paying the fee, but he thought it would be rude to refuse. He did appreciate Max's generosity, and golf was one of the few activities that made life bearable in Randolph Springs.

Twenty-three years old and for the rest of my life this is what I have to look forward to . . . sorting socks and BVDs, folding denims and stacking them on shelves, checking the books, firing a stock boy for stealing . . . waiting on narrow-eyed, snuff-chomping rednecks who smell so bad it's like an oily substance you can't get off your body, even by washing . . .

Philip slowed down as he passed the Town Park on his way home. It looked like something was going on at the dance pavilion. He turned into the gravel area and parked next to a gardener's truck. The pavilion had been closed for the past three summers due to a lack of funds, but carpenters and painters were now busy putting the last touches on the octagonal structure with its gingerbread trim.

"Planning to open 'er up this year?" he asked.

"Yeaup, reckon so. Grand opening Sa'rday night. Buck Williams goin' do the callin'."

Philip thought he might come down to watch the country dancing. Lord knows, there wasn't much else to do around here. The old high school gang had drifted apart, some of them already married, and the men he knew from Randolph College mostly did not live in town. He'd give anything to get away himself, but something held him back. Pa had never said he *couldn't* go to law school. He'd pretty much left it up to his son, but Philip had just known it was the wrong thing to do. He could go even now if he wanted to. Maybe he was afraid to try Chapel Hill, scared he might fail. Not the work—he knew he could do that.

But the rest of it, the stuff that Max thought was so important.

"It's good for you to come to the club, Phil," Max had told him today when he offered to sponsor him. "A businessman needs to make contacts. When you're a member of the club, you'll get to know the right people."

Philip sometimes wondered if he wasn't more comfortable with the "wrong" people.

You could hear the fiddles before you got down the hill. He had asked Benson Miller to come along, knowing he would feel foolish sitting there alone. The dance pavilion was crowded with young people. All the tables were taken, so they leaned against the railing, eating ice cream cones and watching the pairs swing through the sets. Philip recognized some of the fellows he'd known at Randolph High. They looked almost the same, just grown-up versions of the boys they had been, wearing dark slacks and solid color shirts. There was a knowing grace about them as they expertly changed partners, swinging the women in their full-skirted ginghams, following the intricate calls.

"Swing 'er high-ee, swing 'er low, now it's time to do-si-do," sang Buck Williams in his Carolina mountain-boy twang.

"That looks like fun," said Ben, going off to join a square.

Philip threw away the last of his cone and wiped his mouth with a handkerchief. A pretty auburn-haired girl was leaning against the post in front of him. Her profile had a touching delicacy, the lips turning up at the edges in a wistful smile as she watched the couples promenade to the lively mountain music.

Somewhere they had known each other . . . he searched his memory for her name. As if she knew he was staring at her, she turned her head and looked directly into his eyes.

Philip walked over to her, aware that his pulse had quickened. "You look familiar. Do we know each other?"

She smiled and he noticed the dimple at the corner of her chin. "I remember *you* very well from high school,

Philip Jacobson. You were one of the older boys, so y'all never paid attention to me. I'm Anne Elizabeth Weaver."

Anne . . . Elizabeth . . . Weaver! Of all the pretty faces in that dance pavilion, why in hell had he chosen to speak to Jack Weaver's daughter? If he had half a brain in his head, he would make some excuse and go home.

But instead, he asked her to dance.

Chapter 6

"I'M GOING AWAY to school in the fall."

Unprepared for Charlee's announcement, Lauren tried to mask her dismay. "You *are . . . ? Where?"*

"Miss Alexander's, in New York." She struck a typically Charlee pose. "Mama says it's where all the best families send their daughters."

" 'Best' families?"

"You know, Laurie—important, moneyed, Northern, with a dash of Southern and Midwestern for spice!"

The catalogue described the Alexander School as "an outstanding institution of learning and culture for the select few . . . an Alexander education prepares a young woman to assume her future place in society as wife, mother, and community leader." Located in the East Seventies just off Fifth Avenue, it catered for the most part to wealthy Jewish families from outside the urban area who wanted their daughters to be introduced to art, music, the theater . . . and eligible young men.

Reba had been more than thankful when her husband took to the idea of sending Charlotte away to school, amazed that he was willing to be parted from his adored daughter. To tell the truth, she was the tiniest bit jealous of Max's fixation with Charlotte Lee. Well, of course, she doted on her, too—heaven knew, she had lavished the child with affection and attention for her entire life . . .

The next morning, Reba drove over to see Miriam. "Mimi, Max and I want to send Lauren to Miss Alexander's, too. Do you think Samuel will agree?"

"I'm sure he won't consider it, Reba. You know how

Samuel is about accepting gifts of that sort. He feels he alone should pay for his children's education, and we can't afford an expensive finishing school in New York City.''

''We're *family*, Mimi dear, and we love Lauren just as if she were our very own daughter. It's a *wonderful* chance for her and besides, Charlotte would be simply *lost* in New York without her. I want to talk to Samuel, if you'll let me.''

Miriam was tempted. It would be a remarkable opportunity for Lauren to study in New York. They'd miss her dreadfully, but she had so much talent and promise. Miriam realized with surprise that she had no desire for her youngest child to spend her whole life in Randolph Springs, married to some local boy who worked in his father's store on Vance Street. ''All right, Reba, go talk to Samuel. Only, be prepared—he'll say no.''

Much to Miriam's astonishment, Samuel gave his permission for Lauren to join Charlotte in New York. What had Reba said to convince him, she wondered. Her younger sister must have been extremely persuasive, coaxing him not to deny Laurie this opportunity.

''I can't believe it,'' Lauren exulted, hugging her cousin Charlotte when she heard the news. ''Papa really said I can go! Oh Charlee, I'm so happy, I could cry.''

''And *I'm* so happy, because I don't have to go up North alone. What would I do without my Laurie? Those Yankees would eat me alive!''

All summer, the two girls made excursions to the smart shops in Asheville for daytime dresses, pleated skirts and middies, tweed coats and walking suits with matching hats, tea dresses and dance frocks, ball gowns and evening capes, silk pumps for dancing and British Brevitts for walking about city pavements. As Lauren surveyed her mounting wardrobe, she began to believe that she actually was going away to school.

At the end of August on the night of Lauren's nineteenth birthday—an age when her sister Joanna had already been married—Philip said, ''I'm sure going to miss you, Laurie.''

''I'll miss you, too, Phil. I promise I'll write to you

every week.'' She felt guilty that she was the one to be leaving Randolph Springs, while Philip was stuck here. And unhappy. Lauren knew her brother was entranced with Anne Elizabeth Weaver. If Samuel and Miriam ever found out, there would be hell to pay.

Finally, the bags were packed, the trunks had been shipped, their cousins had given them a luncheon at the Randolph Inn, and that night the two families were having a farewell dinner at Aunt Reba's house. In three more days they would board a Southern Railway Pullman car for New York!

Reba and Max were going north with the girls to get them settled and enjoy a week of entertainment and shopping in Manhattan. ''It's important that Charlotte Lee and Lauren get off to a proper start,'' Reba confided to Miriam. ''Maxwell will let them know at Miss Alexander's, in his own particular way, that these aren't just some little nobodies from Carolina.''

On Tuesday morning, just as the working day began, Jack Weaver sauntered into The Liberty Store, sober for a change. ''I'd like to see you alone, Mr. Jacobson,'' he said to Samuel, ''gentlemen's business.''

After forty-one years, Samuel's insides still churned whenever he saw Weaver. He could never quite erase from his memory the confusion and terror he had experienced as a young immigrant lad, cornered in an alley by a gang of hate-filled louts, who shouted epithets he could not understand, but that needed no translation. Jew-baiting was the same in every language.

Samuel climbed the stairs to the mezzanine, leading the way to his private office. ''Be seated—Mr. Weaver. What can I do for you?''

For a moment Samuel closed his eyes, visualizing that long-ago afternoon . . . *Let's see it, Sammy, maybe they didn't cut enough off. Yeah—maybe we'll have to finish the job! Sheeny, sheeny, someone clipped your weenie . . .*

His father had taught him to defend himself when he was a boy. Humiliations and insults had been daily fare in Russia, but he had never been assaulted by so many at once. Greatly outnumbering him, they had beaten him horribly. What he recalled most vividly before he passed out, was being held down by four boys while Jack Weaver sat astride him, smearing his face with horse shit and repeatedly banging his head against the cobblestones. *Dirty Jew . . . shit-eating foreigner . . . how does it taste, kike?*

But he had been consoled that night when Miriam bathed his wounds, shedding tears over him and kissing each place as she bandaged it. The next day, his cousin Abe Jacobson, who was big and tough, had challenged Jack to a fight and knocked the daylights out of him.

A shiftless troublemaker with a face so handsome and a manner so charming that the female teachers had a hard time disciplining him, Jack had gotten the daughter of one of Randolph Spring's leading citizens in trouble and had to marry her. Despite his wife's refinement, Jack Weaver remained what he had always been—a gambling, hard drinking, no-account white trash womanizer.

Weaver came straight to the point. "Your boy's been messin' around with our Anne Elizabeth, Mr. Jacobson."

"My boy?" Samuel stared hard at him across the desk.

"Your son, Philip. He's been screwin' my daughter."

The breath went out of Samuel. "I don't believe you!"

Anger flashed in the watery blue eyes. "Would I be sayin' such a thing about my own little girl, if it ain't the truth?"

Samuel started to rise, but fell back into the chair. "Philip wouldn't—I've taught my son respect for women."

Weaver shrugged dismissively. "She's got some crazy notion she wants to marry him."

"Impossible!" roared Samuel turning pale.

"That's what *I* told her. Impossible." Weaver paused, and Samuel fought against a rising nausea. "But, we've got us a real problem here, Mr. Jacobson. Anne Elizabeth . . . she's in the family way."

Samuel's heart was thudding irregularly and there was a roaring in his ears. He was overcome by a wave of dizziness. "It can't be Philip. He wouldn't—How do I know you're telling the truth?"

"My word of honor, it's the truth."

"Your honor?" spat Samuel. "I wasn't aware you had any!"

"Now, that's a right unfriendly statement, Mr. Jacobson."

Grasping the desk for support, Samuel started for the door. "We'll see what Philip has to say about this," he said in a gravelly voice.

"Hold on there!" Weaver's tone was threatening. "Don't bother calling your son up here. You can believe that Anne Elizabeth is knocked up. And he's the father!"

"You can't prove that, Weaver!"

"I've got witnesses. He's been sparkin' her all summer. Been seen by hundreds of people down in the Town Park."

"What does that prove? I ought to throw you out of here! Or call the police."

"I wouldn't advise that, Jacobson." His eyes were like a ferret's, mean and without lights. "There's a lot of folks I know around here wouldn't take too kindly to a boy like that, spoilin' a nice Christian girl." He picked up a paper clamp from the desk and began to play with it. "They might even take it into their heads to teach him a lesson—*if* y'all know what I mean."

Samuel's breathing became labored. Oh, he knew what that meant, all right! Weaver and his friends had all been nightriders for the Klan. *Philip!* his soul cried in silent anguish. I must protect my son! Even if he's done this awful thing, he's still my son.

"What—what is it you want of me, Jack Weaver?"

Weaver smiled thinly. "There's a doctor I know, across the state line. I think two hundred dollars ought to take care of Anne Elizabeth's predicament."

Anything—anything to get rid of this evil. Samuel reached for his checkbook.

"No checks, Mr. Jacobson. Cash on the barrel, as they say."

Samuel's face was suffused in a deep flush, and he thought he would pass out. He felt a vise-like pressure in his chest, but he pushed himself out of his chair and opened the door to the room where he kept the safe. Instinctively glancing over his shoulder to be certain Jack

Weaver could not see his movements, he spun the combination and removed ten twenty-dollar bills from a cash box. Back in his office he handed them to his visitor.

With an affable smile, Weaver folded the money in a wad and slipped it into his pocket. "Well now, the boy didn't mean no harm, I reckon. I just want him to stay away from my little girl, y'hear?"

"You can depend on it," said Samuel. "Now, get out of here, Weaver!"

Philip had watched apprehensively from the back of the store as his father led Jack Weaver upstairs. He waited a few minutes, then went up to the balcony, trying to hear what was being said behind the closed door, but there was just the drone of Weaver's voice and an occasional word interjected by Samuel. Afraid he would be discovered eavesdropping, Philip retreated.

Half an hour later, Jack Weaver came down alone, nodded curtly at Philip and hurried out of the store. Phil waited nervously for his father to follow, but another twenty minutes went by and Samuel remained upstairs. Unable to stand the suspense any longer, Philip marched up to the office and knocked. There was no response. Slowly he opened the door and peered inside.

Samuel sat at his desk, his head in his hands. "Father?" Samuel did not answer. "Pa . . . are you all right?" Samuel raised his head and Phil saw that his face was gray and covered with sweat. *"What's wrong, Papa?"* Philip rushed to his side.

Samuel clutched his chest, gasping, "You better call Dr. Walters."

"Oh, my God—*Lionel!*" he screamed.

The doctor said Samuel had suffered a mild heart attack. He ordered him to rest in bed for a month, avoiding stress or excitement, and Miriam was terrified at the thought that her husband might die.

Lauren looked at her stricken father and exhausted, panicky mother and knew that she would not be leaving Randolph Springs. On Friday afternoon, she waved good-bye from the platform of the railroad station as Charlee departed for New York with her parents. Sending the Mortimer's chauffeur away, Lauren decided to walk home along the lake.

She gazed at the forest-covered peaks that surrounded Randolph Springs . . . The mountains held her captive here. Left behind, she was hemmed in to the east, to the west, north and south. It had never seemed important before, but now that she was a prisoner, how she longed to get away.

I'm selfish to be thinking of myself when Papa is ill, she thought. With a sigh, she sat down on a stone bench near the gate to Town Park. Lost in thought, she failed to notice the person who approached. "Miss Jacobson?" Startled, Lauren looked up, her reverie interrupted. A young woman stood a few feet away, wearing a straw hat with an enveloping veil. "Excuse me, is it all right if I talk to you for a minute?"

"Do I know you?"

"I'm Anne Elizabeth Weaver." She lifted the veil briefly and Lauren saw that her face was swollen and badly bruised.

"Miss Weaver—Anne Elizabeth! Whatever happened to you?"

Shaking her head impatiently, she replied, "That's not important. I must speak to you. I've been following you ever since you left the station."

"What is it?"

"I'm going away. I'll be gone for a long time—and I won't be able to say good-bye to Philip. Will you give him this for me?" Anne Elizabeth held out a letter. Knowing that Samuel's heart attack had followed an encounter with this girl's father, Lauren hesitated to take it. "*Please!* I'm never going to see Philip again. This won't change anything, but I couldn't leave without explaining."

Lauren waited until Philip was alone that evening before giving him the letter. For some reason, she decided not to mention Anne Elizabeth's bruised face. She was dying to ask him what had happened, but as curious as she was, she knew she would have to wait for her brother to confide in her because he was a very private person.

Feeling restless that night, she sat in a rocker on the upstairs porch. ''Hey, Laurie,'' Phil said softly, coming out to join her. ''I've sure made a mess of everything, haven't I?''

''It's not your fault.''

''Yeah. It is. If I hadn't been such a fool, Pa wouldn't have had his heart attack. And you'd be on your way to New York.''

''Papa will get better, Phil,'' she said. ''And as for New York—I guess it just wasn't meant to be.''

After a few minutes, Philip said good night. Much later, as she was falling asleep, Lauren thought she could hear the sound of his muffled weeping.

Chapter 7

New York
Sunday, September 23, 1934

Darling Laurie,

I haven't written before, because I've been absolutely staggering under the burden of new impressions! Methinks your cuz will be quite happy, once she becomes adjusted to the Alexander School. Like a Carolina mountain fox, I shall adapt by growing thicker fur in this northern clime.

The girls are all very rich "Jewesses," as Mother would say—an expression that is not encouraged here at Alexander's! And she was right—they're all from important families. A few may even turn out to be nice.

There's so much to report, I don't know where to begin. I missed you so dreadfully on the trip up North, I was really in the dumps. Mother and Daddy were dear. For once, Mama didn't keep telling me to sit up straight, put my knees together, stop biting my fingernails, and keep my voice down. She made up for it the minute we hit Washington, though, where we had dinner with a senator and an undersecretary of something-or-other and their utterly borrrring wives. Very ordinary people—tent revival types. Mama practically sniffed through the whole meal, laying on the Old Plantation Act like you've never seen. I do love it when she does that—she can be so wicked!

Aside from being our country's capital, Washington is another hick town, but I did find the White House and congressional buildings exciting. Perhaps it was because the senator had his aide show me around—a cute boy from Raleigh with bedroom eyes!

Finally, New York. Well, Lauren Jacobson, all I can say is if you haven't seen New York City, you are really missing something. I'm sorry, Laurie, I know I should tell you it's too big and noisy and dirty and you're better off in Randolph, but that would be a lie! I was prepared for the skyscrapers, but not the constant excitement. Wherever you look, there's something going on. Mama says I give myself away as a real yokel, the way I stop to stare at everything. The clothes in the store windows! I thought my wardrobe was something special until I saw Fifth Avenue. Daddy said I can go shopping and charge anything, and then of course, Mama had to tell him he was spoiling me and they had a fight.

The Alexander School is quite different from Randolph Academy . . . Since you were supposed to be my roommate, I got put with a girl named Blanche Fields. I learned that I was given Blanche because no one else would share a room with her! She *is* a bit spoiled, but I find her reputation for being impossible to live with greatly exaggerated.

I am chagrined to tell you I'm in a remedial speech clinic. Phil would say our speech coach talks like she has a candle up her ass. "Bird and word rhyme with absurd," she says, pronouncing them in this snotty way, almost like they don't have r's . . .

Charlee's amusing description of her first days at the finishing school were almost like having a conversation with her, thought Lauren, as she scanned the pages filled with her cousin's dramatic, flowing scrawl. She chuckled over the letter, but as much as she missed Charlee, she had to admit the Alexander School did not sound like it was meant for her. She and her cousin weren't at all alike, and if she had accompanied her to New York, she would have been the tail to Charlee's kite, forced to trail along with no direction of her own. It had always been that way, she realized, only it hadn't seemed to matter before.

. . . As for all that culture they spouted about—On Tuesday nights, we attend symphony at Carnegie Hall. On Saturday afternoons, opera at the Metropolitan Opera House. And of course the theater, and endless museum trips.

Oh m'gosh, Laurie, I forgot! We dress for dinner every night. It is such a bore! After dinner, coffee is served in the living room, during which time there is "uplifting conversation." On Fridays, Sabbath candles are lit and a religious leader comes for a discussion of Jewish affairs. The topics so far have been about Hitler and the Jews—I never fully appreciated how awful it is in Germany these days. Occasionally we'll attend services at Temple Emmanu-El on Fifth Avenue. Almost everything of any consequence in New York seems to take place on either Fifth or Park Avenue.

This is a very self-centered letter. I haven't even asked about you or your family. Mama tells me Uncle Samuel is getting better and I am so glad to hear it. Give him my love, and everyone else too, especially Phil.

I miss you, Laurie. It's awful not having you with me. Please write.

Your loving
Charlee

Once Samuel's health began to improve, Lauren passed the time by giving piano lessons to a few neighborhood children. Her mother had been distracted with Samuel's illness, but Lauren already saw signs that the aunts thought something should be "done" about her. She could imagine the conversations that took place behind her back: *Nineteen years old and no prospects!*

"Wouldn't you like to go see Cousin Rose, Laurie dear?" suggested Reba. "There are some fine young men in Chattanooga, and it would do you good to get away."

"No, thanks, Aunt Reba, I don't feel like leaving Mama right now."

Lauren felt it was demeaning to be paraded out for viewing by marriageable men—like being put on the auction block. It was true that her mother no longer needed her here, but she certainly wasn't in the mood for another "road show," and it wouldn't be any fun without Charlee.

The doctor had told Samuel he could go back to work, but her mother continued to fret about his health. Miriam did not think she could go on living if "something should happen" to Samuel. No one in her family ever mentioned dying, Lauren noted, as if voicing the thought would encourage the Angel of Death to descend upon them.

Philip was under a cloud. Samuel had never revealed to anyone what had taken place during his conversation with Jack Weaver, but Phil was convinced he was to blame for his father's heart attack. He tried everything he could think of to redeem his image in Samuel's eyes, applying himself diligently to the business, and even joining his father in attending weekly services at temple. He was also a model big brother.

"If it weren't for Phil, I'd be miserable in Randolph," Lauren wrote back to Charlee. "He's been wonderful, taking me out for dinner and inviting me when he goes somewhere with his friends. He's even been playing golf with me, and you know he's the club champion. It can't be any fun for him to have his kid sister tagging along all the time."

At first Lauren thought Philip was being solicitous because she hadn't been able to go to New York, but soon she realized he was as much in need of companionship as she. "How about taking in a moving picture after dinner, Laurie?" he suggested one Saturday night in mid-October.

"I'd love to, Phil, but please don't feel you always have to take me when you go out."

"I do it for me, kiddo. You're the best company around."

After the movie, Phil drove out to the Old Smoky Tavern, a roadhouse restaurant on Bear Mountain that had been a speakeasy. Although Randolph Springs remained dry after Prohibition ended, Swannoanoa County was embroiled in a political battle, and was likely to go wet in the next election. The tavern's owners had the right connections, and even if the Drys won, the Old Smoky would go on serving beer and bootleg.

"Better not tell the folks I brought you here. They wouldn't approve. I'm in enough trouble these days."

"I know this is none of my business," said Lauren, "but if you ever want to talk about what happened with Anne Elizabeth, I hope you realize you can tell me."

He nodded, smiling sadly. "Sometime, maybe, but I don't much feel like it now." They ordered hamburgers and Phil had a beer, while Lauren asked for coffee. "You know, Laurie, there *is* something I'd like to talk about. What are your plans, now that you aren't going to New York?"

"I wish I knew," she sighed. "I have no purpose, Phil. You at least have your work every day, even though you might prefer to have gone to law school. It's not even that I cared that much about New York, if I had something else. I feel trapped by Randolph Springs—and by the family."

"You know, I never could see you at a finishing school, Laurie. You're much too smart for that. Have you ever thought about going to college?"

"College?" She savored the word and couldn't help smiling. "Somehow it never seemed like I was supposed to, but I like the idea."

"I think you should enroll in Randolph College. It's too late for this semester, but I know everyone in the admissions office and I'll bet they'd accept you for the January term. Let's go over there first thing Monday morning. What do you say?"

Lauren was seized with excitement. "Phil—It's a *fantastic* idea!"

She could hardly sleep that night, thinking about the possibility of beginning college. Philip had been teaching her to drive, and on Monday morning he let her take the wheel when they drove to the new Randolph College campus, on the grounds of an old estate north of the city near Dogwood Mountain. After talking to them, she felt confident she would be admitted for the second semester. "Since your brother is one of our graduates, we'll give it special consideration," the head of admissions told her.

Uncle Max was on the Board of Trustees, but she did not mention that in her interview.

A week later, Lauren received a letter of acceptance for January 1935. With mounting excitement, she broke the news to her parents. Samuel's reaction was predictable. "What do you want to go to college for, Laurie? It's a waste of time for a pretty girl to study so hard."

Miriam soothed him. "Hush, Samuel, let her do it. There's nothing else to keep her occupied, with Charlotte away."

"The days pass so slowly when you're waiting," she wrote to Charlee.

She was marking time until January, when her studies would begin. And then she and Philip met the Stearnses.

They were about five miles outside of Biltmore on their way to Asheville to visit Uncle Julius, who was recovering from an attack of shingles. Lauren had been enjoying the splendid autumn foliage, when she caught sight of a gleaming black Cadillac stranded on the side of the highway in a grove of trees.

"Look, Phil, those people are having car trouble."

The sedan's hood was up and smoke was rising from the front. A man was leaning over looking into the engine, oblivious of his light gray tweed suit, while a woman clad in a smartly tailored outfit of Hunting Stewart tartan stood with folding arms, impatiently tapping her toe. As Philip's Hudson Speedster rounded the curve, she removed a navy silk scarf from her head and began waving it madly.

Philip pulled over. "Need some help?" he called, stepping out of the car.

The woman knotted the scarf around her neck and clasped her hands together. "I *knew* the gods would send a chariot!" She was small and compact with glossy black hair, compelling dark eyes, and a slash of ruby mouth.

The man was cursing as he peered under the auto's hood. He straightened up, and they saw that he had gotten grease stains on his elegant English tweeds. "Damn engine is overheated. We're going to have to be towed out of here. Can you possibly give us a lift to a phone?"

"We'd be glad to," Philip agreed. "Too bad about your suit."

The man glanced down, shrugging indifferently. "Maybe it'll come out with dry cleaning." When the two were settled in the rear seat, he said, "So good of you to stop. Stearns is our name—George and Norma."

"I'm Philip Jacobson, and this is my sister, Lauren."

"Jacobson, eh?" said Stearns. "Well, lucky for us you two came along. It would've been quite a hike to Asheville."

"We're driving to Asheville. It'd be no trouble to drop you wherever you're going."

"We *live* in Asheville. We were on our way to Randolph Springs," said Mrs. Stearns.

"That's where we live!" Philip's voice had new life.

They stopped at a garage in Biltmore where George made arrangements to have his automobile towed. Then he suggested they go to a nearby lodge so he could place a telephone call and wash the grease from his soiled hands.

"You're not Asheville people," said Lauren.

"How could you tell?"

She laughed. "Your accent, of course! It's Yankee, but different. At least Mrs. Stearns's is."

"Boston, my dear—and please do call me Norma," said the svelte woman. "We've taken a house on Kimberly Avenue for the winter. George had pneumonia last year and he's been advised to avoid the cold weather."

Lauren knew "pneumonia" often meant weak lungs or TB among Asheville's perennial visitors. But George Stearns certainly looked fit enough.

"You must have lunch with us—No, I *insist,*" urged Norma when they tried to beg off.

Lauren exchanged glances with Phil. "I suppose we could call Aunt Esther . . ."

"Yes, *do* call, Philip! Aunt Esthers always understand." Norma Stearns certainly was a persuasive woman, thought Lauren.

Philip excused himself and when he returned, he was smiling. "I had to promise we'd stay for dinner, but it's fine." Lauren saw that he was excited. There were few diversions for him these days and he was drawn to the charming Norma.

Soon they were seated on a terrace overlooking the Swannanoa River, with a magnificent view of Beaucatcher Mountain in the middle distance. Norma fitted a cigarette into a holder and, touching Philip's wrist in a familiar gesture, leaned over for him to light it. Sitting back in the deck chair, she inhaled deeply, as if gathering her strength after an enormous physical effort. "There's nothing I'd adore so much right now as a Tom Collins!"

"They make a good imitation planter's punch here," said Philip. "It's almost like the real thing, and with the 'flavoring' I have out in the car . . ." They all ordered the planter's punch, while Phil brought his flask from the glove compartment. After a second round, they ate a lunch of Charleston She-Crab Soup and Plantation Smothered Chicken.

"Quite a fright your town had last month, when that woman's skeleton was excavated," said George, when they were served chicory coffee with their Peach Spice Cake.

"Yes, there's been a lot of concern," said Philip. "It's unlikely they'll ever solve the mystery."

The female remains had been unearthed by bulldozers at the site of a new hydroelectric plant on Dogwood Mountain. Forensic evidence indicated the woman had been murdered at least two years ago. The case had taken on grisly implications when the dismembered bones of several other victims were discovered in a mass grave nearby.

"I know that construction project because my company makes heavy earth-moving equipment," George explained. "We've been selling to the Federal government for some of their WPA projects. I'm hoping to sign a contract with the State of North Carolina." He shook his head with disbelief. "Can you imagine they still use chain gangs down here to build roads? If they were putting family men to work, it wouldn't be half bad—but prisoners in manacles! Most of them are Negroes, of course."

Lauren always felt defensively Southern when someone from the North discussed the plight of black people in the

South. She was glad when Philip answered quietly, wanting to avoid controversy. "The South is poor, George. It costs money to build roads. I guess if a man's a hardened criminal—say, a murderer—it's not so terrible to expect him to work off his sentence."

Stearns studied his hands. "You, uh, your family is Jewish?"

"That's right."

"We are too, so you won't think I'm prejudiced when I say I've never understood Jewish people in the South. I mean, how they can believe in Jim Crow."

Sooner or later it always got around to this subject with Yankees. "I guess some do," Philip admitted, "but it's not really a question of believing. Jewish people certainly had nothing to do with creating the race laws. There are so few of us down here that our opinion doesn't seem to matter—and our parents and grandparents have learned the hard way, they're in no position to change things—the Ku Klux Klan is just as much against Jews as Negroes."

"So I've heard. That's why I should think Jewish Southerners would stand up for the colored people."

"Many of us do, George. We just don't make a great deal of noise about it. If the United States government won't interfere, what makes you think Southern Jews can?"

"Well," George rubbed his hands briskly, "I never meant to get into such a serious discussion on this beautiful fall afternoon. This has been so pleasant, I'm almost glad our car broke down."

Lauren, who had felt the tension, was relieved when George dropped the issue. "So are we. I hope you'll come visit us if you do get to Randolph Springs."

"We'll be there all right. I have to see a gentleman about some logging equipment he ordered. He was expecting us for lunch today, but I called and explained what happened. A man by the name of Mortimer—perhaps you know him."

"Max Mortimer! He's our uncle, married to our mother's sister."

"What a coincidence!" exclaimed Norma delightedly. "We must definitely plan to get together."

In the ladies' room, Norma gazed at Lauren with open admiration. "What *divine* skin! Lucky girl."

Lauren studied her new friend as she sat at the dressing table patting on powder with a fuzzy puff and rouging her lips. Norma's extravagant mannerisms and enormous poise lent stature to her diminutive size. A certain theatricality suggested she might have been an actress. A perfect pale oval, her face was framed by the black hair parted in the middle and rolled at the nape of her neck. Lauren admired Norma's style and meticulously tailored clothes.

George towered over his wife, although he certainly did not dominate her. His prematurely receding hairline lent his handsome features an air of self-satisfaction. The dark brown eyes were lively and intelligent, but there was a hint of petulance about the sensitive mouth, saved from weakness by a firm square jaw. A natty dresser, he wore his expensive clothes with casual elegance.

With promises to meet again soon, they dropped Norma and George at their rented house, an imposing Italianate mansion on Kimberly Avenue. A week later the Stearnses invited Lauren and Philip to a party. "Darlings!" exclaimed Norma, kissing them at the door as if they were the oldest and dearest of friends. Dressed in a simple long black crepe dress trimmed in satin, she glittered with brilliants at ears, throat and wrists. Taking Lauren by the hand, she possessively linked arms with Philip as she escorted them to meet the other guests.

Norma surrounded herself with attractive bachelors who had names like Cap and Justin and Sherman. They came from New York, Boston, Chicago, or San Francisco, and they had vague professions in manufacturing or finance that enabled them to linger in Asheville for weeks at a time.

"They're all quite pleasant, but don't they have to work?" said Philip on the way home. He might have added that he preferred it when he was the center of the charming Norma's attention.

Lauren and Philip became regulars at the Stearnses' frequent entertainments. The couple viewed their stay in Asheville as one continuous house party, with half a dozen visitors in residence at any one moment.

Jules Taylor was one of their perpetual house guests. ‘‘Who's the attractive couple talking to Norma?’’ he asked George when he noticed his hostess laughing with the newest arrivals at a Stearns soirée.

‘‘It's a brother and sister, actually—Philip and Lauren Jacobson from Randolph Springs. They're kin to Max Mortimer.’’

‘‘My, my, the boy's gone Southern on us!’’

George gave him a thin smile. ‘‘It helps to blend with the natives, Jules. Good for business.’’ He watched Taylor heap his plate with Crab Louisiana. ‘‘Would you like to meet her?’’

‘‘Who?’’ said Jules, as he further applied himself to the buffet.

‘‘You know damn well who—the Jacobson girl.’’

Jules studied Lauren, who was by now in conversation with Cap Strauss. ‘‘Rather pretty, isn't she? Yes, why not? Introduce us.’’

‘‘Now there's a match would solve all your problems, old buddy!’’

‘‘Cad! What are you suggesting?’’

‘‘Didn't your daddy ever tell you it's just as easy to love a rich girl?’’

‘‘My daddy never told me anything, George. He died too young.’’

‘‘So, what does a beautiful girl do with herself in Randolph Springs?’’ asked Jules.

‘‘It depends on the girl, I suppose,’’ Lauren answered. She was absolutely incapable of small talk, as this handsome young man was about to discover.

‘‘Lauren Jacobson was the girl I had in mind.’’

‘‘Well, I've been giving piano lessons, but I'm going to start Randolph College in January.’’

His smooth arched eyebrows rose. ‘‘I didn't realize there was a college there.’’

"It's a small school, but one of the oldest in the state. Did you go to college, Mr. Taylor?"

"Call me Jules—you Southern girls are so formal. You don't mind if I smoke?" He took out a monogrammed gold case, offering her a cigarette, and lighting his own when she refused. "I went to Yale, actually," he said in a bored monotone.

Lauren smiled slightly. "Oh, yes, we've heard of Yale down here."

Head held back, he studied her from under his lashes, "Do you suppose I could persuade you to join me for dinner one evening?"

"Why, that sounds very nice," she answered in her best Southern Girl voice. What a conceited man he was with his patronizing Yankee manner, yet he was mighty good looking. It rather pleased her that Jules behaved the way she had noticed new men acting around Charlee. As if he had made a fantastic discovery.

Jules seemed convinced he was irresistible to women. He was skilled at wooing a girl and despite her qualms, Lauren responded to him. In fact, she found she was extremely attracted to him. His longish black hair, brushed back from a patrician brow, waved romantically above dark brooding eyes and a strong straight nose. He had a sensual mouth, beautifully shaped, the lower lip full with a slight notch in its center. His slim body was fit and he carried himself gracefully, particularly on the dance floor.

All through the autumn, the Stearnses and their friends gave parties every weekend and Lauren always went with Jules. Often he would drive over to Randolph Springs during the week to have dinner and spend a few hours alone with her. Once she even took him to meet Aunt Reba and Uncle Max.

Reba put on what Charlee called her Old Plantation Act, giving Jules the full treatment. "Laurie has always been our very favorite niece, Mr. Taylor. Why, I declare, she's just like a daughter to us, isn't she, Max? Ma-ax . . . I was just sayin' to Mr. Taylor, that Lauren is like our very own daughter."

"Indeed," answered Max, bemused by his wife's ramblings. "What was it you said you do, Mr. Taylor?"

"Investments," said Jules, his eyes roving the luxuriously furnished parlor in which they were sitting.

"In Chicago?"

"Uh, yes, in Chicago and elsewhere. At the moment, I'm interested in lumber, here in the Carolinas and Georgia."

"Indeed?" Max looked thoughtful. "And is your father also in the investment business?"

"Yes—well, not the investment business. That is, my father is deceased—but he was interested in investment the way I am—you know, investing his own money."

"Indeed," said Max. He seemed the one person so far who had succeeded in ruffling Jules's tremendous composure. "Taylor? Let me see, I knew a Jonas Taylor in Chicago."

"No relation to my family, I'm afraid. My father's name was Henry."

On the way home, Jules pulled off the curving road into a small landscaped park. "Just what do you think you're doing?" Lauren demanded when he stopped the motor.

He smiled at her lazily, putting an arm around her and drawing her close. "I'm about to make a pass at you, sweetheart." His kisses were exciting and insistent, and for some moments Lauren enjoyed responding to him, but she felt uneasy sitting there necking not half a mile from her home. All her life, she had been taught that only cheap, easy girls allowed men liberties, especially in the seat of an automobile.

"I think you'd better take me home now," Lauren said, her voice a little unsteady as Jules's hands began to wander. She couldn't help being drawn to him enormously, but she wondered whether he could be trusted. He was a smooth operator . . . Her instincts told her not to expose her heart to Jules Taylor.

"Jules has taken my buddy away," Philip teased Lauren on Thanksgiving weekend, but he was pleased that his sister had a beau. Soured as he was on romance, he felt Lauren could use some in her life.

"Why don't you come to the club with us tonight?" suggested Lauren. "I'm sure Jules won't mind, and there might be some new girls at the dance."

"Thanks, but I told Ben I'd have dinner with him."

"Oh . . ." Lauren gave him a guilty smile. She hadn't seen much of Benson Miller since she had started going out with Jules.

Philip was late arriving at the Old Smoky Tavern. He entered by the bar door where the speakeasy customers used to be admitted. Looking around for Benson, he failed to notice Jack Weaver, whose eyes followed him to the booth where his friend was waiting.

"What kept you?" asked Ben.

"I started talking to Laurie and I forgot the time." A waitress came by, balancing a tray for the next booth and Philip craned his neck to see the order. "I'm starved. What are you having?"

"Ribs, I guess." They gave their order to the waitress, who brought foaming tankards of ale.

"Where's Lauren going tonight?" Ben asked, carefully casual.

"Out with some friends from Asheville." Philip knew Ben was interested in Lauren. He was a great guy and a loyal friend—but Samuel Jacobson had never much cared for the Miller family.

"Is, uh, Lauren serious about that fellow, Jules Taylor?"

Philip shrugged. "I don't think so, Ben. They haven't known each other that long."

With a noisy clatter, the waitress set down a heaping platter of barbecued ribs, accompanied by a basket of beaten biscuits, with side orders of fried apples and corn fritters. "Mmm-mmh, will you look at that," Ben exclaimed with relish, helping himself to the ribs.

At the far end of the bar, Jack Weaver sat alone, steadily sipping whiskey, never taking his eyes off Philip. His handsome, dissipated face, ruddy with drink, looked young for fifty-seven years, but the mouth was hard and hateful. There was a disquieting lack of emotion in his blue eyes. Every so often, without speaking, he raised a finger and the bartender would refill his glass.

"How about another beer?" As Philip looked around for the waitress, his eyes met Weaver's hostile stare, and he drew in his breath, realizing the man must have been watching him from the moment he walked in.

"What's wrong, Phil?"

"Nothing."

"You look like you've seen a ghost." Ben signaled the waitress to bring them another round. As he did, he noticed Jack Weaver stare balefully in their direction and walk out of the bar.

"I thought you were hungry," said Ben, seeing Philip's half-eaten plate.

"I don't know what came over me, but I've lost my appetite." He pushed the food away.

"You feeling okay?"

"I'm fine."

"Something happened before that upset you."

He shook his head. "Nothing important. I just saw—that is, I was reminded of something."

Benson looked thoughtful. "Anne Elizabeth?" Philip stared at him, shocked. "Oh, come on, Phil, you didn't think I wasn't aware of it? I watched you two romancing all last summer. What happened to her? I haven't seen her around lately."

"I—I don't know. She moved away, I think."

Philip remained agitated, scarcely paying attention to Ben's conversation. Although Weaver had left the bar, his hostility lingered. *Could he possibly have discovered that his daughter had been telephoning Philip?*

"I think I'll call it a night," said Phil.

"You're not coming to the housewarming?"

"No, I don't feel like a party, Ben. I'll call you tomorrow." Benson frowned as he watched Phil drive away.

His mother was reading in the sitting room when Philip walked in. "You're home early, dear."

"I was tired, Mama." He leaned over to kiss her, wishing he could go straight up to his room, but knowing she would expect him to sit and talk for a while. ''Where's Pa?''

''He went to bed about an hour ago. He still tires easily.'' There was no accusation in her voice, but Philip thought, *It's because of me that my father will be a sick man for the rest of his life.* ''Would you like anything to eat before I go upstairs?'' asked Miriam.

''No thanks, Mama, I just finished dinner. I've got a golf date first thing in the morning, so I think I'll turn in now.''

Lying in bed, Philip tried to read, but he could not stop thinking about the murderous look on the face of Jack Weaver . . . Or the sheer panic in Anne Elizabeth's voice the other afternoon when she had called him.

Chapter 8

THE TRAIN WAS just pulling into the station when Max parked in a spot reserved for official cars. It was typical of him to ignore rules made for mere mortals, thought Lauren. She watched impatiently as each passenger stepped out of the Southern Railway Pullman cars. Half-way down the platform a group of college men in raccoon coats jumped off and turned expectantly, their arms outstretched.

"There she is, Uncle Max!"

Poised in the doorway of the car was Charlee, wearing her favorite shade of mulberry in a soft melton wool coat trimmed with stone marten, and carrying a matching fur muff. As she grinned down at the cluster of upturned all-American faces, they boisterously shouted, *Ta-daaa! Here she comes, Ra-a-andolph Springs! C'mon, Charlee . . . jump!*

Lauren stole a quick glance at Max, who was trying to contain his consternation. She put a sympathetic hand on his arm, "That's *so* Charlee, Uncle Max—doesn't she look wonderful!" She began to run down the platform, waving and calling her cousin's name.

Charlee beamed at her over the heads of the boys who lifted her down and set her feet on native soil. Breaking from the group, she engulfed Lauren in a bear hug. "Laurie—oh Laurie, honey, I'm so *glad* to see you!" She turned to the bemused young men. "Didn't I tell you-all I had a beautiful cousin?" she cried. "This is Laurie—and these boys have been *the* most perfect gentlemen you would *ever* want to meet!"

The perfect gentlemen were staring fixedly beyond the girls at someone who cleared his throat. *"Daddy!"* Charlee shrieked, throwing her arms around Max, kissing him, and knocking his Irish tweed bog cap from Abercrombie & Fitch to the ground.

One of the young men stepped forward to retrieve the hat and shake hands. "Good afternoon, sir, I'm Buddy Wainwright, Thomas Wainwright's son. I believe you know my father."

"Buddy and I hadn't laid eyes on each other since our dancing school days, Daddy, but he recognized me immediately in the dining car. Why, I don't know how I would have managed without these boys. They've been simply *amazing!"*

Even more amazing was the change that came over Max's countenance. He smiled the very special smile he reserved for a favored few—old line Georgians, famous personalities, and the socially prominent. "Well now, wasn't that fortunate? I want to thank you, Mr. Wainwright and all you young gentlemen, for taking care of my little girl. It's difficult for a female to travel without an escort. I might not have been so worried about Charlotte Lee, had I known you-all were on this same train."

"Our privilege, sir," Buddy bowed while his friends murmured their assent. "It's been a real pleasure meeting you."

"You must stop by sometime to visit us," said Max. "Your aunt and uncle, the Randolphs, are our neighbors on Shadow Mountain, you know."

Lauren noticed an imperceptible flicker in young Wainwright's eyes before he replied, "That's very kind of you, Mr. Mortimer."

A porter was hovering at Max's elbow. "Excuse me, sir. The young lady's baggage—?" A pyramid of matched Mark Cross luggage in protective gray suede coverings was piled on the platform next to a steamer trunk.

"My word, Charlotte Lee," said Max, "all that won't fit in the roadster. We'll carry as much as we can in the back and Bertram will have to come down later with the station car to collect the rest." With a flurry of good-byes to Buddy Wainwright and his house guests, they were on their way to Shadow Mountain Drive.

After the first joy of reunion, Charlee was restless. She went through the ritual of visiting all the relatives, and together she and Lauren made the rounds of luncheons, teas, and supper parties. But it was apparent that Charlee was bored in Randolph Springs.

"Mother and her family affairs!" she complained fretfully to Lauren, swinging her foot impatiently and staring at the mountains through the window of the sun parlor. "I suppose we should count ourselves lucky to be let off early from Christmas dinner."

The family did not celebrate Christmas as a religious holiday, of course, but they always gathered at Reba's with all the relatives for a festive dinner on Christmas Day. The season was a time of profitable business and general goodwill for Jewish merchants. Even Samuel, who had childhood memories of bitter Russian anti-Semitism at this time of year, was touched with the Yuletide spirit.

On Christmas Night Lauren and Philip were invited to a supper dance by the Stearnses at their rented mansion in Asheville. When Norma heard that Charlotte would be in town, she told them to be sure to bring her along.

Jules had gone back to Chicago after Thanksgiving on some urgent business. He had called Lauren several times, hinting he might return for New Year's Eve. At first she missed him, but as the days passed, with the excitement of having Charlee home and the rush of holiday activities, Jules was not much in her thoughts.

"So *this* is the famous Charlee," drawled Norma, who was striking tonight in a pearl gray taffeta dress molded to her hips and flaring to the floor in side panniers. Its long close-fitting sleeves and stark low neckline set off perfectly her magnificent sapphire and diamond necklace.

Four months of finishing school had endowed Charlotte with an enviable amount of poise. Shoulders held high, hips slanted forward, she extended a gloved hand, saying in a well-modulated voice, "Mrs. Stearns, thank you so much for inviting me this evening."

"If you don't call me Norma and kiss me Merry Christmas, I'll send you right out the door!" their hostess chided.

Charlee's eyes crinkled in amusement as she kissed the air next to Norma's cheek. Resplendent in one of her New York gowns of rich deep red velvet, Charlotte attracted everyone's attention as she handed her ermine wrap to a maid. Her expression remained cordial, but Lauren detected a skeptical gleam in the smoky-ringed hazel eyes. She thought Charlee was not ready to be taken in by Norma's forceful personality.

"Ducky, I know you've been looking forward to this," Norma called, capturing George's attention. "Let me present my husband . . . Miss Charlotte Lee Mortimer—better known as Charlee."

Taking Charlotte's hand, George looked directly into her eyes. "You're even lovelier than I expected, Miss Mortimer."

Charlee gave him the benefit of her dazzling smile. "That's rather gallant for a Yankee. May I call you George?"

"I insist on it! And now I'm going to play hooky from door duty and dance with you," he said, leading her into the main parlor.

"I could swear George has developed a slight Southern accent," Phil murmured in Lauren's ear.

Norma had a predatory, expectant look, as if she harbored a delicious secret. Her eyes stalked the spacious hallway, coming to rest on one or another of her guests, than darting sideways at Lauren.

"You have something up your sleeve tonight, Norma. You can't fool me."

"Darling Lauren, you know me so well. You'll just have to wait and see." She gave Philip a playful shove. "Take her into the other room, Phil. There's music and champagne, see that you have a *wonderful* time."

Philip danced with Lauren until Cap Strauss cut in. Cap was a superb dancer, leading her expertly through a sultry tango. She knew they made an attractive pair, he in his tuxedo, she in her midnight-blue lace gown shot with silver. "Let's have some bubbly," he suggested, reaching for two glasses as a waiter passed carrying a tray of champagne. He raised his goblet in a toast. "Here's to the prettiest blue eyes south of the Mason and Dixon."

Lauren giggled and sipped her champagne, watching the dancing couples over Cap's shoulder. Suddenly she froze, thinking her eyes were deceiving her. There was her cousin Charlotte, in the brilliant red velvet dress, swirling around the dance floor to the strains of a Viennese waltz . . . in the arms of Jules Taylor.

Noting her expression, something between surprise and chagrin, Cap followed her gaze. He whistled. "Well, well, will you look who's back in town."

Lauren carefully put her glass down on a side table. "Let's dance again, shall we?"

Cap bowed slightly, saluting her with a mock salaam. "Ever your most obedient."

In the doorway of the huge parlor, her glittering eyes bright with excitement, Norma Stearns surveyed the whirling couples with a satisfied smile. She *adored* drama . . . The party was going swimmingly.

Driving to Uncle Julius's house where they were spending the night, Philip was furious. "Charlee's a perfect *bitch* to leave the party with Jules! I have a mind to tell her off when she comes in."

"Don't be silly, Phil. It doesn't bother me a bit, and besides she has no inkling I was seeing him."

"The hell she doesn't! Enough people were talking about it tonight. She must have *some* idea."

Lauren thought so too, although she preferred to believe her cousin (her *best friend,* for heaven's sake!) had been unaware of her romance with Jules Taylor. A very short romance, as it turned out.

She had been tongue-tied when Jules finally danced with her tonight, cutting in on Cap. "Surprise, surprise!" he said, holding her close in a fox trot.

"Yes!" she answered brightly, a fixed smile on her face. "How was Chicago?"

"Co-o-ol. I couldn't get back here fast enough."

"It can get mighty chilly in these mountains during the winter, Jules."

He winced. "But they say the natives are friendly."

She couldn't help laughing. "We like to amuse ourselves with strangers. It helps to pass the time."

She pretended to be asleep when Charlee came into the bedroom they were sharing. Maybe it would have been better to tell her at that moment that Jules was the man she had been dating. They had always been honest with each other. When they were in high school, vamping other girls' beaux had been a game for Charlee. *All's fair in love, Laurie* . . . But surely the grown up Charlotte would not want to take Lauren's suitor away from her! Except, Jules was not *hers*. A few kisses, some easy caresses, a bit of heavy breathing accompanied by murmured endearments, did not constitute devotion or exclusive rights. What a naif she had been to ever suppose they did.

Charlee claimed a champagne headache the next morning, and after a light breakfast, she dozed in the back seat while Philip drove home to Randolph Springs. The cousins did not communicate with each other the next day, but on Friday morning, Charlotte called Lauren. "I'm leaving for New York on the thirtieth, Laurie. My roommate's giving a New Year's Eve party, and I've decided to go back for it."

"The thirtieth? But that's only two days from now."

"Yes, I know it's short notice. Mother and Daddy hadn't wanted me to go at first, but they changed their minds. Anyway, I would've had to leave on New Year's Day because classes begin on the third, and we have to check-in the night before. Most of the girls will be returning to New York early for Blanche's party. It's being held at the Harmonie." Laurie had no idea what the Harmonie was—another of those stodgy clubs, she imagined, like the ones they had visited in Atlanta and Baltimore. "Oh . . . Laurie, honey . . . I hope that boy, Jules Taylor, isn't someone *special* to you. Mama says you've been seeing him. I swear I had no *idea!*"

"Don't worry, Charlee. Jules means nothing to me. He was just another man to go out with."

Charlotte sighed audibly. "I am so-o-o relieved to hear

you say that.'' Her voice took on that intimate, confidential tone that people always found appealing. ''You know, Laurie, I think Jules is something of a *masher.* I'm afraid I had a bit too much champagne that night—well, I don't even want to think about it, but I am *really* embarrassed.'' There was that low, suggestive chuckle again. ''I surely am glad you aren't stuck on him. That would've made me feel even worse.''

''I'm sure it wasn't half as bad as you remember,'' said Lauren lightly. ''Don't give it another thought.''

Bitch! She slammed the receiver down, feeling a vast relief that Charlee was leaving early, picturing with satisfaction the expression on Jules Taylor's face when he learned that Charlotte Mortimer would not be in Randolph Springs for the country club dance on New Year's Eve.

As for Lauren, she intended to go with Cap Strauss!

With her first day of classes at Randolph College, Lauren became thoroughly focused on her studies, to the exclusion of almost everything else. Nevertheless, she went over to the Mortimers' one evening in February when Max invited her to come by to see him. He ushered her into his private study, closing the door, which indicated a subject of serious nature. Oh dear, what if Aunt Reba was ill—or Charlee.

''There's a matter I want to discuss with you, Lauren.''

''What is it, Uncle Max? Is everything all right with the family?''

''Yes, yes, nothing like that,'' he assured her. ''I might as well tell you—there's been something on my mind. This Taylor man you brought to meet us—''

''What about him?'' she asked suspiciously.

''I hope—that is, do you have deep feelings for him?''

''Certainly not!'' She hadn't meant to make her response quite so emphatic. ''I no longer see him, Uncle Max. He went back to Chicago.''

''I'm relieved to hear that. There was something about him—I pride myself on being a good judge of character, Lauren, and that young man just did not ring true. I took the liberty of having him investigated—''

"*Investigated?* But, why?"

"Now, don't go getting your dander up, honey. I didn't set a private detective on his tail. I just made a few discreet inquiries. You know, I have friends all over this country, and I wanted to be certain you weren't becoming involved with the wrong sort of young man."

Lauren found herself growing exceedingly angry. What right did her uncle have to ask questions about any man she was dating? She wasn't *his* daughter!

"First of all," continued Max, "his real name isn't Taylor. It used to be Talpalotsky."

"Plenty of families change their names, Uncle Max," she said calmly, while seething inside. "Jules can't be blamed for that."

"No, I suppose not, but he led me to believe his father's name was *Henry Taylor,* when the man lived and died as Hyman Talpalotsky. He also said his father was an investor—when, in fact, the man was a *tailor.*"

She tried to make a joke of it. "I suppose you could say he stretched the truth—his father was Henry the tailor."

"It is no laughing matter, Lauren. The young man deliberately set out to deceive you and us. He spoke about his own investments, when in point of fact, he's in quite a bit of financial difficulty in Chicago. His debts are significant, and aside from that, he has the reputation of being a—a ladies' man. Why, there's a story one of my contacts told about him and a wealthy young widow from Highland Park—"

Heatedly, she interrupted, "Please, Uncle Max, must we go into all this? I never was in love with Jules Taylor, and I am not interested in gossip about his romantic conquests—be it with wealthy widows—or *heiresses,* for that matter! I can't bear Jules a grudge. He never directly lied to me or took advantage of me."

Max sighed. "Very well, honey, I hope not. I felt it was my duty as your uncle to protect you from a fortune hunter."

"Uncle Max . . . Are you forgetting that I don't have a fortune for anyone to hunt?"

She managed to hide the depth of her anger as she said good-bye. It would do no good to complain about Max's meddling in her affairs, for then it would become a family matter, growing all out of proportion.

In the following weeks, with her full schedule of classes, she had little time to dwell on the incident. Each morning, she drove out to Randolph College, often coming home after dark. Her father was apprehensive about her going alone, especially since that murdered woman George Stearns had once mentioned had been found buried on Dogwood Mountain a few miles beyond the campus. "Be sure to lock the car doors, Laurie," Samuel cautioned, "I don't like you driving at night."

"Papa, you know that woman wasn't killed because she was alone on the highway," Lauren chided him. There was growing evidence that the murder had been connected with illegal night-riding activities of the Ku Klux Klan.

Philip gloated when Lauren finished her mid-terms with excellent grades. "Was that ever a brainstorm, sending you to Randolph!" he chortled. She was willing to give him full credit, because she would never have started college if it had not been for her brother.

She could feel herself gaining confidence as the weeks went by. Meanwhile, Philip became more and more retiring with passing time. Instead of getting out and meeting new people, or making dates with women, he moped around the house in the evenings. Engrossed in her studies, Lauren was guiltily aware of her brother's unhappiness. She made several attempts to draw him out, hoping he would unburden himself. But Philip remained encased in a shell.

Chapter 9

WINTER HAD NOT yet relinquished the mountains to spring when Philip drove across the state line to the wilderness of Georgia's northeasternmost corner. In another month the uplands would be glorious with mountain laurel and wild rhododendron, but as he entered the hideous little lumber town, Philip found its bleakness a demoralizing sight.

The threatening hulk of a burned-out filling station cast a dark shadow on the road where the highway forked. That was his landmark. He pulled into a deserted side street and locked his car. Glancing nervously over his shoulder, he entered a brick-faced building and walked up two flights of stairs.

If you come during the day, no one will be here . . .

The drive down through the mountains had taken him longer than expected. He knew this trip had been a mistake, but how could he say no? *Just this once,* she begged, *I promise I'll never call you again.*

He knocked on the rear door of the third floor. "Who's there?" It was a fearful whisper.

"It's Phil."

The door opened and as he stepped inside, hesitating a moment, Anne Elizabeth threw herself into his arms. She clung to him in a desperate kiss until she was overcome with tears.

"Shh, don't cry, Annie. Come, sit down." He led her across the linoleum floor to a lumpy sofa, handing her his handkerchief. She looked ill, her skin pale, her hair lusterless. "Are you okay?"

She wiped her eyes and nodded. "I guess so."

"Now, tell me what this is all about."

He sat back, trying not to stare, yet unable to believe this was the same blooming girl he had known last summer. Her face looked almost ravaged. Her hands, which she kept twisting in her lap as she spoke, were rough and red, the cuticles raggedy and nails bitten to the quick. Although she had taken some pains with her appearance in preparation for his visit, her dress was worn and stained and her skin showed months of neglect. But worse was the defeat and fear in her eyes.

With growing unease and disbelief, Philip listened to Anne Elizabeth's halting words. He drew a sharp breath, interrupting her. "You're *married?* Why didn't you tell me that before?" She had never mentioned anything about marriage on the telephone. In her letter she had said she was going away to live with relatives. What the hell was *he* doing here if she had a husband? "How—who did you marry?"

"He's older, a friend of my father's."

"Annie—I don't know what to say. Did you *want* to marry him?"

She shook her head. "There wasn't a choice." Her lips trembled and tears spilled down her cheeks. "I had to, Phil . . . I was pregnant."

He was unable to hide his shock. "Oh—I see."

"It's not what you're thinking—It wasn't *my* doing—I was *raped!* And not by the man I married!" She began to cry again. "It wasn't the first time. It had been happening ever since I was fourteen."

"But, Annie! How could you let it go on that long? Why didn't you tell your parents? They would have put a stop to it."

"I couldn't," she sobbed. "I couldn't do that to my mama. She's so sick and miserable as it is—this would've killed her."

"You must have other relatives. Wasn't there anyone you could ask for help?"

"There's never been anyone I could talk to, until you.

I longed to confide in you, but I never knew how to begin.'' She shook her head, unable to continue.

He put his arm around her protectively. ''Poor Annie. Who was it? Who did this terrible thing to you?''

''I want to tell you, but I'm so ashamed, Philip. And I'm afraid. If he ever finds out I said anything—he'll *kill* me! He said he would, and I believe him.''

''You can trust me, Anne Elizabeth, I promise.''

She was shaking uncontrollably. ''I'm scared to tell you. I can hardly say it. It's—it's worse than you can imagine . . . It's the *worst sin in the Bible!''*

Philip had never seen anyone so frightened. He tried to divine what could terrorize her so. Who had that kind of power over her, if not her husband or her—? And suddenly he knew. *''No!* It can't be—*He* didn't?'' She nodded her head insistently. *''Your own father raped you?''*

He had to bend his head to understand her. *''Yes!* He beat me until I gave in to him. And he would beat Mama and my little brothers, so to protect them I let him—And then when he knew I was pregnant, he forced me to marry this man he used to know from the Klan, Jed Hawley.'' Anne Elizabeth shuddered visibly. ''He's *disgusting!* He's big and mean—and he's more than twenty years older than me, Phil!''

Jed Hawley . . . ? He knew that name from somewhere. The sordidness of her story made him feel ill. ''Oh Annie, I'm so awfully sorry. What about the baby?''

''After all the shame and suffering, I lost it. I wouldn't even have had to get married,'' she said bitterly. ''At first my father told me he was taking me to a doctor to—you know, to get rid of it? One day last August he suddenly had a whole lotta big bills—I don't know where he got 'em from. But then he disappeared for two days, and when he came home, the money was gone. I knew he'd been on a binge because it had happened before. He played cards and lost. Giving me to Jed as a wife was part of settling.'' She blew her nose and took a deep shuddery breath. ''It might not be so awful if we could have stayed in Hendersonville, but Jed got in some trouble a while back and he's been hiding out down here ever since.''

What kind of people were these? In his worse visions of what had happened to Anne Elizabeth, Philip had never suspected anything as bad as this.

But it wasn't Annie's fault. She was her father's *victim.* Philip's revulsion gave way to pity. Somehow he managed to say words of comfort, to soothe Anne Elizabeth and get her to stop crying, but he was suddenly impatient to get out of there. If someone had seen him enter the apartment and reported to her husband, or if Hawley came home early from the lumber camp—Philip wasn't a coward, but he knew he was no match for a brutal lumberjack who could count on his friends for assistance.

"I don't know what to say, Anne Elizabeth. I wish there was something I could do to help you. Why don't you leave your husband?"

She shook her head. "Jed said if I ever tried, he'd come after me. I'm even more afraid of him than I am of my daddy!"

It was getting late, and Philip couldn't wait to get going. "I have to say good-bye now."

"Thank you for coming Phil, it was a help just talking to you. Will we ever see each other again?"

He didn't have the heart to say no, for she had the most hopeless look in her eyes. "Maybe, after a while. Take care of yourself, Annie." He ran down the stairs, eager to get far away from that town as quickly as possible. Driving back to Randolph Springs, Philip was burning with rage against Weaver. The bastard! The no-account white trash pig! His heart ached for Anne Elizabeth, but at the same time, he couldn't help feeling she was soiled. He hated himself for it, but everything in him shouted *unclean, unclean!*

So . . . He was beginning to understand what had happened that August day when Samuel had his heart attack. The *money* . . . that was the clue. Where had Weaver got hold of it? Phil didn't buy that gambling story. Jack Weaver must have shaken his father down! But how? Why would Pa have given him so much money? Some sort of blackmail, perhaps . . . but what could Weaver have said to make Samuel fork over the 'whole lotta bills' Annie had seen? It had to be about Philip—that much he knew. Philip and Anne Elizabeth . . . A cold, prickly sensation crept over Phil as a dreadful thought occurred to him. He grasped the steering wheel, afraid he might drive off the mountainous road. Annie had been pregnant . . . *Had Weaver told Samuel that Philip was the baby's father?* Of course! That explained everything—his father's anguish, his refusal to discuss it with Philip, and the loss of the love and trust that had always existed between them.

Phil was full of pain, realizing the burden Samuel had been carrying. No wonder Pa had collapsed that day! What if he had *died* believing Phil had betrayed him? Philip loved his father without reservation, and he could not bear knowing that Samuel had silently been grieving, believing his son had got Weaver's daughter pregnant. He longed to explain, but he had given his word to Anne Elizabeth not to repeat what she had told him.

Philip blinked back the tears that came to his eyes as he drove north through the mountains to Randolph Springs. If only there were some way to let Samuel know his son had not dishonored the family name.

It was fortunate that Philip did not run into Jack Weaver over the next few weeks. He might not have been able to hide his anger and revulsion. At the end of May, he and Benson joined some friends for an evening out.

"What do you say we try the Old Smoky," suggested Ben.

"That's such a dump," said Phil. The last place he wanted to go was the Old Smoky Tavern.

"It's the only place in town that makes a decent barbecue," answered Ben, and the others agreed.

When they walked in, Jack Weaver was sitting at the bar with some men. Philip tried to ignore his presence, but Weaver sat directly opposite their booth, insolently staring in their direction. It was unnerving and had he been alone with Ben, Philip would have walked out. As soon as they placed their orders, he excused himself. "I'll be right back."

Weaver followed Philip to the rear hallway, grabbing his

arm just as he reached the door of the men's room. "Still up to your old tricks, Jacobson?" he growled.

"I don't know what you're talking about, Mr. Weaver," Phil answered, pulling away from his grasp.

"Ask your daddy. Sammy knows."

Philip felt an uncontrollable rage as he turned on Weaver. "You're not fit to say his name! You ever mention my father again and I'll tell what you—"

"What's that you're sayin', boy? You'll *what?*"

Philip took a deep breath. "Nothing. Get away from me." He tried to walk into the men's room, but the older man stood in his path.

"Now, let's get this straight, fella. Were you threatening me?"

"No, I wasn't *threatening* you! Just lay off me."

"One of these days, jewboy, you're goin' to get yours!"

Philip pushed past Weaver and locked the door behind him. His hands shook as he stood at the urinal. What did Weaver know? Looking into the murky mirror above the wash basin, he whispered, *You're crazy, Phil—he couldn't possibly have found out you went down to see Anne Elizabeth.*

Benson was in the hall when he came out. "Hey, Phil, what's going on? What was that redneck saying to you?"

"He was just drunk, Ben. Forget it."

Ben gave him a quizzical glance and shrugged. "Okay. Your food is getting cold."

When they went back to their table, Weaver had left.

Philip had made up his mind not to go to the Old Smoky Tavern again. It unsettled him to see Weaver, and in the heat of anger, he'd come too close to blurting out what Anne Elizabeth had divulged about her father's attacks on her.

Jack Weaver was a nasty customer. If he ever suspected she had told Philip the truth, there was no doubt he would go after Anne Elizabeth—and she had suffered enough.

"I was right, Jack. Anne Elizabeth's been foolin' around with that Jew!"

"Are you sure, Jed? I made her swear on the Bible she

would never talk to him again. I told her what I'd do to her if she did."

"Doesn't he have sort of light brown hair? And doesn't he drive a green Hudson auto*mo*bile? A man answerin' to that description was seen visitin' Anne Elizabeth last month when I was at the lumber camp. A fine thing, fuckin' around when she's a married woman. And with a dirty Jew. I should've known when you passed her off on me, she was damaged goods."

"That's not true, Jed Hawley! She came to you pure and virgin."

"Did not! That child warn't mine, that baby she threw. 'Twas a sickly, mewling little critter, warn't fit to live."

"Whattaya mean? I thought the baby was born dead."

"It died at birth," said Hawley tersely.

Weaver felt a chill. Had Hawley *murdered* the baby? He wouldn't put it past him. He was a violent son of a bitch and it made him mighty uneasy to think of his little girl in the clutches of that hillbilly.

"You've gotta take care of that boy, Jack."

"What—what do you mean?"

"You *know* what I mean. He knows my *name* and where I *live.* Your precious daughter saw to that!"

"*Jesus!* Now hold on a minute, Jed. Don't be too hasty. That family, the Jacobsons, they're a big family in this county. Yeah—in fact, all over the state. There's one in Hendersonville and Asheville—and—and they got kin all through the Carolinas—and Georgia, too. This ain't like the old days, Jed. You can't get away with goin' after Jews or Catholics. They got *power,* those people!"

"That ain't *my* worry, Weaver. If you want your little girl in one piece, you damn well better get rid of her boyfriend."

"Jed—I *can't.* I ain't never done that before—killed a man."

"C'mon, Jack," he cajoled Weaver. "Tell you what. Don't even think about killin' nobody. We'll work together, you and me. Just like it used to be. We'll get us some good ole boys and have us a little fun, a little mischief. We'll just teach him a lesson, that's all."

"I don't know, Jed . . ."

"Well, *I* know, so you just damn well better do what I tell you. You'll hear from me." The telephone went dead.

"Oh, Jesus God!" Tears came to Weaver's eyes and his hands shook as he poured himself a drink.

Why did he ever, *ever* let his daughter marry Jed Hawley? He *loved* Anne Elizabeth! He'd never meant to hurt her, he just couldn't seem to help himself. When he had the drink in him and his wife was too weak and sick to be a proper woman to him, it was hell to see that lovely young girl with her beautiful beckoning body, day after day, night after night—It was *her* fault. She'd bewitched him, turning the whole family against him until he had to punish all of them. *Oh God! Sweet Jesus! Blood of the lamb, forgive me! I have sinned. I have sold my daughter into slavery, to the black devil.*

Be good to her, he had begged. Take good care of my little girl. He must have been out of his mind to let Jed have her! He was pure evil, that man. Surely it was Hawley who had murdered that Quaker teacher who had vanished years ago—the one who set up a school for nigger children. Jack shuddered and took another gulp of Wild Turkey. The teacher's wife had been summoned from Philadelphia to help with the investigation, but she never had reached Hendersonville. Just a few months ago, after these many years, her skeleton, identified through dental records, had been found buried on Dogwood Mountain.

That's when Jed Hawley had taken off for Georgia with Anne Elizabeth.

Chapter 10

June 1935

LAUREN GLANCED AT her wristwatch that Friday evening, thinking Phil should have come home from work by now. He had mentioned he might be delayed because he had to set out new merchandise for tomorrow.

What a luxury to be alone for four entire days, with only her brother for company. Phil had volunteered to mind the store while Miriam and Samuel went to Gastonia for their cousin's daughter's marriage to a boy from New Bern. Lauren had breathed a sigh of relief that morning when her parents had finally departed with Reba and Max. If she had to listen once more to Reba's twaddle about what *lo-o-ovely* people the groom's family were, or how they simply *ado-o-ored* Betsy, she might just puke, to borrow a phrase from Phil.

Of course, they had urged her to come along, but she had endured enough irritating family gatherings in the past year to last a lifetime. It made her blood boil to smile when sundry relatives remarked, "You'll be the *next* bride, Laurie . . ." Or the prize comment from Cousin Rose's husband at the last anniversary party: "Time to get you a husband, Laurie. Fruit that hangs too long, dies on the vine!"

Charlee had managed to wriggle out of the wedding by having her roommate come down to visit from New York. They had gone on an outing to Lake Lure and Chimney Rock today, inviting Lauren to join them, but she had begged off. One afternoon with the haughty, self-centered Blanche Fields had been enough for her!

At eight o'clock, Lauren called the store, but there was no answer, so Philip must be on his way home. She felt guilty keeping Pansy so late, knowing she had another meal to prepare for her own family. As soon as Philip got here, she would ask him to drive her home. When he had not arrived by eight-thirty, Lauren was annoyed. How thoughtless of him not to call! She dialed The Liberty again, but the telephone just rang and rang.

"I'll take you home now, Pansy, and then I'll just go by to see what's delaying Phil. Maybe he's back in the stockroom and can't hear the phone."

After dropping Pansy, Lauren drove up Vance Street, turning into the alley to the rear of the store where there was a loading platform. Phil's Hudson was parked next to the shipping entrance, so he couldn't have left the store. Why hadn't he answered the telephone when she called? It would be quiet with no one else in the building, so even if he was in the stockroom, he should have been able to hear it ring. And then she thought, What if someone had come—*A burglar!* She felt cold fingers of fear along her spine. But that was ridiculous, what a wild imagination she had. Living in the Jacobson family made you a prophet of doom.

It was creepy back there, with just one street lamp illuminating the alley, casting shadows in the parking area. Lauren gave a startled cry as a stray cat ran across the loading platform, leaping down and disappearing behind the rubbish bins. She banged on the steel door with her fist. "Phil! Philip, it's Laurie—open the door!" Her voice rang hollowly through the dark alley, but despite her repeated calls, no one came.

Phil's automobile was unlocked. Fighting her rising anxiety, she looked inside on the seat and dashboard. There was the usual clutter of papers and road maps. *Where could Philip have gone?* It wasn't like him to run off without calling her. Unless there had been an emergency. . . .

As she slowly walked to her father's Packard, her foot

kicked something that scraped across the blacktop. Looking around the pavement, she caught the gleam of metal reflecting light from the street lamp. Bending to pick it up, she felt a chill of alarm as she recognized the monogrammed key ring she had given Philip for his birthday last year. Had he dropped his keys when he locked up—or had some harm come to her brother?

Whom could she call? Everyone in the family had gone to the wedding, except for Charlee, who would not be home. Phil had a number of friends, but she didn't want to embarrass him if he showed up soon with a perfectly reasonable explanation. Benson Miller was the most likely to understand, but she was reluctant to call him, for Ben used every excuse to be in her company and she didn't want to give him any encouragement.

But what if Philip was in danger? He could have been taken somewhere at gun point. Those things happened. Thieves could have broken into the store—or forced him to open up. Maybe they had cracked the safe and left him inside, tied up and gagged. It wasn't crazy, she read such things in the paper all the time. Phil might be lying there, hit on the head, injured—Maybe she should contact the police. Oh, but that would create a *cause celebre,* with their names in the newspaper and all—her family had such a horror of notoriety. Dammit, there was just one person she could call.

A newstand was the only place open in the arcade on the Square. It was a place that attracted loiterers, but it had a pay phone. "Hello, Mrs. Miller, this is Lauren Jacobson . . . fine, thank you . . . uh-huh . . . they went to the wedding. Is Ben home, by any chance? May I please speak to him?"

She grimaced as she heard the woman calling, "Benson! There's a lovely young lady on the telephone for you." Oh Lord, she could hear them whispering.

"Laurie, is that you?" *Is that really you!*

"Yes, Ben. Do you happen to know where Phil is?"

She heard the disappointment in his voice. "No, I haven't spoken to him for a couple of days."

"Well . . . look, Ben, there's no one else I can call. I

don't want you to say anything to your folks, please, but I can't find Philip. He seems to have disappeared."

"Disappeared? What do you mean?"

"He didn't come home for dinner and there was no answer when I called, so I came downtown to look for him. The store's locked and his car's in the parking lot, but there's no sign of Phil." She told Ben about finding the keys on the ground.

"I'll bet he went off with some of the guys. He probably dropped the keys getting in someone's car."

"Phil wouldn't do that without telling me, Ben. Our family's away and he knew I'd be waiting for him." She hesitated. "I was going to look inside the store. I mean, if someone robbed the safe and tied him up—"

"No, don't do that, Laurie," he said in alarm. "I'll go with you. Where are you, anyway?"

"In the arcade smoke shop on the Square."

"Lord! You stand outside there and I'll be right down."

What could Phil be up to, Ben wondered. If he didn't know better, he'd think his friend was with a woman, but Phil had shown little interest in girls since Anne Elizabeth Weaver left town. Something peculiar had happened there. *Hey!* I bet it's got something to do with Anne Elizabeth. Two bucks says she came back to Randolph and gave Phil a call and he's shacked up with her somewhere. He couldn't tell that to Lauren, of course, she'd never understand. But it had to be something like that. He would go through the motions of looking for him and by that time, Philip would show up. He could take his time, for all Ben cared.

"Hey, Laurie." He jumped out of his automobile and helped her in. "Leave your car here and I'll drive."

"I'm sorry to bother you, Ben, but I'm really worried."

"Don't you fret, Laurie, nothing's happened to Phil." He patted her hand, noticing how quickly she moved it away.

Philip was not in the stockroom. They searched the entire store. The offices were in order, the safe undisturbed.

It was apparent that he had locked up in an orderly manner.

"It surely doesn't look like he was rushed when he left," said Benson. "Show me where you found the keys."

Lauren retraced her steps to Philip's car. "What shall we do, Ben, call the police?"

"Let's go back to your house first. He might have left a note after you went out." They picked up Lauren's car and he followed her home.

The phone was ringing as they entered. Lauren made a dash for it, but whoever called had hung up. "Ohh, that's so frustrating! Do you think it was Phil?"

"If it was, he'll call back. He must realize you've been looking for him."

"What time is it, Ben? My watch has stopped."

"Eleven-thirty."

"How did it get so late? Would you like some coffee?"

"No, but you go ahead and have some." He noticed the pots of food on the stove. "You haven't eaten dinner."

"I couldn't eat anything now, I'm too nervous." She shivered and he put his arm around her. "Ben, I *know* something really awful has happened to Philip. I can just feel it . . ."

At first there were flashes of pain, like dabs of a brilliant color—each stroke bearable, but blinding in its profusion. Despite his terror, he was overwhelmed with a sense of unreality. *This could not be happening to him!* In 1935 civilized men did not flog human beings.

With each bite of the whip his body jerked, writhing convulsively. It came whistling into him again and again, and as the successive blows drew blood, he discovered there were no limits to pain.

A part of his mind remained alert, while the rest of him was consumed with the excruciating torture. Focusing on Hawley's tempo and rhythm, anticipating the tone and color of the next stroke, he prepared for a crescendo of searing punishment. He looked for variations in its duration and intensity. How long could Jed continue without a pause?

Never had he imagined it was possible to suffer so. In his agony, his teeth clamped down on the stout stick they had jammed between his jaws. That had been Jack Weaver's idea—To make it easier on him, Philip wondered, or to stifle the sound of his screams? Had there been a flicker of sympathy in Weaver's eyes, a measure of mercy?

There was no mercy in Jed Hawley. He enjoyed this. Hawley derived a sexual pleasure out of inflicting pain. Philip had seen it in Jed's excitation from the moment he dragged him from the rear of the truck and ripped his clothes off. Poor Annie, what she must have suffered from him.

Too late, insight had come to him. After they jumped him in the parking lot, gagged and trussed him, threw him in the rear of the pickup, and covered him with a tarp, he heard Weaver's voice trembling with exertion and fear, "Let's get the hell outta here, Jed. They've got long memories in Randolph. You get caught this time, the Klan won't be there to help you." In a flash he understood what he had not bothered to figure out two months ago. Jed Hawley, Anne Elizabeth's husband, was the klansman who was implicated in those horrible murders! Why hadn't he thought of it before, when Annie had told him her husband's name? He should have remembered and gone to the police.

Philip knew exactly why they had come for him. What he had not foreseen was what Hawley planned to do before silencing him forever.

Oh God! God in Heaven! The wet leather ripped into his flesh, tearing it open. He heard Hawley's grunts as he threw his weight into the lash. *Oh, Lord! Mama! Help me . . .* Philip fainted, and when he revived, his body was one great mass of throbbing torment. A warm stickiness seeped from his back. Slipping in and out of consciousness, he was vaguely aware when the flogging ceased, for the pain remained constant instead of reaching another peak. When they cut him down, each movement was agony. Roughly they carried him into the cabin and threw him on a cot. Was it possible he saw remorse in Jack Weaver's eyes as he removed the gag? *"Water,"* he gasped.

Weaver held his head up, putting a cup to his lips. He gulped and retched.

"C'mon, Jack, cut that out."

"He's had enough, Jed. He needs a doctor—"

Hawley laughed. "Not where he's headed, he don't. But first, I'm goin' get my revenge. Ain't no jewboy goin' father a child outta my wife!"

Despite his stupor, Philip grasped what Hawley intended. *"No!"* he screamed with his last ounce of strength. *"No-o-o . . . not mine! Ja . . . Jack . . . raped her . . . baby his . . ."* He passed out as he saw Hawley's hunting knife gleaming in the light from the oil lamp.

"County sheriff's office," said the night duty officer.

"This is the deputy sheriff down in Rabun County, Georgia calling."

"Yessir, what can we do for you?"

"We've got a young woman brought into County Hospital last night in critical condition, found on the road near Satolah. Someone worked her over and left her for dead. She came round a while ago and told the most *un*believable story. Don't know whether she was out of her head or not, but if there's somethin' to it, I thought we'd best check it out with y'all up there in Randolph Springs . . ."

Through a haze he was aware of shadowy figures and hushed voices, movement and lights. And pain, intolerable pain. Someone stuck his arm with a needle. Then it was dark again.

Sound filtered in and out, far above . . . His eyes opened slowly, closed, then fluttered open again. He was lying on his stomach, unable to move. His arms were tied down and there was an oppressive weight on his back. Where was he? Then he remembered . . . Weaver . . . and Hawley . . . and he began to cry.

This time he was awakened by a woman's voice. "Open your mouth, Philip." Now he was lying on his side, propped with pillows and one of his arms was free. The woman held his wrist. She was a special sort of woman, he knew what she was, but it eluded him. She removed something from his mouth.

"Wha . . . where . . ." His voice was a croak.

Laurie was at his side, stroking his arm and smoothing his forehead, smiling at him through her tears. "Don't try to speak now, Phil. We'll talk about it later. Sister's given you something to make you sleep."

Philip welcomed the oblivion of sleep, sinking down, down into its embrace . . .

"What is that *enormous,* palatial building up there, Charlee, soaring above the forest?" exclaimed Blanche Fields, as they motored down the winding mountainous highway toward Randolph Springs.

Charlotte, sitting in the back seat next to Perry Nathan, did not answer. "That's Mountain View, the Randolph estate," said Perry graciously.

"The family for whom our fair village is named," further explained Sandy Majors, who was driving.

"It looks gorgeous, like a fairy-tale castle! Have you ever been inside, Charlee?"

"No," said her hostess curtly.

"They give tours of the garden and one wing of the main house these days," Perry told Blanche, trying to smooth over Charlotte's uncalled-for rudeness.

"Oh, I'd love to see it!" cried Blanche. "Can't we go?"

Charlee wrinkled her nose disdainfully. "Oh, Blanche, there are so many more fun things to do than to waste our time with a dreary old house like Mountain View."

All the way down the descent, Charlotte remained silent. Periodically she would glance up at the spires of the Randolph castle, her eyes darkening as she relived the humiliating moment of discovery . . .

It had been last spring, when she returned from Palm Beach and was chafing under the homey sameness of each day in Randolph Springs. To relieve her boredom, she had accompanied her father to a reception at a club in Asheville—one of his "obligations," as Max termed the invitations he received from business associates.

Across the crowded room, she noticed him in conversation with a woman, obviously not Jewish. It was not so much her appearance—strong chin, prominent nose—as her manner. She *belonged* there. Everything about her said it, from her confident bearing to her dress—one of those underdone, overpriced little pale crepe frocks. The club was in essence restricted, having only a handful of wealthy Jewish members, mostly Northerners, and as far as Charlee could tell, she and her father were the only Jewish guests at the party. Charlee was certain that was the real reason her mother had decided to stay at home, although she had claimed to be feeling ill. It was not a matter of principle that kept Reba away, Charlee knew, but simply that she felt out of place with the gentile bankers and professional men who belonged here. And with their wives.

Not Charlotte! It would take a hell of a lot more than *this* crowd to intimidate her. She surveyed the room, taking stock of the hearty, redfaced golfers and their lean, sunbronzed wives. Haughtily she scrutinized the women's clothes and makeup. Small-town and tacky. Compared to New Yorkers, they were yokels.

Her eyes were drawn back to her father, absorbed in conversation with the tall, handsome blond woman. Instinctively she knew this was more than a casual acquaintance. Something in Max's countenance alerted her. Normally reserved, he looked *alive,* more animated than she had ever seen him. His eyes never left the woman's face, as she paused in conversation, inhaling on her cigarette, then letting out a stream of smoke with a lift of her distinguished chin. Occasionally they would move nearer, then retreat before touching. Charlee watched them with fascination.

Buddy Wainwright, whom she had not seen since the Christmas vacation, wandered over in a well-tailored blazer. "Where did you disappear to, Charlee?" he asked, as if he had spent the last three months searching for her.

"I just returned from Florida. We went sailing on a friend's yacht . . ." Feigning innocence, she inquired, "Buddy, do you happen to know that woman over there in the beige dress?"

Buddy followed her glance and flushed. "Well, yes, actually,'' he laughed nervously, taking a gulp of his highball. ''That's my Aunt Florence, my father's sister. Her full name is Mrs. Guthrie Randolph.''

Charlotte's eyes widened. ''Guthrie Hayes Randolph's wife?''

''That's right,'' drawled Buddy. ''And I believe that is, ah, your father she's speaking with?''

She felt the heat in her face, but she raised her head and gave him what Laurie called her dazzling Charlee smile. ''Why yes, Buddy, it is. We're neighbors of the Randolphs, you know. They live just beyond us on Shadow Mountain . . .''

Charlotte wondered whether her mother knew about Florence Randolph. If so, Reba would be insanely jealous and completely demeaned. For some reason, the knowledge had made her *angry* at her mother. It was her own fault if Max had turned to someone else! There was a pervasive need among the women of Reba's family to act ''ladylike'' and nonsexual.

Charlee remembered coming in late from a date one night years earlier, to find her father drinking in his study. ''Why are you down here all alone, Daddy?'' she had asked.

''Oh, just sittin' and thinkin', honey.''

''Where's Mama?'' No sooner had she spoken, then she knew they'd had a quarrel.

Max had not answered immediately. He sat there sipping his sour mash whiskey and staring into the fire. She was about to leave when he spoke. ''The women in your mother's family place a mighty high value on their bodies,'' he said, and she had noticed for the first time that his speech was slurred.

Max was not a good drinker. It was the one flaw in the masquerade of Southern gentry.

It was daytime again and Philip stirred in the hospital bed. His upper body was covered in dressings, and he was attached to a mess of tubes. Even worse was the pall of desolation that settled on him as he became aware of his surroundings.

Ben stood at the window, looking out. He turned to find Philip watching him. "You're awake. How're you feeling, buddy?"

Philip closed his eyes again in anguish. He just wanted to be left alone.

"Can I get you something?" asked Ben.

He shook his head, misery clouding his expression. "They cut off my balls, Ben."

For a moment, Ben stared in shock; then he laughed without mirth. "No they didn't, Phil! Hawley knifed Weaver instead."

Philip reached down to assure himself it was true. "You're not fooling me, are you?" He was too drugged and in too much pain to feel any sense of elation.

"I wouldn't kid about a thing like that."

"Where's Laurie? I thought she was here."

"I took her home to get some sleep. She stayed all night."

"Did Hawley kill Weaver?"

"No, the police shot him first. Hawley's dead and Weaver's in jail."

Reacting to Ben's words, he tried to sit up and was seized with pain. "*Shit!* That hurts like hell."

Ben sprang to the side of the bed to help him. "Is that better?"

Phil let out a long breath and nodded. "How did the police know where to find us?" he asked, when he was able to speak.

"Anne Elizabeth told them. She heard Hawley talking on the phone, planning to take you to her father's cabin."

"Annie's a widow, Ben."

"Yeah, Phil." Benson looked away. "You better try to sleep now. I promised not to tire you."

All through the day he drifted in and out of slumber. It grew dark again and still he slept. Before dawn he awakened with a moan, tormented by lurid dreams. Lauren was there, sleeping in a chair. She opened her eyes, coming to his bedside at once. "It's all right, Phil. I'm here." She filled a cup with water from a pitcher on the stand, putting a glass straw to his lips. "Drink some of this, they want you to have liquids by mouth."

"What day is it, Laurie?"

"It's almost Monday. You've been here at Mission Hospital for more than forty-eight hours. You may not be too comfortable lying on your back for a few days, but the doctor says you'll be feeling much better soon."

"Do the folks know?"

She shook her head. "No, I decided not to call them. They're coming home tomorrow night. No one knows, except Ben and the police."

He closed his eyes in relief. "Thank God. I'd rather tell Mama and Papa when they're here and can see that I'm all right."

She touched his hand. "I was so frightened, Phil. The police said they expected you to be dead when they found you."

"They weren't far from wrong. Lucky thing Anne Elizabeth called them. I guess I owe her my life."

Lauren nodded, changing the subject. "Are you hungry?"

"Yes, now that you mention it. When can I have real food?"

"The doctor ordered soft food whenever you asked for it. I'll call the nurse."

Philip was feeling much improved by afternoon when Lauren returned, bringing soup, roasted chicken, and homemade applesauce freshly cooked by Pansy. When he had eaten all he could manage, he eased himself against the pillows, wincing as he put pressure against his back.

"Maybe you shouldn't sit that way," said Lauren, noting his discomfort.

"It's all right. The doctor came in before and told me the cuts aren't very deep. They didn't have to take too many stitches." He managed a laugh. "I guess Jed Hawley wasn't as tough as he thought."

"Oh, he was tough, all right."

Something about the way she said it made him pay attention. "Laurie . . . you're not telling me everything.

What else happened?" She opened her lips, then shook her head and looked away. "What *is* it? *Tell me!*"

She came to the side of his bed and took his hand. "It's Anne Elizabeth, Phil. She—she died." Her eyes filled and she looked at him as if she did not know what to expect.

"*Died?* How?"

"It's—it's horrible! Her husband beat her, fractured her skull. They couldn't save her, but she regained consciousness just long enough to tell what she knew about Jed Hawley—and that he was going after you, intending to kill you."

"My God! *Annie dead . . .*"

"Oh, Phil, I'm so sorry. I guess it doesn't matter who her family is when you're in love with someone."

He shook his head, smiling despite the terrible news. "I was never in love with Anne Elizabeth, Laurie. I was fond of her, but it was never more than a minor flirtation as far as I was concerned." He looked down ruefully. "I'm afraid it was more to Anne Elizabeth, although I never meant to hurt her. Poor Annie . . . what a tragic life."

"I'm afraid there's one thing more."

"Oh no—what?"

"Jack Weaver hanged himself in his jail cell last night. They found him early this morning."

Lauren had taken Miriam home to get some rest, leaving Samuel alone with Phil in the hospital room. "I'm sorry I brought you all this worry, Father. I swear to you, I never did anything wrong with Anne Elizabeth. Jack Weaver knew that."

"I should have known it too, Philip, but I couldn't take a chance. I realized what Weaver was capable of doing to you, and I felt I had to protect you. That was wrong. I should have called you to my office that day and confronted him. If only I had done that, none of this would have happened."

"*If only*—we could play that game forever. I'm just glad it's over and you know the truth."

"Your name won't appear in the papers. Max has seen to that."

Philip threw his head back and laughed. "I guess it pays to have influential relatives."

Ben walked in as Samuel was preparing to leave. "Thank you, Benson, for all you've done to help Philip and Lauren. I don't know what my daughter would have done if you hadn't been with her." There were tears in Samuel's eyes as he put an arm around Ben's shoulders. "You're a fine young man."

When Samuel left, Ben said, "That's the longest conversation I've ever had with your father. I've always had the feeling he didn't much care for me."

"Pa's a rather formal man, but he's loosened up a bit lately." How could you tell a friend like Ben that your father had never thought his family was good enough for the Jacobsons, until something like this occurred?

"Phil . . . may I ask you a question?"

"Sure."

"Do you think Lauren would go out with me?"

Philip had to prevent himself from smiling. This was obviously important to Ben. "Why don't you ask Lauren?"

He sat forward, leaning his elbows on his knees and contemplating his hands. "Afraid of rejection, I guess."

"I don't know what to tell you, Ben. You're a wonderful guy and she'd be lucky to date you. I've always thought Laurie was someone special, from the time she was a little girl. The trouble was, she was never aware of it. She always remained in the shadow of Charlotte Mortimer. Now that Charlee isn't around, Laurie has had to come face to face with herself. There's been an amazing transition in her this year."

"To my way of thinking, Lauren is so much more of a woman than Charlotte."

"Mine, too. But Laurie hasn't realized it yet. I guess that won't happen until she gets what she wants in life."

"What *does* she want, Phil?"

"I'm not sure . . . I don't think even Lauren knows. But won't it be interesting to see."

Chapter 11

December 1935

SOME PEOPLE ARE touched with special fortune. Good looks, wit, charm, luck, and money. And so, it seemed, was Charlotte Lee Mortimer.

Charlee, at nineteen, wasn't beautiful in the usual sense. Long, shapely limbs, a lithe, small-breasted figure, and newly bobbed chestnut hair, silky and unadorned, lent her an intriguing hoydenish air. Yet, there was a cool directness about her, a nonchalance, belied by the exciting, madcap sparkle in her eyes. Generous, assertive, and stubborn, she was a loyal friend, but if crossed, could be unforgiving. When in the wrong, she would never give in or apologize, never admit a mistake. Her elevations and descents of mood could catch anyone off balance—even Lauren, who had made a study of them. Seduced like the others, Lauren never failed to respond to the enigma of Charlee.

"Come on over first thing tomorrow morning, Laurie, and let's just *talk,*" Charlee whispered when they were leaving the Shadow Mountain Club Christmas Gala.

Lauren waved in agreement as she drove off with Benson and Philip, whose date was Ben's sister, Nancy. Nancy was currently between beaux, an untenable position for a girl of her convictions. She was working on Phil, who being especially vulnerable these days, appeared to be taking the bait.

Lauren had not seen Charlee since the summer—a summer she would just as soon forget. Thank goodness, Philip was coming out of his depression, but she feared he would never get over his horrible ordeal. His body had mended, but in his eyes she saw a shadow that should not have been there in her handsome brother. Tomorrow morning she would discuss it with Charlee, who had always cared about Phil and would understand her concern. There was so much she wanted to talk about. Not just the problems, but good things—college, her English professor, and the award she had won for creative writing. She couldn't wait to share all her news.

Lauren slept late on Sunday morning, quickly showered and dressed, and went directly to Shadow Mountain Drive. Aunt Reba and Uncle Max were sitting in the breakfast room with Charlee, expecting her to join them. Max was enjoying a hearty plate of sausages and eggs with grits, and he insisted that Lady serve a portion to Lauren. She had never much cared for hominy, its flavor a little bland for her taste, but Lady's fried hominy cakes topped with homemade praline syrup were irresistible.

"I'll never be the same, Lady. That's more than I eat in a month of breakfasts."

"That's why you're so skinny, Miz Laurie," laughed Lady, whose ample body was a testimony to her delicious cooking.

After breakfast, Max went to his study to read the papers and Reba stayed to visit with the girls in the sunroom while she had another cup of coffee, then excused herself to dress. As soon as her mother had left, Charlee came to sit next to Lauren on the settee, drawing her feet up and hugging her knees. "You remember my roommate, Blanche Fields, don't you, Laurie?"

How could Lauren have possibly forgotten Blanche Fields! Reba had dashed around like a chicken without a head for a week before Blanche came home with Charlee last June. All they had talked about was how important and wealthy Blanche's family was. "Of course I remember Blanche," she replied, trying to summon a modicum of enthusiasm.

Charlotte had that excited, conspiratorial expression on

her face, the mood that had always most captivated Lauren. "Want to know a secret?"

"Yes, what is it?"

"I'm in love."

"Ohh Charlee! *Tell* me about it. Who *is* he?"

"Well, I was invited to Blanche's for Thanksgiving. Her family has a big estate on the Jersey shore, it's *ever* so beautiful—"

"Yes, yes," said Lauren impatiently, "go on."

Charlee's gladsome little smile deepened, her eyes sparkling. "I met Bruce that weekend for the first time—well, actually I *had* seen him at the end of last summer, but that was only for two minutes. Of course, I've been hearing about him for a whole year from Blanche. She simply *idolizes* him. He's a Princeton graduate and ever so handsome." She looked at Lauren expectantly.

"But—what happened? I mean, how do you know you're in love?"

Charlotte gazed through the window with a soulful expression. "I knew it the moment we met. If you could see him, Laurie, you'd understand."

"Is he in love with you?" Of course, that was the most ridiculous question. Every boy who ever met Charlee fell in love with her.

Charlee sighed. "I'm not sure what he thinks of me. He's that hard-to-get type. You know, the kind who seems not to be particularly interested?"

This did not sound at all like the Charlotte who had always enjoyed the chase. "When will you see him again and where is he? That is, when he's not a guest at Blanche's house."

Charlee gave her a playful nudge. "He *lives* there, silly . . . Bruce is Blanche's *brother!*"

Wel-l-l, Uncle Max was certainly going to approve of *this* one.

Charlotte would always attract men. Like moths to a flame, they were drawn to her. She had come to take that for granted. Until Bruce Fields.

Blanche had talked endlessly about her older brother—

his prep school (Taft), his college (Princeton), his friends at Harvard Law School (all tall and devastatingly handsome)—until Charlotte concluded Blanche had an unhealthy fixation on Bruce. "Wait till you meet him, Charlee. He's the most divine man you've ever imagined," Blanche was forever repeating.

The meeting had not been destined, for every time Charlee visited the Fieldses, Bruce was elsewhere. Over the first football weekend at Princeton, he was with friends in New Haven. Last New Year's Eve, the family had waited on tenterhooks for Bruce to make an appearance at the Harmonie Club party, but he never showed. For the Passover seder, to which Charlotte was invited, he was spending his spring break in Palm Beach, and last summer when she and Blanche had passed through New York stopping at the Fields apartment on their way from North Carolina to Maine, Bruce was still on a tour of the West.

After Maine, Charlee had returned with Blanche to spend a few days at the shore before going home. The Fields estate put the great homes in Randolph Springs to shame, except for the Randolph family's Mountain View. Accustomed as she was to luxury, Charlotte never felt so pampered and coddled as she did when visiting Blanche at Fair Fields.

On a sultry afternoon, Charlotte and Blanche had been lounging on a terrace, half asleep after a strenuous set of singles, when an arrogant voice cut through the hot humidity. "Where the hell *is* everyone?"

Charlee glanced up to see a beautiful young man. Yes, beautiful. That was the only way to describe Bruce Fields. Another man might have looked ridiculous in the baby blue yachting sweater and white slacks, but Bruce gave his outfit cachet. He was tall and slim and he moved with an elegant sexual grace. His thick blond sunstreaked hair fell over the aristocratic forehead in a careless fashion above moody eyes of piercing blue. If she had been an artist, Charlotte would have wished to paint him, or preserve his classically molded features in marble. He was that handsome.

"Brucie!" screeched Blanche, jumping up, more ani-

mated than Charlee had ever seen her. "I'm so glad you're home. I didn't think you'd be coming for another week."

"Nicholas cracked up the car, so that was the end of our tour," he answered, allowing his sister to embrace him. He didn't bother to glance at Charlotte. "Is the pater on board?"

"No, he went to Washington."

"Good-o! Where's Moms?"

"In the city. She's coming down tonight." He nodded, slapping her on the rump, and started to turn away. "Wait a minute!" Blanche called. "Don't you want to meet my roommate? This is Charlotte Mortimer . . . my brother Bruce." The way she said it, as if laying out the Kohinoor diamond for viewing. You may look, but do not touch.

"Hello, Bruce." Charlee hoped she had the right amount of cool.

"Hi." He barely acknowledged her as he walked into the house.

"Don't mind Bruce. He's always that way when he first gets home. He says it depresses him and he has to 'acclimatize.' "

Evidently Bruce found the forecast chilly. He did not appear for dinner that evening nor breakfast the following morning, and when the girls returned from the beach in the afternoon, he had left for Cape Cod.

All through the autumn term, although she mentioned not a word to anyone, Bruce Fields had been very much in Charlotte's thoughts. She had always been drawn to good-looking men. "I would only marry someone handsome," she often used to tell Laurie. "If you have to go to bed with the same person all your life, you might just as well choose the best looking man you can find!"

She did not meet him again until Thanksgiving. Max had arranged for her to visit his Baltimore cousins for the holiday, but when he heard that she was invited to Fair Fields, he was more than content at the change of plans.

They drove down to the shore with Blanche's father late that Wednesday afternoon. Adele Fields was waiting anxiously for them. "We're delighted you could come, dear," she welcomed Charlotte warmly. "It's been too long. Have you forgotten this is your home while you're at Miss Alexander's?''

After a simple dinner, the girls accompanied Blanche's parents to the nearby house of a motion picture producer, one of Malcolm Fields's clients, for the screening of a new film. They were back home in bed by midnight.

On Thanksgiving morning Charlee awakened before Blanche. She had always been an early riser, accustomed to riding horseback with her father at sunrise. Max had deplored Reba's habit of lounging in a robe in the mornings. ''Miriam is so energetic,'' he used to say. ''The proof of it is in the children. Look at Philip and Lauren, how lively and industrious they are.'' It had been important for Charlee to prove to him that she wasn't lazy.

She quickly showered and dressed in a sweater and skirt and went downstairs. Wearing riding breeches, Bruce and another young man were seated at the table having breakfast. They rose when she entered the room. Bruce regarded her with surprise. ''Well, hullo. Who are you?''

''I'm Charlotte Mortimer, Blanche's roommate. We met last summer when—''

''I'm Bruce and this is Nicholas,'' he said, as if she hadn't spoken. For the first time she looked at the other boy. He was as tall as Bruce, dark and rather exotic looking. ''Help yourself to breakfast,'' said Bruce, as the two reseated themselves.

Fruit, juices, breads, and smoked fish were spread on a sideboard. Charlee took a plate to the table as a servant appeared with hot coffee. She ate silently while the two young men went on with their conversation, paying absolutely no attention to her. Charlotte was unaccustomed to being ignored by men, no matter how handsome.

Soon Blanche appeared in a robe, and threw her arms around her brother, ''Where were you last night? I waited up for you. Oh—hi, Nicholas.''

The two boys exchanged glances. ''We went to a party in New York. Didn't get in until dawn.''

''And you're going riding?''

''We've already been. Never went to bed.''

''You're nuts! Aren't they, Charlee?''

Nicholas smiled in her direction, saying archly, "Do you agree?" Charlee thought he had an affected manner. She shrugged, dismissing Nicholas, determined that before the weekend was over Bruce Fields would be begging for her attention.

Mrs. Fields's devotion to her children involved a certain blindness to their faults. Adele fussed over her son, obviously doting on him. "Darling," she said that afternoon, smoothing his hair, "I know you have Nicholas here, but please do make an effort with William today. Last time you weren't at all nice to him. Remember, Conrad Hutsel is your father's most important client."

Bruce seemed to take a certain captious satisfaction in bringing Nicholas home with him. The senior Fields did not bother hiding his dislike for his son's friend; in fact, despite their faultless manners, it was apparent that Nicholas was unpopular with all members of the Fields family except Bruce.

Late in the afternoon the other guests arrived. Malcolm Fields retreated to the library with the men for an hour before cocktails were served. He was put out at Bruce, whom he unsuccessfully tried to draw into the discussions.

Charlee was standing at a window looking out over the lawn toward the sea when Adele made her way across the living room with a pale, bespectacled young man in tow. "This is William Hutsel, Charlotte. William is a student at Yale and was most intrigued when he heard that your home is in Randolph Springs."

"Is that so? Have you visited Randolph, William?" she inquired.

"Actually no," he replied in Long Island lockjaw, "but I heard Dr. Morley, the rector of your St. Stephen's Church, speak at an Episcopalian Youth conclave last year. From what he told us, the Randolphs are a most remarkable family."

"Indeed, they are," replied Charlotte, her eyes darkening. Especially Mrs. Guthrie Hayes Randolph. Now, *there* is a truly remarkable lady!

At dinner, Charlotte was seated between Bruce and Nicholas, while Blanche had the arduous task of attending to the sententious William. "Tell me about yourself, Nicholas," Charlee said, leaning toward him and dragging out the intimate, whispery tones she had put in cold storage for her speech classes.

He had grown up in boarding schools in England and Switzerland, Nicholas told her. "Speaking five languages was a help at Princeton. I could always manage a passing grade in French or German lit." His parents were Russian emigrées who had eventually settled in San Francisco, he explained. "I'm a count, actually, if I cared to use the title."

As Nicholas sipped wine, his sallow complexion took on a tinge of color. His looks were unusual, with blue-black hair and dark Asian eyes, almost like a Tartar's. She supposed he was attractive, in a foreign sort of way. He wore an unusual cologne—a spicy oriental scent—and there was a dissolute flavor to him that both repelled and fascinated her. Like most men, she noted, he became totally absorbed when the topic of discussion was himself. Bending her head closer to Nicholas, she gave him her full wide-eyed attention, ignoring Bruce who was leaning forward attempting to be part of their tête-à-tête.

The next night, Bruce and Nicholas took Blanche and Charlotte to a cabaret where they were meeting some of their Princeton classmates. Charlee flirted outrageously with the other men, hoping to make Bruce jealous. The real fun for her had always been the game of romancing. Laurie never had understood when she used to tell her the most exciting part of a new conquest was the challenge and the uncertainty. Until then, Charlee had always won, and quickly lost interest.

Around midnight, she found herself with Bruce. As they danced he pressed himself against her so that she could feel his erection. That had never happened to her before. The boy had always pulled away at such a moment. It was a dilemma. How should she react? If she responded, he would think she was fast, but if she pretended anger, she would discourage Bruce, just as he had started to show an interest in her. She decided to ignore it, deftly sidestepping when he tried to catch one of her legs between his thighs.

Chuckling, Bruce regarded her from under lowered lids. "I don't know about you, Charlee . . . I think maybe you're a phony."

"No doubt *that* is a subject on which *you* are an expert, Mr. Fields!"

Later driving home, Bruce said to Nicholas, "Let's drop the infants off and go out."

Just you wait, Bruce Fields, she vowed, *I will get you to fall in love with me if it's the last thing in this world I do . . .*

Falling in love was not something Lauren had counted on to come between them. They were growing apart, but it was her fault rather than Charlotte's, although she failed to realize it. When Charlee stared into space for long moments, looking dreamy, Lauren would feel strangely alienated and resentful. She was shut out and she didn't want to be. She had always expected that she and Charlee would marry around the same time, probably to men who knew and liked each other. And she wanted to live in the same town with her cousin so they could be together often, the way Miriam and Reba were. When they were young, they had been so close, it had never occurred to either of them that it would not remain that way for the rest of their lives.

Did love make you so self-centered that you lost all interest in other people? Charlee had never once asked about *her* college, or what *she* was doing. There had been no opportunity for Lauren to relate her own news, which seemed trivial now, compared to *falling in love.* But am I being selfish, she wondered. Perhaps the separation from Charlee for so many months has made me too self-absorbed. She promised herself to make an effort to put aside her own concerns and devote the rest of the vacation to Charlee.

There was never a chance . . . Charlee's plans suddenly changed when she received an unexpected telephone call from Blanche urging her to come up to Fair Fields for a

New Year's house party. In the flurry of her hasty departure, Charlee hugged Lauren and whispered, "Happy New Year, Laurie. Wish me luck!"

Blanche met Charlotte's train at Newark station on the last day of 1935. "Thanks for coming, love," she exclaimed as she hugged Charlee. "I don't think I could have made it through this week without you. Daddy is raging at Bruce over his grades and brother dear has been threatening not to stay for the rest of vacation."

Charlee's heart sank. She hated to be in the middle of family disagreements. And she could say good-bye to her romantic plans if Bruce should leave.

Blanche arched one pale ash-blond eyebrow, sucking in her cheeks. "Don't look so down-in-the-mouth, darling. Bruce will stick. He just delights in raising Daddy's blood pressure."

"Well, it certainly makes no difference to me whether he stays or not," she sniffed. Not for the world would she let on to Blanche how she felt about her brother.

It was snowing heavily by the time they reached Fair Fields. The house was humming with preparations for the party. The caterers had taken over the kitchen, but Blanche grabbed some sandwiches, and the two girls went up to her room.

"You have to sleep in with me tonight because all the guest rooms are full. We even have people staying up on the third floor. All the boys."

"What boys?"

"Oh, didn't I tell you? That's why Mother coaxed me to invite you. Bruce asked some of his old friends from Lion's Inn down for the party. None of them has a date."

"Blanche Fields! What is that evil little smirk doing on your face?"

When Blanche laughed, she lost her characteristic aloofness and was quite pretty. "There's one I have my eye on. Wally Westheimer. He's a banker. I trust you will not try to vamp him away from me."

"Why, Blanche," said Charlotte, batting her eyelashes, "you know me better than that."

As it happened, the party was a dismal failure, at least for Charlee and Blanche. Both Bruce and Wally Westheimer spent the entire evening dancing attendance on a motion picture starlet who had been brought to the party by the Fieldses' neighbors, the producer and his wife. Nicholas sulked in a corner. Blanche drank too much champagne and was sick, so Charlee had to get her to bed without letting her parents know.

Coming back downstairs, Charlotte came upon Nicholas in the cloak room, going through the men's Chesterfields. "What on earth are you doing?" she demanded, as she saw him slip something into his pocket.

Unruffled, he took her hand and coaxed her into the game room. "Come, let me teach you how to play billiards," he said. When Nicholas stood behind her, grasping her arms to demonstrate how to hold the cue, she again noticed the distinct, exotic aroma of his aftershave cologne—like the sandalwood box in which her father kept his studs and cufflinks.

Along about midnight, Adele Fields came looking for her daughter. Charlee told her that Blanche had a headache and had gone to lie down. "I should go see her, poor dear."

Afraid Mrs. Fields would discover that Blanche was drunk, Charlee said, "Don't bother, I'll go. Blanche wanted to come down again to welcome in the New Year."

But Blanche was out cold and would not wake up. By the time she came downstairs, Charlee had missed midnight and the toast, and her chance to kiss Bruce Fields Happy New Year.

On New Year's Day, everyone slept until noon. Charlotte's head ached, as it always did when she drank champagne. While Blanche was taking a bath, Charlee went to the kitchen for a glass of milk to wash down some aspirin tablets. She was passing through the hall when she heard Malcolm Fields's angry voice from inside his study. Not exactly meaning to eavesdrop, she couldn't help pausing to listen.

"I want that fellow out of this house *today!* Do you understand?"

"We'll both go, then. It's a bore, anyway."

"You will *not* leave with him. I'm serious, Bruce. You are pushing me too far. Get rid of Nicholas and don't ever bring him back."

"Dad, he made a mistake. Can't you forget it?"

"No, I can't. He is no gentleman. I won't have a sneak or a thief in my house."

"All right. But he's a good friend to me, and it's embarrassing."

"You'll find a way."

At dinner, Nicholas had disappeared and Bruce turned his charm on Charlee. "Would you like to go dancing tonight?"

"Only if Blanche wants to come," she said with a loyalty she did not truly feel.

"Oh, sure. Wally will go."

They met friends at a nightclub and danced until long past midnight. Bruce ordered champagne, and Charlee drank three glasses, feeling giddy. "Cigarette?" he asked, holding out a monogrammed gold case.

"I don't smoke," she answered.

"Try one. You'll like it."

She smoked the cigarette, finding it unpleasant, but she wanted to please him. What had happened to her resolve to make Bruce crawl for her attention? Here she was responding to his every little show of interest.

"Why doesn't your father like Nicholas?" she dared to ask when they were dancing.

"Nicky 'borrowed' a few of my father's excessively numerous possessions, and didn't bother to return them."

"Like what?"

"Like a bottle of seventy-five-year-old cognac, and some leatherbound first editions," answered Bruce, and he threw his head back and roared.

"I don't think that's very funny," said Charlotte demurely, giving him her dimpled smile.

"Let's go out to the car," he whispered.

"No." She wanted to, but knew his sister would notice, and Blanche was the type who would hold it over her head.

Going home, they were alone in his roadster because Blanche and Wally had gone with the others. Instead of pulling in front of the door, Bruce swung around the circle and drove back to the huge garage that was filled with automobiles. "Complete privacy, at last," he murmured as he put his arms around her and kissed her.

It was a kiss different from any she had ever experienced. Sensuous, slow, teasing, building to a passionate intensity. She felt his tongue deep in her mouth and his hands in places where no one had ever touched her. For all her flirting and necking, Charlotte was too imbued with her strict upbringing to have gone beyond the limits of propriety. Within the confines of Randolph Springs, her *reputation* had been at stake, and since coming to New York, there had been no opportunity. Now she was overwhelmed, as softly stroking, insinuating, ever deeper, Bruce caressed her until he slid her down on the seat and slipped his hand inside her satin panties.

"Stop, Bruce! We mustn't do this."

"Please, Charlee, let me. I promise not to hurt you," he said breathlessly, his hands never ceasing their stroking.

For a moment she stopped caring, lost in the new feelings that engulfed her. But her training was too strong, and she had a survivor's instinct for self-preservation. *"No!"*

"Why not?" he groaned.

"It's wrong. We can't do this unless—"

He had taken her hand and pressed it against himself and she could feel a hard swollen throbbing there. "Unless what?" he teased, moving her hand back and forth.

"You know . . ."

"Unless we're engaged? Is that what you mean, darling?"

"I—I don't know. I guess so." Bruce was the only boy who had ever put her at a disadvantage.

"I think that's a *great* idea. Let's get married!"

"Oh, Bruce, *do* stop making a joke of it." At least he had relieved the tension.

"I'm not joking, Charlee," he said slowly. "I think I really do want to marry you."

"You don't even *know* me, for heaven's sake!" she cried, but her heart leapt at his words.

"So what? You don't know me either. How many people really know each other before they're married? Marriage is a gamble—the lottery of life."

"I think you're plastered."

"I am a little, but not all that much. I know I could love you." He kissed her lightly on the lips. "Sleep on it."

But she scarcely closed her eyes all night. Never had she been so challenged by a man. She lay awake thinking of Bruce down the hall just a few doors away, reliving how it had felt to be in his arms and savoring the remembered excitement of his kisses. She couldn't wait for tomorrow, when she would see him.

But in the morning, he was gone.

He had left a sealed envelope with her name on it. Puzzled, she ripped it open and read: "Darling Charlee—I had to go back to Cambridge. Don't despair. I *will* fall in love with you. Bruce." His handwriting was a large scrawl, angular and flamboyant.

How did she feel? Excited at his words, hurt that he hadn't waited to say good-bye, and engulfed with a new kind of physical longing he had awakened in her.

When would she hear from him again, she wondered. Not for two weeks. Then four dozen red roses arrived for her at the Alexander School and the girls were eager to hear who had sent them and what it meant.

Blanche guessed immediately. "Brother dear! He always was wildly extravagant. Didn't I tell you, Charlee? Isn't he the most *divine* man?"

Charlee was on her guard. There was something almost dangerously unhinged about Bruce Fields. She would regret it if she told Blanche the truth. That she had fallen madly in love with him.

Chapter 12

THE RETURN ADDRESS, engraved in a discreet Spencerian script, said: *Fair Fields, Deal.* Just that.

Impatiently, Reba slit open the pale lavender envelope. With mounting excitement, she scanned Adele Fields's letter.

March 15, 1936

My dear Mrs. Mortimer,

I simply must write to say how much we've been enjoying your precious Charlotte, who has become quite like one of the family. Malcolm and I have grown to love her as if she were our own.

We are delighted that our girls have formed an inseparable bond. Charlotte is such a stabilizing influence on Blanche, who tends to be flighty at times. It appears that Charlotte also has a salutary effect on our son! Bruce has spent more weekends at home in the past three months than ever before.

Charlotte tells us that you and Mr. Mortimer will be coming to New York in April. We would be honored to have you as our weekend guests at Fair Fields, or if you are unable to fit a trip to New Jersey into your schedule, perhaps dinner at our New York apartment. As soon as you know your travel plans, drop me a note. I do hope you will join us. We are so looking forward to meeting Charlotte's parents.

Yours sincerely,
Adele Fields

"Isn't it a *warm* letter, Max? Just as if we were old friends. Wasn't that a *gracious* thing to write . . . about Charlotte Lee being like their own daughter?"

Reba reread Mrs. Fields's message. Charlotte Lee a *stabilizing* influence? Well, perhaps the child was settling down. "Max, what do you suppose she means about their son? Charlotte has never said very much about him." Reba referred to the letter again, "Bruce . . . a Southern name. *I* once knew a boy named Bruce Cone whose family was—"

"Reba, let's try to concentrate on one family at a time, shall we?"

"Well! of *course,* darling . . ."

"You should write to her—not immediately—wait until the end of the week. We don't want to appear eager. Make a draft of the letter and let me see it before you send it off. Use the engraved social notes. I think you should say we'd be pleased to have dinner in New York. At this time your husband's calendar is crowded, but it's possible we will extend our stay in Manhattan beyond one week, in which case, we would be privileged to pay them a visit in New Jersey." Max frowned. "It's probable, Reba, that this is an overture."

"An *overture?"*

"I wouldn't be surprised, my dear, if the Fieldses are entertaining the prospect of having Charlotte Lee as their daughter-in-law."

"Max!" Reba's mouth flew open and she clasped her hands reverently. "That would be too good to be *true!"*

Max shook his head emphatically. "The wrong attitude, Reba. Absolutely wrong. Why, young Fields would be lucky to breathe the same air with our daughter."

"If you don't calm down, Reba, you'll collapse before you get on that Pullman car tomorrow."

"Oh, Mimi, I don't believe I've ever been this nervous. You *know* I sailed right through Charlotte's coming-out party and the girls' tour without batting an eyelash. But, somehow, this is almost beyond me."

The two sisters had spent the better part of the week

shopping in Asheville. Or rather, Reba shopped while Miriam consulted. They had been delayed today waiting for the seamstress at Ivy's designer salon to further ease one of the new dresses. Driving back to Randolph Springs, the trunk and front seat piled high with boxes, Reba said, "I can't *imagine* that a black dress is right for dinner, Mimi. Even if it did cost a fortune. I would have thought the apricot lace . . ."

"The black is perfect, Reba."

"But it's so *plain!*"

"With your pearls and diamond clips and the small fur cape, you will be properly dressed for the city. If you go down to the ocean, then you can wear one of the softer prints."

"Are you *sure?* I so want Max to be proud of me. I've gained a bit of weight lately and . . . well, he's always admired slim women."

Miriam's throat tightened with sympathy for her sister. She wondered whether the rumor was true about Max and the Randolph woman, and if Reba suspected. She hoped not. Reba was so tender and vulnerable, it hurt to think that Max would betray her. The fact was, she had let her figure go. Reba was too inactive and indulged in rich foods. Maybe Miriam should resume those morning visits to the Shadow Mountain house. Years ago, after Joel died, when she was in the habit of going over there for coffee, Reba would be up early, dressed and bustling about. Lately, though, whenever Miriam dropped by unexpectedly she found her sister in her negligée, or even in bed, as late as eleven o'clock. Lying there amidst rumpled sheets, with her large, fleshy breasts spreading flat under a nightgown and her distastefully heavy breath, it was understandable that Reba might have lost her appeal for her husband. Yet, Miriam could not tolerate the thought of Max's unfaithfulness. While it was true men had needs that were different from women's, a husband should be considerate of his wife's feelings. She and Samuel still loved each other in that way. In fact, in some respects it was better, now that she had passed the change.

They had reached her house, and Miriam kissed Reba

good-bye. "Have a wonderful trip, dear, and give our love to Charlotte."

"Thank you for your help, Mimi. I don't know how I would have managed without you." She waved as the car moved off.

A week and a half later, the Jacobsons had just finished Sunday supper when the telephone rang. Lauren ran to answer.

"Is that you, Laurie, honey?"

"Charlee! How *are* you?" Her cousin hardly ever telephoned from New York, and it had been ages since she'd written a letter. "It's wonderful to hear your voice. How's the visit going?"

"It's all over, thank goodness! There were some trying moments, but we made it through." She laughed mischievously, and Lauren could picture the crinkling of her eyes. "I just saw Mother and Daddy off at Penn Station an hour ago, and I *had* to call you. Laurie . . . I'm *engaged!"*

Lauren's breath caught. "To Bruce?"

"Of course, to Bruce, honey! Who else?"

"Well—golly, that's great," she said lamely. Why was she shocked? Hadn't she known this was bound to happen one day? She forced herself to sound enthusiastic, despite a sinking feeling within. "It's really wonderful news, Charlee."

"Oh, Laurie, I'm so in heaven! I can't wait for you to meet him. Please be happy for me, darling."

"I *am*—you *know* I am! You—you caught me by surprise, that's all. I wasn't expecting it this soon. The first I ever heard of Bruce Fields was in December, and here you are, just a few months later, telling me I've practically got a new cousin!"

"I know, but it seems I've been in love with him forever."

"Oh Charlee, dear, I'm so glad for you. Truly I am. What do Aunt Reba and Uncle Max think about all this?"

"Mama's in ecstasy, except she's upset there won't be

time for a proper engagement party. The wedding's in June, right after Bruce graduates from law school."

"So soon!" Lauren felt dismayed, as if the world had speeded up and left her behind. In two months' time Charlee would be a married woman.

"I'm petrified. There's so much to plan and so little time. I'm really counting on you, Laurie. Will you be my maid of honor? Blanche will be jealous, but she'll just have to be satisfied with being a bridesmaid."

"Of course I'll be your maid of honor," she said, beginning to feel a pulse of excitement. "And don't worry, Char, I'll help. We'll get you launched into matrimony like no other bride in history!"

But after she hung up, Lauren could not stop thinking that her own life seemed to have ground to a standstill, while Charlee continued step by step along the charmed path of her existence.

The wedding invitations were out.

Feverish excitement reigned as bids for prenuptial luncheons, teas, and showers arrived in Asheville, Memphis, Charleston, Atlanta, and all through the South. On Shadow Mountain, a gaggle of gardeners was kept busy planting and pruning and cultivating the wedding set. Under two prized magnolias whose branches formed a canopy, Charlotte and Bruce would exchange vows. Max plotted the path he would tread through azaleas, rhododendrons, and flowering dogwoods to hand his beloved daughter to her bridegroom. Fifty extra servants were engaged to prepare for and serve the four hundred guests who would be coming from as far away as Canada and California. Wedding gifts began to arrive daily from New York, Upper Montclair, Philadelphia, and Chicago.

The groom's parents were traveling from New York by Pullman, intending to spend a week beforehand at the Randolph Inn. Bruce was driving south with his best man and the ushers in a caravan of automobiles, making a last bachelor holiday of it. The bridesmaids, including Blanche Fields, would be staying at the Mortimer house. Their dresses and matching hats in a soft mauve-pink organza, were appliquéd with silk roses, while Lauren, as maid of honor, would wear a deeper mulberry rose of similar design. Charlotte's bridal gown, custom-made in New York, was a fabulous creation of gossamer ivory silk inset with bands of antique lace. Its heirloom veil formed a flowing train that trailed from a Juliet cap of reembroidered lace encrusted with seed pearls.

Charlotte's trousseau filled five steamer trunks and eleven pieces of hand luggage. Bruce had made a mystery of their wedding trip. The honeymoon destination was a secret, even from the bride. All Charlee knew was that they would be gone for three months and she should be prepared for any type of weather and every variety of activity.

"I wonder where we're going . . . Isn't it thrilling, Laurie?" exclaimed Charlotte, scrunching her shoulders. They were sitting on the floor in her room amidst mounds of tissue paper, dress boxes, and half-packed luggage.

"I thought you didn't like surprises."

Charlee laughed, a wicked gleam in her eyes. "Bruce can surprise me all he wants, just as long as it's with gifts . . . or sex!"

Lauren flushed. "Uh . . . aren't you a little nervous about that—I mean sex?"

"*Nervous?* Honey, I can't wait! I nearly *haven't* waited."

"Charlotte Lee Mortimer! What do you mean?"

Charlee grinned. "I mean that Bruce and I have indulged in some pretty heavy petting that leaves little to the imagination!" She extended her left hand to admire her five carat emerald-cut diamond engagement ring. "He's been trying to get me into bed for the past six months, and I must admit, I've had a hard time resisting."

"Oh, Charlee, you'll never change!" Lauren shook her head in amusement. "Do you know, my mother still insists that nice women don't really like it all that much?"

"Honey, don't you believe it! That's just the women in her family she's talking about, and it's pure nonsense." Charlee strode across the room and snatched a sheer nightgown from the window seat, holding it against her body and posing in front of the mirrored wardrobe. *"I* must take after Daddy, for I intend to enjoy every last minute of it. With Bruce, that shouldn't be too difficult!"

Bruce *was* the most attractive man Lauren had ever seen. More handsome than a movie star, she thought, watching him admiringly all that week as he charmed everyone at the prenuptial receptions and dinners. The women of Randolph Springs could not stop talking about his dazzling smile and hazy blue, long-lashed eyes. Gracious at tea time, suave in a receiving line, graceful on the dance floor, superb on the golf links, and sensational in tennis whites, Bruce captivated all of them.

"What a dreamy man," sighed one of the bridesmaids, a classmate from the Alexander School. "Lucky Charlee!"

Bruce's sister clung to the bride, following her around the house from room to room until Charlee was getting prewedding jitters. "Laurie," she finally begged, "will you please keep Blanche company this afternoon while I go for my fitting? It's bad luck for her to see my gown."

Lauren diverted Blanche by taking her on a drive around Randolph Springs. "You should see their apartment," said Blanche. "It's a positively gorgeous duplex on Park Avenue."

"I didn't realize they'd already decided on an apartment."

"Daddy found it for them through a client. Charlee hasn't been there yet, but she'll be wild about it, I know. Mother and I are going to supervise the decorating while they're on their honeymoon. It'll be all ready for them to move right in when they return in September."

The Fields family certainly were partial to surprises, weren't they, thought Lauren. "Do you know where they're going on their honeymoon?" she asked.

"Yes . . . but I'm not supposed to say." Blanche gave Lauren a sidelong glance. "Oh well, I suppose I can trust you if you promise not to tell. You wouldn't spoil Charlee's surprise, would you?"

"Not for the world."

Blanche leaned forward, mouthing the words in slow

definition. "They leave for New York right after the wedding—Daddy has arranged a private railroad car for them. On Tuesday, they're sailing on the *Normandie* for Cherbourg. After a tour of northern France—Paris, Normandy, the Champagne district—they'll cross the Channel to England. From there to the Low Countries, then Switzerland and Italy, before ending with two weeks on the Riviera." With a self-satisfied smile, Blanche sat back. "Daddy didn't think they should go to Germany because of Hitler."

"How sensible," pronounced Lauren. There was a tepid smugness about Blanche that brought out the worst in her, she thought, as they turned into Shadow Mountain Drive.

It took three of them to dress the bride on her wedding day. The other attendants were banished from Charlotte's room, but Lauren was there to help Pansy spread out the billows of lace-banded ivory silk, while Miss Odile, who had been called in to do all the last minute pressing and stitching, fastened the dozens of tiny buttons.

Lauren lifted the heirloom veil, setting the Juliet cap of Alençon lace and seed pearls on Charlotte's perfectly coifed head. As she had on countless occasions throughout their girlhood, Charlotte turned for her approval.

"Well, Laurie, how do I look?"

"You're just . . . absolutely the most magnificent bride I've ever seen." She was overcome with emotion. "Charlee . . . I'm going to miss you so!"

"Don't go getting all weepy on me, Laurie, or I'll cry, too. Wouldn't that be something, if the bride and the maid of honor walked down the aisle with their eyes all red!"

Blinking back tears, Lauren smiled. "There, is that better?"

"Much better. You look beautiful today, Laurie. I just know one of the groomsmen is going to fall for you! Be sure you catch my bouquet, hear?"

"You'd better throw it to me, then," she answered with forced gaiety.

Suddenly, for no reason at all, she was aware of that

old tightness creeping over her. How she hated it, that smothered compression, as if she were holding something in. Today of all days, she wanted to feel joy, only joy.

Reba's excited voice could be heard in the hall calling to one of the servants. "Oh Lord," exclaimed Charlotte, "please do something to keep Mama out of here, Laurie. I'm nervous enough, without having her fluttering around like a pouter pigeon."

"I'll go head her off until you're ready," Lauren assured her, grateful for the chance to escape.

Later, standing under the canopy of twin magnolias, flanked by six bridesmaids and eight groomsmen, Lauren watched Charlotte Lee on her father's arm, gliding with stately grace along the white-carpeted garden path. A murmur rippled through the assembled guests as they rose and turned toward the radiant bride.

The groom moved a few steps from his place to take Charlotte's hand. When Lauren reached for the bridal bouquet to hold during the ceremony, from beneath the gauzy veil, Charlee met her loving glance with a sly wink. Lauren felt the prick of tears and a welling deep within, of love and laughter and longing and sadness, all mingled in one confusing brew of emotions, as her cousin, her dearest friend, entered the sacrament of marriage.

After the receiving line, after they had posed for the photographers, they joined the champagne reception on the terrace, followed by a seven-course dinner under an enormous striped tent. It was a magical wedding, elegant and tasteful down to the smallest detail. Watching Charlotte blissfully waltzing in the arms of her new husband, Lauren was truly happy for her cousin. If she was feeling the slightest discontent, it was simply that she had this need for something . . . *someone* . . . of her own.

The moon was almost full and the sky was filled with stars when the entire wedding party hopped into roadsters to follow the bride and groom to the station. Charlee and Bruce dashed aboard the train under a shower of rice and rose petals. The private railroad car belonged to Conrad Hutsel, a tycoon client of Malcolm Fields, Max explained. It had arrived in Randolph the night before, waiting on a siding to be joined to the Southern Railway passenger train.

Lauren tried to suppress the wave of desolation that swept over her, as she watched the tail end of the train disappear far down the track with a last echo of the locomotive whistle. Something had ended. Once again, she had been left behind. She had a vision of herself spending her entire life here in the Carolina hills.

Powerless, that was how she felt. All her life she had been unable to decide anything for herself. Everything was determined by the family. Papa ruled over them, like a benign dictator. Ever since Samuel's heart attack, Philip had been afraid of making a move that would upset him. Mama did whatever he wanted, whether or not she agreed with it, and Joanna had married the first man who asked. Given other opportunities, Lionel might still have chosen the store, for he seemed to thrive on dealing with the mountain farmers who were their customers. But what choices had Lauren ever had?

She spent the next three weeks helping Reba send out wedding announcements and notices that gifts had been received by Mr. and Mrs. Malcolm Bruce Fields, Jr., who would be At Home at their Park Avenue address after the first of September.

The rest of the summer loomed ahead. College was closed, but she used the library and continued writing, ignoring the whispered conversations around her. *What shall be done about Lauren?* seemed to preoccupy everyone in the family.

Ben took her on picnics and excursions to Chimney Rock or Looking Glass Falls, and they played golf at the club. Eligible bachelors called to invite her out. It became apparent to her family she would never marry any of them. Whenever she was introduced to a new man, Reba or Lionel's wife Fay would ask eagerly, "Would you like to see him again?" Or, "Didn't you think he was attractive?"

As another birthday approached, she began to believe she was indeed an overripe fruit on the vine. If only she could get away, she might find the solution. She felt she had to discover her life's purpose. On the day she turned twenty-one, Lauren promised herself that soon a train would be carrying her away from Randolph Springs.

Book II

MAGNOLIA BLOSSOMS

1937—1941

Chapter 13

Greensboro, Autumn 1937

LAUREN NOTICED HIM immediately across the crowded room. Tall and striking, his bearing set him apart from the other men. When he bent his head, a soft wave escaped his neatly brushed dark hair. I want to meet him, she thought, as she watched him lead a stylish brunette onto the dance floor.

She had been haunting the punch bowl, affecting a brave nonchalance, wishing someone, *anyone*, would invite her to dance, and asking herself why she had let Ruth Felder persuade her to attend the Sunday afternoon social. This was only her fourth week since transferring to the college in Greensboro, and she was anxious to keep ahead of her assignments.

"I have a lot of work to do, Cousin Ruth," she had tried to beg off. "I think I'd better stay in the dorm."

But Ruth accused her of being a grind. "You have all week long to study, Laurie. How will you ever meet anyone if you don't socialize on the weekends?"

It infuriated Lauren that her family insisted on viewing college as a matrimonial lottery. "If I get behind in my reading, I'll have to drop the extra course. I may need it if they don't accept all my transfer credits."

"I don't see what your hurry is, honey. You can just as well finish next year."

"If I'm going to get my masters degree after I graduate, I don't want to take any more time than necessary."

"She's *far* too serious-minded for a girl," Lauren overheard Ruth say to her husband, Jay. "What's she going to do with all that education?"

A short, thick-set boy appeared at Lauren's side. "Would you like to dance?" With a weak smile, she followed him onto the floor. He had an embarrassing mannerism of swiveling his hips in a grinding motion to the music's beat. "I've never seen you at the club before," he said, slowing to a normal two-step.

"I go to Women's College. My cousins invited me to the dance."

He resumed his peculiar gait, like the coupling of an exotic species of insect. Just as she was trying to come up with a plausible reason to excuse herself, Stanley Eisen cut in. He was a lawyer who had graduated from Chapel Hill, one of the more agreeable boys Ruth had trotted out years ago to meet her and Charlee when they were shipped around for their Great Road Show.

"How're the studies going, Laurie?"

"I'm working a lot harder here than I did at Randolph," she replied, thinking he was very like the boys she had grown up with, friendly and unassuming, with curly brown hair and warm spaniel eyes.

"You know what they say about all work and no play!" And he was just as unimaginative.

Over Stanley's shoulder the tall young man she had taken notice of glided by, still dancing with the attractive brunette. Perhaps they were married, although Lauren thought the girl did not look like she belonged with him. A little too made up, and not sufficiently refined. *Good grief, I'm thinking just like my parents.*

Up close, he was even better looking than she had thought. There was a momentary flicker in his eyes when they met hers above his partner's head—almost as if they should know each other. Lauren felt her pulse skip, but then Stanley whirled her in a circle and tried a complicated break. Her concentration broken, she stumbled and they ended up colliding with the other couple.

"Sorry, old boy," Stanley apologized with elaborate courtesy.

"My fault entirely," the stranger replied solicitously in a deep voice with an edge of Yankee accent.

"You better watch yourself with this guy, Susie," Stanley kidded the young woman, who was leaning against her partner in a possessive way.

"Oh, he's not all that dangerous, Stan," she answered in one of those sugar-coated drawls affected by females who excel at attracting men.

"So how are things at Duke?" Stanley asked, clearly reacting to her charm.

"Couldn't be better," she answered breezily, giving him a toothy smile.

I'll never learn to flirt like that, thought Lauren. The stranger was watching her and raised a quizzical eyebrow at Stanley.

"I'm forgetting my manners. Susie Winkler and David Bernard, meet Lauren Jacobson, who has just come to Women's College," said Stan. "David was my roommate at Chapel Hill."

He had dreamer's eyes, deep set, dark blue pools, under a square forehead and straight shaggy brows. His navy suit fit his broad shoulders well and the clean, strong line of his jaw was appealing. Not until he smiled would she have said he was truly handsome. A solid, reassuring, earthly beauty, quite different from the classical perfection of Bruce Fields's looks. She wished he would ask her to dance, but had not the slightest idea what to do about it. Charlee would have known.

"Why don't we switch for the next dance," proposed Stanley.

Lauren felt a flutter of excitement, but at the same time was painfully aware it had been *her* partner's suggestion. Stan had probably been doing his duty, taking a turn with her at the urgings of her cousin, and he could hardly wait to dump her and dance with clingy, honey-voiced Susie Winkler. It was apparent to Lauren that Miss Winkler did not share Stanley's enthusiasm for the exchange.

David Bernard was either a fine actor or a perfect gentleman, for he began to dance with an air of happy anticipation. "It worked," he said.

"Worked?"

"Bumping into each other. I planned the whole thing."

"You didn't!"

"Oh yes, the minute I saw you dancing with Stan, I contrived a way to meet you. But it took my rather dense ex-roommate a while to take the hint."

"You mean—?"

"I gave him the signal."

"I didn't realize men did that."

"We do. I learned early in life that you have to make your own opportunities." He drew back, gazing down at her, and her heart lurched at his smile.

"You went to law school with Stanley?" she said, to prevent his knowing how flustered she was.

"We were roommates in college. I went to medical school."

"Then you're a doctor?"

He smiled again. "That's what they tell me."

She could imagine the enthusiasm among the cousins. *A doctor!* Laurie's going out with a doctor . . . Idiot, cretin, stupid moronic fool—one turn about the dance floor, and you're already spinning daydreams. "Do you have a practice here in Greensboro?" she asked.

"I'm a second-year resident at Duke, with at least four or five more to go."

"Why so long?"

"I want to do orthopedic surgery and that takes forever. We start out with general surgery and then go on to the specialties."

"You ought to be an extraordinary doctor after all that training."

He looked at her thoughtfully for a moment. "I'm getting some extra practice in medicine these days as a team sawbones for Carolina. Do you like football?"

"I don't know. I've never been to a real football game."

"Now that seems a shame. We'll have to do something about it."

Did that mean he would ask her for a date? She prayed he would. He seemed to like her and they certainly danced well together. She could tell he enjoyed music from the way he moved effortlessly with the rhythm. He drew her closer, and it was the most wonderfully cared-for feeling.

Susie Winkler was looking daggers at them from across the room! But Lauren didn't care. She could have gone on dancing with him for hours. She understood what Charlee had meant when she said she *knew* the moment she first saw Bruce. No one had ever intrigued her as much as David Bernard, although she couldn't have said why. Surely a man's appearance didn't mean that much to her, and that's all she had to go on. That, and his beautiful smile . . . and the marvelous excitement she felt from his closeness. She hardly remembered the rest of their conversation, but by the time the afternoon was over, Lauren wondered if she was falling in love.

He called a week later. The hallway in her dormitory was crowded and noisy with girls getting back from their weekend dates. "This is David—David Bernard. Do you remember me?" *Remember* him? She had thought of nothing else since last Sunday. "Will you meet me in Chapel Hill for the Homecoming game next weekend? There's a dance on Friday night."

For the rest of the week her feet scarcely touched ground. She had to have written permission to visit a man, of course. The Felders served *in locus parentis* for her at Women's College. "Who *is* David Bernard?" asked Ruth, when Lauren requested the note.

"He's a doctor. I believe he lives in Durham. I met him at the country club dance, Cousin Ruth. Stanley Eisen introduced us."

"Jay, do you think I should give Helene Eisen a ring and ask about this boy?"

"Oh *please,* you wouldn't do that?" Lauren cried, dismayed. "It would get back to him and he'd never ask me out again. I can tell he's a very nice boy—I mean, man. He graduated from Chapel Hill, went to medical school at Duke, and he has good manners."

"Jay has a niece in Durham who's married to a dentist. I wonder whether they know a Bernard family . . ."

"Cousin Ruth, *don't you dare!* I'll never forgive you if you do. Besides, his family doesn't live there."

"Where *do* they live?"

"I haven't the slightest idea. What *difference* does it make?"

"Well, dear, we know nothing about this young man. How can I let you go off to Chapel Hill with him?"

There was steel in Lauren's voice. "This is the most ridiculous thing I have ever heard! I am *not* a child. I am twenty-two years old and I am going to a *football weekend,* not an assignation!"

"I declare, Laurie, I know just what your dear mama means. There are times when I don't understand you at all."

Lauren had to struggle not to lose her temper. She knew what *that* little reference was all about. No doubt everyone in the family had been informed that she had transferred from Randolph College against her father's wishes!

It had taken her a whole year to convince him.

"I want to go to the university at Chapel Hill to finish college, Papa," she had told him after her sophomore year at Randolph. "They have the best English department."

"Chapel Hill is for men, Laurie."

"No, Papa, they admit a few women in the junior year."

"My daughter will remain under my roof until she marries," he replied. Then he had softened it by saying, "Your mother and I would be very lonely without you, Laurie."

"But you were going to let me go to New York with Charlee. Why not Chapel Hill?"

She had continued to campaign for months. It was Philip who had in the end persuaded their father to permit her to leave Randolph Springs for her senior year. Samuel had insisted on a woman's college, however.

Lauren finally agreed to stay with friends of the Felders, since Chapel Hill appeared to be the one town in all the South where the Jacobson-Mortimer chain of relationships did not extend. David had arranged a room for her at a friend's house, but he accepted her explanation without comment when he met the bus from Women's College in front of the Carolina Inn. He was even taller and more handsome than she remembered, dressed casually in a V-neck sweater under his herringbone tweed jacket. She noticed how deeply blue his eyes were, and his brown hair had golden glints in the bright fall sunshine.

It was a short drive to the home of Ruth Felder's friends, Selma and Oscar Rosenbloom, who owned a popular Chapel Hill clothing shop that catered to university men. Gravely courteous, David conversed with her hostess while Lauren unpacked and hung up her evening dress. When she joined them in the living room, he said, "If it's all right with you, ma'am, I'd like to show Lauren around the campus before it gets dark."

"Why, certainly," smiled Selma Rosenbloom. "Such a nice young man," she whispered when they were leaving, loud enough for David to hear.

As soon as they had walked to the end of the block, Lauren said, "David, I'm very sorry about all this, but it wasn't worth fighting with my entire family."

He looked down at her quite seriously. "You don't know how lucky you are to have a family that cares." She sensed a sadness behind his smile, and she realized her cousin was right. She really knew nothing at all about him.

"Where do you come from, David?"

"I grew up on the North Carolina coast," he said, "but I was born in Philadelphia."

"And where do you live now?"

"I just left Durham for Strickland Hospital where I'm starting my new rotation. It's eight miles from here, in Oakland Hills, but I've spent so much time in Chapel Hill, it seems more like home than any other place."

It still didn't explain him. "I meant—where is your family?"

"What's left of it. I was raised in a little dot on the map outside of Wilmington by my father's brother and his wife. Uncle Sydney still lives there."

Lauren was afraid it was rude to ask too many questions, but she was eager to know everything about him. They walked along Cameron Avenue under a canopy of golden maple trees. David took a brick footpath through the center of the campus. "What's that little dome over there that looks like a Greek temple?" she asked.

"I'm forgetting our tour. That's the Old Well, venerable

shrine of UNC." He led her over to the graceful wooden structure. "You're standing right in the center of the original university. That's Old East over there, the first building. Straight down is the Wilson Library, and just behind it is the Bell Tower, which you will become accustomed to hearing if you ever spend any time in Chapel Hill."

"I hope I will," she said with enthusiasm. "I'd like to come here for my masters."

"A scholar, no less. I would never have guessed."

"That was a patronizing remark!"

He laughed. "I suppose it came out that way, I didn't mean it to be. Actually, I think that's pretty terrific. It's fairly unusual for a beautiful girl to want to go to graduate school, at least, in my experience. Most of them seem to have one ambition—"

She nodded and they mouthed it together, *"To get married!"*

"Everyone wants to get married," Lauren said when she had stopped laughing. "There's no law that says a woman can't be married *and* go to graduate school."

"None except the law of motherhood."

"What's that supposed to mean?"

He sighed. "Maybe I better keep my mouth shut, I'll just get in trouble. What I meant was that if a woman has an advanced degree, she'd probably want to use it in some way, professionally. It's difficult to have a career and a family. That's all."

"Difficult, but not impossible."

He slanted his eyes downward at her. "Are you one of those females who always has to have the last word?"

"Absolutely!"

"Come on," he said, grabbing her by the hand. "I'll show you the amphitheater. It's almost time to get dressed. We're invited to a bunch of parties before the dance."

The "Tin Can," as the huge indoor sports facility was called, had been transformed into a festively decorated ballroom for the Homecoming Ball that evening. Masses of balloons and streamers in Carolina blue hung from the girders, lowering the ceiling of the cavernous gymnasium, which was already reverberating with music, laughter, and the hum of conversation when they arrived, after stopping at three cocktail parties beforehand.

Seldom had Lauren seen so many gorgeously arrayed women gathered in one place. As they swayed to the music, their filmy full-skirted ball gowns, reminiscent of the Old South, in hues of rosy pink, soft lavender, daffodil yellow, and persimmon swept around the floor in a revolving wheel of color under the glimmer of hundreds of flickering paper lanterns. Lauren's evening dress of French blue chiffon—a new style brought back from New York by Reba—had a low cut back and form-fitting bodice that flared out below the hips in gores of shaded blue. She carried the nosegay of tiny pink tea roses, violets, and lilies-of-the-valley that David had given her. "You're beautiful, Lauren," he murmured as he took her in his arms to dance. She wondered whether he was as affected by their nearness as she, and if he sensed the delicious pleasure that engulfed her.

The evening passed too quickly. Smiling with happiness, she conversed with David's friends, meeting professors, graduate students, and alumni, always conscious of David's eyes on her. The exhilarating effect of the jubilant crowd, the collegiate spirit, and her constant awareness of David set her nerves tingling. Around midnight, the mood reached a peak of excitement, couples swirling to the increased tempo of the band, as the assemblage was caught up in a delirium of nostalgia, good spirits, and anticipation of the gridiron contest ahead. Through it all, sensitive to David's presence, Lauren was seized with a buoyant joy. As they moved to the last slow waltz, she wanted to remain in his embrace for the rest of her life.

"Unfortunately, I have to teach a class here at the med school first thing tomorrow morning," said David, when they were parked on the dark, quiet street in front of the Rosenbloom house. "I think you'd enjoy walking around the campus, and you should go into the library. Do you mind meeting me downtown? That way we'll have time to grab some lunch before the game."

At the door he leaned down, taking her face in both his

hands, to kiss her gently. "I knew it would be a wonderful evening," he said.

She wobbled up the stairs to her room, a lopsided smile on her lips. Floating in the arms of a phantom David, she turned her head to watch her skirts fan out and fill the full-length mirror. Moving to the glass, she stared at her reflection. "It's happened," she whispered, "it's really happened. I'm in love!"

At noon on Saturday, Lauren was sitting on the stone wall under a poplar tree, memorizing a selection for her Nineteenth-century Poets course. She looked up to see David drinking from a water fountain marked "Colored."

"Hey there," he grinned, wiping his mouth with the back of his hand. His defiant, masculine swagger warmed her. Taking the book from her, he examined its spine, then opened to the page where his thumb saved her place. "Thackeray. Are you a Lit major?"

She nodded. "When I began college, I thought I would major in Music, but I discovered I like to write."

"Are you any good?"

"Not yet."

He laughed. "That sounds like me, except in my case it's surgery."

"I would say your stakes are a little higher. Bad writing can't do much harm."

He grinned. "I'm not so sure." When he stared at her that way, his eyes seemed to go straight through her and she felt a stirring inside. She had a desire to reach out and touch his face, wanting to trace the outline of his mouth and feel the texture of his skin.

As if David could read her thoughts, he took her hand and kissed the fingertips. "I'm starved," he said, suddenly brisk. "Let's go have lunch."

They ate chicken salad sandwiches and chocolate shakes at a tiny lunchroom called The Hole-in-the-Wall, and then they rushed to Kenan stadium just as the Carolina marching band struck up "I'm a Tar Heel Born," high-stepping their way onto the field.

David assisted the official team doctor at home games.

"I get two free tickets for my efforts," he told her. Their seats were up front on the fifty-yard line where he could be near the players in case there were any injuries. Lauren wondered who had sat with him in her place at previous games.

The Tar Heels were meeting the undefeated Tulane Green Wave before a throng of twenty-one thousand in the University of North Carolina's great egg-shaped football arena. Although the opposing team was not UNC's arch-rival, Duke, there was ample enthusiasm for the contest among the students and alumni gathered on this beautiful fall Saturday. It was fairly cool for late October, and old grads wore class sweaters and fraternity ties under their blazers, hailing classmates in the crowded bleachers as they made their way up the steps with their ladies.

With shining eyes, Lauren watched the colorful spectacle, and David watched Lauren. He spread a blanket over the hard seats for them to sit on. "I'll be right back," he excused himself, reappearing in a few minutes carrying a UNC pennant and a giant yellow chrysanthemum which he pinned to the lapel of Lauren's heather blue tweed suit. "Now you are officially initiated into the rite of the college football weekend."

She smiled up at him, aglow with happiness. "Thank you. You must think I'm a real hillbilly, never having done this before."

"I thought everyone from Randolph Springs was a hillbilly!" He put an arm around her shoulders and hugged her. "Having fun?"

"Yes, I think I love football."

He threw his head back and laughed. "Wait! The game hasn't begun. The best is yet to come."

The band marched into the stands and the cheerleaders took up their positions, performing gymnastic feats. Suddenly there was a roar from the bleachers, and the Carolina team ran out to the center of the field to begin warming up. From the visitors' side of the stadium came a thunderous cheer as Tulane appeared. The players stretched and sprinted and practiced feints, while the officials waited on the sidelines for the moment when the captains would toss for the kick.

"How will I ever know what's going on?" Lauren asked.

"It's easy," he assured her, as he explained the basic rules. "You'll get the idea once the game starts."

There was a blare of brass from the band. *Everyone up for the kickoff!* Lauren rose with David and watched the pigskin sail through the air. She felt the electricity in the crowd, as she tried to remember David's rudimentary sketch of the game.

At half-time, Carolina led 13–0. David said, "Come on, let's go up in the bleachers to see some of my friends." They were all alumni, some of whom Lauren had met the night before.

No one scored in the second half. David went down to the field twice to examine players who had been roughed up, but there were no serious injuries. By the time the game ended, a strong wind was blowing and half the stadium was in shade. David wrapped an arm around Lauren's shoulders as they forced their way through the victorious fans to catch up with Stanley Eisen, whom David spied outside the gates with his date, Elaine Martin.

"I once met you and your cousin at a dance in Charleston," Elaine said when they had been introduced.

"I'm sorry I didn't recognize you," Lauren apologized. "That was three years ago. How can you remember?"

Elaine laughed, a pretty sound, "Everyone knew Charlotte Mortimer! She was a legend in those days. Whatever happened to her?"

"Charlee's been married for over a year now to a boy from up North. They live in New York."

"There must have been a slew of broken-hearted Southern boys left behind when she became a bride!"

"What's this about broken hearts?" asked David.

"We were speaking of my cousin Charlotte. She has always had an interesting effect on men."

"Interesting!" snorted Stanley. "That's one way of putting it."

"How would you describe it?" asked Elaine, laughing.

Stan shook his head. *"Formidable!* Even in those days I knew my limits. Charlee was too much for me."

"Well," said David, "I guess I'll have to meet this *femme fatale."*

"I hope you will someday," said Lauren, even now relieved that Charlotte Lee was safely married and living in New York with her handsome husband.

Dry leaves crunched underfoot and a crimson arch of oaks and maples cast a ruddy glow above their heads. They were going to the Pi Lambda Phi house for a post-game bash. "When I first came to Chapel Hill, I didn't want to join a fraternity," David told her, as they walked along Columbia Street behind Stan and Elaine. "I couldn't really afford it. But this guy," he gave Stanley a playful punch on the shoulder, "talked me into Pi Lam."

Stan grinned back at David. "Hell, we needed a piano player, that's all. You don't think we would've taken a 'shmuck' like you otherwise, do you?"

"Hey, watch your language around my girl!"

His girl! Did he mean it, or was that just an expression? "You play the piano?" she said aloud.

"Yeah. Sort of a hacker, but I earned all my spending money in college playing with a group of guys for fraternity dances. We called ourselves the Noblest Obliges."

"That's why you dance so well, you have a musician's sense of rhythm."

"I never had too much practice dancing. I was always up on the bandstand. My dates got to dance with all the other guys—they loved it."

Lauren doubted that. Any girl who had been lucky enough to be asked out by David Bernard would certainly have wanted to dance with *him,* not his fraternity brothers.

As dinner time neared, couples began leaving the party in groups to go to the Carolina Inn, if they were feeling flush, or to Swain Hall or one of the frat houses if they were on a tighter budget. Stanley and Elaine, who were expected back in Greensboro for the evening, said goodbye.

"Ralph and Gretchen Nelson have invited us for dinner tonight," said David. "They're the people whose house you were supposed to stay at. That is, before your cousins questioned the honorableness of my intentions."

"David! That's not why—"

"Oh, isn't it? I never had a sister, Lauren—well, actually I did once, but I didn't grow up with one—however, I do understand how Southern families go about guarding the virtue of their womenfolk."

She saw that he was teasing, and replied in kind. "You seem to know an awful lot about women, Dr. Bernard!"

On their way across campus to pick up David's car, they met Dr. Thomas Sayles, professor of orthopedic surgery at Duke and chief of orthopedics at Strickland Hospital, where David had recently started his surgical assignment.

"Tom! I didn't expect to see you here today," David greeted him, shaking hands and introducing Lauren.

"We came over for the game. Helen went to Sophie Newcomb, if you remember. I'm afraid this was not Tulane's finest hour." The youthful surgeon told Lauren he had spent many summers of his boyhood in Randolph Springs. "I used to go horseback riding on the trails near Shadow Mountain. That's beautiful country you come from, Miss Jacobson."

"Are all of your professors so friendly?" asked Lauren after they had parted from Sayles.

"Tom's one of the best. Everyone wants to be on his service."

"I'm surprised you call him by his first name."

"Duke's a pretty informal place. They've only had a medical school for seven years and most of the teaching staff are young. Tom's still in his thirties."

They had reached his automobile. "Do you want to stop at the Rosenblooms' before we go to dinner?" he asked, opening the door for her.

"Not unless you think I should change for the evening." She looked down at her tailored suit, which she wore with a cream-colored silk blouse.

"No, you're fine. This is a pretty casual group, all young faculty, with no spare money."

They drove past a university hall under construction.

"That's the new medical building. It'll be finished by next year," said David.

"Where's the hospital?"

"There is none. That's why they don't have four years of medicine here. You can't train doctors unless you have a teaching hospital."

"But you said they *do* have a medical school."

"The University of North Carolina has only two years of med school, the preclinical years. There's been talk for ages about expanding it to four years, but the state has never approved the funds. There's an infirmary, of course, but the closest hospital is Strickland, which maintains an affiliation with Duke."

"What happens to the medical students after their second year?"

"They go on to finish at other schools, some of the best in the country," David explained. "I took my first two years here at Chapel Hill and then I matriculated to Duke. Good thing, too, since I might not have met Tom Sayles if I'd gone somewhere else."

"Is all your work in orthopedic surgery?"

"Not yet. It's been general surgery and pathology so far, but I'm starting to get into some of the exotic stuff." He grinned and she was again aware of how handsome he was. "Tom is building a strong group, and I want to do my residency in orthopedics with him next year. I'm hoping I'll get a Russell fellowship."

"What's a Russell fellowship?" Lauren asked.

"An award for postdoctoral training at the Russell Clinic, which has just been established at Strickland. The grant is part of a new Cartwright Foundation program that pays a stipend to residents. Otherwise, we get no salary, just an allowance to cover the basic costs of living."

"Do you have a good chance for the fellowship?"

"I think so, but I won't know until the spring. It's very competitive. Tom likes my work, and he would have a lot to say about it, since he'll be chief of orthopedics at the new clinic. It would be difficult without a grant because I'm up to my ba—eyeballs in hock, paying off loans." He was offhand about it, but she sensed it was a matter of some concern to him.

They parked on a hilly street in front of the Nelson house. "Ralph's in the history department," David mentioned, as they walked up the steep stone steps. "He and I became friends when he wrote his thesis on medical history and asked me to critique the draft. He's expanded it into a textbook that will be published next year."

David kissed Ralph's wife, presenting her with a box of chocolates. Lauren felt an immediate warmth toward Gretchen Nelson, a freckle-faced young woman with a generous smile and an impudent, lively breathlessness. She wore her wavy auburn hair piled on top of her head, secured with something that looked remarkably like a knitting needle. Charlee would have called her Bohemian. In her all-enveloping smock-like garment of South American Indian design, Lauren would never have guessed Gretchen was pregnant if David hadn't mentioned it.

While the men settled down with bourbon and branch water in the sparsely furnished, book-lined living room of the Nelsons' compact university-owned house, Lauren followed Gretchen into the kitchen, offering to help with the dinner preparations. "You can do salad, if you like. The Strouds probably won't be here for an hour, which is nice, so we can talk. We're only six for dinner, the rest are coming later for dessert and coffee. I thought it would be better if I kept it small, for you to get to know some of David's best friends." The way Gretchen spoke, it sounded like David had told her he especially wanted his friends to meet her, as if she really *was* his girl.

Lauren busied herself cutting up vegetables on the wooden counter, which was jammed with cookbooks, memo pads, mail, ceramic pots filled with green avocado plants and rootings, and an assortment of scissors, pencils, and balls of string. Gretchen kept up a steady chatter about Chapel Hill and the university. ". . . so Ralph decided at the last minute not to go to Michigan, but to stay on at Carolina. It's a good thing, too. Otherwise we would never have met. I came down from Boston that year as a grad student. I was studying for my masters in English."

"That's what I plan to do after I graduate."

"I advise you to do it in a hurry." Gretchen's tone was rueful.

"Why?" asked Lauren uneasily.

"Once we got married, I had to work full time because we needed the money. It is *not* true that two can live as cheaply as one, and soon we'll be three." Gretchen tried to look serious, but her grin was irrepressible. "I had hoped to go on for my Ph.D., but I still haven't finished my masters thesis, and now with the baby coming, I'm usually too tired at the end of the day to do any writing. The old fire just isn't there, I guess." She shrugged philosophically. When she saw the expression on Lauren's face, she said, "Please don't misunderstand. I *adore* Ralph, and we're happy as clams, but, we all have our dreams."

Ralph came into the kitchen. He was attractive in a scholarly way, with sandy blond hair and gray eyes behind horn-rimmed glasses. "Do we have anything for snacks, hon?" He kissed Gretchen, patting her belly as he went by.

"Cheese and crackers, over there on the counter."

Ralph put a chunk of cheddar cheese on a plate and dumped some Ritz crackers around it, then rummaged in a drawer.

"Where's a knife?"

"Here." Gretchen rinsed off a paring knife in the sink, dried it, and handed it to Ralph.

"Are you two girls coming in for a drink?"

"In a minute, soon as I get dinner in the oven." Ralph disappeared into the living room with the cheese platter. "We're having tuna casserole. I hope you like it," Gretchen said to Lauren.

"Oh . . . yes. Tuna is one of my favorites. How do you prepare it?"

"Simple. Come watch."

She drained boiled noodles and combined them in a buttered casserole with canned tuna fish and Campbell's Cream of Mushroom Soup. What will she do with the corn flakes? Lauren wondered, as Gretchen reached for a box on the cupboard shelf. Fascinated, she watched the snub-nosed girl-woman crush a handful of dry cereal and sprinkle it over the top, dot it with butter, and place the casserole in the oven.

"Done! I think I'll write a book called *Faculty Meals*. Nothing will cost over fifty cents." She dusted her hands together with an emphatic nod of her head. "Let's go have a drink."

Ralph and David rose when they entered the living room. "What can I get you, Lauren?" asked Ralph.

"Something nonalcoholic, please."

"You're not Temperance, are you?"

"Good heavens, no! I just don't like the taste of liquor."

"What about sherry?"

"That would be nice," she said, preferring a soft drink, but not wanting to make a fuss about it.

"Come sit here next to me," David patted the couch. When Gretchen reached for her highball, he said, "Does your obstetrician approve of you drinking during pregnancy?"

She looked surprised. "I never asked him. Why? Is it bad for me?"

"Not for you, but I wouldn't overdo it. It can't be good for the baby."

Gretchen sighed. "Why is it, anything that's fun is bad for my pregnancy?"

Ralph tweaked her nose and winked. "Not *everything!*"

Lauren felt herself blush, but the room's lighting was dim, so she thought no one would notice. The easy, unaffected banter, the outspoken frankness and camaraderie she had noticed among the graduate students and young faculty in Chapel Hill were new to her. She wondered whether she would ever enjoy that kind of affectionate intimacy with a husband. Ralph and Gretchen were obviously very much in love.

A bell sounded and Ralph opened the door for the Strouds, who had driven over from Durham. "I baked brownies, Gretchen. I hope that was all right." Grace

Stroud, a tall, sunny woman with the apple-cheeked freshness of a farm girl, set down a large platter piled high with fudgey squares.

"Wonderful! they look yummy. How are you, Tony? Bad day?"

"Awful. I wasn't sure I'd be able to come tonight. Gil Rogers agreed to cover for me."

"Tony is chief resident in surgery at Duke," David explained to Lauren.

"How often are you on duty?" she asked the rangy, tired-looking man.

They all laughed. "Twenty-four hours a day, seven days a week, fifty-two weeks a year," said Grace, rolling her eyes. "It's heaven, let me tell you."

"Hey, Grace, that's not fair! You'll frighten her away from me," David joked.

"Is it really true?" asked Lauren.

"I'm afraid so," David nodded.

"How were you able to get away this weekend?"

"We cover for one another. I'll have to make up for it. But don't worry, it just means I'll go without sleep for weeks and wreck my health . . ."

Lauren giggled. "Are you trying to make me feel guilty?"

"Who me?" David pulled her against his side, kissing her forehead.

She noticed Gretchen and Grace exchange significant glances. If this were Randolph Springs, the rumor mill would be gearing up. It was probably the same here among the academic crowd, but Lauren didn't care. Her heart was singing, and she felt an amazing sense of freedom in Chapel Hill.

After dinner, the three women cleared away the dishes and set out coffee cups and dessert plates. Soon the other guests began arriving, walking in without ringing, tossing coats on a bench in the hall or over the banister, until the small rooms were crowded. Four of the couples were engaged or going together and the rest were married, except for one lone bachelor, who deposited a jug of wine on the kitchen counter, planted a kiss on Gretchen's cheek, and rejoined the party in the living room.

"That's Kyle," Gretchen told Lauren, smiling and exchanging looks with a woman named Carol Lawrence. "He's a classicist."

"Ahh, really?"

"He's—you know." Carol wet her pinky with her tongue and made as if to groom an eyebrow.

"Beg pardon?"

Gretchen gave a little laugh, playfully elbowing her. "He doesn't go out with women, Laurie," she whispered. "He's a fairy."

"Uh . . . I see." She didn't *quite*, but she thought she got the general idea. There had always been a dark, mysterious area, something she couldn't imagine. The girls at school sometimes joked about men who were like that.

"Oh, but he's really very nice," Carol hastened to add. "Everyone likes him."

Each wife or fiancée had made some sort of dessert, which she had brought on a plate covered with waxed paper. Lauren was glad to see Gretchen had put out a dish of David's candy. The women placed their pastries on the table in the dining room, wandered into the kitchen, helping themselves to cheese or a roll, then lounged on the couch or floor, as comfortable as if they were in their own homes.

Gretchen lit candles, placing them on tables around the living room and Ralph brought out folding chairs, started a cheerful fire to take off the chill of the night, and opened the wine brought to dry Chapel Hill by Kyle. The house took on a wonderfully warm atmosphere of mellow spirits and sharp conversation, as historians, political scientists, doctors, English professors, and artists talked at, around, and about one another.

Many of the wives were Lauren's age but they were far more worldly than the college girls in her dorm or her friends in Randolph Springs. Some came from the North and they all spoke up without hesitation, joining in the conversation when the men discussed politics or medicine. These women were knowledgeable and had strong opinions about the economy, the war in China, the brewing crisis in Europe, the Roosevelt administration in Washington, and campus affairs at Duke and Carolina. You could tell they cared about what was being said. They drank and smoked cigarettes and used strong language, all of which would have caused her mother to disapprove. Most were attractive and feminine, but some seemed careless of fashion, and unconcerned with their own appearance. Reba would have said they were too forward, and Charlee would turn up her nose at their lack of style.

After a time, David invited her to go out on the porch to escape the thick cigarette smoke inside. "You seem to get along well with the wives," he commented. "I can tell they like you."

"I like them, too, they're easy to talk to. You have nice friends, David."

He nodded, glancing through the windows at the group inside engaged in animated conversation. "My friends mean a great deal to me," he said. "Unlike you, I do not have a large family. My parents and younger sister died when I was eleven."

"How dreadful! That must have been heartbreaking for you."

"Yes, at the time it was. But my aunt and uncle were wonderful guardians. Uncle Sydney was my father's only brother. He sent Dad through medical school and he was so proud of him. You see, he had always wanted medicine himself, but he had to settle for being a pharmacist."

"What about your mother's relatives?"

His jaw hardened and a darkness came into his eyes. "I never see them. My mother's family did not acknowledge her marriage."

"Why not?" she said in surprise. "The Jewish families I know would be thrilled to have a doctor for a son-in-law."

"I guess that explains it," he said lightly. "They weren't Jewish."

"Oh . . . I see." Embarrassed, she tried to think of something to say to cover her confusion.

He quickly caught her hand. "But *I* am, Lauren. My

father was Jewish, and I was brought up as a Jew, more or less. I even had a Bar Mitzvah."

For a moment, she had panicked. Her father would never approve of her marrying anyone who wasn't Jewish—*There she went again, weaving daydreams!* She was as bad as her relatives, thinking about marriage when she hardly knew this man. "So, you're fulfilling your uncle's dream, by becoming a doctor," she said.

"He's very happy about it," David admitted. "I was supposed to go to Hopkins, but the depression made it impossible. I was lucky to get through Carolina."

"Why did you prefer Johns Hopkins?"

He shrugged. "Because my father went there, I guess. When you don't have a father, he tends to become a mystical godhead figure. No regrets, though. I'm quite satisfied with the education I received here and at Duke. And Chapel Hill's a lot prettier than Baltimore."

"Do you go home often to visit your aunt and uncle?"

"Aunt Ethel died the year I started college and Uncle Sydney lives at his club in Wilmington now, with all his cronies who are widowers. It's like an old folks home. I'm afraid I don't visit him nearly often enough."

"Aren't there any other relatives?"

"Distant cousins, I suppose. I don't know any of them."

"That seems so strange to me, David. My family must make up half the Jewish population of the Carolinas and they're all constantly visiting one another."

"I had a Yankee friend in college who used to say the reason people in small Southern towns had such big families is there's nothing else to do but procreate."

Lauren laughed. "Small town or not, it was fun growing up with lots of relatives. Charlee and I—that's my cousin Charlotte, the one Stanley and Elaine knew—we always did everything together. She and I used to go all over the South visiting aunts and uncles and distant cousins. There were always dances and parties and outings. Those were wonderful times!" Her face glowed as she spoke, recalling the happiness of her girlhood. She was unaware of how lovely she looked to him, with her sparkling eyes, shining hair, and flushed cheeks.

"It must have been," he answered. "I want a big family some day. It's no fun to grow up alone." He looked at her searchingly. "What is it that you want, Lauren Jacobson? There's something, I can tell."

"If only I knew," she sighed. "I guess what I want is . . . to find out what it is."

He took her hand. "You will."

"Hey, you two, time for dessert." It was Gretchen. "I hope I wasn't interrupting anything *important!*" She gave them a pixie grin.

"What could possibly be more important than dessert?" David answered.

An hour later they said good-bye to the Nelsons. "Next time, come stay with us," Gretchen told Lauren.

"If I had known it would be with you—"

"Say no more, we all have our families."

When they reached the Rosenblooms' street, David parked under some trees away from the house and put his arms around her. Drawing her close, he softly kissed her hair, her eyelids, and finally, her lips. Lauren was unprepared for the intensity of it, the warm liquid feeling deep inside. Over and over again, they kissed . . . deep, wild, marvelous, tempestuous kisses. Dizzy with the wonder of it, she gasped when he released her.

"Lauren . . ." he kissed her again, and his hands brushed her breasts, but then he drew back. "I can't believe we just met two weeks ago. It seems we've known each other so much longer."

"I know," she whispered, wishing it could be forever.

"There's another game next Saturday."

Next Saturday? *Philip!* "I'm sorry, David, my brother is coming to visit me in Greensboro. I feel a little guilty about him, since I'm the one who went away to school."

He looked regretful, but he smiled. "I wasn't sure how I would get the day off, anyway. It's kind of difficult to make dates ahead of time, with my schedule."

She lay awake half the night fantasizing about David. *Please make him love me,* she prayed. *If only he'll fall in love with me.*

In the morning, when Lauren thanked Selma Rosenbloom for her hospitality, the motherly woman replied, "I hardly saw you, dear. Remember, any time you come to Chapel Hill, you must stay with us. I'm going to call Ruth and tell her what a pleasure it was to have you." Lauren could just imagine that conversation.

They lingered overlong at Sunday brunch and just made the bus. David drove up to the Carolina Inn honking his horn, much to the disapproval of some gaping Chapel Hillians out for a Sunday stroll. There was no time for goodbye, which was just as well, because he might have kissed her, and all the girls from Women's College were peering out the windows to see who had held them up. Flushed and breathless, Lauren thanked the driver for waiting and fell into a seat halfway to the rear.

A sophomore, Shirley something-or-other, who was in her Western Civilization seminar, moved forward to sit beside her. Lauren would have preferred to be alone on the return trip, but she was stuck. "Hi, Laurie," said Shirley. "Did you have a nice weekend?"

"Yes, what about you?"

She grimaced. "It was all right. Umm, wasn't that David Bernard I saw you with?" she asked, all innocence. Shirley was the sort of girl Lauren loathed—sugar sweet on the outside, hard and calculating on the inside.

Lauren concealed her annoyance. "Yes, it was."

"I thought so. Have you known him long?"

"Not all that long," said Lauren. "Why?"

"No particular reason, just curious. He goes out with my cousin Susie."

Lauren smiled. "Oh, really." Now she remembered Shirley's last name. *Winkler.* She had no doubt that Susie would hear about her date with David before the sun had set.

"Yes," Shirley continued in saccharine tones, "they've been seeing each other for quite some time now. Well over a year."

"Ah."

"He's *crazy* about her. I expect they'll be engaged one day soon."

For the briefest moment Lauren's spirits sank. Susie had

looked awfully sure of David that day at the club dance. But then she remembered David's words last night, and his kisses.

With a polite smile, she turned to look out the window. *Don't bet on that, Shirley!* she whispered silently, as the bus rolled along the highway to Greensboro.

Chapter 14

THE SHARP RINGING of the telephone aroused David. He groped for the receiver in the dark.

"Bernard speaking." He felt the crackling surge of adrenalin as he listened to the intern's urgent voice telling him a crisis had developed. It was the compound fracture case and it sounded bad. "I'll be right there!" he said, already out of bed and reaching for his clothes.

A nightmare coming true. Four soused-up fraternity boys from Chapel Hill had wrapped their car around a telephone pole on the Raleigh Road in the early hours last Monday morning, after an all-night beer bust. The driver and one passenger had been killed instantly, another escaped with only minor injuries, and this boy, with his smashed body, was still on the critical list. Multiple shatter fractures of his arms, both legs, ribs, and pelvis, and a torn bladder—Christ, what a mess! After eight hours in the OR, with relay teams of thoracic, orthopedic, urological, and neurosurgeons piecing him together, the eighteen-year-old college sophomore had been doing all right. Assured he would survive, his family had left for home last night.

When David reached the surgical floor, one of the nurses was in tears. The intern who had called him was bending over the patient with a stethoscope. Wide-eyed with disbelief, he looked up and shook his head. "He's dead."

David grabbed the stethoscope, shoving the intern aside. "Jesus Christ! *What happened?*" He searched for a pulse.

"He was having chest pains and labored breathing. The nurse alerted me about an hour ago."

"Why the hell didn't you call me immediately?"

"I was sure I could—with fractured ribs, I thought—I loosened the tape, and he was breathing better . . ."

"Okay, it's okay." He didn't want the kid falling apart now, when he needed his help. "Have them call Dr. Withers, it's his patient. Tell those nurses to stop crying and give us a hand in here. Get me oxygen and epinephrine hydrochloride, one-tenth of one percent solution. Come on, *come on,* speed it up!" The staff scurried in and out, following his orders.

David clamped an oxygen mask over the boy's face. He couldn't use pressure on those smashed ribs . . . While a nurse filled a syringe with an ampule of adrenalin, David cut through the chest tape over the heart. Grabbing the syringe, he injected the powerful vasopressor directly into the heart muscle. With luck, it would stimulate the stopped heart to start beating again. He pumped up the blood pressure apparatus that had been placed on the patient's upper left arm, above the cast. With all that plaster, it was a hell of a problem to get at him. David put the stethoscope to the chest, straining his ears, keeping his eyes on the boy's face.

Had he heard something? No, nothing.

Wait a minute . . . a faint thumping tone. Lup . . . lup . . . lup-*dup*. "Come on, *come on!*" he urged. Again, an almost imperceptible tremor, a flutter. Three fairly steady, weak heartbeats, followed by vermicular contraction.

"He's fibrillating," said David, trying to keep calm. "Check the oxygen, will you? If only we could get a respirator on him. I'm afraid those ribs would separate and puncture the lungs."

Lup-*dup*, lup-*dup*, lup-*dup* . . .

"I think he's breathing," said the young house officer, his voice tense with excitement. "He is! He's *breathing!* He *made* it!"

"Not yet," cautioned David. "Did you reach Dr. Withers?" he asked one of the nurses, who appeared at that moment.

"There's no answer, doctor."

No answer at 3 A.M.? "Keep trying. They must be sound

asleep over there." He bent his head again, listening. There was a heartbeat, slow and faint, but nevertheless, a heartbeat. Should he give more adrenalin? Better not. It could send him into spasm.

Lup-*dup*, lup-*dup*, lup-*dup*, lup-*dup*, lup-*dup*-puh . . . Uh-oh! lup-*dup*-puh . . . lup-*dup* . . . lup, lup-*dup*-puh . . . Heart failure.

"He's failing again, he's stopped breathing!" cried the intern, practically sobbing. "Oh God, Dave, he's not breathing . . . *Breathe! Breathe!*" Either this kid would learn to handle stress better, thought David, or he'd have to become a dermatologist!

"We'll try another half dose of adrenalin in the vein," ordered David. There was nothing to lose.

For an hour they worked over the youth before David gently let go of the limp hand. It was too late, the boy was gone. He felt the familiar despair at losing a patient, the anguish that caused him to dread trauma cases.

David forced himself to remain stoic as an example to the distraught intern, who was just five months out of med school. He placed a hand on the dejected young man's shoulder. "I'm sure you did everything you could. We'll talk about it later," he told him, trying to keep his own voice from shaking. "I'm betting it was an embolism. We'll try to get the family's permission for an autopsy. They live in Edenton. Probably just got home after the week's vigil." He closed his eyes, thinking of the attending unenviable task of informing them their beloved son was dead. "Did anyone reach Dr. Withers?"

"He's away until tomorrow, Dr. Bernard," a nurse reported. "The patient's family were informed that complications had developed and they're on their way back here. Since you pronounced him dead, I guess you'll have to speak to them . . ."

David sighed with resignation and followed her to the desk to sign the death certificate. How could Withers have gone out of town, when he had a patient on the critical list? Why had the nurse waited? And why in hell had the inexperienced intern tried to handle it alone?

He wondered whether the boy would have pulled through

if they had called him at the first sign of trouble. Probably not—but you never knew. He couldn't really place the blame on the intern. The system was at fault, the practice of requiring interns and residents to work endless, grueling hours without rest for days on end. Just last week, he had said to Dr. Sayles, "How can a man go without sleep for thirty-six hours and be expected to function properly or use good judgment?" Tom was always ribbing him about questioning the order of things. But he couldn't help it, that was just the way he was.

He returned to his room, knowing he would be unable to go back to sleep even though he was exhausted. This had been a hell of a week, with one emergency after another. It was just as well that Lauren had made other plans for the weekend, because he would never have been able to keep a date with her. Was it really her brother she was seeing? Of course it was. He was too inured to the wiles employed by girls like Susie Winkler. Unless he was way off the mark, Lauren Jacobson was that rarity, a woman completely lacking in guile.

As soon as she spied her brother, Lauren waved and ran toward him. She had been waiting all morning for Philip to arrive. With a big smile, he engulfed her in a bear hug, lifting her off the ground.

"Sorry to be late, I got tied up." He held her away from him. "Let me look at you—just as pretty as ever."

"It's great to see you, Phil." She couldn't contain her impatience. "Did you bring it?"

Grinning, Philip held up a letter. "Uh-uh, I should make you pay for this," he laughed, pulling it out of her reach.

"Philip, let me have it!" She snatched the envelope from him. "I can't believe Mama really signed it. I should call to thank her."

"Maybe you better not, Laurie. Pa doesn't know and she might have a change of heart."

"What did you say to convince her?"

"I told her you'd end up being an old maid!" He ducked, laughing at the expression on Lauren's face. "Actually, it was Ruth's calling about your date in Chapel Hill that clinched it. You know how Mama hates gossip."

"Listen to this," said Lauren. In a voice heavy with pomposity, she began to read the printed form: "I, Miriam Jacobson, hereby grant permission for my daughter, Lauren, to take unlimited overnight absences from the campus of Women's College during the 1937–38 academic year . . .

"Get this, Phil. She must have loved this part:

"At all times my daughter will remain subject to the rules and regulations of Women's College and if on any occasion she is guilty of an infraction of those rules," Lauren paused dramatically, "this permission will be revoked and she will be subject to appropriate disciplinary action, including dismissal.

"Well, that surely must have impressed her." She folded the letter and replaced it in its envelope. "Thanks, Phil, you're a dear."

"Sounds like this place is a convent," said Philip.

"Come on in and see if you think it looks like one." On their way through the lobby, Lauren slipped the envelope into the slot of a locked wooden box outside a door marked Head of House. "Shall we go out for lunch, or would you rather eat here in the dining room?"

"I suppose I ought to have at least one college meal," he answered. "I'll take you to a restaurant tonight."

"Ruth will have a fit if we don't have dinner with them."

He shook his head. "I absolutely refuse to go over there. I get enough family in Randolph."

"All right, but I'll have to call her and make some excuse," Lauren said, making a face.

Saturday lunch was always informal at the college. In the dining room, after introducing Philip to her house mother, they found seats at an empty table.

"Now tell me about this guy, Dr. Bernard," he said, folding his arms.

She smiled. "There's really nothing to tell. David's training to be a surgeon. He's nice, Phil, we had a good time together."

"You really like him, don't you? I can tell."

Lauren pushed the creamed chipped beef around on her plate. In a way, it would be good to confide in Philip. As a man, he could probably give her some helpful advice. But she was afraid to make too much of it, as if talking about David would put a jinx on any future dates.

"Yes, I like him. But I don't even know for sure whether he'll call me again. I haven't heard from him since last weekend, although he did ask me to go to the game today."

"And I got in the way," said Phil, putting down his fork. "You could have told me to come another time, I wouldn't have minded."

"But I wanted to see you. You're the one I really miss, Phil. I wish you were closer so we could get together more often."

"So do I. The house is lonely without you." With a grimace, he pushed his plate away. "God, how can you eat this crap?"

"Now you know why I've lost weight," she laughed. "What's new at home? How's Papa feeling?"

"He seems fine. The doctor now says he's not even sure he had a heart attack that time. It could have been angina."

"But that's wonderful!" she cried, at the same time feeling dismay. If they'd known Samuel hadn't had a heart attack, maybe all those terrible things wouldn't have happened to Philip. It had all been connected—her brother's guilt, the furtive trip to Georgia, and the final brush with death. Phil looked so much better to her; she hoped he was putting it behind him. "And what about you? How's the store?"

"Not bad." His enthusiasm surprised her. "We're thinking of investing in a new business, manufacturing uniforms. Father turned the project over to me."

"You mean you're *leaving the store?*" she asked, shocked.

"Not right away, certainly. I wouldn't want to burn my bridges until I know it will succeed. Right now, we're talking about an investment, a share in the company, in return for the use of some property we own."

"What property?"

"Believe it or not, that worthless parcel on the far side of the river, down by the hollow. Those abandoned warehouses from the tobacco days are perfect for setting up a factory; there's a built-in labor supply right there, with all the people out of work." Philip leaned forward, "I tell you, Laurie, it could be a very good thing, not only for us, but for the town. Well, it's nothing definite, so don't say anything to Ruth or Jay."

"Are you kidding? That would be like publishing it in the *Randolph Mountaineer!* But I notice you're talking in a very proprietary fashion, brother."

Having been away from Philip for two months, Lauren saw him with new objectivity, reminded of what an attractive man he was. Every girl who passed their table had looked at him with interest, no doubt assuming he was her date. Perhaps she should have asked one of her friends to go out with them for the evening. *Now why hadn't she thought of that before?* There was Jeanette Greenthal, who was also a senior, and quite pretty. Maybe it wasn't too late. Lauren decided to check with Jeanette before mentioning it to Philip.

"Any romances lately?" she asked.

He shook his head. "Not really. I think Nancy Miller's about given up on me. Marriage is what Nancy has in mind. I sometimes think I'll never find someone to marry, Laurie."

"That's up to you, Phil. It's so easy for a man—all you have to do is go after a girl you like. A woman has to wait for someone who wants her." She wondered whether she didn't sound bitter.

"That's not the way Charlee's sister-in-law did it—" He clapped his hand to his forehead. "I forgot to tell you—Blanche Fields is engaged, and you'll never guess to whom . . . Jules Taylor. And from what I heard, she did not sit around waiting for him to pursue her."

"Jules Taylor! Blanche is going to marry *Jules?* Where did you hear that?"

"From Reba, the other evening. Charlee had called just before I stopped by after playing golf with Max."

Lauren was more than surprised. "I didn't even know they *knew* each other. How did they meet?"

"Charlee introduced them—I suspect with the connivance of our old pals, Norma and George Stearns. You didn't know?"

She shook her head, puzzled. "No . . . no I didn't. Charlee hasn't written in ages, and I've been so busy with classes. You mean they're friends with Norma and George?" Lauren had neither seen nor heard of the Stearnses for almost three years—since that ill-fated Christmas party at their rented mansion in Asheville.

"Evidently so. Reba says they're all part of the same New York crowd." Philip rose and helped her with her chair.

Lauren shook her head. "Too small, this world. Imagine Charlee having Jules Taylor for a brother-in-law." No doubt Uncle Max believed Jules had found his fortune at last. She wondered again why her cousin had never mentioned that she and Bruce saw the Stearnses in New York.

"Let's go for a walk," suggested Philip.

"I'll get a jacket," she replied, thinking she would catch Jeanette Greenthal on the way to her room.

It was good to get outdoors and relax. The bright sunny weather and spectacular foliage put Lauren in an optimistic frame of mind. She realized she had been tense with worry about her upcoming midterm examinations. And about not hearing from David Bernard.

At dinner that evening, Lauren observed her brother and Jeanette with a feeling of satisfaction. Phil had been more than mildly annoyed when she told him her friend would be joining them, and she had been afraid he might be in one of his silent moods. But from the moment Jeanette walked into the front parlor that evening, looking awfully smart in a russet wool dress that complemented her rich auburn hair and warm coloring, Philip had been his most agreeable self.

After dinner, they headed for The Scat, where the band

was exceptional. The place was packed with the college crowd, but Phil managed to get them a tiny table off to the side, close to the dance floor. The tumult of flying hands and feet was matched only by the frenzy of the music and the enthusiasm of the patrons keeping time on table tops.

"Why don't you two dance?" said Lauren, seeing how both Philip and Jeanette were unable to keep their feet from tapping out the beat as the musicians swung into a spirited rendition of "When the Saints Go Marching In."

"Are you sure you don't mind?" said Phil, while Jeanette looked hopeful.

"No, honestly, go ahead—I mean really! I love just listening. I'll order the drinks."

One thing could be said for crowded dance floors: There was no alternative to being locked close together, especially when the music quieted to the slow, mournful blues the group was playing after the energetic Dixieland. With a glad heart and a pang of yearning, Lauren watched her brother dancing with her friend. Every once in a while Philip would gaze down at Jeanette and then place his cheek against the side of her forehead with a contented smile.

Just a week ago, she had been held that way in David's arms. Longing to be with him, she wondered where he was tonight.

David sat in his room brooding, unable to rid himself of the image of the dead student's face.

There had been a resemblance to another face, one he had viewed years ago through a haze of tears, the first time he had looked upon death, as a boy of eleven. It had been his father's still form that time, lying on a neighbor's couch, dead of smoke inhalation after trying in vain to save his pregnant wife and young daughter from their burning house. David had been at school when the fire broke out.

"You're to live with your Uncle Sydney in North Carolina," the lawyer had explained in his Scottish burr, trying to avoid the pureness of the troubled dark blue eyes.

What kind of people, he wondered, could reject this handsome lad, their own grandson?

The tender mouth had trembled as the boy fought hard not to weep. "But how will I find my uncle? I don't remember him."

"It's all arranged, laddie. He's cummin' to Philadelphia to fetch you."

Vividly David recalled his shock during that melancholy train trip from Philadelphia, when he had first seen White and Colored signs above waiting room doors. "I heard about that in school," he told the kindly stranger who was his uncle. "I just didn't believe it was true."

How life had changed. His father's medical practice was just getting established when he died, and David's inheritance had gone up in flames with the house. Uncle Sydney and Aunt Ethel gave him a full measure of affection, but it was an adjustment for them, too. They were childless and his uncle lacked an understanding of young people. David helped out in the drug store after school, on Saturdays, and during vacations. It was a sober upbringing for a boy in an alien land.

For the first year his chief amusement had been the piano lessons Aunt Ethel gave him on the Chickering upright in their small parlor. "You have a gift for music, David," she told him, "but I can see you lack the discipline to become a classical pianist." She had encouraged him to play for enjoyment, teaching syncopation and improvisation, and introducing him to ragtime, blues, and stride piano.

As a school teacher in Fayetteville before her marriage, Ethel had often been criticized for her racial views. Once she had been brought before a disciplinary committee when she was discovered reading to her class from the memoirs of Frederick Douglass, the emancipated slave. "Ideas can never hurt young minds," was the defense she had used on that occasion, and the philosophy with which she had endowed her nephew. David came to adore his aunt and her prim, mannerly ways. All he learned of music, his passion for ethics and fair play, his liberalism, and his love for the South, he felt he owed to her.

At school they made fun of his Yankee accent, but he was large for his age, so no one dared pick a fight. In the spring, David joined the junior high baseball team and became an instant hero when he hit a home run his first time up at bat. "Hey, Davey, what's doin'?" Dokey Poole hailed him in the hall the following Monday before classes. Dokey, the acknowledged leader in the junior high school, was president of the Rebels, a mysterious fraternal order.

David was sworn into the Rebels in a secret ceremony held in the shed behind Dokey Poole's house on Myrtle Street. The Confederate flag nailed on the wall was a little disconcerting, but club activities consisted mostly of playing cards, holding spitting contests with chewing tobacco, collecting dirty pictures, and sitting around talking about girls.

Sometimes they would chase the trolley, hopping on back to hitch a ride to Wrightsville Beach. On the first afternoon they went swimming bare, David noticed how the other boys kept sneaking glances at him. It wasn't something you could talk about to a woman, and he found it hard to approach Uncle Sydney.

"There's something bothering the boy," Sydney told his wife. "I can't seem to get to him, but you know how to speak to youngsters."

From her years of teaching, Ethel had a knack of sensing a boy's confusion. David was not born of a Jewish mother, but Ethel had never been one to follow protocols. "Soon you'll turn thirteen, David, and you should be Bar Mitzvah," she suddenly announced one morning.

He had almost forgotten about Bar Mitzvahs. His aunt and uncle had taken him to the Kol Nidre service in Wilmington the previous fall, but he had not set foot in a synagogue since. Now he began classes in preparation for his Bar Mitzvah. At school he had known only one Jewish boy, Leonard Weinberg, a quiet, scholarly fellow who did not hang around with the Rebels. He met other boys at Hebrew School, but none of them was as much fun as Dokey and the gang.

Late in the springtime, when the Southland is ablaze with crab apples and dogwoods in bloom and the sweet nectar of jessamine and honeysuckle hangs overpowering, the Rebels went on a camping expedition on the Cape Fear River, but David was not included. It got back to him, of course, and Dokey kind of kicked his toes in the dust and mumbled, "Y'all weren't around, Davey, and it being last minute and all . . ." but David knew it was something else. They had discovered he was unlike them, and even if he could slug it out on the baseball diamond with the best, he no longer belonged.

At his Bar Mitzvah, David shared the pulpit with two other boys. There was a *kiddush* in the social room and afterward they were invited to a reception at Leonard Weinberg's house. More than ever that night, among the large clan of Weinberg relatives, he had felt his aloneness.

When his parents were alive, they had talked often about the future, when he would become a doctor, like his father, but it had been his misfortune to begin college just as the country slid into the worst depression in its history. That winter, Aunt Ethel died suddenly of pneumonia and only then did David discover she had regularly put away money for medical school. But in his junior year at the University of North Carolina, the bank failed, obliterating the education fund and his hopes for Johns Hopkins. His only alternative had been to apply for a scholarship at Chapel Hill, where he completed the first half of his medical studies . . .

David came awake with a start. He had dozed off in his chair and if he didn't hurry, he would miss being there when the dead boy's family arrived. How he dreaded having to talk to them. One of the hardest parts of medicine for him was conquering his cowardice in dealing with bereaved families.

As he showered, alternating the hot and cold spigots to get rid of the logey, hung over feeling, he reflected that last week at this time, he had been preparing to take Lauren to Sunday brunch. When would he see her again? Not next Saturday, since weeks ago he had accepted Susie Winkler's invitation to go to a wedding in Greensboro. Lauren was lovely, he mused . . . special. She was different from the other women he knew. He would have to be careful with her, though, take it slow, for she was vulnerable. He sensed it could move very quickly, and he wasn't ready to get serious. Maybe he had been a little hasty last weekend, getting carried away so easily.

David wrapped himself in a towel and lathered his face. When Lauren said she was busy this Saturday, he had considered asking Susie to the game, but he'd put off calling her until it was too late. Miss Winkler did not go for last minute dates.

What was he going to do about Susie? It was complicated . . . Susan Winkler was a Magnolia Blossom. A carefully cultivated daughter of the South—genteel, feminine, nurtured by her mother to demand the best of everything, and the most of a man. There were certain rules you had to follow, if you dated a Magnolia Blossom. Calling on Thursday for Saturday was not one of them—nor was breaking a date, even for good reason, like being held up in emergency surgery. You had to watch it with Magnolia Blossoms. Susan had not liked it one bit when he danced so long with Lauren that first Sunday afternoon in Greensboro.

How had he ever let himself get so involved with her? It had just happened, somehow. Susie was pretty . . . very pretty. And sexy. She was a tease. She used it to get what she wanted, and David had the most uncomfortable feeling that *he* was what Susie wanted.

A lot of guys he knew would say there were worse fates than ending up married to Susan Winkler. How would he extricate himself, he wondered. And did he really want to?

Patting his face with after-shave, David brushed his hair, went to his room and dressed quickly in whites. Taking his watch, he saw that he had just enough time to grab some juice and coffee. Then he would have to meet the parents of the accident victim.

Chapter 15

LAUREN SPRINTED UP the steps and yanked open the front door, narrowly avoiding a collision with another student. "Sorry," she flung over her shoulder. "Are there any messages for me, Nellie?"

"Yes, Miss Jacobson, I put them in your box," the maid answered with a knowing smile. She was accustomed to the breathless inquiries of the girls at Women's College. They all had social anxieties, even the pretty ones. Particularly the pretty ones.

Lauren eagerly sorted through the papers and envelopes in her mailbox, but there was nothing from David. Two-and-a-half weeks since their first date, and still he hadn't called. Each day she would rush home to the dorm after classes, passing the front desk to see if there had been any calls for her, making sure the maids knew she had come in, then studying in her room with the door ajar. The telephones seemed always to be in use. Maybe he had tried to reach her and couldn't get through. She couldn't expect that he would go on trying all evening if he kept getting a busy signal, could she? After all, he was a resident and his time wasn't his own. Having just recently transferred from Duke Hospital to Strickland, he must be exceptionally busy . . .

After dinner, she sat at her desk to study, but her thoughts kept wandering to David. She closed her eyes, trying to picture him in a hospital setting. Mission was the only hospital she had ever entered—when her father and Philip had been patients there. Did David have his own apartment with a telephone, or did he share a room with other residents? Would he wear a white suit, or did he go around in street clothes like the doctors who came to see their patients at Mission? Surgeons wore special socks when performing operations. How would he look in his surgeon's gown, with a cap and mask?

She glanced down at her notebook where she had been doodling. *David Bernard, Dr. David Bernard, David Bernard, M.D. Mrs. David Bernard . . . Lauren J. Bernard . . . LJB.* She ripped the page out of the notebook, crumpling it into a ball and throwing it across the room. This was the most idiotic, frivolous waste of time! How could she permit herself to indulge in these daydreams about a man she scarcely knew? Her first midterm exams in Latin and Medieval History were coming up in four days, and there was so much material to cover.

It was impossible to concentrate here in the dorm when she had one ear tuned to the sound of the elevator opening, the slow approaching footsteps of the maid, the pause at someone else's door—There was a knock. "Miss Jacobson? Phone call on line two."

Oh, good Lord! Please make it be him, *please, please!* "All right, Nellie. Thank you." She ran down the hall to the booth, her pulses racing. "Hello? *Hello!*"

There was static on the line and then she heard a woman's voice. "Laurie, is that you, dear? I can hardly hear you. It's Cousin Ruth."

Oh, no—sweet, motherly Ruth was a chatterbox, and a total bore. Half the time Lauren never paid attention to her prattling. How had Jay and their children put up with it all these years? She sat numbly as Ruth droned on about a wedding she and Jay had attended on Saturday night, members of the club whose daughter had married a boy from Atlanta. What did she care about the stupid wedding of a girl she had never met. She ground her teeth and raised her eyes heavenward. Would Ruth *never* stop talking?

". . . and I was so *surprised!* He was there with the Winkler girl. She looked simply *gorgeous* in this heavenly shade of pink ninon. That gown must have cost a *fortune*—it had sort of a Graecian effect, draped and gathered on one shoulder. Marjorie Winkler has always spent money on clothes, and especially for Susan. They're anxious for her to make a good match. She will, of course—those glamorous girls always do. I must say, he *did* look mighty handsome in his formal clothes. Has he called again?"

What was Ruth saying? "—um—has who called, Cousin Ruth?"

"Why, that young doctor, David Bernard, of course. Who did you think I was talking about? I *told* you, Laurie, we met him with Susan Winkler at the Siebert wedding . . ."

Her throat tightened until it pained. "I'm sorry, Cousin Ruth, I couldn't hear you, this is a terrible connection. I'm afraid I can't talk any longer now, I'm studying for a big exam. I'll call you the week after next, as soon as my midterms are over."

Back in her room, Lauren picked up her history text and resumed the chapter on the Carolingian Empire. Halfway through the second section, she stopped, realizing she had not absorbed a single fact in the passage she had been reading about the Frankish kings. With leaden resignation, she sat staring out her window at the lighted campus. A huge harvest moon hung low on the horizon, pulling at her senses with its romantic aura. She tried being angry—at David for not calling, at herself for letting it mean so much. But all she could do was indulge in self-pity until the tears spilled over and rolled down her cheeks.

Ruth's words seemed to echo in the room, mocking her. "I think that must be a *serious* romance. Everyone was remarking on what a lovely couple they made. She certainly was looking at him with adoring eyes." It appeared that Shirley Winkler had known what she was talking about, after all. David was in love with Susie, and soon they would become engaged.

It hurt so much, she despised herself for the constricted oppression in her chest. How patently ridiculous it was for her to have fallen in love with someone she hadn't known five weeks ago, and who obviously didn't give a damn that she existed. She should have learned by now, after her experience with Jules Taylor, that a man can lose himself while kissing a woman without its meaning anything.

"I wish I had never met David Bernard!" Slamming her books shut, she put on her robe and went to take a shower.

Standing under the hot stream, she concentrated on clearing her mind of its torpor. Never before had any boy so disturbed her, intruding on every waking hour of her thoughts, and interfering with her studies. When Jules had dropped her to run after Charlee, she had been disillusioned and offended, but she had quickly thrown it off, considering the exercise a good lesson in the ways of scoundrels. But David wasn't a scoundrel! Instinctively she knew he was sincere and he had seemed more than passingly attracted to her. In fact, he had practically verbalized it that last evening. But if that was so, why hadn't he called her?

It was always the boys she didn't want who pursued her. Ben constantly telephoned and somehow *he* always managed to get through to her. He wrote letters, and was forever sending flowers and gifts. In September he had driven her to Greensboro, loading up his car with her suitcases, typewriter, boxes of books, and bedding, tying her rolled up carpet on top. Poor Ben had to lug everything up two flights of stairs because the elevator was out of order that day. Not once had his good humor failed, even when the bottom of a carton had opened, spilling its contents down the stairway. In fact, he acted grateful for the opportunity to exert himself on her behalf; and the more eager and affectionate he became, the more he irritated her.

Ben dreaded the men she might meet while she was away from Randolph Springs. He had declared himself the night he left her at Women's College, putting a sort of security on her, a down payment on the future. "I just want you to know how much I love you, Laurie," he had said, his eyes wet with emotion. "Maybe it's not the right time to tell you, but if I didn't say it now, and—and something should happen," (he made it sound like a death in the family) "I would always wonder whether it would have made a difference."

"Ben, I—I don't—" she had stammered.

"Shhh," he put a finger to her lips. "Don't say it.

Please, don't say anything. Just remember, I love you and I'll be there waiting for you." He had kissed her passionately, desperately, moaning low in his throat with his frustration. And she had felt nothing other than a sweet tenderness for him, more pity than anything else.

What was so different about Ben and David? Ben was wise and intelligent, and he had a fine character. Like David, he had graduated from Chapel Hill. He was tall and nice looking, in an unexciting way. And he was totally devoted to her. But where the idea of spending the rest of her life with Benson Miller caused her to feel smothered and claustrophobic, thrills of excitement ran through her at the mere thought of David Bernard.

When she came out of the bathroom, her flighty next door neighbor was in the corridor. "Oh, Laurie, you had a phone call," she said in her high, shrill voice. "I didn't know where you were."

How many times have I gone looking for you when you had a call, she wanted to scream. She tore down the stairs in her robe, since it was after hours and no visitors would be in the building. There was no message notice in her box. "One of the girls said there was a call for me," she told the maid, who was about to leave the desk for the night.

"Yes, Miss Jacobson. A gentleman called about ten minutes ago, but he didn't leave his name."

"Did he say anything about calling again?"

"No, miss. He just asked for you, but when Nellie went up, you weren't in your room."

"I was taking a shower. Doesn't Nellie check the bathrooms?"

"Usually she does. Perhaps you didn't hear her."

It could have been anyone—Philip, Ben, her father, Cousin Jay, or that creep she had met at the dance who kept calling her. Surely it wasn't David, for he would have left his name, unless . . . When she thought about it, why would he leave his name? He wouldn't expect her to call him. Oh, this was impossible! She had never been on such a course of ups and downs. If this was what it meant to be in love, she could just as well do without it.

For the rest of that week Lauren studied at the library, where she would be undistracted by hysterical hen sessions in the dorm, the shrieks of girls who received letters from their boyfriends or went racing down the hall to answer the telephone. She was sorry to miss afternoon tea, which was always a pleasant way to take a break, but discovered that she accomplished twice as much in the library. By the following Thursday afternoon, she had finished her last exam and had only one more paper to write.

It was already growing dark when she walked across the quad. There was a nip in the air and the trees were losing their leaves of scarlet and gold. Swept by a wave of homesickness, she was glad that soon it would be time to return to Randolph Springs for Thanksgiving. How wonderful it would be to go home again, to see her parents and the rest of the family. This was the longest she had ever been away from them.

The lights from the dormitory looked inviting and the pungence of a wood fire in the living room welcomed her as she entered the door. Someone was playing the piano and a group of girls were harmonizing. Lauren glanced through the mail she collected from her box. Among the college memos and notices were three letters, one from Ben, another from her mother, and a big, fat envelope from Charlee. It had the heft of the long narratives Charlee used to write from the Alexander School. There was just time to read it before dinner. Running up to her room, she threw her books and coat on the bed.

As she settled on the window seat with her letters, a slip of paper fluttered to the floor. She was going to ignore it, but saw that it was a telephone message. Bending to pick it up, she read with elation, "Dr. Bernard called. He will try to reach you this evening. If not, would you please call him." A telephone number and extension were written at the bottom in the maid's painstaking hand.

David had called! He had actually called, and she would be speaking to him later on. Filled with joy, she turned to Charlee's letter.

Her brow furrowed as her eyes scanned the first paragraphs in Charlotte's flamboyant curling penmanship. Was it her imagination, or did Charlee sound restless, less than content? "I seem always to be pulled in different directions," her cousin had written. "Between Bruce's family, Bruce's law groups, our social obligations, the tiresome women's organizations I am expected to join, the luncheons, gallery openings, museum committees, and a different dinner party or theater benefit every night of the week, there's so little time for the people I really care about."

Lauren was relieved as she read further, realizing how impulsive she had been to doubt Charlee's happiness. "You mustn't think I don't love my life. Most of the time, I'm on cloud nine, but there are days when I long to just *breathe,* and I think if only my Laurie were here so we could have one of our sessions!"

We all have those days, Charlee, she thought. Letters were so unsatisfactory, when what you really wanted was to have a long chat with someone you loved.

> . . . Have you heard that Blanche is going to marry your old friend, Jules Taylor? It's a long story, which will have to wait until we're together, but the wedding will be at the Plaza in the spring. She's so madly in love with him that any doubts I have about Jules being good husband material must be kept to myself. Bruce and I are giving a party in their honor on Christmas, which is a Saturday. Mark it on your calendar because you will receive an invitation. We want you to come up for a visit over the holidays. You've never seen New York, which I find hard to believe. I long to show you all my favorite places . . .

It would be such fun to visit Charlee and Bruce in New York. She would love to see that enthralling city. A picture of what it must be like formed in her mind. Tall, glistening skyscrapers, broad avenues lined with smart shops, alive with excitement; elegant women in long gowns and fur wraps, and handsome men handing them into swank automobiles. Lauren did not relish the idea of meeting Jules again, or the Stearnses either, for that matter. She had suspected Norma of playing a role that time when Jules dropped her to make a play for Charlee—but it did seem childishly petty to bear a grudge for so long. Well, she would see how she felt about the trip in December.

The warning bell rang for dinner. Lauren doubted she could eat much, she was so keyed up, but she quickly washed and combed before going down to the dining room. They were about to sing grace by the time she entered. Her friends had all taken their places. "You're certainly in high spirits tonight," Jeanette said, her eyes dancing.

"I'm just relaxed because my exams are over," Lauren replied. She knew that Philip had been corresponding with her friend, but thus far she had refrained from discussing David with Jeanette.

Skipping after-dinner coffee in the living room, Lauren returned to her room. What time would David call, she wondered. If he didn't reach her by ten o'clock when the switchboard closed, she would go to the pay telephone to call him. Rolling a fresh sheet of bond into her typewriter, she began typing her term paper, determined to finish it that night. At the end of each page, she glanced at her watch, conscious of the passing time.

At nine-thirty he called. "Do you know how hard it is to reach you? I've been trying all week, but the lines are always busy."

"With ninety girls and three telephones, you're lucky you got through at all," she replied gaily. The sound of his voice filled her with unspeakable bliss.

"I've missed you, Laurie," he said, with that warm mellowness she remembered.

"Have you?" She closed her eyes, knowing she sounded breathy and sophomoric. "I've been studying. We had midterms this week."

"Are they over?"

"Yes, I'm writing my last paper tonight."

"Then, how about celebrating with me this Saturday? I could come there, if you prefer, but there's not much to do in Greensboro. If you meet me in Chapel Hill, you can stay with Gretchen and Ralph."

"I'd love to come to Chapel Hill," she said quickly,

not at all interested in having David show up in Greensboro.

"That's swell." He sounded happy. "Gretchen will be excited, she really took a fancy to you."

"I liked her, too. And Ralph," said Lauren. "Is there a football game this weekend?"

"No, the game's away. I'll try to provide some other entertainment."

If only David knew, being with him was all the entertainment she could ask for. Thank goodness she had her blanket permission. There would be no need to inform Ruth she was going to Chapel Hill again.

They lingered at their table until they were the only remaining customers in the restaurant. "I think they want us to leave," David finally said. "It's kind of hard, not having a place to go, I mean an apartment of my own, or—well, I guess you wouldn't go to a man's apartment anyway, would you?"

Lauren giggled. "I never have, but then, no one's ever asked."

She loved the slow way he smiled. "I tell you, ma'am, given the opportunity . . . I would ask."

In the Nelsons' darkened front room they at least had privacy. Lauren knew that nothing short of the house catching fire would cause Gretchen or Ralph to come down those stairs. They were so obviously eager for Lauren and David to become a couple.

"I think David's really crazy about you," Gretchen said that afternoon when she had shown Lauren to the guest room. "I hope you get married so we can be friends. Well, we can be friends anyway, especially if you come to Chapel Hill next year, but you know what I mean. It's nice when married couples all like each other." She noticed the color in Lauren's cheeks. "Am I embarrassing you? Ralph says I'm always poking my nose in places it doesn't belong. But you two just seem so right together."

Lauren couldn't think of what to reply. "We haven't known each other very long, just six weeks."

"Ralph and I got married two months after we met."

"You did?" She couldn't imagine such rashness.

"You can close your mouth, Laurie!" Gretchen was rolling on the bed with laughter. "Honestly, we did. I slept with him on our second date. I know that probably sounds awful to you . . . I can see you're in shock, poor thing! There are some things you just *know,* and I knew five minutes after I said hello to Ralph Nelson that I wanted him."

"I can't get over that you would marry someone you had only known for two months, Gretchen. Even Ralph, who I think is wonderful."

"Don't you know that forty or fifty years ago, almost everyone married someone they hardly knew? Ralph's grandparents had never even seen each other before their wedding. The fathers arranged it."

"Yes, but didn't your families object?"

"Mine still does. They disowned me." She tilted her chin up defiantly. "They're sitting up there in Sudbury, richer than Croesus, but I'll never get a cent from them."

"That seems a little extreme," said Lauren. "I mean, you've been married for a while—"

"Three years in April."

"Now that you're expecting a baby, don't you think they'll change their minds?"

Gretchen shook her head. "Never."

"What makes you so sure?"

"Because Ralph's Jewish and they're the most ardent anti-Semites you've ever met. I mean, with them, it's a religion!"

"Oh, Gretchen . . ."

"Don't look so sad. If you want to know the truth, we're not missing much. I don't recall ever being kissed by either one of my parents, and I sure as hell never saw them kiss each other. I think I must have been an immaculate conception."

"What about Ralph's family?"

Gretchen smiled. "Herman and Minnie? In the beginning, they went through the tearful what-have-we-done-to-deserve-this routine, but when all was said and done, they love their son, and I think they've grown quite fond of me.

Especially now that I'm carrying the heir.'' She rubbed her pregnant belly. ''Ralph says they'll be excellent at the grandparent thing. Fortunately, they live in Detroit, so they can do it at a distance.''

Lauren had been horrified at Gretchen's parents. She couldn't imagine her mother and father disowning her for any reason, even marrying the wrong person. ''Gretchen told me about her family disapproving of their marriage,'' she said to David when they were alone in the living room, sitting on the couch. ''I didn't realize that Ralph was Jewish.''

''Yes, it's a pity about her parents. Ralph's a great guy.''

''It doesn't seem to bother them.''

''I'm not so sure. What a waste when families deny their love.'' He kissed her lips softly. ''There's not nearly enough love in the world to go around,'' he said, holding her and stroking her hair.

Lauren couldn't remember ever being so happy. ''Are you staying in Chapel Hill tonight?'' she asked.

''No, I'll go back to the hospital. It only takes about fifteen or twenty minutes. Next time I'll take you there.''

Next time. ''I'd like to see it,'' she answered.

He kissed her again, cupping her breast with his hand. As she stiffened, Lauren sensed David's hesitation, and for a moment she was transported back in time. She was lying in her room on Lenoir Avenue, the room she had shared with her sister. Listening to the litany she had heard over and over all during her childhood. The catechism of ladylike behavior that Miriam Jacobson had repeated every night to Joanna, never suspecting that her youngest child was wide awake in the next bed.

Lauren could not have been more than seven or eight when Miriam delivered those bedtime lectures to her doltish adolescent daughter. By the time it was her turn for indoctrination, she had committed the sermon to memory: ''Never let a boy become intimate with you, Joanna. Never let him touch your body or become too familiar . . . he'll lose his respect for you. Remember, men want the women they marry to be ladies.'' Joanna, of all young women, had never been in need of such advice, but Miriam had a horror of one of her daughters developing a *bad reputation.*

Lauren pushed the memory of her mother's words to the back of her mind. That was another life, another time. This was David and, with luck, he would be her future. She had never been kissed like this, this deep penetrating soul-embracing . . . going on and on . . . tender enveloping wrenching, from which they both emerged trembling.

He stared into her eyes. "What if I hadn't gone to Greensboro that Sunday? Do you know how close I came to staying in Durham?"

Her breath was tremulous. "I wanted to study. My cousin practically had to drag me there."

"Maybe it was destiny," he said, with a hint of laughter. She prayed he wasn't joking.

Chapter 16

New York, December 1937

THE PORTER DEPOSITED Lauren's suitcases alongside the sleeping car in Pennsylvania Station.

How would she ever find Charlotte in this throng? She had never seen such a mass of humanity pressed into one contained area. Unsmiling, gray, and purposeful, they moved in streams in the dark cavern, heading for the exits or boarding the train on the next track.

For the first time in her life, Lauren had passed over that invisible divide between the South and the North. As the train sped northward, gradually the slow graciousness of life had slipped away and the tempo quickened. She felt it in the changes of speech patterns and clothing, in the closed inwardness of the faces. Through the train window, the people became harder and the land corrupted. Poverty may have been worse in the South, but it wasn't as ugly. Long stretches of track were lined with shanty-towns, and at station stops along the way she had seen men who should have been working in offices, selling pencils or shining shoes.

A Negro man jostled her without apology and crossed over to enter a coach on the opposite track. With a start, she realized that white and black people were sitting together inside the lighted car. But, of course . . . she was *up North!*

Suddenly she caught a glimpse of Charlotte further down the platform. "Charlee! Charlee, over here," she cried, waving and jumping a little. Tall and elegant, Charlotte kept turning her head in every direction, straining to find her among the detraining passengers.

Lauren was afraid to leave her bags for fear someone in this enormous crowd would walk off with them. The porter called for a red cap who began loading luggage onto a handcart. "That's all right, miss," he said, "go and find your party. I'll follow along." The way he was piling suitcases on the dolly, her baggage was getting all mixed up with others'. She wondered whether she would ever see her belongings again.

"Laurie! Oh, darling, how wonderful to see you," cried Charlotte, throwing her arms around Lauren. There was the delicious scent of gardenias as she was smothered by Charlee's fluffy sables, worn around the shoulders of her seal-lined, plum-colored melton military greatcoat.

"Fletcher will collect your bags and see that they get to the car," Charlotte indicated a liveried chauffeur, who touched his hat and followed the red cap down the platform. "How was the trip? I always love the train coming up, you meet such interesting people in the dining car . . . somehow men are more handsome when they travel, aren't they? It was the same on board ship. What a *high time* I could've had on the *Normandie,* if I hadn't been on my honeymoon."

"Charlee!"

"Oh, darling, I do so love to get a rise out of you," Charlotte laughed merrily, relishing Lauren's reaction. "You're positively *radiant,* Laurie, the most beautiful you've ever been. Are you sure you're not in love? Stand still for a minute and let me look at you. What a *divine* shade of lavender-blue," she exclaimed, inspecting Lauren's new beaver-trimmed winter coat and hat, her parents' Chanukah gift, which she and her mother had selected at Worth's in Asheville.

Glancing at her diamond-encrusted wrist watch, Charlotte linked arms with Lauren and began walking rapidly toward the exit. "Heavens, we've got to *dash!* Bruce will be waiting for us. We're dining with friends tonight. I hope you're not too tired . . . did you get any sleep on the train? I always love sleeping in a berth, I feel positively *hypnotized* by the rocking motion and the sound of the wheels on the tracks . . ."

Grinning, Lauren let Charlotte ramble on, knowing it wasn't necessary for her to comment. Eventually her cousin would wind down, and they would have something resembling a normal conversation, but right now, she was intoxicated with the excitement of their reunion. A wave of love for Charlee swept over her. They truly were closer than sisters, just as they had been for all of their lives.

Somehow they made it to the automobile, an immense steel gray Chrysler Imperial town car, which Fletcher had pulled up to the station entrance. The red cap was unloading Lauren's suitcases, setting them inside the trunk. She was relieved to see that all three pieces were accounted for.

"Drive up Fifth, Fletcher, so Miss Jacobson can see the shops," Charlotte ordered, fitting a cigarette into a holder and lighting it as soon as they were settled in the sedan. They turned north on the famous avenue, passing all the well-known stores that had been just names to Lauren until this moment: Lord & Taylor, Arnold Constable, Peck & Peck, and Saks Fifth Avenue.

"It's every bit as I expected it to be," Lauren exclaimed, sitting forward in the seat to peer out at the city. "Is that the RCA Building? Oh look, Charlee, the *tree!*"

Fletcher pulled over and stopped the car opposite Rockefeller Center so that Lauren could see the huge Christmas tree ablaze with lights. She rolled down the window to catch the strains of the skating music from the ice rink, the ringing of Salvation Army bells, and the joyous hum of Christmas shoppers that was the musical heartbeat of New York, even in this ninth winter of the Great Depression.

"We'll come back tomorrow," Charlotte promised. "The only way to see New York is on foot. Look up here on the right, Laurie, that's St. Patrick's Cathedral. Bruce took me to midnight mass there the Christmas after we were married. It was magnificent, so *grand!*" A haggard-looking man in a threadbare coat with the collar turned up walked hesitantly toward the automobile. His face was red with cold and his breath made a cloud of vapor in the frigid air. Charlee dropped a bill into his outstretched hand, then quickly rolled up her window and settled back in the seat. "All right, Fletcher, thank you."

They drove north as far as 59th Street before turning east, with Charlee pointing out Best & Company, Tiffany's, Jay Thorpe, and Tailored Woman along the way. "And there's the Plaza! It's still my favorite hotel in New York. Blanche's wedding is going to be in the Grand Ballroom. It will be the last word, you can be sure. If there's anything Adele Fields knows, it's how to throw a party."

Charlotte's tone was a trifle sharp, bordering on sarcasm, but then most women were a little critical of their husbands' mothers. Sadly, if Lauren married David, she would not have a mother-in-law. At the thought of him, she suppressed a wave of loneliness.

"And here it is, *Park Avenue,*" cried Charlotte, as they turned onto the sparkling boulevard, its center island an unending string of twinkling silvery lights as far as the eye could see.

"It's so glamorous, Charlee! This is how I always imagined New York. Just this."

"It *does* seem to be the essence of the city," Charlotte agreed. "I really do love it."

They whizzed past one imposing apartment building after another. In the fading daylight of the crisp winter afternoon, uniformed doormen rushed to the curb under awnings to assist passengers from taxis and limousines. Fletcher drove into the courtyard of an immense rococo building, pulling around a circle to the entrance. A doorman hurried to open the car door and two hall porters came scurrying to take up Lauren's luggage. With surprise, she noted that all of them were white men.

"Mr. Fields came in a few minutes ago, madam," the doorman told Charlee.

"Oh good," she responded. "We'll need the car at about eight, Fletcher. Come on, Laurie, you'll want to have a drink and relax a bit before we dress."

The elevator had emerald green carpeting and was paneled in dark, rich mahogany, with a polished brass railing.

Charlee spoke in a low voice behind the back of the operator. "Blanche and Jules will be there tonight, I expect. I'm not sure about Norma and George Stearns, she's not been well. You do remember them, don't you?"

"Certainly I do." Did Charlee really think she might have forgotten the Stearnses?

At the penthouse, the elevator doors opened quietly with a luxurious swoosh, directly into a private entry leading to a white and black marble foyer, where a butler waited to take their coats.

"Thank you, Winston. This is my cousin, Miss Jacobson."

"Good evening, miss," murmured Winston, his granite visage registering no human emotion.

"How do you do, Winston," said Lauren. Winston looked like he wasn't certain whether *she* would do at all. That would never happen with the colored help in the South, she thought. They were warm and friendly, taking pride in knowing how to make a guest feel welcome.

The foyer opened onto a large circular gallery in the center of which stood a heavy round marble-top pedestal table of Empire design. The walls were hung with tapestries of English hunting scenes. To the left was a curving staircase and the entire space was dominated by an enormous crystal chandelier which hung suspended in the stairwell from the carved ceiling of the second floor.

Charlotte led the way into a magnificently furnished living room. The walls, covered in a dull green Chinese silk, contained a number of large landscapes hung above the fireplace and at intervals along the opposite wall, with those little brass museum lights attached to the frames. Lauren had an impression of row upon row of period pieces. Sheraton cabinets flanked by Georgian side chairs covered in needlepoint. Nests of Chinese Chippendale occasional tables separating conversational groupings of Hepplewhite arm chairs. Gigantic twin rounded sofas upholstered in deep midnight blue velvet faced each other across the fireplace, with its ornate Regency mantle. An array of porcelain urns and crystal vases had been transformed into silk-shaded lamps whose rosy light cast a soft glow over the expanse of ankle-deep celadon green wool carpeting. From tremendous windows at the far end of the room, there was a fabulous view of Manhattan looking west to the Hudson River.

Lauren let out her breath slowly. "So this is where you live? It's so . . ."

"Overdone, opulent, excessive—any one of those will do," said Charlotte with a wry twist of her mouth.

"I didn't say that, Charlee. It's absolutely beautiful."

Charlee shrugged in an offhand way that brought back so many memories. "I certainly can't claim it as *my* taste, since I had nothing to do with the design. Adele and Blanche were good enough to take care of all that while we were on our wedding trip." She riffled through some mail that had been stacked on a silver tray in a small hallway. "Gradually, I'll get it toned down and under control. I've already begun in the upper regions," she indicated the floor above with a lift of her head. "An apartment is meant to be *lived* in."

They were interrupted by a male voice that Lauren would have described as insinuating. "Well, if it isn't our little cousin from the Southland . . ."

Bruce strolled toward them across the lush carpet, martini in hand. He was still the most startlingly good looking man. His sky blue eyes and blond hair were brilliant in the subdued light of the room. In his perfectly tailored three-piece gray pin-striped suit, he was a little intimidating, reminding her of the socialite captains of industry she had seen pictured in prestige magazines. After kissing Charlee, he patted her on the bottom and winked, then set down his drink and turned to Lauren. "Welcome, dear girl. I thought we'd *never* get you up here to visit us." He kissed her on either cheek.

"Thank you, Bruce. Now that I'm here, I wish I had come sooner."

"We'll try to make it such fun that you'll never want to leave."

He was playing the perfect host, but Lauren had the uncomfortable feeling his words were empty. That's unfair of me, she chided herself. He's being friendly and here I am trying to find fault. Still, she sensed a false note there, unless that was the way sophisticated New Yorkers behaved.

"I see you got a head start on us," Charlee murmured as they went into the library. A smaller, cozier room lined with books, it had a baby grand piano in one corner, and an abundance of comfortable overstuffed sofas and club chairs. Bruce headed for a built-in mirrored bar that must once have been a closet.

"What can I fix for you, Lauren?" he asked in a hearty voice, adding to his glass from a cocktail shaker on the counter.

"Some sherry, please, if you have it." It had become her standby when she knew it was gauche to ask for a soft drink.

"Somewhere-oh-somewhere on these premises, we must have a bottle of sherry," he said, as he stooped to look into the recesses of the cupboard below.

"If you can't find it, I'd just as soon have ginger ale," she called.

"Over my dead body! How about rye and ginger ale? That's an easy thing going down."

"That would be fine," she said quickly.

Bruce handed her a tall glass filled with amber liquid. He had prepared a batch of Manhattans in a second shaker, serving Charlotte without asking what she wanted. I suppose that's what marriage is, Lauren thought, knowing each other's tastes. She watched Bruce light Charlee's cigarette and then his own. It was obviously a familiar routine with them. Was it Charlee's habit to drink a Manhattan cocktail every night, while her husband got pleasantly sloshed, she wondered.

"Tell us about college," said Charlotte, who had kicked off her high heels and was sitting with her slim, shapely legs slung over the arm of the chair, inhaling deeply and blowing out a stream of smoke. "Are you having fun?"

"Yes, actually," she replied. "I'm taking a new writing course next semester, which I'm greatly looking forward to. They've just agreed to accept all my transfer credits from Randolph, so I hope I can graduate in June. I'll know when I go back after the holidays."

"That's splendid," said Bruce, sounding forced. "Then what?"

"I want to go to Chapel Hill for my masters in English."

"You don't mean it!" said Charlee, as if she had told them she had a rare dread disease.

"Yes, I *do* mean it. Why should that surprise you?"

"Well, what's the point? You don't want to be a teacher, do you?"

She shrugged, feeling irritated. "Possibly. I think I would enjoy teaching high school or college students. I might even like to write." She sipped the highball, which she found sickeningly sweet. "You know, it's not that unusual. There's a whole university full of people who are doing graduate work down there."

"She's right, Charlee. *I* think it's nifty. Good for you, Laurie," Bruce said heartily. Too heartily. He headed for the bar again to refresh his drink. Lauren noticed Charlee frown as he poured the rest of the martini into his glass.

"Umm . . . would you two mind if I took a bath and got myself together? My hair must look a fright, after traveling."

"Oh, darling, of course. How thoughtless of me. I'll take you up to your room. Bruce, don't forget we have dinner at the Richmans'. It's going to be a long evening, sweetie."

Bruce guffawed. "Why do you think I need a drink?"

"Poor dear, he works so hard, he has to unwind at the end of the day," Charlee whispered on the way upstairs, but Lauren could tell she was annoyed.

While Lauren removed her travel clothes, Charlotte lounged on one of the twin beds, smoking another cigarette. "Are there any men within ten miles of Women's College?" she asked, wrinkling her nose. "What a grim-sounding name for an institution."

"There's a decent social life, if that's what you mean," Lauren answered carefully.

"Mother mentioned you were seeing someone—a doctor."

"I wonder where she got that information," Lauren said, her voice heavy with sarcasm. "Ruth Felder couldn't keep anything quiet if her life depended on it!"

"Is it meant to be a secret?"

"Not necessarily, especially from you, but I don't see why the entire family has to hear when I've only had a few dates with him." On the train, she had so looked forward to telling Charlee about David, knowing how her cousin adored romance, but somehow this conversation wasn't going at all the way she had anticipated. Nothing was, really, so far. Maybe tomorrow. "Ruth was all set to inquire into David's background before I'd gone out with him the first time," she said, as she brushed her tangled hair.

"Lord spare us, I am *so glad* to be away from all that, I must say." Charlotte uncoiled from her curled up position and straightened her skirt. "I'd better get ready, too. We're due at eight. Just ring for the maid if you need anything, Laurie."

All of her needs had been anticipated. Her clothes had been unpacked and pressed, the dresses and suits hung neatly in the closet, and everything else put away in drawers. On the night table between the beds were magazines for bedtime reading and several of the latest novels. As she prepared to bathe and dress in the comfortably appointed suite, she noted the bathroom and dressing room had been stocked with imported soaps and shampoos and dusting powders and perfumes and colognes, and every face cream, body lotion, mouth wash, and beauty supply imaginable. Everything was cheerfully decorated in the currently popular combination of pink and spring green—not what she would call a Charlee color scheme. This must be one of the areas her cousin had not yet tailored to her own persona.

Not a bad life, she thought, as she relaxed in the deep, sudsy tub. She would enjoy the luxuries and the beautiful apartment well enough, but she could not possibly live with the underlying tension she had sensed between Charlotte and Bruce. Perhaps she was too sensitive. Two people of their finely tuned temperaments were bound to have occasional differences. Many couples sniped at each other and were difficult to be with at times, especially for an unmarried woman. She certainly knew from her own experience that Charlee had always been high strung, with all that excess energy, and accustomed to having things her way. Bruce had no doubt been equally indulged. Was that the word?—spoiled and self-centered seemed too harsh. She supposed his job did put a strain on him, and having his wife's cousin as a house guest must seem an intrusion. Yet, if she were honest, she would say that after only a year and a half of marriage, something did not seem right between them . . .

The steam from the hot bath had revived her, bringing color to her face and some curl to her limp hair. Seated at the dressing table, she lifted the top and considered the array of makeup in a tray. *Why not?* She had never used anything other than lipstick, but now with the tip of her little finger, she applied a touch of soft blue to her eyelids and brushed mascara on her long lashes, which had always been too light. She sniffed the various French perfumes and decided on a cool, fresh-scented eau de cologne called Félicité. On that optimistic note, she slipped the new black crepe dinner gown over her head, brushed and smoothed her hair—a thankless task, since it seemed to have a mind of its own tonight—and appraised herself in the long dressing room mirror. Deciding the result wasn't half bad, she ran down the stairway.

From the small hallway before entering the library, she heard Bruce saying in a testy voice, "Dammit, Charlee, what would you *expect* me to do? I *had* to ask him along."

"You could have said we were busy—"

"Hello," Lauren called from the doorway, "I hope I haven't kept you waiting."

"Not at all," Bruce said, obviously relieved at the interruption.

"You look smashing, Laurie," cried Charlotte. "I don't think I've ever seen you wear black before."

"You're right. Mama insisted I had to buy it. Somewhere she read that a black dinner dress is *de rigeur* for New York."

"She's absolutely right. You look more like a New Yorker than I do."

Charlotte was outstanding in severely tailored floor-length white satin with a high neckline and long sleeves. A triple strand of large matched pearls with a decorative clasp of rubies and diamonds encircled her throat. A slim diamond bracelet and diamond and ruby earrings completed the elegant outfit.

"You are positively fabulous," Lauren said quietly.

Miriam had rejected several dresses Lauren had planned to bring on the trip. Her mother was wise in unexpected ways. "Charlotte and her friends will be wearing the most expensive, tasteful designer clothes, Laurie. You can't begin to compete with them, so keep your wardrobe simple and understated." Fortunately, she owned several attractive suits, and a number of good evening gowns brought back from New York by Reba—probably selected by Charlee, now that she thought of it. Tonight's long black crepe dress with cap sleeves was more sophisticated than most of her wardrobe, perfect for a dinner party. With it, she planned to wear the gray fox jacket Reba had given her.

"Oh, there you are!" Bruce called in the loud, over-hearty manner he had used earlier when he was trying to head off a confrontation. Lauren turned to see an intense young man with snapping dark eyes, who looked quite elegant in dinner clothes.

"Darling Nicholas," drawled Charlotte, moving to his side. She took his arm and brought him across the room to Lauren. "I'd like to introduce our *dear* friend, Count Nicholas de Georgenov. You haven't met before because Nicky stood us up for our wedding. He was meant to be best man."

"Nonsense, Charlotte, I didn't stand you up. Malcolm would never have countenanced my coming to Bruce's wedding." He spoke with an odd inflection, not quite British—Lauren never had been good at placing accents. Nicholas bowed over her hand, bringing it just short of his lips. He openly studied her, not even trying to be subtle about it. "She's really quite charming," he said to Charlee. "I believe they've told me everything there is to know about you, Lauren."

"Is that so?" If it was, why had she never heard of Nicholas until this moment? She remembered there was a bit of a flap about the best man at Charlee's wedding, but Bruce's father had stood-in and it seemed unimportant at the time.

Just then, Winston appeared in the doorway. "Fletcher is waiting with the car, Mr. Fields."

"We'd better get going," said Bruce. "We're already late."

In the general fuss of putting on wraps, Charlotte whispered to Lauren, "Don't worry, we do not mean to pair you with Nicky."

The thought had never occurred to her.

The first person she saw at the Richman apartment, standing in the foyer beside the silver and gold Christmas tree, was Jules Taylor. He looked exactly the same, except for his astonishment. "I can't get *over* you, Lauren. You've become a *really beautiful* woman!"

Once, she would have been nonplussed by that remark, especially coming from Jules. "Little girls grow up to be women," she answered lightly, deflecting his kiss to her cheek. "Congratulations on your engagement," she added. "Where's Blanche? I must tell her how delighted I am to know you two are going to be married."

His smooth brow clouded for the briefest moment. "Blanche couldn't make it tonight. Poor girl has a migraine."

"Ohh, I *am* sorry. I hope she'll be all right for the party on Saturday."

"Don't worry, she will. Blanche's headaches have a certain predictability. They come only at moments of convenience." Jules flashed his toothpaste smile to show he wasn't being serious, then turned to Charlotte and Bruce.

"For as long as I've known Blanche, she's never had

migraines,'' Charlee murmured under her breath when they were in the cloak room. ''Not until she became enamored of Jules.''

Cornelia Richman, the reigning hostess of Charlee's group, greeted them as soon as they walked into the living room. She was a statuesque blonde in her late thirties, as tall as Charlotte, but whereas Charlee bore her height with graceful elegance, Cornelia hunched her shoulders forward in an attempt to disguise her rather amazing bosom. ''The Stearnses won't be joining us this evening,'' she said immediately. ''Norma tells me they're old friends of yours, Lauren.''

''Yes, they used to winter in Asheville, but I haven't seen them in years.''

''That's because Norma's a business woman and she can't get away all winter.''

''Really? I wasn't aware of that.''

''Well, what was the poor thing to *do?* George lost all his money in the market. Imagine surviving the crash and then taking a flyer on some stupid oil stock. Fortunately, Norma has a talent for trade. It's been keeping them afloat.''

The delight in Mrs. Richman's voice couldn't have been more transparent. ''Exactly what is it that Norma does?'' Lauren inquired.

''Of course, you couldn't have known. She sells estate jewelry, which these days means she's just a little this side of a pawn shop. All sorts of women in the city are turning their jewels into cash. Norma has always had her finger on the pulse of New York society, and it's turned into a lucrative little pastime.'' She fingered her necklace, a heavy chain of old gold with a topaz pendant that was worth a fortune if it was real. ''I bought this piece from Norma, as it happens. It's quite old.''

Jules was making his way through the guests carrying two glasses. ''Here's your drink, Lauren,'' he said, handing her a rye and ginger ale.

''I didn't—''

''Bruce told me what you're drinking these days. I must

say, it's a step up from orange squash, or whatever it was you used to order.''

''Orange Crush,'' she said, and could have bitten her tongue. She did not want to do or say anything to reestablish auld lang syne. What was Jules up to, anyway?

He leaned over and whispered in her ear, ''You're sitting next to me at dinner. I changed the place cards.'' Her mouth flew open. The nerve of him!

''A shame Blanche couldn't come this evening,'' said Cornelia Richman, eyeing the two of them.

''She was devastated to miss your dinner party, Cornelia. I'm sure she'll give you a ring tomorrow.''

''We'll miss her. Usually I don't mind if a woman can't come at the last minute, but tonight we happen to have two extra men. I've put them on either side of you, Lauren; you're the only single girl. No doubt you've met Count de Georgenov, since Charlotte and Bruce brought him. And there's an awfully interesting young man, a professor of English literature at Columbia, whom Herbert met through one of his committees. His name is Peter Wise. You'll recognize him if you look for horn-rimmed glasses and a pipe. Now, if you'll excuse me, I must go check the tables. With these last minute changes, I want to be certain the seating is right—boy, girl, boy, girl. Of course, we *do* have the extra men . . .'' Mrs. Richman hurried away, her brow wrinkling with the burden of her task.

''Uh-oh,'' said Jules, ''I hope she doesn't find me out. I performed a noble deed by saving you from the English professor.''

''It just so happens, Jules, that I *like* English professors. I'll be spending the next few years with them, since I plan to get my Ph.D. in English!'' She turned her back and moved through the crowded room, looking for Charlee.

What had she just said? *Ph.D.!* Where had that come from? Suddenly she found herself face to face with a lean man of youngish years and medium height who was holding a cocktail and at the same time trying to light a pipe.

''It's much too crowded in here to smoke,'' she said, ''but if you insist, I'll hold your drink.''

He looked up, surprise on his face. It was a nice face.

"You're absolutely right," he said. "The pipe is a social crutch. I use it when I can think of nothing else to do."

"Do ladies ever smoke pipes?" she asked, giving him a sidelong glance.

"Not that I'm aware of," he answered, his eyes twinkling. They were very nice eyes behind his horn-rimmed glasses. "And the name of the lady?"

"Lauren Jacobson."

"I'll bet you're a Southerner."

"And I'll bet you're an English professor."

He grinned, shaking his head in disbelief. She thought he had an extremely nice smile. "You just promoted me," he said. "I'm an assistant professor."

By the time dinner was announced, Lauren fervently hoped that Cornelia Richman had restored Peter Wise to his rightful position by her side. Confusing though it was—after all, she was in love with David, wasn't she?—she found him a very attractive man. Peter taught modern literature and creative writing at Columbia University and he had written a novel that was about to come out.

"I see you two have discovered each other!" Cornelia Richman's strident voice was an intrusion. "Come along, children. We're going to dinner now." She linked arms with them and led the way to the dining room where four large round tables for eight had been set with silvery cloths and centerpiece arrangements of silver and gold Christmas balls and tinsel.

"Lauren, you're right over here, and Peter's on your right—What's this? That's a mistake, I *definitely* put Jules next to Hortense. They both come from Chicago and that should keep them going. Never mind. Peter you just sit right down here and I'll take this," she deftly palmed the place card with Jules Taylor's name hand-lettered in gold and proceeded to the table in the opposite corner of the room, where she exchanged cards. As she turned, she cast a curious, rather disapproving glance at Lauren. Did Cornelia suspect *her* of switching the place cards so that she could sit next to Jules? Her instincts to stay as far away from him as possible were right on target.

"How long will you be in New York?" Peter asked,

when the appetizers of pastry shells filled with creamed lobster had been served.

"About ten days. I'm not sure exactly when I'm leaving." She had been hoping David would call to say he was off for New Year's Eve. As the only unmarried and least senior resident at Strickland Hospital, he would have to wait for the other men to determine who was on duty. Or so he had said.

"Bruce Fields's wife is your cousin? I was surprised when I met her."

"Why so?"

"I don't know exactly . . . Bruce was in my eating club at Princeton—I was two years ahead and didn't know him well. Charlotte's an extraordinarily attractive woman."

Lauren smiled broadly, "Of course she is, but so's Bruce. An attractive man, that is. In fact, he's very handsome."

"Yes. They make a good-looking pair. I don't know why I brought it up." As if he had just remembered, he said, "My publishers are giving me a little party tomorrow. Will you come?"

She had never been to a publishing party. "I'd *love* to! I suppose I should ask Charlee and Bruce first. I just arrived today, and it may interfere with their plans."

"Bring them along. Five o'clock at the Scribner Building, second floor. In any case, I'd like to see you again while you're here."

"That would be—" She couldn't seem to get out an answer.

His expectant expression faded. "Well," he said, looking down and touching his silver, "I must be slipping. I can usually tell when a woman isn't interested." He picked up his wine glass and sipped.

"I'm sorry, Peter, I was thinking about something else. I'd enjoy seeing you, too."

He looked at her squarely. "Honestly?"

"Honestly."

Peter smiled and squeezed her hand, then turned to speak to the woman on his right, leaving Lauren to Nicholas de Georgenov.

"You couldn't be more different from Charlotte," he said. A rather enigmatic opening to their conversation.

"So I've been told. But then, I've never known anyone quite like Charlee, have you?"

Nicholas was the strangest looking man. With his lean, elongated head, he seemed to have been stretched on the outer edges, so that his ears were flat against his skull, with high tops and long lobes, and his watchful black eyes slanted upward at the corners. Despite his full sensuous lips, he had a cold, almost Mephistophelian quality. And yet, he was very handsome, the kind of man who might be cast as the romantic villain on the stage. She wondered whether his title was genuine.

"So, you know all about me, do you, Nicholas?"

"Perhaps not. On meeting, you don't quite fit the representation of Charlotte's little cousin from Randolph Springs, North Carolina."

She felt hurt. Is that how Charlee and Bruce had described her? It couldn't have been meant as a compliment. "It's a bit unfair. You know so much about me, when I've never even heard them mention your name." She thought she saw his facial muscles contract. Good! She hoped she had wounded him.

At the evening's end, as they were leaving the Richmans' party, Jules took Lauren aside. "Are you free for lunch tomorrow? I must see you alone."

"I'm all tied up, Jules. Besides, you're wrong—the one thing you must *not* do is to see me alone!" She hurried to the elevator, squeezing in next to Bruce and Charlotte, who gave her an inquiring glance.

It bothered Lauren that Charlee smoked in the morning, but she refrained from saying anything. They were having breakfast in the solarium in their robes, just the two of them, since Bruce had left early for his office. She told Charlotte about Peter Wise's invitation.

"Well, *of course* you should go, Laurie. A publishing party—what a treat! How clever of Cornelia to seat you with an English professor. Bruce says he knew him at

Princeton. I thought he was rather sexy behind those spectacles!''

''Oh, Charlee,'' she laughed, but she had to admit they were in agreement there. She had found herself strongly attracted to Peter. Since she had started dating David, she was much more attuned to men and their sex appeal.

''I thought we would go shopping this morning, Laurie, and then meet Blanche for lunch. We'll do the Metropolitan in the afternoon, and then I'll come home and you can take a cab right down Fifth to Scribner's.''

''Don't let me take all your time, Charlee. You must have lots to do for the party. I can go around to the museums and stores by myself, if you'll just point me in the right direction.''

''Darling! I'm looking forward to showing you the city,'' Charlotte protested. ''There's almost nothing I have to actually do for Saturday and I still have all week to take care of the last minute errands. It's being catered and the servants will supervise everything. We're going to trim the tree tonight after dinner, so if you want to bring Peter home, he might enjoy that.''

The tree? Charlotte had not grown up with a Christmas tree, even in Maxwell Mortimer's house. ''Peter mentioned something about dinner. Would it be all right if we came back afterward?''

''Of course, love. You must do exactly as you wish, just as if this were your own home.''

Charlotte went back to her *Herald Tribune,* while Lauren looked through the *Times.* There were so many exciting things to do in New York—plays, concerts, ballets, the opera, and any number of art exhibits and lectures. Just one of these attractions would have Randolph Springs turning out in force. She could imagine how exciting it would be living here and having it all available every day.

Lauren finished a second cup of coffee. ''If we're going to do everything you mentioned, I'd better go get dressed.''

Long before one o'clock, she was exhausted from their shopping expedition. She loved the glamour of New York, especially in the midst of the cheerful Christmas shoppers. It had begun to snow and she was glad she had let Charlee talk her into buying a pair of warm fur-trimmed boots at Saks. Sometime this week, she thought, she would select a gift for David, but thus far, nothing had struck her as being right.

"It looks like we're going to have a real snow for Christmas," said Charlee, when they came outdoors.

"My feet," groaned Lauren. "How can you walk all morning in this city and not drop of fatigue?"

"This is *nothing,*" laughed Charlotte. "I've slowed down for your benefit. Most days I go tearing around all over the city—Henry Street and Mt. Sinai Hospital for my volunteer work, luncheon meetings for my various committees—up to the Museum for my lecture series. Then, there are the afternoon recitals at Carnegie Hall and usually a matinée on Wednesdays."

"Stop! I can't take any more," cried Lauren. "You must fall into bed every night right after supper."

"Not at all," replied Charlotte, steering her across the wet, snowy pavement of Fifth Avenue toward the Plaza where they were meeting Blanche for lunch in the Palm Court. "We're out almost every evening. We have our Tuesday night concert series at the Philharmonic and there's always some sort of benefit dinner or theater party. Most people entertain during the week because so many of them go away to the country on weekends . . . Did I tell you Bruce and I are buying a house in Connecticut?"

"That's great. How far from the city is it?"

"It takes a little more than an hour by train and almost two by car. It's a wonderful old farm house. We take possession in February, and I can't wait 'til spring to start on the alterations and furnishings. This will be all mine, I can assure you," she said firmly, then cautioned Lauren, "Don't say anything to Blanche. I don't want my mother-in-law getting wind of it until it's completely finished." She laughed gleefully. "They're not the only ones who can keep secrets!"

Lauren need not have worried about avoiding the topic of Charlotte's country house. Whenever she met them at the numerous gatherings she attended that week, neither

Blanche nor her mother was interested in discussing anything other than the plans for the wedding.

On Christmas night, the splendidly turned out guests poured into the Park Avenue penthouse, embracing as if they had not seen one another at half a dozen affairs over the past week. They consumed case after case of Dom Perignon, gorged themselves at the seafood bar on Cherry Stones and Blue Points, Alaskan King crab legs, and Louisiana prawns, and feasted on an assortment of imported patés and Beluga caviar presented in such abundance that one might have concluded Manhattan was in the grip of enormous prosperity.

Charlee and Bruce received in the marble foyer with Blanche and Jules, who looked made for each other. They put Lauren in mind of a perfectly matched pair of highly bred wolfhounds, streamlined and decorative. Regal and pale in an ice blue satin gown, Blanche was resplendent in the sapphire and diamond earrings and necklace that were her parents' engagement gift. She gestured constantly with her left hand, displaying her large heart-shaped diamond ring. Greeting the guests with a ceremonial smile, her only obvious emotion appeared when she looked at her fiancé. Dapper and urbane in a tuxedo, Jules could have been born to this role.

Everyone agreed that Charlee and Bruce's party was the highlight of the season. Adele Fields hovered nearby, not the smallest detail escaping her fastidious eye, while Malcolm had wasted no time in bringing together the head of a prominent banking house and a Federal judge in the farthest corner of the living room.

The Stearnses were among the earliest arrivals. George looked much the same, but Lauren would never have recognized Norma as the chic, glittering hostess she had last seen in Asheville three years ago. Norma had gained an enormous amount of weight, which distorted her features, giving her the aspect of a faded beauty who might once have borne a resemblance to Norma Stearns. She was still immaculate in her dress, but whereas formerly she had given the impression of a sleek panther, crafty and somewhat dangerous, now she had the benign and comical mien of a St. Bernard. ''Lauren Jacobson!'' she fairly shrieked, waddling forward with arms outstretched to envelop Lauren in an embrace. ''How *are* you, darling?''

''It's good to see you, Norma. And George,'' said Lauren, extending a hand. He leaned over to kiss her cheek.

''Tell us about *Philip,*'' cried Norma, ''I always had a weakness for your brother.''

''Phil's just fine, going with a marvelous girl from Rocky Mount. I introduced them.''

''And you, love . . . still not married?'' That, with a knowing little laugh.

''That's right, Norma. One thing at a time. I haven't finished college yet.''

Norma turned toward the receiving line. ''What do you think of our engaged couple? Your old beau, Jules . . .'' the eyes glinted, and for that moment she was pure Norma.

''They're absolutely ideal for each other.''

''I couldn't agree more,'' said Norma. ''Blanche is *exactly* what Jules has been searching for in a wife.''

Up close, George looked strained around the eyes and Lauren noticed quite a bit of gray at his temples. Charlee had told her that Malcolm Fields was barely on speaking terms with him—something about a bad stock deal George had involved his friends in. But it seemed cruel to kick a man when he was already down on his luck. If what Cornelia Richman had said was true, the Stearnses had been going through hell.

''Let's have a toast to old times,'' said George, signaling a waiter for champagne. ''Here's to the pleasure of meeting our lovely little friend again.''

Lauren melted, feeling ashamed of blaming them for an old slight they probably had nothing to do with. ''Thank you, George. It's wonderful seeing both of you, truly it is.''

Norma had always been quick to catch nuances, and Lauren was surprised to see her eyes moisten. ''Oh, Laurie, I was always so fond of you . . . I'm sorry we drifted apart.'' Glancing down at herself, she said, ''Look what's happened to me, will you? Pure nerves. When I'm fidgety, I eat."

"There's plenty to be fidgety about these days," Lauren answered quickly. "There's bound to be a war in Europe."

George nodded. "And you can bet we'll get into it."

"Do you really think so?" she asked in dismay. "Why would we?"

"Just like the last time, we'll eventually have no choice. There are those who think it would be good for the economy."

"That's outrageous!"

"Come, George, this is far too serious a subject for a party," Norma interjected.

"Sorry, Norma, I started it," said Lauren. "If you'll excuse me for a few minutes, I promised to telephone my parents tonight."

"Give them our love," Norma called as Lauren started up the stairs. "And to Philip."

Slipping into the study where the din of conversation would not interfere, Lauren dialed the operator. She was worried about her father, who had been a little under the weather the other day when she'd spoken to them.

"Are you having a good time, dear?" Miriam asked.

"Wonderful, Mama! Charlee and Bruce have been such terrific hosts. I've been going to a different party every night."

"I hope you have the right clothes," Miriam said anxiously.

Lauren smiled, thinking it was more like Reba than her mother to be concerned about fashion. "Thanks to you, Mama, my wardrobe is perfect."

When her father got on the telephone, he sounded so *old* . . . After they hung up, she sat at the desk in the softly lit room thinking about her parents. What would happen if her father became ill again? She feared she would have to go home to be with her mother, and she dreaded the possibility.

Downstairs again, Lauren looked around for a familiar face, briefly joining Audrey and Steve Burns, a couple she had met the night before at Adele Fields's annual Christmas Eve Open House. Nicholas lurked about, avoiding Malcolm Fields. He sought Lauren, remaining at her side, probably for lack of other company. While she talked to him, she kept one eye on the door, expecting Peter Wise to arrive any minute. Charlee had invited Peter when they came home the night of his book party, after having dinner at the Algonquin Hotel with his editor and other hangers-on. Lauren had been seeing a great deal of him ever since.

She had not heard from David. For the first few days, she had come home each afternoon and evening, expecting there would be a message from him, but when there wasn't, she forced herself not to think about him. Perhaps he was too busy amusing himself with Susie Winkler to call her in New York! The time was passing so quickly and pleasantly, with Peter free to take her sightseeing, or to concerts and the theater, since Columbia was closed for Christmas vacation.

"Let's celebrate New Year's Eve together," Peter had urged, mentioning that there were several parties. Tonight as she was dressing, Lauren had made up her mind she would stay, and planned to tell him so as soon as he walked in.

On Thursday night, their third date, they had been sitting alone in the library after Charlee and Bruce said good night, when Peter kissed her. She moved away after the brief pressure of his lips and he said, "I have a feeling there's a special fella waiting down there in Dixie."

"I'm not engaged or going steady, Peter. I wouldn't have gone out with you if I were," she answered. "What about you? You're twenty-eight and not 'involved?' "

"I have recently become disinvolved," he said, tamping his pipe. "It was all for the best, although I don't think either of our families will get over it for a while."

"Ah, one of those. Are the families good friends?"

He nodded slowly, rolling his eyes. "Worse than that. Our fathers are law partners. This has been planned from birth. I don't know which one of us fought it harder, Deborah or I."

It had made her like him even more to know he had

struggled with the necessity to please his family. She sensed that it would not take much encouragement on her part for this to become what Cousin Ruth might call a "serious romance." For heaven's sake, she couldn't even trust her own feelings! Last week at this time she had been madly in love with David Bernard, and here she was, eagerly awaiting the arrival of Peter Wise.

"Excuse me, Miss Jacobson," Winston the butler was actually addressing her by name. "You have a long distance telephone call."

"Thank you, Winston. I'll take it up in the study." For a moment she was alarmed, thinking perhaps something had happened to her father. She'd had a premonition before when she heard his careworn tone. Hurrying upstairs to the study, she closed both doors before picking up the receiver.

"Hello, Lauren . . . it's David." *David!* "How's New York?"

"I'm having a wonderful time," she answered, feeling breathless.

"Not too wonderful, I hope. We'll never be able to keep you down on the farm."

She was grinning, irrationally happy, feeling a glow of warmth. "No need to worry. Two weeks of this life is about all I can handle."

His voice dropped. "I miss you, Laurie."

She closed her eyes and whispered, "I miss you, too."

"I was hoping I could talk you into coming back for New Year's Eve. Fairfax Reynolds, good man that he is, said he'd take the duty. He's a big golfer, so I have all summer to cover for him."

She could tell he was using bravado to deflect a possible rejection. Did he sense her dilemma? But all of a sudden, she realized there *was* no dilemma. Her confusion had evaporated. The minute she heard David's voice, all doubts had vanished . . .

Sleet lashed against the windows as the train sped through the night. Somewhere south of Baltimore, the snow changed to freezing rain. Lauren slept soundly in her berth, waking only once when her sleeping car was being switched to the Southern Railway locomotive. After raising the shade to peer out, she lay back for a moment, considering her visit with Charlotte and Bruce.

This was the first time she had been alone with them for any sustained period, and what she had seen did not bode well for the marriage. Bruce was drinking far too much. He was arrogant and moody, creating dissension in the household. And despite Charlee's obvious pleasure in the luxuries and diversions of her life, whenever her face was in repose, Lauren detected an expression of unhappiness. Even in private moments, her cousin's nervous restlessness was evident. And a new cynicism.

"What did you think of the Burnses?" Charlee had asked on the last morning when she and Lauren had been lounging alone in the small upstairs study.

Steve Burns was Bruce's friend and colleague in the Fields law firm, so Lauren replied carefully. "They seemed nice." Actually, she had not much cared for the couple, finding them overbearing, but she felt it would be rude to say so, even to her cousin.

Charlee was curled up like a cat on the windowseat, chain-smoking. "Audrey can scarcely bear to be in the same room with me."

"I'm sure that's not true! She told me you were one of her closest friends."

Charlotte made a little laughing sound. "Did she? How *terribly* sweet." There was an uncomfortable silence. "Would you say that she was attractive?"

"Quite attractive," replied Lauren.

"Well, she *ought* to be! She's had everything made over. Her nose has been bobbed, of course. And she just had something done to her jaw."

"Really? What was wrong with her jaw?"

"She had a weak chin." Charlotte gave her an amused smile. "What she really has is a weak husband. He has a weakness for other women."

"But they seem too young for that! I mean, wouldn't you think the romance hadn't gone out of their marriage this early?"

Charlotte exploded in hilarious laughter. "Sweet, darling Laurie! You still believe in prince charming and happily ever after, don't you?"

It distressed Lauren to hear her cousin speak in that brittle, superior, New York manner. She was offended, but managed to laugh it off. "I've grown up some in the past two years, Charlee. I am no longer your little Sleeping Beauty!"

"Oh dear . . . now I've gone and hurt your feelings," said Charlotte, sounding only half sorry. "But you must admit, Laurie, you *are* a babe in the woods when it comes to men. Moonlight and roses, hearts and flowers, knights in shining armour—Well, let me tell you, honey, marriage isn't like that. I can vouch for it!" Angrily she flicked the ash from her cigarette. "If I had it to do over again—"

She turned her head away and closed her eyes, and Lauren was immediately at her side with her arms around her. "Charlee! Oh, darling, you don't really mean that, do you?" Her heart was beating rapidly, and she felt real fear. If Charlotte's storybook romance was a failure, what hope was there?

Charlee drew herself up, taking a deep breath. "Oh, Laurie, you must think I'm terrible, carrying on so. Why, I don't know what came over me! Too much partying all week. You know how champagne always puts me out of sorts." She forced a smile, the dazzling smile Lauren knew so well. "What a way to end your visit! Just forget what I said, honey. Promise?"

"Of course! I'm so relieved. You really had me scared there for a minute." But she hadn't been relieved at all. This was just Charlee's pride preventing her from unburdening herself. She had always been loathe to divulge her weaknesses.

Lauren had ended the visit by not telling her cousin about David. Charlee had always been the one to hand out advice in matters of the heart. Once it would have been natural to confide in her. But unable to recapture their familiar intimacy, Lauren had left New York without revealing that she was in love.

The mesh storage hammock in her berth swung violently as the Pullman section was uncoupled and shunted to another track. Lauren lowered the window shade and turned over in the berth. By the time they were again rolling south, she was fast asleep, lulled by the insistent rhythm of the train wheels.

Chapter 17

A WINTER STORM was raging all through Virginia and the Carolinas, causing flooding where low-banked streams had overflowed. The winds had reached near gale force by the time Lauren's train crossed into North Carolina.

David was waiting on the station platform in Durham on Friday afternoon. The moment she saw him, Lauren found it incredible that she could ever have doubted she loved him. But then, it wasn't *her* love for him that was in question; it was David who had never said he loved her.

"The driving is awful," he warned, after kissing her warmly. She clung to him, thinking public embraces seemed perfectly acceptable at railroad stations in bad weather.

"The faculty dance has been canceled," said David. "There's a party at the Lawrences', but I wonder whether we shouldn't sleep in Durham tonight."

"Where would we stay?"

"I have lots of friends who would put us up, but Ralph and Gretchen are expecting us in Chapel Hill. Gretch wasn't feeling so great when I called, and I think she likes the idea of having a doctor around, in case she goes into labor."

"Oh, my goodness, do you think she will?"

"Supposedly she's not due for another two weeks, but you never know." Turning up his coat collar, he lifted her suitcases. "Whattaya say, shall we chance it?"

"I'm game if you are."

"I think we'll be all right. You wait here while I bring the car around."

Lauren shivered in the penetrating damp. She had put on her warm overshoes and taken out her umbrella, which was useless because it would break in the strong wind. "I think I prefer the snows of New York to this crazy weather," she said, when they were seated in the automobile.

Brushing the moisture from his hair, David regarded her with that lopsided grin she so loved. "Just as long as that's all you prefer," he retorted, pulling her closer for a quick kiss before starting for Chapel Hill. "I kept thinking all week that you might decide to move to New York."

"I did give some thought to going up there for graduate school," she admitted. "I met some terrific people, and I can't tell you how much I enjoyed the concerts and museums. And the *theater!* It was hard to leave."

"That's just what I was afraid of. I didn't really expect you to agree to come back for tonight," he said, "but I'm glad you did."

"So am I." The truth was, although New York was a fascinating city, there was no place on earth she would rather have been at this moment than driving through the storm with David Bernard.

Rain beat against the windows, painting a steel-gray watery landscape. The trip to Chapel Hill, ordinarily no more than twenty-five minutes, took over an hour. They crawled along through deep puddles, stopping frequently for David to wipe the fogged windshield. Lauren could feel the force of the wind buffeting the automobile and at times the rain was so heavy, David was unable to see even a few feet ahead. The highway was deserted, as most people heeded the weather bureau's warnings to stay at home. As they drew closer to Chapel Hill, the temperature dropped dramatically and the rain turned to sleet. The streets were icy by the time they pulled up to the Nelson house.

"Whew! glad that's over," said David. The wind howled and the freezing rain came down in sheets as they ran for the porch, sliding over the glaze of ice on the stone steps. There were lights in the house, but no one came to the door. Finding it unlocked, they walked in. "Ralph? Gretchen?" David called. No one answered.

The house had an uninhabited feeling. "I don't think they're here," said Lauren. "Look, David, there's a note."

It was propped up on a table in the living room, written in a hasty scrawl: "The waters broke. We're going to try to make it to Duke, otherwise Strickland. Call you later. Ralph."

"Well," said David happily, "I guess we're going to have a baby. Poor kid, imagine having a birthday on New Year's Eve."

"You mean she's in labor?" said Lauren.

"If she isn't, she will be soon. Ralph said her water broke—the amniotic sac ruptured."

"I thought he meant the rain, that it was getting too heavy. What . . . ?"

"*Land's sake,* as my Aunt Ethel used to say. Don't they teach you girls anything about how babies are born?" he laughed.

"That's not funny, David. I've never been pregnant, so how do you expect me to know? I gather it has something to do with the onset of labor," she said, picking up her suitcase and heading upstairs to the guest room.

"Here, let me take that," he offered.

"Never mind," she said coolly. "I can manage quite well on my own."

"Come on, Laurie, don't be so sensitive." He grinned. "If you like, I'll give you a crash course in the anatomy of human reproduction!"

Lauren sniffed and put her nose in the air, and David followed her upstairs, stopping at the master bedroom, where a hasty departure was evident. Ignoring him, Lauren proceeded to the guest room where she usually slept when she visited the Nelsons.

Gretchen had prepared for her arrival. A set of towels had been laid out on the dresser, and the bed was made up with fresh linens and a colorful handmade coverlet. It was a charming room, with a hooked rug and homespun tier curtains at the dormer windows. A framed grospoint of a windmill in a field of wild flowers hung on the wall above the bed and handmade baskets filled with dried grasses sat on the window ledge.

Opening her suitcase, Lauren took out a box from F.A.O. Schwarz and went across the hall to the little bedroom that Gretchen had furnished as a nursery. David was standing with his hand on the bassinet, looking serious.

"Is something wrong?" she asked.

"I hope not. I called both hospitals. Gretchen and Ralph haven't checked in at either Duke or Strickland."

"They must be driving slowly, and the weather's even worse now than it was earlier. Remember how long it took us."

"I guess you're right," he answered. "We have no idea what time they left. It could have been just a few minutes before we arrived, although I think we would have seen them when they passed."

"Not necessarily. Not if we weren't expecting them to be on the road."

"I'll feel a hell of a lot better when I hear from Ralph— What's that?" he asked as Lauren placed the package on top of a chest of drawers.

"It's a baby gift. I bought it in New York."

"Laurie . . ." In one motion he was across the room, embracing her. "You're so great. I'm sorry I made fun of you before."

"You're forgiven," she smiled, holding him around the waist. "I brought something for you, too." Breaking away, she went back to her room, with David following. There was another small gift-wrapped package in her bag.

Lauren had deliberated about whether to bring David something from New York. Chanukah and Christmas had already passed, it was true; however, people brought gifts back for their friends when they took long trips. But since he probably would not have one for her, would it embarrass him or make her feel uncomfortable? For days she had debated. In the end, she decided she wanted to give him a present, and that was sufficient reason.

Conscious that this was to be her first gift to David—indeed, the only gift she had ever given a man outside of her family—she had selected it with considerable thought. It was important that it be personal and yet not presumptuous, something that would last forever and remain a symbol of the first gift if he should become her husband. But, on the other hand, if he had no intention of marrying her, it would never do to leave him with a tangible reminder of her foolish hopes and lost pride. Consequently, she had rejected a toiletry kit from Crouch & Fitzgerald made of soft glove leather (too intimate, and therefore not in good taste), a gold pen and pencil set from Dunhill (too expensive and therefore not in good taste), a pair of thin gold cuff links she had seen at Tiffany (surprisingly affordable, but she had been taught that a well brought-up young woman did not give jewelry to a man unless they were engaged), almost deciding on a soft camel's hair cardigan at Brooks Brothers (which she loved, but if David married the Winkler girl, she would not want Susie's husband lounging around the house on weekends in her sweater). Finally, she had decided on a miniature Swiss clock from Mark Cross, with its own burgundy leather case. It was embossed with his initials, and could be used on his night table at the hospital or for traveling.

David was very touched. "Lauren, how thoughtful. I never expected you to bring me anything. It's a beautiful clock, and I really need one. Is it an alarm?"

"Yes, and it has the mellowest little chime that won't jar you awake. Let me show you." She loved the happiness on his face; he really did like it.

David was fumbling in his pocket. He brought out a square box wrapped in gold paper and tied with a blue ribbon. "I wasn't going to give this to you until midnight, but this seems like an appropriate moment." She just sat there looking at him, afraid to say anything. "Well, aren't you going to open it?"

Nodding, she untied the ribbon and let the paper fall away. She lifted the lid of a blue velvet jewelry box to reveal a slender gold bracelet embossed with a delicate scroll design. David opened the catch and showed her the engraving on the inside: *Lauren and David—October 10, 1937.* "That was the day I met you," he said, closing the bracelet on her wrist.

"Oh, David—" she threw her arms around his neck, kissing him. "Thank you so much, I *love* it! It's the most beautiful bracelet I've ever owned." Her eyes were shining with happiness.

"You know, you're wonderful to give a gift to. The way you look, it's incredible."

He kissed her again and they fell back on the bed against the pillows, their kisses deepening until she became aware of his arousal as he pressed himself against her. A piercing excitement went through her, and she was filled with an aching desire for him. As David slid his hand under her sweater and brushed his fingertips across the skin above her slip, she held her breath. Lost in his nearness, she was hardly aware when he moved to turn off the lamp. Slipping off her shoes and then his, David threw his jacket on a chair and opened his shirt. Then lying down beside her again, he kissed her gently, removing her sweater and pushing her slip down to her waist.

For a moment she panicked when he unhooked her brassiere, but then he caressed her breasts, kissing them and whispering incoherent words, and she no longer cared that she was half naked and that he had taken off his shirt. She loved the feel of his strong, muscular hardness against her, running her fingers up and down his back and into his hair. His hands were stroking and caressing her, kneading her lower body through her clothing. As he parted her legs and softly stroked her with his hand, she closed her eyes, feeling hot and dizzy and wanting nothing so much as to allow the tide of passion to sweep over and engulf her.

"Laurie," he gasped. "Darling . . ."

"David, I . . . oh, David!" Why didn't he say he loved her? *Why?* If he said it, she knew she would do anything he wanted, *anything*.

"You're so beautiful," he whispered. "I want you so much, darling."

Never let a man . . . he'll lose his respect for you . . .

nice girls don't let men take liberties . . . a man will never marry a girl who allows him . . . never, never . . .

Somewhere a telephone was ringing. Slowly David became aware and sat up. "I guess I have to get that. It might be Ralph." He hurried out of the room in his stocking feet.

Lauren felt like she had awakened from a long, deep, dream-filled sleep. It was almost dark now and the wind was higher, driving the rain against the house. Through the window, the trees were tossing and bending. She put on her bra and slip, and then her sweater. Closing her eyes against the brightness, she pressed the switch on the bedside lamp, flooding the room with light. As she was straightening the bed, David came in.

"That was Ralph," he said. "They never made it to Duke or Strickland. They had to take a detour, going miles out of the way. Then he drove through some water and shorted the wires. The car stalled and Gretchen started having labor pains—"

"Oh no! What did they do?"

"It's the damndest thing. Some Negro men came along in a truck and drove them to the nearest hospital, which happens to be Booker T. Washington. It's for colored people." David shook his head, giving a funny little laugh. "Now, I can tell you that I have personally seen Negro patients—emergency cases—turned away from Strickland and made to go on to Washington Hospital. But Gretchen was put right into a labor room and they notified her obstetrician at Duke, who may or may not be able to get there. Meanwhile, the chief o.b. at Washington came right over as soon as they called him."

"You mean she's going to have her baby there at the colored hospital?"

"I would say that is an accurate assessment of the situation. I can assure you, that little baby doesn't know from beans about segregation!"

"No, of course not," she laughed. "It's just kind of funny—and sweet, isn't it?"

"It's *damn* sweet, I *love* it!" he shouted. "Ralph says they couldn't possibly be any nicer."

"Is everything all right with Gretchen?" she asked.

"She's fine, but the doctor told Ralph they should be prepared for a long labor."

"How can he tell?"

"I gather this doc has had lots of experience." Suddenly aware that she was dressed, he sat on the bed and put his arms around her, pulling her to him. "We were getting a little carried away there for a while, weren't we?"

Lauren nodded, smiling tentatively. Was her mother correct—had he lost his respect for her?

"I guess you could say we were saved by the bell." He smoothed her hair and kissed her gently. "It was beautiful, Laurie. You're wonderful."

The trees were covered with ice when they inched their way over to Jim and Carol Lawrence's house that night. "You *have* to come," Carol had wailed when David called to say the driving was so bad he thought they should cancel. "What'll I do with all this food? None of the Duke crowd will be able to get here."

"I think it's crazy," he answered, "but we'll try."

David put on a dark suit and Lauren wore her wine velvet dress with the white lace collar. When she had finished dressing, she fastened the clasp of the gold bracelet, wondering at the significance of the inscription. It seemed so romantic, and yet she was afraid to attach too much meaning to it.

The entire Chapel Hill crowd showed up, full of good humor and regarding the weather as a great adventure, one couple even bringing their six-month-old baby in a basket because the baby sitter could not travel from Carrboro. "The extremes to which some people will go for a good time," David said to Lauren disapprovingly. But Lauren understood, because she had observed how sparing the lives of these young wives of graduate students and junior faculty were. *Of course* they would bundle up their infant and take him along, even in this freak storm, rather than miss a party on New Year's Eve.

Each couple had chipped in for the wine, everyone carried a platter of canapés or a casserole dish, and several brought extra glasses and place settings of china and silverware. What a contrast it was to the elaborate entertainments she had attended in the elegantly appointed apartments of Manhattan, with servants and caterers, caviar and champagne, magnificent dinner tables and extravagant epicurean menus. Charlee and her New York friends would call this tacky, smiling at the make-do furnishings of the Lawrence house and the homesewn "faculty dresses"—made-over, much-used creations of taffeta, silk, brocade, or velvet, ill-fitting and out-of-date. Lauren had discovered it wasn't that these women did not know and appreciate fine furniture and *haute couture*. On the contrary, most of them were artistic and had a highly developed sense of esthetics. Many had grown up in privileged circumstances, but they had learned how to sort out the essentials and do without.

"Tell us about your trip," they asked eagerly. "Did you go to the ballet or see any shows?"

"Yes," she said, almost apologetically. "My cousins splurged. It was my first time in New York, you know."

"That's a beautiful dress, Lauren. Did you buy it up there?"

"Thank you, I've had it for ages . . ."

"Is unemployment as bad as it is here?"

"Worse, I think. At least, you see more people on the streets looking for a handout."

Many of them were not Southerners. They came from all over the country—Ohio, Indiana, Pennsylvania, Michigan, New Jersey. The *real* Southerners, those who had lived in Chapel Hill and the surrounding communities for generations, often regarded the university families as a little outré, a shade too free-thinking. As for these young newcomers, they considered *them* downright liberals. In fact, among themselves they speculated that it wouldn't be at all surprising if there were some *pinkos* amongst them!

"No baby yet," David reported, after calling the hospital and speaking to Ralph.

"Poor Gretchen," commiserated the mother of the baby

who was peacefully sleeping upstairs in a bedroom, "what a way to spend New Year's Eve."

"Yes, but she'll feel like a million tomorrow morning when it's all over and she has that dear little bundle in her arms," said a sweet-faced woman who had left several little bundles of her own at home.

Carol Lawrence rolled her eyes and whispered to Lauren, "The original earth mother, that one! Gretchen's days of freedom are a thing of the past."

Despite everyone's determination to make it a festive evening, the party had an air of forced gaiety. In the middle of dinner, the electricity went out, which meant no heat since the furnace had an electric thermostat. They lit candles and the men brought in firewood from the back porch. Soon they had a blaze going, but the chimney did not draw well and the smoky air burned their eyes.

Frightened of the dark, the Lawrence's two-year-old son woke up screaming, and in all the commotion, the plum puddings that Carol was warming in the gas oven burned. The power came on in time for her to scrape off the singed crust and disguise the damage with hard sauce. "Oh well, as long as it tastes all right," she sighed. They all assured her the dessert was delicious and they turned out the lights again, because candlelight was much more romantic.

Just before midnight, Jim poured champagne in the living room where everyone was dancing to phonograph records. Someone switched on the radio so they could hear Guy Lombardo.

"This has been one disaster after another," said David to Lauren. "I bet you're sorry you didn't stay in New York."

"Oh, no! There's no place I'd rather be than here with you," she answered, lightheaded from two glasses of wine and the champagne.

"Get ready," shouted Jim, passing out noisemakers and paper hats.

Someone started counting the seconds, "Ten . . . nine . . . eight . . . seven . . . six . . ."

"There's no one I'd rather be with than you," said David.

". . . three . . . two . . . *ONE!* HAPPY NEW YEAR!"

Lauren's head was spinning and the room seemed to be turning in circles as David kissed her and whispered, "Happy New Year, darling. What a wonderful way to start 1938."

A mixture of rain and snow was falling when they crawled back to the Nelsons' house. "Ralph isn't here yet."

"I'll call the hospital to see how it's going," said David. He went to the telephone closet under the stairs, returning in a few minutes, with a huge grin on his face. "Gretchen had a boy about an hour ago. Eight pounds! And Ralph is sacked out."

"A boy! That's wonderful. Gretchen wanted a son."

David removed his suit coat and sat next to her on the couch. She leaned her head back, closing her eyes. "You must be bushed after your trip," he said. "Ready to go to bed?"

Lauren raised her head. "Are you . . . that is, where will you stay?"

He shrugged. "If it'll make you happier, I'll sleep down here on the couch."

"You mean we're *both* going to stay here, without anyone else?" For the first time, she realized she would be spending the night—what was left of it—alone in the house with David. Her mother would swoon! And Papa—well, she didn't even want to think what *he* would say if he knew.

"What would you suggest, Lauren?" David answered in a reasonable tone of voice. "I don't relish driving to Strickland in this weather. I could go back to Jim's, but I think that's pretty stupid. Besides, do you really feel like being here alone if the electricity goes again?"

"No, but if anyone knew we were here—" She felt idiotic, but what else could she say? "It just doesn't look right, David."

He sighed, resigned. "All right, Lauren, if it means

that much, call the Rosenblooms and I'll take you over there."

"I can't call them at this hour. Besides, I think they went to Florida."

They were silent and David put his arms around her, intending to kiss her, but she pulled away. "This is really foolish," he said bitingly. "What *is* it about you Southern women? You have an obsession with sex! I can assure you I won't throw you on the bed and rape you, Lauren. I've seen plenty of women's bodies, and they're pretty much all the same!"

"You needn't be insulting! It has nothing to do with sex. I didn't make the rules, but I have to live by them. *Good night!*" She ran up the stairs and slammed the door to her room.

David lay on the couch staring into the darkness. Why had he been so hard on Lauren? Was he disappointed that she had turned out to be another variety of Magnolia Blossom? Not spoiled and demanding like Susan Winkler, but sheltered and bound by convention.

It wasn't surprising. Lauren came from a conservative family and besides, she wasn't wrong . . . In Randolph Springs or Durham, if people knew that they had stayed alone in a house all night it *would* damage her reputation. But in Chapel Hill it was different. They were not part of this community, and all of their friends here were young transplants, with that same unfettered sense of freedom, the lack of ties and strictures that he had always loved about the village. No one would know or care that they had stayed together. Except Lauren.

Admit it, Bernard—the real reason why she got you mad. He had realized Ralph would be staying at the hospital that night, and all through the evening, he had been looking forward to returning home with Lauren. To making love to her.

He must have been dreaming! A man did not make love to a Magnolia Blossom. Not until he was married to her. And, as he had recently learned only too well, he could not continue to date a Magnolia Blossom indefinitely without marrying her.

He sure was having his difficulties with women lately . . . Susie had lammed into him two weeks ago, taking him to task for leading her on all this time. *Leading her on!* Half the time they went out, it was she who invited him—to dances, weddings, and engagement parties.

"Are you coming to Greensboro for New Year's?" she had asked when they were parked in front of her sorority house the night before she left Duke on Christmas vacation. What a cost that must have been to her pride.

"No, Susie, I can't. I'll probably be on call, but in any case, I won't be coming to Greensboro."

She had remained silent, while David grew more and more uncomfortable. "Will I see you at all over the holidays?" she finally said, her voice trembling—with anger, he thought. "I just want to know, David, so I don't hold open any special dates for you."

"I think you'd better not count on me," he answered quietly.

"You are . . . the most *outrageous, ungentlemanly* boy I've ever known," she shrieked, starting to cry. "You've been leading me on for over a year, taking up my time, making my whole family think we were—Ohh, I can't believe you would do this to me!"

He had never known how to deal with girls and their tears. "Susie, I'm truly sorry, I never meant to lead you on. I like you and enjoy being with you, but it was never anything more than that."

"You *bastard!* You know very well you made me think—You've taken up the best time of my life! Now, I'll *never* have the chance to meet someone. All the boys think of me as your girlfriend."

"Not from me, they don't. I haven't asked you to stop dating other men."

"I hate you!" she screamed. "I never want to see you again!"

He'd felt rotten afterward and he kept asking himself whether he had in fact been unfair to Susan. On more than one occasion, she would have gone to bed with him, but he had never taken advantage of her. Careful not to let it get out of hand, he had known instinctively she would expect a commitment if he did.

He never had been in love with Susie—and he knew now he never would be. Because he loved Lauren. The admission filled him with joy and a tremendous longing to hold her in his arms and declare his love. But if he told her now, what would she expect? What could he offer her?

They were fragile, Magnolia Blossoms, not up to the rigors of living on a shoestring. You did not ask a Magnolia Blossom to share the life of a resident, with his twelve-hundred dollars a year. Even the couples they had been with tonight lived on larger incomes than that. Most of his fellow residents had families who helped them out during these years, but he could not take any more money from Uncle Sydney. There was no hope—unless he got the fellowship from the Cartwright Foundation. He would know in the spring.

Poor Laurie, lying up there angry and unhappy. She would get over it by morning. Should he go make up with her? No, that would only lead to trouble, with the powerful physical attraction between them. He had been surprised this afternoon, not suspecting she would be such a passionate woman.

David closed his eyes, wishing Ralph were home. He sure could use some advice on how to deal with women.

Upstairs in the guest room, Lauren tossed restlessly, unable to sleep. She had cried when she got into bed, lamenting how dreadfully the night had turned out. It had been wonderful all through the evening. And in the afternoon, they had been so close, right here on this bed. As close as lovers. They had made love, really, even though they hadn't gone all the way.

She knew now that her mother was wrong about lovemaking. A woman could enjoy it every bit as much as a man, perhaps even more. She had been just as excited as David, just as carried away by his kisses. And when he had caressed her body, touched her the way he had, never had she felt anything like that before. Never had she felt such joy, so full of bliss.

David must be uncomfortable down there on the couch. She hoped he was warm enough. The furnace was off and it was freezing in the house. Perhaps she should take a blanket to him, in case he didn't have enough covers . . . Slipping out of bed, she searched for her robe and slippers in the dark. When she opened her door, there was a dim light from the lamp in the lower hall. Quietly she crept down the stairs.

He was lying on his side asleep, covered with an afghan. Lauren shook out the blanket and laid it over him, smoothing it around his shoulders. He sighed in his sleep, burrowing into the pillows like a contented child.

I love you so much, she whispered under her breath. Kneeling to caress his head, she leaned over to kiss him. He stirred and slowly opened his eyes. "Laurie . . ."

"I'm sorry we quarreled, David. I was such a prig."

Still groggy, David smiled. "It was my fault, honey. I said some stupid things." She shivered involuntarily in the cold. He lifted the covers, holding out his arms. "Come under here with me."

He enveloped her in his warmth, briskly rubbing her arms and back, his touch becoming more gentle and sensuous as their breaths mingled and their lips finally joined.

"You're not at all like other women," he murmured. "I don't know why I said that."

"I acted like a child."

"No, that's the way you were taught to be, the way all respectable girls are brought up."

"If you knew my family, you'd understand me better. My parents—I guess you could say their standards are a little old-fashioned. They've always been obsessed with a fear of scandal. The worst thing I could do would be to disgrace them with disreputable behavior."

"You would never do that, Laurie. I would never expect you to do anything you don't want to."

He kissed her again, and then he began to fondle her until they were both full of desire. When he raised her nightgown, she whispered, "Come upstairs to my bed."

That seemed to break the spell. ''No, darling. I'll take you up, but I won't sleep with you. I want to—Lord, how I want to! But I know you'd regret it tomorrow.''

Together they walked upstairs and Lauren climbed into the cold bed. David sat on the edge, pulling the covers tightly around her, and kissing her good night. When he left, padding down the stairs in his socks, she wondered whether she was relieved or disappointed.

Chapter 18

CHARLOTTE FIELDS PACED the length of the sumptuous living room, nervously dragging on a cigarette. Dark and discontented, her glance lighted on a Fragonard painting—one more example of Adele's insipid taste imposed on her.

"Lord deliver us from mothers!" she muttered, casting her eyes at the ceiling.

Telephone conversations with her own mother often had an abrasive effect on her, and today had been no exception. After rambling on with the usual Randolph Springs gossip, Reba had tendered her oft-repeated petulant request for Charlotte and her husband to visit them.

"I don't understand why you won't come down home, Charlotte Lee. You and Bruce go off to Europe at the drop of a hat."

It just didn't work! Hadn't her mother seen that by now? Bruce was simply not a smalltown type. After one round of golf with Max, he was ready to leave.

"Did Laurie tell you about her new beau?" Reba had asked.

"Not really. I assume you mean the *doctor.*" She was aware that her tone sounded disparaging.

Oblivious, Reba continued, "She's been seeing a lot of him. Of course, *I'm* not supposed to know anything about it. Ruth swore me to secrecy."

"Then, why are you telling *me* about it, Mother?"

"Well, Charlotte Lee, I thought you would be *interested!* You two are so close, I'm surprised she didn't talk about him when she was there. But then, you *know* how peculiar Lauren is about her private life."

"We all like to guard our privacy, Mama! There is nothing *peculiar* about that!"

"Why must you speak to me in that way?" Reba complained in that wounded voice calculated to instill guilt.

But there had been something else . . .

"I hear Joanna's going to have another baby," her mother said, in what she considered her subtle manner. "Four children now."

"Good Lord, she's just like an old brood mare, isn't she!"

"That's unkind, Charlotte Lee. After all, she *is* your first cousin."

"Mama, Joanna is and always has been the least fascinating person I've ever known. How she and Laurie could be sisters is a mystery to me."

"Darling, you always seem so out of sorts lately. Maybe if *you* had a baby, dear . . ."

"Good Lord, Mama, I'm only twenty-one! There's plenty of time for babies. Why can't you leave me alone?" And once again she had ended the conversation by hurting her mother's feelings.

Damn it to hell! Why did everything in her life turn out wrong?

It was three months past her twenty-first birthday, a year and a half since the fairy-tale wedding. She was fabulously wealthy, had every luxury that anyone could possibly desire, and was the envy of every woman she knew. With an exasperated sigh, Charlotte threw herself into a chair, thinking back to the afternoon when she had stood on the deck of the *Normandie,* ready to sail to Europe on her honeymoon . . .

She clung to her new husband's arm as he leaned over the ship's railing to wave. Amid the streamers and confetti, the music and strident farewells on the decks of the *Normandie,* Charlee almost believed she was living a dream.

In the melée, she was jostled by a tall, rather attractive man. "I beg your pardon, ma'am—Well, *hel-lo!* It's Charlotte, isn't it?"

Not wishing to lose sight of Blanche and the Fieldses

in the crowd on the wharf, she smiled, half-turning to see who he was. Somewhere she had known him.

"I'm George Stearns," said the man, raising his voice to be heard above the brass band. "We met in Asheville a few years ago."

"Oh yes, I remember now." She tried to introduce Bruce, but the noise was deafening and he was still distracted by his Princeton buddies who had made it off the ship just as the gangway was being raised. She shrugged helplessly as George mouthed "later" and moved away.

Slowly the ship was pulled from the pier and turned into the harbor. She felt a surge of excitement at the realization that she was leaving the United States for the first time in her life. They stayed on deck past the Statue of Liberty into the Narrows, and as the other passengers began to take shelter from the brisk wind in the Lower Bay, Bruce suggested they go to their stateroom.

The cabin was filled with baskets of fruit, flowers, and candy from friends and clients of the Fields law firm. The steward had already cleared away the glasses and plates from the bon voyage party. Bruce immediately headed for a tray where a new bottle of champagne sat chilling next to a tin of Beluga caviar on ice. Charlotte examined the heavy ivory card on which there was a scrawled message: "Have a toast on me, N." *Nicholas Alexander P. F. de Georgenov* was engraved under an embossed crest.

Bruce was already pouring champagne into two goblets. "Darling," she protested, "you're not going to have another drink now! Please wait until dinner."

"The trouble with you, Charlee, is you don't know how to relax. This is supposed to be a honeymoon, remember?"

She turned away from him, biting back the words that sprang to her lips. *A honeymoon, yes!* And thus far, they might as well not have been married.

On the train it was perhaps understandable. Bruce had drunk too much at the wedding and the motion made him queasy. He had fallen asleep, never waking until the following morning, when Charlee had a headache. But last night in the hotel, she had expected—

"Come on, sweetie, Nicky would be terribly hurt if you didn't help me drink his gift."

"Nicky certainly doesn't worry about offending *us*, does he? I never before heard of a best man not showing up for a wedding."

"Sssh," he soothed, "let's forget about it. He couldn't help being sick." He pressed a glass into her hand.

"Bruce, you know I get headaches from champagne."

"Not from the good stuff you won't, and this is the best. Just one glass."

"All right," she sighed, "but no more than one, promise?"

There was a knock on the door and a steward delivered an envelope on a silver tray. Bruce tore it open. "Ahh!" he said, sounding pleased, "we're invited to dinner at the captain's table. Please tell him we are delighted to accept."

They were the only Jewish couple at the captain's table. Charlotte could tell because Jews did not have names like Van Renssalear and Whittingham. Malcolm's client, Conrad Hutsel, had arranged it, Bruce told her.

George Stearns, who was traveling alone on business, came over to them after dinner and Charlotte made the introductions. "Congratulations," he said, "I read the announcement of your wedding in the *Tribune*. Lovely photograph, Charlotte."

It turned out that he and Bruce knew many friends in common, and although George was considerably older than Bruce, she noticed he treated her new husband with deference. That was when she began to understand just how much the Fields wealth and influence meant.

There was no question that she had made a brilliant marriage, but something was *terribly* wrong. Was it her fault, she wondered. Perhaps she wasn't sexually attractive, or—or Bruce wasn't in love with her, after all.

All the time they were courting and engaged, Bruce had pressured her to go to bed with him. But, raised to believe that nothing was more disgraceful than losing your virginity before marriage, she had resisted, even though she was dying to. So, now that they were married, why didn't he make love to her? What had happened to his ardor?

It must be her fault. There must be something she was supposed to do or say. Oh, *why* had her mother not talked to her about sex? Surely Reba could have been helpful. After all, she had *done* it, she had conceived and given birth! Not a word. Not a blessed syllable of advice or instruction.

Clutching her when she was ready to leave on the wedding trip, choking on her tears, Reba had cried, "My poor baby, my beautiful daughter! Remember, darling, we've all gone through it and men can't help it." Wonderful. Terrific. If only her mother knew how much she was looking forward to having sex! But what was she to do? Each night since they were married, her husband had been either drunk or hung over.

The last night out, Bruce wanted to go back to the stateroom, but Charlotte refused to accompany him. She was tired of his half-hearted, groping advances. As soon as she became aroused, he would roll away from her, groaning and falling asleep. "I'm staying at the party," she told him. "If you want to go to bed, you can go alone." And he had.

Around midnight she went to look in on him, but he was deeply asleep. She turned off the lights and went out on deck. It was a still, balmy night, the sea a placid sheet of silver under a magnificent full moon. From the ballroom she could hear the orchestra playing "Lover Come Back to Me," and suddenly the tears were spilling down her cheeks. She hugged her silk shawl around her shoulders, wishing she were back in Randolph Springs, never having met Bruce Fields.

"Lovely night, isn't it?" It was George Stearns. "I'm sorry if I startled you, Charlotte." He looked at her intently. "Uh-oh, a lover's quarrel. And the honeymoon's just begun."

When she turned her head and did not respond, he apologized. "Forgive me for being flippant, my dear. I'm sure you think it's worth crying over, but believe me, whatever it is, by morning, you'll forget about it. All honeymooners have spats. It takes time to get used to being married."

He handed her his handkerchief. "Thank you," she murmured, wiping her eyes, "I don't believe I've cried since I was a child."

He smiled. "To me, you're still a child. A very beautiful and lovable child, if I may say so."

She glanced up at him. He was a powerful looking man, smooth and assured, but with an underlying roughness. There was a knowing, sexual quality about him.

"Where's your husband?" he asked.

"Gone to bed." He raised one eyebrow. "Passed out, if you must know."

"With a magnificent bride like you? He must be out of his mind." When he saw the expression on her face, he said, "You're not going to cry again?"

She shook her head. Just then someone came out of the ballroom and the strains of the orchestra swelled. George drew her into his arms and began to dance with her in the shadows. He moved slowly and gracefully and she had a faint recollection of having danced with him years before at his home in Asheville. Then she had thought of him as an older man, someone she could never be attracted to. But as he pressed against her she felt his hard, strong body and a surge of excitement ran through her.

George's hand was on her bare back, lightly stroking the skin under her wrap. His lips brushed her forehead, and she raised her face to look at him. For a long moment their eyes held, and then he bent his head to kiss her, and his lips were smooth and soft, suggestive and questioning. With a small sigh, she returned the kiss and he danced her into an alcove where it was quiet and dim. They stood there swaying, kissing, his mouth gently moving on hers.

"Will you come with me?" he murmured, and she nodded her assent, giving one last, regretful thought to the girl she had been, who had saved herself for her bridegroom.

His stateroom was even more luxurious than theirs, with a separate parlor and a large bedroom. He took his time undressing her, pausing to stroke and kiss her, exclaiming with delight at the sight of her body. She was unashamed, finding his touch pleasurable, enjoying the slow, romantic way he stimulated her. When she was lying on the bed, he removed his own clothes quickly but without seeming to hurry, and when she saw his well-formed body and his maleness, she understood how it was meant to be.

He continued to arouse her, in no hurry to satisfy himself, until he discovered that she was still a virgin. "Ah, no . . . ah, dear God, no! You poor kid." And he became even gentler and more tender, and when she thought she could stand no more, she begged him to do it. He went into the bathroom and returned with something he put on himself, like a deflated rubber balloon, and then he pushed inside her and there was no pain, no pain at all. Just a wonderfully mounting flush of warmth that began deep within and spread to her fingertips and toes.

As the marvelous sensation crested, Charlotte discovered she did not have to love a man in order to enjoy sex. In fact . . . she scarcely had to know him at all.

Paris was better for them. With her newly gained insight and assurance, Charlee seduced Bruce in their suite at the George V. It wasn't perfect, but he was able to complete the act.

"Don't let him drink," George had cautioned that night on board ship. "Alcohol is the worst thing for sex. It kills the ability to keep an erection." He had taken hold of her hand to teach her. "For God's sake, Charlotte, look at me! How else will you know what to do?"

"But what if he can't?"

"Patience and understanding, my dear—and perhaps a few little secrets I can show you," he had answered, demonstrating some imaginative techniques. "Too bad young Fields will never know what I've done for him. He'd be forever in my debt." When hours later she had left his quarters to return to her own stateroom, she had been a vastly more experienced woman.

Charlotte was returning from a fitting at Chanel when she thought she caught sight of a familiar face in the lobby of the George V. Something about the way he walked and the angle of his head alerted her, but he was gone before she had really seen him.

Bruce was in the room, just finishing bathing and shaving for the evening. "Hello, darling, how was the fitting?"

"Boring. I detest standing still for so long. I'll never again buy so many outfits at once." She kicked off her shoes and lay on the chaise. "What did you do this afternoon?"

"Nothing much. Just puttered around looking in shop windows and stopped for an aperitif."

"You know, I thought I saw Nicholas de Georgenov down in the lobby just now, but that's ridiculous."

Bruce paused for the briefest moment. "Actually, it isn't. He's here in Paris. I bumped into him this afternoon on the Fauborg-St. Honoré."

She felt a flutter in her breast. "You 'bumped' into him? Just like that?"

"Yes, well, it happens often to Americans in Paris. We all seem to haunt the same places." He began to whistle a tune under his breath. "You'd better start your bath. We have cocktails with the Dohrmans in an hour."

A few moments ago, she had been happy, deeply in love with her husband, thinking how promising the marriage now looked. Suddenly, that nagging anxiety had returned. She dared not even consider what might have happened to change it.

Two months later near the end of their tour, they were in Monte Carlo. Charlotte suggested a scenic ride along the Riviera to Toulon, but Bruce had been there before and said it was a bore. He liked the casino, but Charlee hated gambling. It made her nervous to see Bruce's excitement when he played baccarat or roulette. To add to her displeasure, Nicholas had shown up in Monaco and she was tired of having to share Bruce's company with him. They actually quarreled about the trip, and finally Bruce arranged for her to go along with the Dohrmans, the American couple they kept meeting who were friends of his parents. Charlotte took a suitcase, for they were to stay overnight.

The drive along the Corniche was wild, and Charlee thought their chauffeur a madman. They had gone as far as St. Tropez, where they stopped for a late lunch, when she told the Dohrmans she had changed her mind and was going back. They put up a fuss, but she hired a taxi and they reluctantly went on their way, uneasy at leaving her. Before her driver had gone half a mile, they developed motor trouble, and by the time she found another car and reached Monaco, the sun was setting behind Mt. Agel.

She let herself into their suite, surprised to see the rooms unlighted in the dusk. Perhaps Bruce was napping, she thought, not turning on a lamp. Tiptoeing to the bedroom, she noticed a faint sweetish odor she could not immediately identify. She had no time to think what it might be, for she stopped suddenly, catching sight of her husband standing in front of the mirrored wardrobe, admiring himself. He was entirely naked, except for the pale blue silk peignoir he had bought for her in Paris. It was fashioned like a cape and quite sheer, with panels of handmade ecru lace going around the neck and bordering each side. He wore it carelessly, so that the front fell open, exposing his body.

Charlotte's hands flew to her mouth to stifle her gasp, but Bruce heard her and turned his head. He was smiling, a curious rapt smile, as he put down a glass of champagne and held out his arms to her. Her heart was pounding and she thought she might not be able to catch her breath.

"I'm glad you came back, darling," said Bruce in a dreamlike voice. "Come . . . come over here to me. Can't you see how I want you?"

In a trance she moved toward him. The elusive aroma was slightly stronger in here. The room was in shadows, except for a shaft of fading daylight from the open curtains.

"Why are you wearing that?" she whispered.

"Just a whim," he said, shrugging off the negligee and tossing it aside. He kissed her and began to undo the buttons of her linen frock. "Come, lie here with me."

He pulled her down on a satin comforter that had been spread on the floor in front of the mirrors. A dark dread hovered over her, like great gauzy bat wings, bearing down, suffocating, terrifying.

As if he were performing a ballet, Bruce made love to her, kneeling over her, artfully bending to kiss her lips, her closed eyelids, her throat and breasts. His tongue trailed over her flanks and thighs, to the soft, tender place within. Gradually her pulse changed from the beat of panic to the beat of desire. She was suffused with her need for him, conscious only that he was at last as full of love as she.

In the growing darkness, her eyes fluttered open. Bruce's head was thrown back as he thrust himself deeper inside her in the act of love. Poised above her, he was transported with passion . . . but his eyes were fixed beyond her, watching himself in the mirror. He glanced down then and smiled, that odd half-smile again.

She closed her eyes, turning her head into the folds of the quilt. As she felt the beginning of her climax, she breathed deeply the traces of a familiar scent, exotic and spicy. Not hers . . . not Bruce's. But she knew what it was now.

It was the sandalwood cologne that Nicholas always wore.

Chapter 19

LAUREN LEFT HER advisor's office, immensely pleased to learn that she would be graduating in June. Crossing the campus on her way back to her dorm, she ran into Shirley Winkler.

"Did you go out with David Bernard on New Year's Eve?" the young woman demanded without ceremony.

Lauren regarded her coldly, "I don't think that's anyone's business except mine."

"I *warned* you he was my cousin Susie's beau, and you made up your mind then to *take him away* from her!"

"That's preposterous! I don't even *know* your cousin. Why would I want to take anyone away from her?"

"You shouldn't have gone out with him after I told you about them. Nice girls don't date someone else's boyfriend."

"Shirley . . . if David were really Susie's boyfriend, why would he ask me out? He's the one who invites me, not the other way around."

Lauren dismissed the unpleasant incident as unimportant. During the remaining winter months she concentrated on her studies, for she was determined to graduate with honors. Except for her dates with David, she had few outside interests. Benson had dropped out of sight after she discouraged his attentions, but Peter Wise telephoned every week from New York and in several letters he urged her to apply to Columbia for the masters program in English. But Lauren had no desire to go to New York and in any case, she doubted that her father would permit it.

She had filled out the application for the University of

North Carolina, but she began having some doubts about her plans. Would David think she was pursuing him if she came to Chapel Hill next year? They had been going out for five months, but he had never mentioned marriage.

Her love for him had grown steadily from that first afternoon she had danced with him, until a future without David Bernard seemed bleak. Each time they were together and he embraced her, she struggled not to tell him how much she cared for him, fighting not to give in to her desire. The erotic feelings David had aroused in her on New Year's Eve continued to enflame her, but she had almost made a grave mistake that night. She was determined it must never happen again. Not until they were married.

As the weather turned warmer, the Carolina countryside was glorious with azaleas, rhododendrons, and laurels coming into bloom. When David had time off on the weekends, they went riding or hiking, and if Philip came to Greensboro to visit Jeanette, they often joined them for picnics. Phil and David got along well, but Lauren was reluctant to dwell on matters of the heart with her brother these days. There was too much of a parallel between them. Jeanette was plainly in love with Philip, but he had not yet proposed marriage. How Lauren envied men the prerogative of declaring their feelings!

In a few days it would be time for spring vacation, and then only two months remained until graduation. Lauren was hard at work writing the mid-term paper for her Shakespeare course when David called. "If I come to Greensboro tomorrow night, will you have dinner with me? There's something I want to tell you."

"How important is it?" she asked. "I have an exam the next day."

"I guess it can wait."

Something in his voice made her say, "I know the material and I have all day tomorrow to study."

"Are you sure?" he said, but she could tell he was relieved that she would see him.

All through dinner, David seemed edgy; however when

she asked him what he wanted to tell her, he just smiled and said, "We'll talk about it later."

"Can't you give me a hint?" she teased.

"It has to do with my residency," he answered, but would say no more.

She hadn't expected his news to be about work. She tried to imagine what it could be. Her heart fluttered as she thought, What if he's going away? David was always talking about wanting to take surgical training at Hopkins or the University of Pennsylvania. Her curiosity gave way to apprehension and she wondered why she always expected the worst. Like the Ancient Mariner, she walked in fear and dread of something that might never happen. Was she becoming like her mother, who worried constantly about health and death and danger?

After dinner, David drove to a nearby park and stopped the car by the side of a lake. It was balmy, with a high sliver of moon in the night sky. Through the open windows, the freshness of the season came to them, green, fragrant, and full of promise. David was silent, looking out across the water; then he turned to her. "I got the fellowship," he said. "The dean called me yesterday."

"David, that's wonderful! Congratulations. I'm really pleased for you." So that was what he wanted to tell her. It was very good news, but why the mystery?

He looked at her, his eyes full of emotion. "I didn't realize until now how much I was counting on it. It was the only way we could—" He lifted her chin and kissed her, his lips lingering. Stroking her hair, he said, "I wasn't going to talk about marriage, Lauren. With years of residency ahead of me and a pile of debts, I can't even support a wife properly. But I love you so much, and I don't want to lose you."

Tears of joy and relief stung her eyes as she clasped her arms around his neck. "None of that matters to me, David. We'll manage, darling, I can get a job. I love you . . . Oh, how I love you!"

He brought a small box out of his pocket. "This was my Aunt Ethel's," he said, showing her a ring with three rose-cut diamonds, the center one a little larger than the others. "I told Uncle Sydney about you when I went to visit him last month. I had no idea he'd kept this for me." Her heart contracted as he smiled at her uncertainly. "I had it cleaned and reset—I hope you like it." Lauren's hand was trembling as he slipped the ring on her finger.

"It's perfect, David, I adore it! I didn't expect to have an engagement ring, darling."

"Someday, I'll give you all the beautiful things you deserve, my love," he whispered.

"As long as I have you, that's all I'll ever want or need."

Charlotte called the moment she heard. *"Laurie!"* she shrieked. Grinning, Lauren held the receiver away from her ear. "You sly boots, you never said a word!"

"I was afraid to, Charlee. I knew I was in love with David, but we'd only known each other since October and honestly, I had no idea how he felt about me. It's all been kind of a dream."

"Peter Wise will be *devastated.* I saw him just the other night and he said he was going down to see you soon."

"Oh no! I'd better drop him a note." She had never answered Peter's last letter.

"What are your plans for the wedding?" asked Charlotte.

"Nothing yet, except the date, but I want you to be my matron of honor. It's the first Sunday in June, the fifth. That doesn't leave a lot of time after graduation, but there won't be much to do. We want to keep it simple."

"In our family, my dear, there is no such thing as a simple wedding."

Lauren let her happiness wash over her, not caring about anything else. David came to Randolph Springs to meet her parents and for the formal announcement of their engagement. Miriam and Samuel warmed to him immediately, and it was obvious he felt affectionate and at ease with them. When Samuel learned that David's only relative was Uncle Sydney, living alone in his men's club in

Wilmington, he called to invite him to Randolph, but the old man said he was unable to make the trip alone.

"I'll bring Lauren to meet you in two weeks," David promised his uncle. "He sounds much more feeble than he did in February," he told her in a worried voice after they hung up.

It was the beginning of Passover, and all the close relatives were expected at Aunt Reba's for the seder. In years past, Miriam had always invited the family for the Jewish holidays, while Reba had presided on all other occasions. Since Samuel's illness, however, Reba had completely taken over the role of family hostess. Samuel grumbled that Max had made the seder into a secular feast, but Miriam was relieved to be rid of the responsibility and Samuel was still accorded the honor of conducting the ritual.

Miriam supervised the making of the gefilte fish, matzoh balls, and sponge cakes ahead of time in her own kitchen. Lauren and David delivered them to the big house on Shadow Mountain Drive on the morning of the seder. Lauren thought it would give them a chance to have a visit with Reba and Max before David had to face the entire family.

She could tell Max liked David immediately. This was his kind of man—just Southern enough, and not too "Jewish." Reba appeared surprised and approving, threatening to get carried away with her enthusiasm. "Of course, Laurie darling, you'll have the wedding right here in the garden, just like Charlotte Lee! And you'll wear her wedding gown. That's such a *nice* sentiment, don't you think? It can be taken up with a French tuck without damaging the lace. Oh, you'll make a *beautiful* bride!"

There did not seem to be a choice. Lauren prickled at the familiar closed-in feeling, but she decided she was being foolish. Reba was loving and generous and it was a perfect solution for the wedding. Her own family's house and garden were suitable for only a small number of people, whereas all the relatives and friends would fit comfortably at the house on Shadow Mountain. They did not want a lavish affair, though, and she made certain Reba understood that.

There was little to plan, other than ordering the invitations and going to the dressmaker for alterations on the gown. Charlee and Jeanette would be her only attendants, since Joanna was in the advanced stages of pregnancy. David had asked Philip and Lionel to be his ushers, as well as Ralph Nelson and Tony Stroud. Stanley Eisen, who had just become engaged to Elaine, was best man. Stan offered to travel with Uncle Sydney from Wilmington, and all of David's friends from Durham and Chapel Hill would be coming. Lauren's own family was so vast that it seemed strange and sad to her that David had no other relatives to invite to his wedding.

Lauren returned for her last weeks of college, happy in the knowledge she would soon be Mrs. David Bernard. "I hope you and Phil—" she almost said when Jeanette embraced her, but bit the words off before she had spoken. Whatever it was that prevented Philip from asking Jeanette to marry him, was between the two of them. All of the other girls at school were excited about Lauren's engagement, exclaiming over her ring, and eager to hear her wedding plans. Even Shirley Winkler offered her best wishes.

They wanted to find a place to live in Chapel Hill so that Lauren could take courses toward her masters and find a part-time job at the university, while David would start his new Russell Clinic residency in orthopedics at Strickland on the first of July.

Apartments were scarce in Chapel Hill and were often passed along by word of mouth. David had been consulting the listings at the university's housing office and he called to report he had seen a nice sunny two-bedroom in an old frame house on West Rosemary Street. It belonged to a widow who lived on the ground floor, and had been rented for the past two years to a graduate student and his wife.

The next Friday afternoon, she met David in Chapel Hill and he took her to see the apartment. "The rent is forty dollars a month, Laurie, but I think it's worth it," he told her on their way over. Lauren did some quick mental calculations and estimated that too much of David's total compensation as a resident would be used for rent if they took this apartment. She might have to get a real job, not a low-paying, part-time position.

The gray-haired woman who opened the door was from an old Chapel Hill family that had fallen on hard times. All she had left was her house and her dignity. Forced to share the former with others, she refused to sacrifice a drop of the latter. "Good afternoon, Dr. Bernard. Please come in."

"Thank you, Mrs. Hilton. This is my fiancée, Miss Jacobson."

Mrs. Hilton eyed Lauren speculatively, acknowledging Lauren's courteous greeting with a curt nod. "I'll show you the rooms," she said in a cold voice.

"I'm afraid I won't be able to stay, Mrs. Hilton," David interrupted. "I have to go back to the hospital, but I'm sure you and Lauren will get along just fine. The decision is hers, since I've already seen the apartment."

Lauren walked out on the porch with David. "She seems kind of unfriendly, doesn't she?"

"Yeah, I noticed that," he answered in a puzzled tone. "Funny, she was just fine when I was here before."

"Maybe she likes men better than women."

"She can't help but love you," he said, giving her a hug. "See you later at the Nelsons'."

The apartment was ideal. It was a floor-through with a large, airy living room and dining alcove, an eat-in kitchen, two bedrooms and a bath. There was a separate stairway entrance from the side of the building and a large screened porch in the rear overlooking a garden. Beyond, through the trees, one could see rolling fields and farmland.

"It's a lovely apartment, Mrs. Hilton. I'm sure we would be happy living here."

"The rent is fifty dollars a month," said Mrs. Hilton, drawing her mouth into a tight little pucker.

"Oh—but David said it was forty."

"That's what the last tenants paid. I'm entitled to an increase," she replied, setting her face in a determined manner. "I thought it over and I must get fifty."

"I'm afraid we can't afford that. A resident doesn't make

much money, Mrs. Hilton. Can we sit down for a moment to discuss it?''

''I'm particular who lives up there, being in the same house and all,'' said Mrs. Hilton as they walked downstairs.

''I can assure you, we'll be excellent tenants. We expect to lead a quiet life.'' What was bothering the woman? She had definitely agreed on the rent with David. ''Is it something else, Mrs. Hilton?'' Lauren asked when they were seated in the parlor.

The landlady was looking out the window, her attention seemingly absorbed. She lifted her chin, her eyes still turned away from Lauren. ''Jacobson—is that a Hebrew name?'' she asked.

Taken aback, Lauren did not answer immediately. Why should she have been surprised? It wasn't her first experience with anti-Semitism. She had seen prejudice all her life, but somehow she had not expected it in this idyllic academic village, nor in this form. She regarded Mrs. Hilton, taking in the shabby shoes and threadbare cardigan. ''That's not a question the university housing office would approve of, is it? But as it happens, the answer is yes. Both Dr. Bernard and I are Jewish.'' She picked up her purse and headed for the door.

''Wait!'' Biting her lower lip, the landlady hurried after Lauren. ''Miss Jacobson,'' she said breathlessly, ''there—there's no need to take offense. Some folks won't rent to you people, but I have nothing against the Hebrews. After all, they're the People of the Book. I'm bound to believe y'all are the Chosen.''

Lord deliver us! How badly do we want this apartment? ''I'll have to discuss it with David, Mrs. Hilton.''

As she went down the brick walk, she turned back. The old woman was standing in the doorway looking after her, an expression of utter dejection on her face. Why should I feel sorry for her, thought Lauren. ''If we were to take it, what would the rent be?'' she asked.

''Forty,'' the woman replied in a barely audible voice.

''I think you are entitled to an increase,'' said Lauren.

"Would forty-two be satisfactory—that is, if we decide to rent the apartment?"

After stopping on Franklin Street to buy tulips from the flower ladies, Lauren walked slowly across the campus, feeling that some of the brightness had gone out of the day.

"Maybe we should reconsider," David said that night when she told him what had occurred. "At least Durham is a city with a Jewish community and a synagogue. All they have in Chapel Hill is the university."

"Which is exactly what we like about it. I'm sure Mrs. Hilton's not typical of Chapel Hill. There must be other apartments, David."

"There's one building and everything is taken. The best housing is owned by the university and I'm not eligible for it. We'll just have to keep looking."

"I really don't want any other apartment," Lauren said in a small voice. "It's so perfect for us, David . . ."

The next day they signed a lease and gave Mrs. Hilton a deposit. "Poor old soul, she was so relieved. You could just see it in her eyes," said Lauren when they were driving to Durham to have dinner with the Strouds.

"Poor old soul! If you hadn't fallen in love with her damned apartment, I'd tell her to shove it."

"I think she regrets what she said. Maybe she'll learn to love 'Hebrews' after she sees what nice people we are!"

"I doubt it. It's been my experience, that bigots are unredeemable."

One of Lauren's first acts when she returned to Greensboro after she became engaged was to call Ruth and make a date for the Felders to meet David. Although Ruth had already seen him with Susan Winkler at their friends' wedding, no one referred to that meeting. Lauren suspected Ruth had been feeling slighted, thinking she should have been the first in the family to get to know her fiancé since the romance had developed right under her nose, but Lauren had been determined not to take David there until her parents had met him.

"He's just *precious*, Laurie," Ruth said, as she fluttered

around the pantry after dinner preparing a fruit bowl to accompany the coffee tray. Of all the words Lauren would have chosen to describe David, "precious" would not have been among them.

"Everyone in the family has fallen in love with you, darling," she told David, when he was driving her back to the dorm.

"How many more cousins do you have?" groaned David.

"Dozens," she laughed. "But there's only one who's really important to me. I simply can't *wait* for you to meet Charlee!"

Chapter 20

Randolph Springs, June 1938

STANDING BEHIND THE screen, Charlee observed the handsome, broad-shouldered young man who bent to kiss her mother on the front steps.

His smile caused her a pang of envious admiration. She remembered how she had reacted the first time she had seen Bruce on the patio of his parents' home, how she had made up her mind immediately to get him, to dazzle him until he wanted her. In those days it had been a game, the challenge of attracting an exciting new man. She wondered whether she could still do it . . . Squaring her shoulders, Charlotte lifted her head and strode out across the veranda with the old slant-hipped panache, her lips parted in breathless surprise, the arched brows raised in that wide-eyed, stop-'em-in-their-tracks esprit.

"And this is the one I've been dying for you to meet, darling," said Lauren. "My cousin and dearest friend, Charlotte Lee. I just know you two are going to love each other."

Charlee extended her hand, gazing directly into his eyes for a long moment. Her shimmering smile lit the air between them as her alluring gardenia perfume rose in David's nostrils. For an instant he remained rooted, his lips parted in wonder. Quickly recovering himself, he took her hand, "Lauren's told me so much about you, Charlotte."

"I should kiss my new cousin hello," she said in her low, breathy voice, as she touched her lips to his cheek. Observing the firm jaw sag a little and the answering light in his eyes, Charlee smiled to herself. If Lauren noticed, filled with love and pride in her prospective husband, she paid no attention.

Despite Lauren's protestations, the week was filled with festivities. They were fully occupied with a plethora of luncheons, showers, teas, buffet suppers, and the rehearsal dinner for the family and out-of-town guests, to be held at the Shadow Mountain Club the night before the wedding.

The wedding gifts were spread out on a large table in the music room. Lauren thought it vulgar to display their presents, even if as Reba insisted, it was an old Southern custom. She closed the double doors every time she went by, while Reba kept opening them. Among the china, silver, crystal and linens they had received was a set of cordial glasses from Benson Miller. "Lifelong happiness to you both," was written on his card. Benson had been invited to the wedding, because of course, he had to be, but he had declined, saying he would be away. Lauren was sorry when Philip told her the news of her engagement had been hard on Ben.

The day before the wedding, Reba insisted Lauren come over one last time to try on Charlotte's gown, which had been altered to fit her. "The dress has to be taken in a little more, Laurie. You've lost weight from all this excitement."

"It seems so much trouble for such a little amount, Aunt Reba. No one will notice."

But Reba was adamant. "*I'll* notice, and that's sufficient. We'll just go down to Miss Odile and she'll have it done in no time."

"Will you come, Charlee?"

Charlotte was lying on the bed with a cold cloth on her head. "Not I! I've got the most dreadful headache. All that champagne last night."

"Where's Bruce?"

"He went to the club to play nine holes with Daddy. They asked David, but he didn't feel like golf."

"Poor darling, I think he must be bored out of his mind. He's so used to his medical friends."

"Doctors don't play golf?"

"His kind of doctor doesn't do much of anything except work."

"Talk about boring. Ohh . . ." she groaned, "maybe he can cure my headache."

"We'll see you later, darling," said Reba, taking the gown in its linen bag. "Come along, Lauren."

On the way out, they found David sitting on the side veranda. Reba rushed into the car, holding the dress as if he could see through the clothing bag.

"I'm going to the dressmaker, David. Charlee's lying down upstairs with a headache."

"How long will you be?"

"About an hour, maybe a little longer. Aunt Reba has a couple of errands. What will you do?"

"I might take a walk up the drive. How far does it go?"

"All the way up to Mountain View, the Randolph family estate at the summit. There's a beautiful view from the overlook. Use the footpath. It's easy to find if you go out the back gate."

David waved as the car drove around the circle and down the sloping driveway. He walked behind the house where he saw a gardener at work. "Can you direct me to the footpath that goes up Shadow Mountain?" he called.

The man stopped hoeing. "Yessuh. Just beyond to the left, behind the rose garden. There's a gate and you just follow your nose."

"Thank you."

In an upstairs window, a curtain dropped in place. Charlotte slipped on her shoes and bent to check her hair in the looking glass. Grabbing a silk scarf from the dresser, she ran down the back stairs.

David stopped at a fountain to drink the cold spring water. Tomorrow at this time, he would be preparing for his wedding.

He sure would be glad when all this was over. The Randolph Springs family was rather overpowering. Not the Jacobsons; Miriam and Samuel were good solid people, and he liked Philip and Lionel. But the Mortimers were a breed apart. Max was one of those Southern men he could never quite figure out—snobbish, assured, acting like the old family plantation was just a few years in his past. In Reba he saw a soft fluff of a woman with a hard inner core. The sugary voice was enough to slay you, but he was willing to bet she was one tough cookie underneath.

And Charlotte. Talk about surprises! Despite what he had heard, and all that Lauren had told him about her cousin, nothing had prepared him for her staggering beauty . . . or her sheer sex appeal. He could have sworn she came on to him in the split second when they first met, yet that was absurd! He must have been hallucinating. Why would Charlotte, who was the bride's cousin and best friend, try to attract the man who was going to marry Lauren? It made no sense at all and it must have been that *he* was attracted to *her,* not the other way around.

It had bothered him so much that he had thought of nothing else last night when he was unable to sleep, imagining her two doors away in her husband's arms. No chance that she would flirt with him when she was married to Bruce Fields. Bruce was the sort of fellow every guy envied at college, who has women falling all over him.

After the party last night, when Lauren had gone home with her parents, they had sat around the sun parlor playing cribbage and listening to records. Charlotte had been all over Bruce, leaning against him from behind, putting her arms around him and kissing his neck. It didn't seem to affect Bruce much, but it had nearly driven David from the table. He had actually become horny, watching her stroke her husband and listening to her rich, intimate laugh. They had climbed the stairs together at the end of the evening, pausing with their arms around each other to say good night to him at the door to their room. In his own bed, he had envisioned those two beautiful bodies down the hall, making stupendous love.

This is absolutely crazy! I am going nuts with bridegroom jitters. I should be thinking about making love to *Lauren*, not Charlee. And tomorrow night I will. One more night and I'll be a married man.

Lauren had said this was an easy walk, but he was

winded. These mountain people seemed to think nothing of hiking uphill for miles. Lauren told him that she and Charlee had gone on climbing expeditions with their friends almost every weekend when they were younger. A sign pointed to a lookout eight hundred feet ahead. There were two paths; the one to the right looked less challenging.

David rounded a corner and beheld a needle-shaped promontory jutting out at the end of a rocky cliff. His breath caught as he realized a woman was sitting on the tip, her feet dangling over the sheer drop. It was Charlotte.

She sat suspended above the world, leaning forward on her hands, her long slim legs crossed at the ankles, swinging gently. Her profile and the line of her throat were pure. He stood watching her for several seconds, not saying anything, until she slowly turned and smiled at him, as if she had been waiting. "Come see the hawks," she said in a low voice, extending her hand.

He climbed out on the narrow ledge, amazed at her daring. "Do you like the thrill of danger?" he asked, only half in jest.

She grinned and he noticed again that shimmering tremulousness, and the way her eyes crinkled at the corners. "It used to scare Laurie to death when we were kids."

"You enjoy that, don't you, frightening Lauren?"

She did not answer, but pointed to a lone tree trunk projecting from a craggy shelf below them. A family of chicken hawks had made it their home, the large, somewhat untidy nest filling a hollow in the tree. Six fledglings, their outsize beaks open and squawking for nourishment, crowded one another in the nest while the mother hawk made regular food forays to a meadow far below.

"That nest has been there for years," said Charlee. "Like a family house."

"How do you know it's the same nest?"

She looked directly at him, the dark pupils huge in her hazel eyes. "Because if I were a bird, I'd be one of them. Hawks are unsociable. They don't travel in flocks, and they prey on their own kind."

He laughed uneasily. There was barely room for the two

of them on the ledge. David balanced himself on one hand, placing it behind her.

She stretched her arms and lifted her face to the sky. "I love it here. Sometimes I wish I could come back and never leave."

He glanced down at her. For one long breathless moment their eyes clung together and they moved imperceptibly closer. If Charlotte had not closed her eyes and turned away, he feared that he might have taken her in his arms and kissed her.

"Come on," she said, pushing herself backward and standing. "I'll show you a short cut home."

The next twenty-four hours passed in a haze for David. The rehearsal dinner that evening at the Shadow Mountain Club, the interminable sleepless night, breakfast on the terrace to the sound of morning larks with smiling blacks serving coffee and hot pastries. And finally, his best man, Stanley, helping him with his studs and cuff links as he prepared himself to marry Lauren Jacobson.

Standing under the twin magnolia trees that formed a canopy, he watched Charlotte Fields walk toward him along the white carpet, followed by his bride on her father's arm.

"May your marriage be as beautiful as you are today," said Charlee, gazing at Lauren's reflection in the wardrobe glass. She unfastened the tiny buttons of the magnificent dress she had worn at her own wedding three years before.

"Thank you for saying that, Char. I know we're going to be as happy as you and Bruce." Lauren turned to embrace her cousin, glad that her old sweet Charlee was there in the room with her. The marital problems that had been evident when she visited them in New York seemed to have disappeared. Charlotte and Bruce had behaved like starstruck lovers, dancing at the wedding.

Charlotte lowered her eyes, bending to help Lauren step out of the bridal gown. "Tiffany's will ship the extra coffee spoons as soon as they're monogrammed," she said, reaching for a padded silk hanger.

"Charlee, you're outrageously generous, giving us our entire silver service!"

"I wish I could give you *everything,* Laurie. You've always been the person I've loved most in the world."

Lauren's eyes misted and she touched Charlotte's cheek, unable to speak, but they had never needed words to express their devotion for each other.

"I promised myself not to be maudlin today," Charlee laughed, wiping her eyes. "Here, let me help you with the dress." She slipped the blue linen frock to Lauren's going away outfit over her head. "Will your apartment be ready when you get back to Chapel Hill?"

"Yes, but I do wish we had a little longer to get used to each other before David's residency begins." For their wedding trip, they were taking a leisurely drive to Cape Lookout in the gray Chevrolet sedan that was Reba's and Max's wedding gift. David had always loved the Outer Banks and wanted to show the coastal area to Lauren, who had never been there. "It isn't as glamorous as your honeymoon, but we'll have to save Europe for the future."

"American beds are more comfortable anyway," said Charlee blithely, "and that's where you'll be spending most of your time. Touring is wasted on honeymooners."

Lauren was aware of a rush of heat to her cheeks. She was married now, and yet, despite her deep love for David and their attraction for each other, she felt ridiculously unprepared for her wedding night. Her mother, of course, had been no help. "Don't get pregnant right away," was all the advice Miriam had offered.

It had been ages since she and Charlotte had exchanged confidences, and there was no one to whom she felt closer. "Is it really wonderful making love, Charlee?" she asked, laying the silver-backed brush on the dressing table.

Half reclining with her long slim legs thrown over the arm of a chaise longue, Charlotte lifted her face toward the ceiling. "Glorious, darling . . . absolute heaven."

"I'm a little—well, unsure, truthfully. I know it's silly, but I'm not certain I know what *I'm* supposed to do. I mean, besides the obvious." She laughed self-consciously.

"For God's sakes, Laurie, David's a doctor. He'll know *everything.*"

"I suppose so. But isn't the woman supposed to know how to do certain things . . . I mean, it's not really all up to the man, is it?"

Charlee sprang from the chaise. "I assure you, it all comes naturally," she said, giving Lauren a hug. "You'll be fine, sugar. Just lie back and enjoy it—or, as Queen Victoria is supposed to have said, Think of England."

Charlee could always make her laugh. "You nut! I've never been to England."

"Well then—think of *me!*" She grinned, handing Lauren the spray of lilies and trailing stephanotis. "Come on, love. All those unmarried maidens are dying to catch the bride's bouquet."

The two cousins descended the circular staircase to the front hall where David and the wedding guests were waiting. Amidst squeals of laughter and outstretched hands, Lauren tossed her bouquet to Jeanette. Quickly she embraced Reba, Max, and her parents, and then she and David, pelted with rose petals and rice, made a run for the ribbon-festooned automobile.

A chorus of good-byes sounded as they turned to wave to everyone assembled on the lawn. Their last impression was of Charlotte and Bruce standing with arms entwined, smiling and blowing kisses, madly in love, as anyone could see.

"We made it!" exulted David, putting his arm around Lauren when they had rolled out the driveway and turned onto the winding, woodsy road.

"You held up beautifully, darling." She picked grains of rice from his lapel. "I wasn't sure you'd get through the week."

"There were moments," he agreed, "but it wasn't so bad."

"I thought it was a beautiful wedding."

"Especially the bride." He pulled over and stopped, taking her in his arms. "I don't want to drive another foot without kissing you and telling you how much I love you, Mrs. Bernard."

And then she knew it would be all right.

* * *

Lauren slept in David's arms, blissfully unaware of her new husband's unrest.

He had known Lauren would be inexperienced. She was a virgin and naturally reticent—in fact, he found her somewhat old-fashioned innocence one of her most endearing qualities. Except for that one wildly abandoned New Year's Eve, she had imposed strict limits to their premarital loving, and he had respected her all the more, realizing that he wanted his bride to be a virgin. Once they were married, he had been certain it would be fine, for there was such an intense physical attraction between them, waiting to be unleashed.

Despite the heated interludes of kissing and petting during their courtship, he had expected her to be shy on her wedding night, and he had been prepared to be patient. When Lauren emerged from the bathroom in a white bridal nightgown and matching negligee, he had taken her into his arms to kiss her, but she had freed herself from his embrace.

"Would you like some champagne?" he asked, pouring two glasses from the bottle sent by Charlotte and Bruce. He watched her sip the sparkling wine, her eyes avoiding his.

"Look, Laurie," he took her hand and kissed it. "We have all the time in the world. I promise I won't rush you." He put his arms around her and looked into her eyes. "Darling, what's wrong? Hey, this isn't my girl. Aren't you happy?"

"Oh yes, David, I couldn't be happier—it's not that at all. I honestly don't know what's gotten into me." She attempted a little laugh. "Bridal nerves, I guess."

He took the wine glass from her and put it on the table. "Don't worry, honey. Just come to bed and relax. There's nothing for you to be afraid of, I promise."

He held his desire in check, kissing her for the longest time, gently caressing her neck and back, softly stroking her breasts and finally her hips and thighs. Gradually he felt her grow less tense. She responded passionately to his kisses, just as she always had, and when she let him slip the gown off, she pressed her body against his. As he ran his hands over her silky skin, he could tell that she had become fully aroused.

After what seemed like hours, he could stand it no longer. "I can't wait—I've got to, Laurie," he cried. "Oh, darling . . ." He thrust into her and felt her push toward him in response, but then suddenly she lay still with her arms around him. Once he heard her gasp. "Am I hurting you?" he asked, trying to gentle his motions.

"No, no . . . it's fine," she whispered. Her breathing became ragged and uneven while her hands made feathery little beating motions against his back. He closed his eyes and lost himself in the sensations of love.

When it was over, she asked hesitantly, "Was it . . . all right?"

"Oh, yes," he told her. "It was wonderful."

He kissed her and held her to his heart, awash in a soft contentment. All the while, he longed for a storm of passion, a tempest.

Chapter 21

Chapel Hill, March 1939

LAUREN WAS OUT of breath by the time she reached the second floor apartment and deposited the heavy bag of groceries on the kitchen counter. She had stopped to shop on her way home from work, knowing that David would be tired and hungry when he finished at the hospital.

Dinner was always special, the table set with their second-best china and sterling silver. With few weekends off and only an occasional night during the week, their evenings were important to them. David loved his work, but the hours were ungodly and the pay criminal. Lauren's salary from her job in the Bull's Head Bookshop supported them, since every spare penny went to reduce his loan at the Carolina Trust.

Lauren put the groceries away, then kicked off her shoes and lay on the couch, thinking she should really spend the next hour drafting the term paper for her Chaucer course. But she had no energy this afternoon. She placed a hand on her swollen abdomen, reflecting that the baby's arrival would bring to a halt her plans to complete her master's degree and go on for a doctorate in English literature—at least for the immediate future. Just as Gretchen Nelson had once warned.

The pregnancy had not been planned. They would both have preferred to wait another year or two before having a child. Nevertheless they were excited, especially David, even though he was worried about money.

The obstetrician, a full-time professor at Duke, had said

Lauren could stay at her job as long as she felt well. But once the baby was born, her income would stop. *Unless* she could hire someone to take care of the child so that she could continue to work. The woman who did their cleaning and laundry was not reliable enough, however Lauren was certain she could find the right person. David would object, but she intended to convince him.

Lauren fell asleep on the couch, awakening when David let himself in. "Hello, darling," she pushed herself up. "I must have drifted off. I haven't even started dinner."

Sitting on the couch, he put his arms around her, and kissed her. "That's all right," he said, "dinner can wait."

She took his hand and placed it against her belly. "He's kicking!" Smiling at the delight on David's face, she said, "I don't know why I say 'he'—it might be a girl. Why isn't there a neuter pronoun?"

"There is. *It.*"

"That sounds so—so inanimate. This child is anything but that."

He began to kiss her again, and immediately his kisses became deep and demanding. His hands moved over her breasts and down to her hips. He was always easily aroused when he came home after being away from her for a night. "You're so beautiful when you're pregnant," he murmured.

His words made her self-conscious, but she returned his kisses ardently. More than ever she was in love with him, truly and wildly in love, as she had never thought it possible to be. She waited eagerly for him to make love to her, but after nine months of marriage, she still—foolishly, she knew—had a reticence with him. Part of it was that David prized her refinement. "You have such elegance, Laurie," he had said recently when she was dressing to go out. "I'm always so proud of you. My Aunt Ethel would have said I married a real lady."

Sometimes when they were making love, she ached to express the need that came over her, to ask him to slow down, to wait for her . . . to teach her. How she wished she could articulate what she felt, knowing there must be ways she could please him, but afraid he would be shocked, or consider her unladylike, if she did some of the things that she had an impulse to do.

David smelled so clean and masculine, his shaving cream blended with the faintest odor of surgical scrub and anesthesia. She sensed her body responding to him, the warmth spreading. Caressing his neck and shoulders, her hands moved down to stroke his back, and she felt him harden against her. "Let's go to bed," he whispered, and she followed him to the bedroom.

An urgent, passionate lover, he was especially tender with her because of the pregnancy. Lauren closed her eyes, feeling the pleasure sweep over her and mount, wanting to cry *Wait for me, wait!* until David entered her body and found satisfaction there.

"Wonderful," he gasped, "I love you, Lauren."

"I love you, darling," she echoed, wishing she could get closer to the ecstasy that remained always just beyond her reach.

Amanda Baker was the first person to answer the newspaper advertisement. Lauren made an appointment to see her at the apartment on an evening when David was on call. Amanda's friendly, energetic personality impressed Lauren. She had a warm, round, smiling black face and she spoke in a lovely, well-modulated voice.

"I can't help admiring your perfect diction," Lauren commented.

"My father is a minister, Mrs. Bernard, and he always insisted on proper speech." Her husband was away from home much of the time, Amanda explained, since he was a dining car steward on the Southern Railway. "Times being as hard as they are, we can use the extra money."

"Do you have references?" Lauren asked.

Amanda hesitated. "I've never worked as a domestic before, Mrs. Bernard. However, I do have character references."

Lauren was embarrassed. "Do you think you will mind this type of work? You would have to do the cleaning and laundry as well. We can't afford to pay a maid and a nurse."

"I'm not too proud to do honest work, ma'am. I love babies and I don't have any of my own."

Amanda was almost too good to be true. Her mother would have told her that if it seemed that way, she probably was. "Can you come back tomorrow night? I'd like Dr. Bernard to meet you."

When David reached home the next evening, Lauren had dinner all prepared. The table was set with flowers and candles. She had bathed and put on a fresh blouse and jumper, the only garment that fit her in her eighth month. David's eyes lit when he saw her preparations. "Are we celebrating something?"

"Yes we are. At least, I hope so." She told him about Amanda.

At first, he was resistant. "I don't want to leave our baby with a maid all day, honey. Poor little thing won't know who its parents are."

For a moment she did not reply, thinking of her own childhood, shunted back and forth between her mother and Reba. Then she realized how different this situation was. "The baby will be four months old when the fall semester begins, David. I won't go back if Amanda doesn't work out, but by that time I'll know."

"Don't you want to stay home with your own child?"

She thought about it. "Not especially," she answered, a note of self-discovery in her voice. "I think I'll be a better mother if I'm doing something interesting during the day. I really don't like housekeeping and cooking very much."

David agreed to meet Amanda.

"It's a good thing! She'll be here in an hour. Let's eat dinner."

David and Amanda liked each other immediately. He would never have stood for a servile woman taking care of his child. He admired Amanda's spirit, pride, and obvious intelligence. If she had not been black and living in the South, he thought, she might have been applying for a different kind of job.

Amanda came to work the following week, the day the bookshop staff gave Lauren a surprise baby shower. In the three weeks before she went into the hospital, there was plenty of time to show Amanda everything in the apartment. Together they opened all the packages of baby clothes and diapers, preparing the nursery. Miriam and Reba had knit dozens of sweaters, hats, booties, and receiving blankets. Charlee had sent an enormous layette from Best & Company, all in yellows, blues, and aquamarine, "because you can dress a girl in any color, but a boy would look like a pansy in pink," Charlee had written. David chucked when he read her note.

Lauren noted a wistfulness in Charlotte's voice when she first heard they were expecting a baby. "Ohh," she said, with uncharacteristic softness, "Oh, lovely. I can just see you as a mother . . ."

Most people hurried through long distance calls, rushing every sentence, as if there were an invisible meter ticking away in their heads. Not Charlee. She would go on chatting for half an hour, just as if they were teenagers back in Randolph Springs. Nowadays she called even more often, wanting to know every detail of Lauren's pregnancy.

"Are you *huge*, Laurie?" she inquired eagerly.

"I *feel* like a beached whale."

"Maybe you're going to have twins."

"Bite your tongue! That's all we need," she laughed. "The doctor can only hear one heartbeat."

"Ohh . . . he can *hear* it?"

"Yes. He puts the stethoscope in my ears so I can hear it, too."

"Oh, Laurie!"

Afterward, she felt really sad, for it was obvious to her that Charlee wanted to have a baby. "I think they're trying," she told David. "Aunt Reba had trouble conceiving."

"Infertility is not hereditary, honey," he said. It took her a minute to realize he was teasing.

It had always seemed to her that Charlotte was born lucky. "This is the first time I can remember that I've had something Charlee wanted," said Lauren.

* * *

They nearly lost Barbara. It was a breech presentation and Lauren's labor was hard and protracted. The infant kept turning, making the delivery difficult. David was growing more and more concerned as the hours passed. He asked the obstetrician whether they should consider a Caesarean section, but the doctor preferred to wait.

"She's young and healthy and the baby's heartbeat is strong. We'll give it a little longer."

It was a high forceps delivery, with Lauren anesthetized. The baby had to be resuscitated, but all of her signs were normal and both mother and daughter were in good condition an hour after the birth.

Lauren awakened to find David kissing her.

"The baby . . . ?" she whispered.

"She's perfect, darling. A wonderful little girl."

They had decided if the baby was a girl, she would be named Barbara Ethel after David's mother and aunt. When the nurse brought her daughter to her, showing her how to put the baby to her breast, Lauren was suffused with love. "Isn't she marvelous, David?" she asked, her face radiant.

David contemplated the mystery of his wife suckling their child. "I love you both so much," he said, his eyes moistening. "My beautiful girls."

An enormous bouquet of pink roses and baby's breath arrived. "A thousand kisses and hugs for bonnie Barbara and her proud parents," said the note, "Love, Charlee and Bruce."

Once they arrived home from the hospital, Lauren was eternally grateful for Amanda, who proved to be a gifted baby nurse. She managed the household perfectly, cooking delicious meals, cleaning, washing and ironing, and following David's strict sanitary rules in the nursery.

Miriam arrived with Reba to see her new granddaughter. Philip drove them from Randolph, depositing them at the Carolina Inn, since there was no room for guests in the apartment. Phil made the proper laudatory remarks about his niece before departing for Rocky Mount to visit Jeanette.

"Isn't it about time you decided to get married?" Lauren got the courage to ask him before he left.

"One of these days, I guess," he answered, avoiding her eyes.

"Seriously, Phil, why the delay? Jeanette won't wait forever."

For a moment, there was a flash of sorrow in his eyes, a bleakness she did not understand. He sighed and a chill ran through her as he said, "There are things you don't understand about me, Laurie. I'm not sure I'd make a very good husband."

Samuel had been suffering from high blood pressure since the previous winter and was unable to come to Chapel Hill, but Lauren planned to take the baby to Randolph Springs to see him as soon as they were able to travel. After two days, the women began to get on Lauren's nerves and she found herself having small arguments with her mother. Reba had a pitying expression in her eyes whenever they came to the apartment. It was plain to see she deplored their living arrangements. After all, in Charlee's New York abode, one climbed the stairs *after* entering the apartment.

Reba, and probably Miriam, too, thought it was a reflection on a husband if his wife had to work outside the home, so Lauren said nothing about going back to her job in September. They would have blamed David. At least she can't say Charlee has a more wonderful daughter than I do, she thought tearfully. Then immediately felt contrite, knowing how much her cousin wanted a baby.

Amanda saved the day. "She's a gem," declared Reba when they had been served one of Amanda's delicious dinners. "How ever did you find her, Lauren?"

David, ordinarily the most imperturbable man, was getting testy by the end of the week when Miriam and Reba finally departed for Greensboro and Winston-Salem to visit relatives. "I see what your Uncle Max means when he jokes about the Jacobson women!" he told Lauren after he returned from putting them on the train in Durham.

"Mama's all right alone. It's only when she teams up

with Aunt Reba that I have trouble getting along with her. She thinks Reba's an authority on everything."

David looked at her thoughtfully. "I noticed something this past week. You don't defer to Reba any more."

She stared at him, surprised. "Don't I? I guess I must finally be growing up."

He grabbed her and kissed her hungrily. "How long did that doctor of yours say we had to wait?"

"Two more weeks," she smiled.

"I'll never make it."

She held out her arms to him. "Maybe we can find another way."

"I do believe you *are* growing up," he murmured lovingly, his lips tracing the outline of her neck and shoulders. Gently she pushed him over on his back. Filled with adoration and a daring sense of her own power, Lauren made love to her husband, then fell asleep in his arms, wishing their lives would always be as happy and uncomplicated as this.

As if she had been clairvoyant, those few days proved to be a last peaceful lull before the intrusions of family problems. Lauren had been trying to gradually switch the baby to formula in preparation for returning to classes and her job, but Barbara developed colic and kept them awake almost every night. In addition to nursing the baby, Lauren usually was the one to get up to walk the floor with their daughter, since David needed a good rest if he was going to be alert for surgery in the morning. Amanda sometimes stayed over to relieve them of the constant interrupted sleep.

During the day, Barbara slept like an angel, while Lauren moved around in a state of perpetual exhaustion. To get away from the apartment, she often pushed the carriage, accompanying Gretchen Nelson and Carol Lawrence when they took their children for walks to play in the many woodsy knolls in Chapel Hill.

"You look awful!" exclaimed Gretchen. "Why don't you put cotton in your ears and let Babs cry it out for a few nights?"

"How could I do that? She's so tiny and helpless. If she cries, it's because she needs me."

"Uh-oh. I can see you're going to be one of those mothers whose whole life is wrapped up in her children," teased Carol.

"No, I'm not!" Lauren insisted vehemently. "I'm going back to work in September and as soon as I can, I'm going to finish up my master's."

"That's what I said," Gretchen reminded her gently. "It's not as easy as it sounds."

Barbara was less than a month old when on the sixth of June, a day after Lauren and David's first anniversary, Uncle Sydney died in his sleep. Leaving Babs with Amanda, they drove to Wilmington where Sydney was buried next to Ethel in a touching service attended by an extraordinary number of ancient-looking men and women. His uncle's attorney asked David to come to his office that afternoon. David was Sydney Bernard's sole heir, and much to his astonishment, the value of the estate after all debts and funeral expenses, was more than enough to pay off his medical school loan, leaving them with a comfortable sum in their savings account.

"He must never have spent a cent on himself," said David, full of wonder. "How could he have managed to save all that money?"

"I'm sure he did it because he loved you, David," Lauren told him tearfully. "He told me he was so proud of you. You were all he ever dreamed of your being."

Troubles always seemed to come in multiples. No sooner had they returned to Chapel Hill, than they received an early morning telephone call from Philip. David, who spoke to him, looked sad when he hung up. "Your father has had a stroke, darling," he told Lauren.

"Oh, David! Is he . . . ?"

"He's alive, but he's in serious condition." He took her in his arms. "I think we'd better go there."

Tears flooded her eyes. "Will he die?"

"I don't know, honey. I think you have to be prepared for that."

They drove to Randolph Springs that day, bringing the

baby with them. Amanda came along to take care of Barbara, insisting she could be away because her husband, with his job on the railway, was seldom at home and her sister would look after their father. "You'll need me to help, Mrs. Bernard. With your poor papa dying, you'll be spending all your time at the hospital."

But Samuel did not die. He remained on the critical list for a week and then rallied, although the stroke had left him aphasic and paralyzed on one side. After a few days, when it appeared that Samuel's condition had stabilized, David returned home. His fourth year of residency was about to begin, and he was chief resident.

When Lauren entered Samuel's room the next morning, he stared at her, trying to speak, but the words were garbled and the attempt cost him a tremendous effort. "L . . . l . . . l," was all he could manage.

"Yes, Papa, it's Laurie," she whispered, taking his hand and kissing him. She could hardly contain her tears, but she did not want to upset him.

In the second week, the doctor permitted her to bring the baby to see him, and Lauren took his good hand, placing it against Barbara's cheek. He petted the sleeping infant and when she stirred and opened her eyes, Lauren was afraid she would start to cry and disturb him, but Barbara just lay in her mother's arms, making sweet baby noises, and looking around the room, seeming to fix her gaze on her grandfather. A one-sided smile crossed Samuel's face.

Lauren put Babs in the padded wicker basket they used as a traveling bassinet and went back to her father's bedside, taking his hand. He grasped hers with surprising strength. "L . . . uh," he said, staring intently at her.

She looked at him questioningly. "What, Papa?"

"L . . . lo . . . ve!"

"Did you say 'love,' Papa?" Samuel smiled and repeated it once more, the tears standing in his eyes.

"I love you, too," she said softly.

Just then, the nurse came in to give him an injection and told Lauren she must leave. "We don't want to tire ourselves, do we?" she said, as if speaking to a child.

Even with his facial paralysis, Lauren could recognize her father's grimace. He held onto her hand with an imploring expression on his face. She leaned over to kiss him good-bye and smiled. "I'll see you in the morning, Papa."

But by the next morning, Samuel had lapsed into a deep coma, and that evening, with all of his family around him, he died. Through tear-filled eyes, Lauren gazed at her father's still face, remembering his last word to her. *Love* . . . What had he been trying to say, she wondered. That he loved her? That love was the only thing of any importance in the end?

David came back for the funeral, and Lauren asked him to call Jeanette, who traveled from Rocky Mount to be with Philip. They stayed for the week of *shiva*, and at the end of that period of mourning, they were preparing to go home to Chapel Hill when Philip took Lauren aside.

"This is probably not the right moment," he said, "but I want you to know, Jeanette and I are engaged."

"Oh, Phil!" Lauren embraced her brother. "I am absolutely thrilled to hear that. When did it happen?"

"Yesterday, when I took her to the train. With Papa gone . . . I don't know, something happened to me. I suddenly realized life is very short and we ought to grab all the happiness we can."

Lauren smiled at her brother's new elation. "If anyone deserves happiness, it's you. When is the wedding?"

He grimaced. "Not for a while, I guess. Now that she's alone, I'm not sure how Mama's going to take to this turn of events."

Chapter 22

June 1940

LAUREN STOOD QUIETLY in the nursery gazing with adoration at her sleeping daughter. The infant who had cooed at her grandfather in his hospital room was now a spunky thirteen-month-old. Barbara was unusually bright and quite beautiful, with soft brown curls, dark blue eyes, and an enchanting smile. Sometimes Lauren could detect a resemblance to David, but Babs was cast from her own mold.

Tonight when she bathed her, Lauren had been overwhelmed with love, finding it difficult to believe this perfect creation was really theirs, hers and David's. She had smoothed the wash cloth over the tiny back, delighting in the way the child smiled up at her.

"Did you have fun today, lovey?" she asked.

"Fun, have fun, Mommy!" Barbara dashed her hands up and down in the water, splashing her mother. With a sly little glance, she trickled water on the bathroom floor.

"Don't, Babsy, that makes a mess and it will leak through to Mrs. Hilton's ceiling," said Lauren, leaning down to wipe up the puddle and thinking that was all their grouchy landlady needed to cause a fuss. Grinning, Barbara showed her tiny even teeth, then scooped water into her cupped hands and threw it on the floor.

"*Stop* that, Babs!" Lauren scolded her sharply.

Barbara studied her mother's changed expression gravely, then said in a plaintive voice, "Smile at Babs and call her lovey." Unable to resist, Lauren hugged the small, wet body against herself, reflecting that soon she would not be the only baby in the house.

Lauren told David about the incident when he came home late from the hospital. "She's such a little minx," he laughed, as he pulled back the covers and got into bed. "I don't know whether I want a son this time or another daughter."

"I suppose Babs would enjoy a sister, but I'd prefer a boy." She sighed, thinking that regardless of the baby's sex, it would be another year until she could register for the doctoral program. The baby was due in October, just the wrong timing for the next semester. "I wish it were now, during the summer, so I could at least start *some* classes in the fall."

David reached for her. "I'm sorry, sweetheart. I'm sure it's all my fault," he said contritely. But she knew he was not sorry in the least. He could hardly wait for the new baby to be born. And after that, he would want more!

David was such a loving husband, she asked herself how she could possibly find fault with him. After her father's death, he had known exactly what to do and say to comfort her. When they returned to Chapel Hill after Samuel's funeral, Lauren had experienced a delayed depression, and David had been there for her whenever she needed him. Recalling the loss of his own parents, he told her how it had haunted him throughout his childhood and into his college years.

"Even now, a feeling of longing sometimes comes over me," he had assured her, "a need to connect with my parents and have them see what has become of me, to know my wife and my children . . ." Once it had been Charlee who was her best friend, the one she could turn to for comfort and solace. Now it was David. She was able to tell him anything. In some ways they were better friends than spouses.

They were also better friends than they were lovers. That part of their marriage, she knew, was a disappointment to David. To her also, but she seemed unable to do anything about it. Wouldn't it be nice to be able to go to a doctor and say, *My sexuality isn't working right. Fix it.*

She had tried. One day she had asked her gynecologist whether there was anything wrong with the placement of her genitalia. She had read a paper in one of David's medical journals, a review of sexual dysfunction in the female. Some women had a thickened membrane that covered the clitoris, the study disclosed, preventing easy stimulation during sexual intercourse. According to the article, there was a simple surgical technique to correct this condition. It could be performed in a doctor's office under local anesthesia, ensuring immediate improvement in sexual relations.

Lauren had hoped Dr. Gorman would announce that she had this condition (it had an erudite Latin name, but was more commonly referred to as a *nun's hood*) guaranteeing marital ecstasy in the years ahead. Instead, without examining her, he had answered brusquely, "Everything is quite normal, Lauren." It had taken all her courage to ask that question, and afterward she was sorry she had. Now he would know she did not have a satisfying sex life, that she and David had a "problem." Would he write it in her medical history, she wondered. Would anyone else see it? His nurse, perhaps. Would he ever discuss it with any of his colleagues at the medical school? ". . . Oh yes, it's quite common for young women not to achieve orgasm. Lauren Bernard, for example, is unable to attain sexual satisfaction. No physical reason for it, some women just can't. Poor David."

What a fool I am, she thought, putting aside the book she was reading. David, exhausted as usual, had fallen sound asleep with the light on. She studied his face on the pillow next to her. He was undoubtedly the most handsome man she knew . . . well, she supposed many people would say Bruce Fields was better looking, but not to her. David was more masculine. Bruce reminded her of a matinée idol, so controlled and always perfectly groomed. There was an artificiality about Charlee's husband, but David was real and vital, both dynamic and sensitive at once. Wherever they went, it was noticeable how people responded to his presence. Women especially.

"Don't you ever worry about David in the hospital

around all those nurses?'' Carol Lawrence had once asked her.

''No,'' Lauren answered, surprised. ''It never occurred to me. Do you worry about Jim with his students?''

''You *bet* I do!'' And then she had told Lauren the latest scandal involving a professor and one of his women graduate students. Lauren always felt disloyal listening to campus gossip, knowing how much David deplored it.

She turned out the light and adjusted her pillow, and within a few minutes, had fallen asleep. Stirring when the telephone rang in the middle of the night, she was vaguely aware when David got up to answer a summons from the hospital, but soon she fell back into a deep slumber.

Lauren came to the breakfast table looking rested and radiant, with the same lushness David remembered from her first pregnancy. ''Good morning, everyone.'' She kissed him and Barbara. ''Why didn't you wake me?''

''Since it was Saturday and you don't have to go to work, I thought I'd let you sleep. I'm glad it's the end of the term next week and you'll be finished.'' He had wanted her to quit her job as soon as she became pregnant, now that he was making more money, but she enjoyed working at the Bull's Head, and it had paid for her courses.

''Are you going to be able to come to Randolph Springs with me?'' she asked.

''I really can't, honey. It's right in the middle of Boards and we'll be short of staff.''

''Well then, do you mind if I invite Charlee to come back here with me? It seems so strange that she's never been in our home.''

He hesitated for only an instant. ''Mind? Of course not, why should I?''

''That was just an expression, darling. There's no reason in the world why you should mind if my cousin visits us.''

Lauren left for Randolph Springs with Babs on the twenty-second of June, 1940, the day France surrendered to Germany. They stayed at her mother's. Since Samuel's death,

Miriam and Philip had been living alone in the old house, with Pansy as their housekeeper.

Phil and Jeanette had ended their engagement last fall, after three months. Lauren suspected there had been disharmony between Miriam and Philip's fiancée. Miriam had claimed it was too soon after Samuel's death for wedding plans, but Lauren questioned whether her mother really wanted Philip to marry at all. It was a very convenient arrangement for her, having her unmarried son share this house.

Philip's uniform manufacturing business was prospering beyond his expectations, now that he had signed contracts with the U.S. Navy. At thirty, he was beginning to look a little like a middle-aged man, with a receding hairline and the glasses he now habitually wore. Lauren felt sad that Phil had broken off with her college friend. At first devastated, Jeanette had recently announced her engagement to a dentist from Norfolk. Lauren was certain it was a romance on the rebound.

Babs quickly became attached to Uncle Phil, and he never came home without bringing some little gift for his niece. "You'd make a wonderful father," Lauren told him, feeling a fond sympathy for her brother. He smiled, but there was a pained expression in his eyes.

"I wish Philip would find a nice Jewish girl," Miriam repeated so often that Lauren was tired of hearing it.

"He was *engaged* to the nicest Jewish girl imaginable, but you didn't seem terribly enthusiastic about that!" she retorted. Her mother had become impossible lately.

Relatives were always inviting Phil to come for a special occasion, offering to introduce him to women. But the light had gone out of her brother, and he seemed to prefer his books and classical records or a night of playing contract bridge at the Randolph Inn. Lauren wondered whether there was a new woman in his life, but she hesitated to ask. He had been deeply in love with Jeanette, and now that she was engaged to someone else, Lauren thought he regretted not marrying her.

The level of energy picked up with the arrival of Charlotte and Bruce. Charlee still carried her own brand of excitement as part of her baggage.

The cousins spent every day together, sitting on the terrace at the big house and watching Babs chase butterflies over the velvety lawn, while Bruce perfected his suntan on the golf links with Max. One afternoon Charlee lit a cigarette and lay back on the chaise longue, regarding Lauren with an appraising look. "Pregnancy becomes you."

"David says I must come from good peasant stock because I feel wonderful when I'm pregnant. It was the same with Babs, except the delivery was rough. I was in labor for forty-eight hours."

"Ugh—I would never stand for that!"

"Charlee, dear, I have news for you. There wouldn't be a goddamn thing you could *do* about it!"

"I'd insist on a Caesarean. That's the first question I'd ask an obstetrician before I hired him."

Lauren stared at her. "First of all, you don't 'hire' a physician. And what makes you think any doctor would agree to that beforehand?"

Charlee gave her head a toss and took a deep drag on her cigarette. "They do it all the time in New York. Women have their babies by appointment."

"If that isn't just like New York!"

Charlee exploded in laughter. "If you only knew how provincial you sound, Laurie!"

Lauren tried not to show she was hurt. I suppose we must all seem a little hometown to Charlee, she thought. After all, she's been living up North for seven years, ever since the Alexander School.

Charlotte's mood swings troubled her. She was often restless and at odds with herself and everyone around her. One day she would be the old sunny, loving, amusing Charlee. And then there would come a period, like today, when she was irascible. She and Bruce bickered continually, embarrassing Lauren and causing a speculative expression to cross Max's face. Reba, blithely unaware as usual, chattered on constantly about her last visit with Bruce's parents at Fair Fields, or the addition to the farmhouse Charlotte and Bruce had bought in Connecticut.

Realizing she had offended Lauren, Charlee was anxious to make amends. "How was the good doctor when you spoke to him?"

"Just great. He's been made chief resident, which means more pay. Good thing, too, since we'll have to move when the baby comes. David would like to find a house."

"You're happy, aren't you?" Charlee's face softened in love for Lauren.

"Yes, very happy." Lauren smiled, forgiving her instantly. "I do wish there had been more time between babies, though."

"I wouldn't complain, if I were you," said Charlee, with a rueful smile. She rubbed out her cigarette, immediately lighting another.

"I didn't mean to complain, Charlee . . ." Lauren could have bitten her tongue. What a tactless thing for her to say, when Charlee and Bruce—She wondered whether they had consulted a doctor who specialized in infertility, but she hesitated to ask. It was a very personal subject, more tender than almost any other. "It's just that I wanted to enroll for the doctoral program, but I'll have to delay that for at least a year. It would be impossible with two children and my job."

"Why do you still want a Ph.D.? I should think marriage would have changed all that."

"I want to teach and maybe write," she answered, feeling a little defensive. "Living in an academic community, you get to value advanced degrees. Besides, I like to study."

"Is it absolutely necessary for you to work? I mean, do you really *need* the money?"

"Yes, Charlee, we need the money," she said evenly. "David thinks we can get along without my salary because he'd prefer me to stay home with the children, but I know better. I pay the bills and balance the checkbook."

"You *do?* I wouldn't know how to balance a checkbook to save my soul. Bruce has his accountant take care of all that."

Lauren realized anew how broad the divisions between her life and Charlee's really were. Charlotte lived in a world so disparate from her own that there was no basis of comparison. She wondered how her cousin spent her days when she was at home in New York. Surely she wasn't as idle and frivolous as she had been three years ago when Lauren had visited them.

She visualized the relationship between Bruce and Charlee, comparing it to her own marriage. They seemed to go their separate ways, almost as if they were pulling on different oars. Their night life was one round of parties, openings, and events. Did they ever spend a quiet evening at home, she wondered, just talking and confiding in each other, the way she and David did? Even with Amanda's presence, they had the nights to themselves. Those were the best times, when David shared his dreams of the future with her, and they talked of the trips they would take, the house they would buy when they could afford it, their plans for their children's education. They were so much in tune, it was like they were part of the same individual sometimes.

She missed him dreadfully. This was the longest they had been apart since their marriage. He'd been calling every night for the entire two weeks, even when he was at the hospital. Maybe it hadn't been a good idea for her to visit Randolph Springs without him, after all. "When are you coming home, honey?" he had asked last night, sounding forlorn.

"Actually, darling, if you don't mind my staying another week, Charlee said she would come back with me. Bruce is returning to New York and we can all travel together as far as Durham. Is that all right?"

"I guess it'll have to be. I miss you, sweetheart. This is the longest we've been separated, do you realize that? I can't fall asleep at night without you."

"Yes, I know . . . me too." She kept her voice low because the telephone nook was in a hallway right off the sun parlor where everyone in the family was gathered.

"How's Babs? I bet she's forgotten me."

"Not a chance! She kisses your picture every night." Then she whispered, "So do I."

"I love you, Lauren. Kiss the baby for me."

She was always depressed after she talked to him, wishing they were together. And yet, she *did* enjoy coming home. Charlee seemed disappointed whenever she returned to Randolph, finding it smaller and less picturesque than she remembered. But there had always been a special warmth and beauty here awaiting Lauren.

She had spent many hours in the past two weeks talking with Philip, renewing their closeness. He was concerned about Miriam's health, and Lauren was distressed to see that her mother was indeed aging, looking older than her sixty-three years. There were few diversions in Miriam's life. It gave her such pleasure to be with Lauren and little Babs, and that alone was worth the trip.

But David was the center of her life now, and Lauren longed for him, counting the days until they would be together again. He was waiting eagerly when the train pulled into Durham the second week of July, engulfing her and Babs in his embrace. Bruce got off to say hello, supervising the unloading of the luggage, most of it Charlee's. Half of her wardrobe was going home with Bruce, yet they had to tie two bags onto the luggage rack when the trunk could hold no more.

"How long does she plan to stay?" whispered David when he and Lauren were alone for a moment.

"I'm not sure. Probably not more than a few days. I can hardly set a limit, darling. After all, I've stayed at Reba's for weeks on end."

"I suppose so," he answered, but Lauren could tell he was not overly enthusiastic about their house guest.

Amanda had made up the spare bed in Barbara's room and moved the baby's crib into the master bedroom. She helped unpack and hang Charlotte's clothes in the closet. "I hope y'all will be comfortable in here, Mrs. Fields."

"It's perfectly *divine,* Amanda. How clever of you to have arranged all this alone!" Amanda had moved toys and baby clothes aside to give her a bureau and dressing table. Soon Charlee had taken over the bathroom and was submerged in a foamy bubble bath.

In the living room, Lauren had an overwhelming sense of love and contentment as David took her in his arms and kissed her. "I don't care who's visiting us," he growled in an undertone. "Tonight I intend to make mad, passionate love to my wife."

He handed her a sherry, then poured a drink for himself. They sat on the couch holding hands. From the bathroom came strains of Charlee throatily singing *"Bei Mir Bist Du Schön,"* while fumes of gardenia bath salts wafted through the apartment.

Throwing Lauren a wry glance, David clinked her glass with his. "Well . . ." he toasted, "here's to family ties."

Chapter 23

October 1940

MAX MORTIMER LUXURIATED under the needle jets of his custom-built shower. Flexing his right biceps, he kneaded the shoulder that sometimes caused him trouble on the golf course. Terry had given him a real workout on the table today, and his muscles were still tingling. Max always arranged for the club masseur to be waiting at his house when he returned from New York.

For all these years, Max had enjoyed the long train trips to and from the North, but lately he was becoming impatient with slow journeys, feeling achy at the end of them. One of these days, he would have to try flying. There were no scheduled flights from Randolph yet, but he could charter a plane. He was convinced that air travel was the wave of the future.

Max had a nose for picking the right industry. Years and years ago, when he had bought Ford Motors stock, he remembered Samuel saying, "Max, I don't understand how you can invest in any business owned by an anti-Semite like Henry Ford." At first he ignored Samuel's comments, but when the automobile tycoon published that scurrilous anti-Jewish tract, he had sold his Ford stock (at a profit), putting that money and more, into General Motors, Chrysler and Standard Oil. He hadn't been wrong in 1919. And he wasn't wrong now.

The week in Manhattan had been productive. Two days ago, after discussing his investments with Malcolm Fields, Max had instructed his broker to start accumulating shares of Lockheed and Douglas, as well as airline stocks. The country would eventually be dragged into the war and airplanes were bound to play a strategic role in modern warfare.

Max switched to a cold rinse, exhilarated by the icy spray. It was a rare luxury for him to be alone in his own home. Reba had stayed on in the North to spend more time with Charlotte Lee. When she first mentioned the possibility of remaining longer, Max had encouraged her to do so. "After all, dear," he said, trying not to sound too eager, "Charlotte *is* our only daughter and you deserve to see as much of her as possible."

"You won't mind, Max?"

"Well of course, I'll miss you, but it won't be nearly so bad, knowing you're with our little girl."

He meant that. Charlotte Lee needed more contact with her parents. Max had not liked what he observed in New York. Hadn't liked it at all. He harbored deep concerns about that marriage. Bruce's drinking was worrisome and Charlotte did not look happy to him. He wished Malcolm would take his son in hand. Bruce was pampered and indulged by Adele, who fawned on him to a disgusting degree. It must drive Charlotte crazy to have her mother-in-law making such a fuss over Bruce.

There was even more there that troubled Max, yet he hoped his darkest fears were exaggerated by a father's natural concern for his only beloved daughter. He had tried to broach the subject with Malcolm, but it was a hard row to hoe, suggesting to a man that his son was lacking in moral fiber. Calling in a private investigator seemed like a drastic step, but Max was almost prepared to take it. He would give it a few more days of consideration before acting.

Turning off the water, Max stepped out of the shower and reached for a thick Turkish towel. As he dried his back, he studied himself in the mirrored wall. Not bad for sixty-one, he thought, slapping his flat abdomen. He kept in shape by riding and golfing, and had the body of a man in his forties, as Florence was always telling him. A flicker of excitement ran through him at the thought that she was waiting for him at Mountain View. On the massage table, he'd damn near had a hard-on as her cultivated, caressing voice came over the telephone. "Hayes has gone back to Philadelphia, lover. We'll be all alone . . . you can even stay the night."

He would come home to sleep, of course. Otherwise, the servants would know he had been out all night. If he kept up the charade, Max liked to think no one suspected that he cheated on his wife. It was important to maintain appearances and to protect Reba, to whom he was truly devoted. His wife had denied him her body for so many years, it had become their way of life, having nothing to do with the genuine affection and loyalty that existed between them.

What he felt for Florence was something altogether different. It was not a frivolous affair—Max did not play around. He and Florence had been lovers for more than nine years and they sincerely cared about each other, but there was never a question of a further commitment. She had her obligations and he had his, and they both agreed part of that was to respect the sensibilities of her husband and his wife. The secrecy lent excitement to their liaisons, and as long as no one was hurt, Max did not feel he was being unfaithful.

He slipped into a terry robe and rang for Bertram to shave him. The butler had laid out fresh clothing in the dressing room. Max exchanged the sober navy foullard for a natty red bow tie, then settled himself in the reclining chair as Bertram worked up a lather in the shaving mug.

Half an hour later, behind the wheel of his silver Cord Sportsman 812, Max skillfully maneuvered the hairpin curves leading to Mountain View, smiling with anticipation as he neared the summit of Shadow Mountain.

Lauren was on her way to Durham to see her obstetrician when she felt the first twinges of labor. She wasn't certain at first because they were mild, so she kept on driving, wishing she had followed David's advice that morning when he suggested she call Gretchen to go along with her. Usually she visited Dr. Gorman at Strickland, but this was one of his days at Duke Hospital, when he saw patients at his office in Durham. By the time she passed Hope Valley, she knew she was going to have her baby.

Nothing about this delivery was the same as Barbara's birth. It was all fast and simple. David barely reached Duke in time to scrub and accompany her into the delivery room. She was awake throughout and despite the searing pain, she had never experienced anything so movingly beautiful as the elation in David's eyes when the obstetrician handed him their son. Over the head nurse's objections, David placed the infant in Lauren's arms, embracing both of them.

"Hello, Mark," she whispered.

"Are you *sure?*" David's voice trembled with emotion.

"Absolutely certain. Now that I've met him, he is definitely a Mark."

When she was settled in her private room and had been given some sedation for pain, David went home to tell Babs about her new baby brother. He promised to return that evening, but got tied up in emergency surgery at Strickland, thus it was the next afternoon when he finally came back to visit her.

The moment he walked into her room, Lauren knew there was bad news. "David, what is it?"

"Nothing, darling."

"There's something you're not telling me. The baby! What's wrong with him—?" She could feel her heart beating rapidly.

"No! It's not the baby—he's perfect."

"Babs . . ."

"Oh, Laurie," he kissed her, fondling her head, "it's nothing to do with either of the children." Sitting on the edge of the hospital bed, he held her hand. "I didn't want to spoil your happiness today. Your Uncle Max was in an accident, darling . . . He's been killed."

She marveled that she could feel relief and sorrow at the same time. *Max dead*—that vigorous, powerful, confident man! It did not seem possible. "Poor Aunt Reba. And Charlee—she worshiped her father. What kind of accident?"

David looked out the window, remembering Philip's words on the telephone . . . "The damn fool, speeding down that road at night! He was up seeing his woman. Her family will keep it out of the papers, of course, but everyone in town knows he was with Florence Randolph."

"She wasn't in the automobile with him, was she?" David had asked.

"No, but she was first on the scene," said Philip. "Max had just left her house and evidently he lost control on a curve. His car went off a cliff. I was the only one of the family around, so Bertram called me and I went over there. It was not a pretty sight, Dave."

"Was he killed instantly?"

"Unfortunately not. The police said he regained consciousness and said something to Mrs. Randolph before he died. She became hysterical—I arrived just as she started screaming how it should have been her."

"What a mess. How is Reba taking it? And your mother?"

"Reba's still in New York. They've got her under sedation, and she hasn't been told the details. Mama's okay. She's a little lost these days. It's very strange, I was going to talk to you about it. Most of the time she's as sharp as ever, but sometimes she doesn't seem to be completely *aware.*"

"That sounds worrisome, Phil. She ought to be seen by someone at Duke."

"If I can talk her into it. She doesn't think there's anything wrong. Well, let's get through the funeral first—Say, congratulations! How's Laurie doing?"

"She's wonderful. The baby was a bruiser, eight pounds, three ounces, and she came through it beautifully."

"What are you going to name him?"

"Mark Samuel, for the two grandfathers." He hesitated, "I'm not sure what to tell Lauren about Max. Women get depressed easily after childbirth."

"Wait until she's feeling stronger, then. She can't come to the funeral anyway. I'll call to let you know what's happening. Give my love to Laurie."

* * *

At Charlotte's suggestion, Miriam had moved over to the Mortimers' to be with Reba, who was prostrated by Max's death. The entire family protected Reba from the truth, hovering nearby whenever friends came to pay their respects during the period of mourning. No one would be so heartless as to mention . . . but still, you never knew. People could be thoughtless, or deliberately cruel.

Shortly after Lauren came home from the hospital, David drove her to Randolph to visit her Aunt Reba. A pall of bereavement hung over the great house. Everyone, from Lady and Bertram to the maids and gardeners, wept when they first saw Lauren. Reba flung herself at her niece, "Oh, Laurie, Laurie! He's *gone* . . . gone *forever,*" she shrieked.

Charlotte, who had stayed to be with her mother and help write acknowledgments for the mountain of condolence notes and contributions in Max's memory, tried to calm Reba. "She was carrying on like this all the time at first," Charlee told a shaken Lauren. "She's been much better this last week, but seeing you set her off again."

Charlotte looked pale and interesting in black.

"I wish you had brought the children, Laurie," Miriam kept repeating.

"It would be a nuisance for everyone to have them around now, Mama. They're better off at home with Amanda."

Reba's bereavement had brought Miriam out of her peculiar lethargy. According to Philip, she had been purposeful and energetic since moving over to Shadow Mountain.

"I think Phil's happier with Mama out of the house," Lauren told David that night when they were lying in the old four poster bed in her former room on Lenoir Avenue.

"I wonder whether it isn't something else that's cheered him up," said David. "He told me this afternoon he's spoken to Jeanette a couple of times."

She felt a little envious that Philip had confided in David and not her. "Really? He didn't mention a word about that to me. Tell me what he said. Did he call her, or did she call him?''

''Now, hold on, Laurie,'' he laughed. ''Poor guy, no wonder he hasn't told you. He called Jeanette about Max, and they just talked for a while.''

''Is that all?''

''Well, he did say he might go to Rocky Mount to see her.''

''Oh, David, wouldn't it be wonderful if they got back together! I just *know* she isn't in love with that dentist.''

''I swear, Lauren, you must be descended from a long line of matchmakers.'' He drew her into his arms, kissing her and cradling her head on his shoulder. ''Go to sleep, sweetheart. This has been a long day.''

It had been an exhausting day for Lauren, who still tired easily after giving birth. She was glad they had left the children in Chapel Hill, even though it would have been nice for her mother to see the new baby. They should really invite Miriam to go back with them, and at the same time, she could have a complete examination at Duke. On the other hand, the apartment was crowded and it might be too disruptive to have her staying with them just now. Even in the few days since Lauren had come home from the hospital, they had seen how much more complicated it was having a second child in the house.

From David's deep, even breathing, she knew he had fallen asleep. She nestled against him, thinking it was really quite wonderful being his wife and having two children.

The next morning Lauren went over to Reba's, while Phil invited David to visit his newly expanded manufacturing plant. Lionel had recently joined Philip in the uniform business. After fifty-eight years, The Liberty Store had closed its doors, and now the offices and sales department of Liberty Uniforms, Inc. occupied its premises.

Philip showed David through the factory, where piece-goods workers were assembling fatigues for the Army Supply Corps. ''We've been swamped with orders since the draft,'' said Phil. ''They're working overtime six days a week.'' The Selective Service and Training Act had become law a month ago, in September. "We're preparing for war, Dave."

David heard the seriousness in Philip's quiet voice and he paid attention. If a man supplied the armed services with uniforms, he knew what was going on.

When they left the factory, Phil drove out toward Dogwood Mountain. It was a clear, sparkling autumn day with a bright sun warming the crisp mountain air. It was obvious that Philip had something on his mind, probably his mother. David had been alert to Miriam's behavior, but although she was aging and often repeated herself, she appeared pretty normal to him.

But it wasn't his mother Philip wanted to discuss. He parked at a scenic overlook. "I—uh—I'd like to talk to you about a personal matter, Dave. Can I trust you to keep it confidential? You know what I mean . . . from Laurie."

"Of course, Phil. I'm used to that. I never discuss my patients with Lauren."

"That's why I thought you'd be a good person. I mean, because you're a doctor."

"Are you having a medical problem?"

"Not exactly. Well, maybe." Phil drummed his fingers on the steering wheel and stared across the ravine. "Dammit—it's kind of embarrassing, but it's screwing up my life something terrible."

"Let me guess," said David, when Philip remained silent. "Is it connected with women?"

With a look of amazement, Phil turned to him. "How did you know?"

David smiled. "When a young man tells me something is screwing up his life, it usually has to do with sex."

"Is it that common?"

"More than you think. Of course, that's not my specialty, but when you take medical histories all the time, it often comes up." Philip already looked relieved. "Why don't you tell me what you're having difficulty with and I'll see if I can help you, or direct you to someone who can."

"It's hard to describe. I think I might be—that is, I

don't seem to . . ." He pounded his fist on the seat. "Ah hell, Dave, I just can't get it up."

David gave a noncommittal grunt. "Since when?"

"Since . . . *always!* Well, that's not entirely true. But, for the past few years, anyway." He looked glum. "There's never been much opportunity for me to be with women, living at home with my folks. And now, Mama."

"You were engaged not too long ago."

"When I was going with Jeanette, we didn't—well, I wouldn't expect her to—"

"Of course not. I didn't mean that you would have had intercourse, Phil. Did you neck with her?"

"Sure."

"Did you ever have an erection when you were with her?"

"Yes, but you know, with a girl like Jeanette, I tried to hide it at first." Philip looked away and sighed. "Pretty soon, there was nothing to hide."

"Did the thought of having sex with her worry you?"

"Yeah, after a while. I was afraid I wouldn't be able to—you know what I mean—perform, when the time came."

"Is that why you broke the engagement?"

"Basically, yes." He smiled ruefully. "I was really in love with her. In fact, I still am."

"Lauren says Jeanette has never stopped loving you. She thinks she's marrying this dentist on the rebound."

"That doesn't solve my problem, does it? What can I do, Dave?"

David was lost in thought. "Do you masturbate?" he finally asked. He could tell the question made Philip uncomfortable. Reaching into his pocket, he removed a notepad and fountain pen. "Maybe it would be helpful if I took a short history. Just forget I'm your sister's husband and think of me as a doctor."

Philip seemed to relax as he responded to David's dry, straightforward questions. His medical record was uneventful. Except for the childhood diseases, he had been exceptionally healthy.

"When was the last time you had intercourse with a woman?"

"I never really have." David controlled his surprise as Philip continued. "When I was younger, there were the usual parties. Once when I was about twenty or so, some of my friends invited me to a stag bash where there were girls—I don't think they were prostitutes, but they were available. One of them brought me to a bedroom and stripped, then she took off all my clothes. I thought I would do it, but at the crucial moment . . ." He shook his head.

"You lost your erection." Phil nodded. "That happens to lots of guys. When was the next time?"

"There was a girl I liked, she wasn't Jewish. Didn't Laurie ever tell you about what happened to me? The whipping?"

"Yes, but I didn't know it was connected with a woman."

"It wasn't, directly. But the men who did it were her father and her husband. She and I never slept together, but we came pretty close to it. Funny," he mused, "I've always thought it would've been all right with her . . . I mean, I didn't lose it. She—"

"Yes, go on."

"Well, she did it to me with her hand, and her—"

"Mouth?"

"Yes."

"There's nothing to be embarrassed about, Phil. That was how long ago?"

"Almost six years. God, it doesn't seem that long. It's almost like yesterday. And then, when I saw her after she was married and realized what kind of people they were—*lowdown trash!* I don't know, Dave, it did something to me. Made me feel rotten, like I'd been up to my neck in *shit!* Then, when those two came after me and one of them tried to castrate me—" David gasped. "You didn't know about that? Well, of course, I didn't tell Laurie. Anyway, I haven't had much desire to be with a woman since then . . . At least, I think it's since then."

David read through the pages of notes he had taken. The picture that emerged was one of sexual repression from childhood, an atmosphere in the home where normal sexual appetites were considered dirty and contemptible. The more he learned about the Jacobson family, the more David wondered how any of the children had emerged with a libido intact.

He sensed that Philip had not voiced his deepest concerns. "Are you worried that you might be a homosexual, Phil?"

After a frozen moment, Philip buried his face in his hands, shoulders shuddering as he sobbed. David reached out to touch him, keeping his hand on his back until he was quiet. "Am I, Dave? Am I queer?" Phil asked, in a strangled voice.

"You've given me no reason to conclude that. Have you ever found yourself sexually attracted to another man?"

Recovering his composure, Philip shook his head. "No. But when I've been out with girls like Nancy Miller, who was my girlfriend before I met Jeanette, I never had much desire for her."

"I don't wonder you've had problems, Phil. That's pretty strong stuff you've had to deal with. On the basis of what you've told me, you seem perfectly normal, and you said your doctor has examined you and never found anything physically wrong. But the thing that strikes me is, you've had no real experience with women."

Except for the required introductory courses in medical school, David had never made a study of psychiatry, but Philip's problem, he was certain, had an emotional basis. David wasn't all that sold on psychoanalysis, but in the right circumstances, it was useful. He could recommend that his brother-in-law see a psychiatrist and Philip would probably then spend the next few years in analysis. Meanwhile, his youth was slipping away . . .

"You know what I think, Phil?"

"What?"

"I think you need to get laid."

Two days later, Lauren and David returned to Chapel Hill. David had made an appointment for them to look at a house on Laurel Hill Road. David had seen the house when

Lauren was in the hospital, before it was listed with an agent, and he couldn't wait to show it to her. "We'll have to do a little interior work," he explained on the way over. "The second floor was never completely finished after the Depression came along."

Lauren was immediately charmed by the white brick colonial with its dark green shutters. The rooms were spacious, with beamed ceilings and wonderful details like corner cupboards and built-in bookshelves. "Can we afford it?" she asked, wondering how they would manage if she worked only part-time.

"Of course. We have my inheritance from Uncle Sydney, and the bank will give us a mortgage."

"But what about the unfinished bedrooms and bath, and the cost of maintenance? We've never had to pay for heat and electricity before."

"Don't worry, honey, we'll manage. In another year, I'll be making a decent salary." David had become less cautious than Lauren in the two-and-a-half years since they had been married.

The lovely house belonged to them by Election Day, and Lauren's spirits were buoyant as she supervised the carpentry and painting of the bedrooms. Although they had planned to wait, the plumber was urging them to install the fixtures that were standing upstairs in the empty shell of the second bathroom. "Better do it now, Mrs. Bernard, while I can still get hold of pipe. Government's shipping everything to Europe for the war."

With Gretchen Nelson's help, Lauren selected wallpaper and fabric for curtains, which Gretchen stitched on her sewing machine. "Are you sure you want to do them, Gretch? I can take the material to a seamstress."

"This'll be my housewarming present," replied her talented friend. "I need a project, Laurie. Keep my mind off other things."

Strangely uncommunicative of late, Gretchen was pregnant again. She seemed preoccupied and joyless. Lauren wondered whether there was any truth to the disturbing rumor she had heard that Ralph was involved with another faculty wife. He couldn't be, not with their third child on the way!

Lauren and David gave a housewarming reception on New Year's Day of 1941, inviting all of their many friends from Duke and Chapel Hill. The afternoon before the party, a floral centerpiece and a gigantic silver punch bowl arrived from Charlee and Bruce, who were off on a holiday cruise in the Caribbean Islands. "No one stays in New York for Christmas these days," Charlee told her when she called from New York just before they sailed. Her voice had lacked the joy of anticipation, and Lauren recognized the signs of her earlier discontent.

"I do hope she gets pregnant soon," she told David, as she helped him fill the elegant punch bowl on the afternoon of their housewarming. Although, she was beginning to wonder whether not having children was the real reason for Charlee's discontent.

The Nelsons came through the back door, the first guests to arrive. "Where's the greenhouse?" called Ralph, carrying in an armload of potted plants. Gretchen followed, hugely pregnant, bearing homemade fruit cakes, and looking as weary as Lauren had ever seen her.

"Gretch! You shouldn't be standing on your feet baking in your seventh month!"

"Good therapy," she retorted in her most doughty New England manner.

Lauren was talking to Stanley and Elaine Eisen who had driven over from Greensboro when the Lawrences arrived, so she missed the rather tense encounter between Gretchen and Carol in the dining room. A few minutes later, Jim came to say good-bye. "But you just got here!"

"Sorry, Lauren, I'll explain another time," he replied, looking distressed.

She had no time to wonder what that was all about before David claimed her attention, "We need more ginger ale for the punch, honey." For the next two hours, it was hectic, with more and more guests arriving. Lauren and David were kept busy seeing that everyone had a drink and the new people met one another, while Amanda constantly refilled the platters with her delicious food—and even little Babs got into the act, toddling around offering people her beguiling smile. Finally it was calm enough for Lauren to have a sherry and chat with the Rosenblooms, who had been her first hosts in Chapel Hill. And, of course, with her cousins, Ruth and Jay Felder, who had brought an embarrassingly expensive house gift. "It's a *precious* little house, Laurie," declared Ruth, and David had to leave the room to keep from laughing in her face.

When their guests had left, they lingered over coffee and fruit cake in the living room, then helped Amanda clear up. Putting her arm around her husband's waist as they looked in on the children before going to bed, Lauren thought how sweet they looked, sleeping peacefully. *I am so lucky to be me, having David and these two wonderful babies.*

And in ten days, she was going on with grad school. As long as Amanda was there to help care for the children, she would be able to get her Ph.D.

Chapter 24

November 1941

IT WAS LATE afternoon, eleven months after the house-warming party, when Lauren finished proofreading her term paper for Renaissance Studies. The interdepartmental seminar was given by two of the best scholars in the English and history departments, one of them a remarkable woman who had just been turned down for tenure by her mostly male colleagues. In her second term as a doctoral candidate, Lauren was learning something about the politics of academia.

Stacking the pages in order, Lauren fastened them into a binder, intending to drop the paper in the history office on her way out. It got dark so early, if she didn't hurry, the children would be falling asleep by the time she reached home. She glanced at her watch. *Damn,* she'd missed her ride again.

Her attention was caught by a movement across the hall. Through the glass in the door of the seminar room, she glimpsed Carol Lawrence walking past. Giving a quick glance over her shoulder, Carol ducked into a side door leading down the stairs to an exit. We can walk home together, thought Lauren, gathering her books and hurrying to catch up, but before she could call out, Carol had vanished. Strange, she had acted almost furtive, sneaking around as if she was concealing something.

Come to think of it, this was the second time Lauren had seen Carol leaving this building late in the day, the last occasion on a rainy afternoon several weeks ago. Carol had waved, calling hello, and hurried off without stopping for conversation. What would she be doing in the history department, anyway? Her husband Jim's office was over in MacNider and Carol wasn't taking courses at the university, as far as she knew.

Of course, Lauren hadn't been keeping up with her friends over the past year, had scarcely seen Gretchen since the end of summer. Fulfilling requirements in history, languages, and philosophy, in addition to 400-level studies in writing and English literature, did not leave you much time for anything else. Last summer she had taken a vacation from the bookstore because David insisted. He said it was too difficult for her to work year-round, and of course it meant she spent less time with the children, which was his *real* concern. It was a subject of growing antagonism between them. She would love to quit her job, but she was loathe to give up the pay check that covered Amanda's salary.

There would be another fight with David when he learned she had registered for three courses and agreed to work four half-days during the next term, beginning in January. She knew what he would say, could repeat the words before he got them out: *It's not as if I have a nine-to-five job, Laurie, one of us has to be home for our kids, if you didn't want to be a mother why did you have them . . .*

If she didn't *want* to be a mother! She hadn't had much choice, had she? Sometimes she felt it would have been better if they had waited to marry. She could have been *finishing* her Ph.D. by now and they would just be starting out. Like Philip and Jeanette.

As soon as Phil had begun to call her again, Jeanette had broken her engagement to the dentist, and now their wedding date was set for the first Sunday in December. Lauren envied them the joy of beginning their lives together. All too soon, the excitement wore off and you came to take each other for granted. She sighed, thinking how quickly romance dissipated with marriage. At least, it had with her and David. Hardly romantic anymore, making love only once every other week or so. Mostly because of David's long hours and night duty—but of course, her own late-night studying and worrying about another pregnancy didn't help.

Lauren shivered in the cold air, wishing she had worn a heavier jacket. She hated walking home alone after dark. Some of these streets didn't have lights yet. It wasn't far, but it was hard going uphill carrying a stack of books.

"Hey, lady, want a lift?"

Startled, Lauren was relieved to see that it was Ralph Nelson in his old Chevrolet coupe. "Oh, it's you, Ralph. Thanks—my usual ride left and this bag is getting heavy."

Ralph leaned over to swing the door open and she slid in next to him. "Do you always go home this late?" she asked.

"I had a student conference."

"I was in the history seminar room. If I'd known that, I would've come to your office. I didn't notice any lights."

"I was using an advisor's cubicle downstairs," he said quickly. Too quickly. She knew he was lying. "Gretchen was just saying we haven't seen you and David for weeks," Ralph continued nervously talking. "He must be pretty busy now that he's full-time at the Russell. I've been meaning to call . . ."

But Lauren wasn't paying attention. It was suddenly so clear, so obvious! Numbed by her discovery, she was unable to do more than nod in response to Ralph's words. Could she possibly be wrong? No, there wasn't a doubt in her mind . . . *Ralph was having an affair with Carol Lawrence.*

David had reached home ahead of her and was playing with Mark on the living room floor. Babs sat at the piano picking out tunes with one finger.

"Hi, sweetheart," David called, smiling to see her. "I was wondering when you were coming home. I would've come by for you if I'd known where you were. We really should try to find a second-hand car for you to use— Darling, what's wrong?"

She put down her books and burst into tears, turning away so the children wouldn't see. David set Mark in the playpen. "Be back in a minute, sport." He quickly came to Lauren's side and put his arms around her, leading her into the little den off the front hall. "Hey, now, what's this all about?"

"Oh, David—Ralph brought me home. I think—that is, I learned something I never suspected. Ralph and Carol . . ."

He tightened his arms around her. "Yes, I know," he said quietly.

"It's really true, then. How long has it been going on?"

"A long time—over a year."

David recalled the day six months ago when Ralph had called to say he needed to talk to him. It was on a Sunday morning and they had met in David's office at the Russell Clinic. "Gretchen and I—well, things aren't so great between us, Dave," Ralph had begun haltingly, and David had been dumbfounded because he thought theirs was an idyllic marriage.

"I'm sorry, and surprised, frankly."

"Yeah, I guess you would be." He sighed and ran his hands through his hair. "Jesus! I've made a mess of it, but I'm in love with someone else."

He had looked so bleak that David almost, but not quite, felt sorry for him. *A married man doesn't fall in love with another woman unless he's looking for it!* he wanted to shout. Instead, he had quietly asked questions and listened to his friend make excuses for screwing around.

"I know now it was just a physical attraction between Gretchen and me," Ralph's smooth, persuasive manner was almost convincing. "Once we started having kids—*three,* for Christ's sake! One after the other—"

"You can hardly blame Gretchen for that, Ralph," he had managed to say.

"I suppose not. She said she didn't want to get pregnant again so soon, but—anyway, she let herself go, never took off the weight after the second baby, the house was always a mess. I don't know, she lost her attraction for me. Let's face it, Dave, mothers are not sexy!"

He had been really pissed off at Ralph. But he referred him to a counselor who worked with couples to try to save their marriages, knowing all the time that what Ralph really wanted was exoneration.

"But Carol is Gretchen's *best friend!*" Lauren was saying tearfully. "How *could* she? How could *he?*"

"I honestly don't know, honey, I don't understand anything about it. I guess it just started and somehow they're powerless to stop."

"That's *ridiculous!* No one is *powerless,* they're just selfish and pleasure-seeking. Gretchen and Ralph have *three children,* and the baby's just eight months old!" She blew her nose in David's handkerchief. "And what about little Jimmy Lawrence?"

"It's terribly sad for both families. I hear Jim won't give Carol a divorce."

"*Divorce?* Oh, my God! Then Gretchen knows about it?"

"If not, she's the only person in Chapel Hill who doesn't."

Lauren planned to go over to talk to Gretchen—to indicate in some way that she was on her side—but there was no time the following week because her mother came to visit them for Thanksgiving.

Miriam was fretful after Philip deposited her in Chapel Hill before driving on to Rocky Mount to spend Thanksgiving with Jeanette's family.

They were getting married, after all. She knew in her bones Jeanette was the wrong wife for him! The girl was too headstrong, too dominant. Miriam, who thought she understood her son better than anyone else, was absolutely certain what was good for him . . . But you couldn't tell young people anything these days. No one would listen to an old woman.

When David suggested that his mother-in-law have a checkup at the Russell Clinic while she was in Chapel Hill, she went along with it because she worshiped Lauren's husband. It was a family joke that because David was a doctor, Miriam put him on a pedestal and he could do no wrong. She loved the way he called her Mother. Joanna's husband called her Mimi, Mrs. J., or nothing; but then, he was only twelve years younger than Miriam, so she wouldn't have liked to be called Mother by someone almost as old as she . . .

"Just a few more tests to run, Mother," David assured her when she complained about the amount of time she was spending at the hospital. "I'll bet it's been years since you had a thorough physical."

It *was* years. In fact, Miriam had never had this kind of examination before. Why did they ask her all those foolish questions? Word-association tests they called them. And why were they taking X-rays of her head and pricking her legs with pins? The things doctors could dream up to do to their patients, it was like some sort of medieval torture!

"After all that, what did they find?" she asked David when they were driving home.

"Nothing more than what the internist told you. You have to watch your diet, not eat too much sugar or salt. Your blood pressure is a little on the high side and your blood sugar could be lower." He patted her hand, "You're a perfect specimen."

He would wait until after the wedding to talk to Lauren about the clinical report. They would have to run more tests, of course. They knew so little about *Alzheimer's dementia,* but if the neurologists were right, Miriam would not be able to live alone for long.

Miriam was displeased because the number of guests at Phil's wedding was so small, a hundred and twenty people. That meant only first cousins could be invited, offending all the relatives scattered throughout the South. There were so many of the Jacobson clan, they wouldn't know where to stop, explained Jeanette, who did not want her family to bear the expense of a huge affair. Miriam was also dissatisfied with her accommodations at the hotel. She put up such a fuss that she ended by staying with one of Jeanette's relatives, thus causing everyone last minute inconvenience, which embarrassed Lauren.

"This is supposed to be the bride's day," she whispered to David. "I don't know what has happened to Mama, she's become so domineering. Nothing pleases her anymore."

"Many people become difficult as they grow older," David reassured her.

"She's not that old. Grandpa lived into his eighties, but even when he was sick, he wasn't as bad as this."

"Your mother hasn't only lost her husband, Lauren. Her entire purpose was to take care of her family and now she feels they're deserting her."

"It isn't fair of her to hang onto Philip just because he's the last one to get married. Poor Jeanette will have to put up with her, living in Randolph."

At least Jeanette would not have to share a house with her mother-in-law. Miriam's personality was changing for the worse, and it was unlikely that she and Jeanette could live harmoniously in the same house. In the last difficult year, Philip had worked out some of his problems with the help of a psychiatrist in Asheville, recommended by a colleague of David's. A good, solid, sensible man, not one of those Freudians who forced you to drag out all sorts of garbage you had buried. Phil had come to understand that his difficulties were not so much sexual as filial. His mother had him bound to her by ties of guilt. One of the results of Philip's therapy was that he had bought a Mediterranean-style bungalow in the new Shadow Mountain development.

Lauren was Jeanette's only attendant. The wedding took place at noon and was followed by a reception and luncheon at Ricks Hotel. In the excitement of the occasion, no one listened to the radio. The bride and groom were dressed in their going away outfits, ready to leave on a honeymoon trip to California, when a hotel porter was overheard saying, "It's a mighty sad day, with America going to war."

As everyone clustered around to hear the news of the attack on an American naval base in Hawaii, Miriam burst into tears. "It's a bad omen! I *knew* it, I've had a terrible premonition all along."

Lauren hushed her mother, taking her aside so the Greenthal family wouldn't hear. "Mama, that's an outrageous thing to say! What has the Japanese attacking Pearl

Harbor got to do with Philip's wedding? Please, try to act like you're happy for them."

The wedding party followed the bride and groom to the train station just across the way. They flung rice and streamers at Philip and Jeanette as they boarded the Pullman that would carry them west.

Forever they'll remember that we went to war on their wedding day, thought Lauren, as she waved to her brother and his bride.

Book III

BETRAYAL

1943—1945

Chapter 25

New York, Winter 1943

AN ICY WIND swept off the Hudson River on a bitter cold evening in February, when Captain David Bernard, U.S. Army Medical Corps, returned to his quarters in a grand old building on Riverside Drive, within view of the dimmed-out George Washington Bridge. After a grueling day in surgery at the Columbia University Medical Center, he was looking forward to a hot shower, a double bourbon, an early dinner, and a good night's sleep.

The United States had been at war for fourteen months: The President had met with Prime Minister Churchill in Casablanca, calling for unconditional surrender by the Axis; the Allied invasion of North Africa had caught the German High Command completely by surprise; the last Germans had surrendered at Stalingrad; and American forces in the Pacific had finally secured Guadalcanal, but at a terrible cost.

This was David's first free evening in the four weeks since he had arrived in New York City for an intensive course in "The Surgical Management of Battlefield Casualties." Thus far, it had meant twelve- and fourteen-hour days, filled with nonstop lectures, clinics, and surgery. Today's session on arthroplasty, the restoration of motion to a damaged joint, had turned out to be more complicated than anticipated when they encountered fibrous ankylosis in a patient suffering from rheumatoid arthritis—a condition he was unlikely to encounter in vigorous young men wounded in action.

In the lobby of his building, the desk sergeant handed him several letters and a telephone message: *Call Mrs. Fields today. Urgent.* Laughing, he thought how like Charlotte that was. In her opinion, anything concerned with herself and Bruce was of vital importance. Thank goodness Laurie wasn't that way—he couldn't stand self-absorbed women.

So far, he had managed to put off contacting Lauren's cousin. Whenever he called home, two or three times a week, he was hard put to explain to Laurie why he had not yet seen Charlotte. She never could accept that David had not developed the same close family feeling with Charlee as he had with Philip and her parents. "If you'd just give her a chance, you'd see what a truly wonderful person she is," Lauren told him whenever he remarked that Charlee and Bruce were shallow people.

The elevator creaked upward to the fourteenth floor. David let himself into the spartan studio apartment assigned to him, and tossed his mail on the desk. For a moment, he considered returning Charlotte's call. It was a solitary life up here and he did have the evening off, but he really did not want to get involved with the Fieldses and their socialite friends. This was only the second time in his life he had been in New York and he intended to enjoy his freedom. There were some tickets for Broadway shows at the desk and he was tempted to ask for one of them—but he would probably do better to spend the evening reading the material for tomorrow's lectures. Removing his jacket and tie, he unbuttoned his shirt, preparing to take a shower.

It was lonely in the city. He missed Lauren terribly and, despite his initial anger, had forgiven her for refusing to accompany him to New York. It turned out that she had been right, after all. She would have been stuck in a dreary apartment with the children during this miserable winter weather, waiting up for him until all hours. Unless Amanda came along to care for Babs and Mark—impossible, since Mandy lived with her ailing father—Laurie wouldn't even have been able to enroll in graduate courses at Columbia.

Like everyone, their lives had been disrupted by the war. Soon after Pearl Harbor, David had been commissioned as a reserve captain attached to the 65th General Hospital, a North Carolina unit from World War I that had been reorganized and affiliated with Duke Hospital. As part of the regional staff at Duke, he had remained at the Russell Clinic until called to active duty in July of '42. Once finished with the five weeks of basic training at Fort Bragg, he had been able to get home to Lauren and the children every weekend.

Bored out of his mind at Bragg, with little surgery to perform, his duties had been mainly administrative. When he had been detached for special surgical training at Columbia, David welcomed the temporary assignment in New York. He would be here for a minimum of four months, possibly longer. He knew his working hours would be impossible. It was probably crazy, but he had wanted his family with him.

"You always said you'd like to live in Manhattan, honey," he announced to Lauren as soon as he received his orders. "Here's your chance."

Perhaps he should have been prepared for her reaction. "Me, go to New York *now?*" she had cried, aghast. "You don't mean it! Where would we live?"

"I'll find an apartment when I get there and then you can bring the children."

"There's a housing shortage in New York, David. Everything's ridiculously expensive and I hear living conditions are terrible."

"It won't be so bad. I'm sure Bruce can help us find something, maybe in the suburbs. That would be good for the kids."

But Lauren had not wanted to leave Chapel Hill because it would mean dropping out of graduate school once again. "Couldn't we wait, David? I'll come up in the summer if you're still in New York."

"If I'm not there, I'll be overseas."

There was hurt in his voice and guilt in hers, but she would not back down. "I just started planning my dissertation with my advisor. You know what it will be like for us if I come to New York—you'll be tied up at the hospital every night, just as you are here, and I'll see you on the occasional evening, whenever you can get off."

"Thanks a lot, Laurie! I didn't realize it was such a sacrifice."

She glared at him, "Am I supposed to drop everything to follow you around the country with the children, just so you can spend a few hours a week with us? Is that what you expect of me?"

"I was under the impression that's what wives did—most wives, anyway. I guess I was wrong."

The hell, he had thought bitterly, forgetting all about his own doubts. Obviously, getting her degree meant more to Lauren than *he* did! He might as well face it, the romance had gone out of their marriage. It had happened almost without his realizing it. Maybe that wasn't unusual after five years, but he longed for more.

On the tedious train trip north, sitting up all night, he'd had time to view the situation more rationally. Being married to a surgical resident had not been easy for Lauren. For years she had been an uncomplaining wife, putting aside her own ambitions when the babies were born. Now she felt it was her right to finish her degree. The fact was, he was proud of Lauren's achievements and admired her determination. Certainly he loved her and knew she was devoted to him and the children. But that incandescent fire was missing between them. Had it ever really been there, he asked himself. *Yes,* in the beginning. For one night, one forgotten night, long ago . . .

What they had was probably better than most of their friends, he reflected. Look at Ralph and Gretchen—they had been crazy in love, and now Gretch wanted to take their children back to Massachusetts, if her parents would have her. Ralph had been drafted, Jim Lawrence was 4F, and Carol had decided not to leave him after all, when he refused to give up their son. Two families would never be the same because Ralph couldn't keep his pants buttoned up, for that's what it amounted to.

By the time David reached New York, he had almost convinced himself that an absence from each other might improve their marriage. Practically speaking, Lauren and the children would be more comfortable and safer at home in Chapel Hill. If the Germans were to bomb any American cities, it would be New York or Washington. Even so, he did wish she were the sort of wife who would willingly join him wherever he was sent.

While he was still in the shower, David heard his telephone ringing. Wrapping himself in a towel, he walked dripping across the room to answer it.

"I have the feeling you've been avoiding me," said a velvety female voice.

"Charlotte?"

"The same."

"I just came in a little while ago and I received your message."

"Naughty boy! You've been here for months and you haven't called."

"Barely one month, Charlee, and I'm sorry. They've kept me standing on my feet ten hours a day."

"I'll forgive you if you come to dinner."

"Not tonight!"

"Yes, *tonight.*"

"Charlee—I can't. I have some reading to do and—"

"There's no way you can get out of this, David. Be here at seven. Do you have the address?"

He sighed. "Yes, I have the address."

"See you, then." And she rang off.

Dammit, he did *not want* to go to Charlotte's Park Avenue apartment for dinner. He did not wish to make empty-headed conversation, or endure Bruce's snide New Yorker put-downs. But Bruce would not be there, of course, for he was stationed in Washington with army intelligence . . . If David refused to go, it would get back to Lauren and all the family. Charlee was right, there was no way he could get out of this one.

At seven o'clock, arriving in the courtyard of the ponderous rococo building with its mansard roof and carved pink marble facade, he felt the country boy. An ancient doorman saluted him as he opened the cab door, and in the lobby, a gray-haired, elderly attendant (all the young ones had been drafted) noted his uniform respectfully.

"Mrs. Fields is expecting me," David said, conscious that the softness in his diction marked him as a Southerner.

"Yes sir, Captain, it's the elevator to the right."

He had never been inside a Park Avenue apartment building before. In taxis, driving past block after block of impressive granite and brick structures, he had felt little curiosity about the buildings or the people who lived in them. This was grander than most from the outside, its lobby more imposing than the Hotel Pennsylvania where he had stayed on his first night in New York. He took in the dark woods, lofty carved ceilings, and thick silencing carpets. Discreet sconces flanked gilt mirrors that reflected careful arrangements of fresh flowers. Such permanent elegance and stability seemed to stand in defiance of swings in the economy or wars among nations.

A maid waited in the penthouse foyer for David to emerge from the elevator. He handed her his hat and military overcoat, and passed through a hallway to enter a round gallery, just as Charlotte shouted his name from a balcony and came flying down the stairs like a school girl. Fresh, sparkling, and vibrant, she threw her arms around his neck, kissing him exuberantly. For a moment, there flashed before him the memory of the first time they'd met, and he knew there was a reason why he had been avoiding her.

"*Wow,* Dave," she exclaimed, holding him away from her, "you're even more handsome in uniform—there ought to be a *law!*" Flattered in spite of himself, he smiled.

Wearing a garnet and gold silk brocade jacket over a velvet hostess pajama, with her glossy dark hair falling loose and shoulder-length, she smelled of some glorious gardenia-like fragrance. Her speech had lost much of its drawl, but then, she had sounded less Southern than the rest of her family ever since he'd known her.

"Come, let me show you around and then we'll have a drink," she said, and he allowed her to take his hand to lead him through the light, airy rooms all done in the most restful and subtly beautiful tones of white, beige, and mushroom, with faded antique Oriental carpets underfoot.

On the walls were paintings like those he had seen only in modern art collections of museums or in the folios Lauren collected. Brash, bold, and innovative, they startled the eye. The library was more mellow, a room to be lived in, with stacks of books, deep, comfortable loungy couches and chairs, and good lamps for reading. A baby grand Steinway stood in one corner, and a fire crackled cheerily in the grate.

Charlotte outshown everything in the exquisitely furnished penthouse.

Now that he was here, it was both better and worse than he had anticipated. "It's a beautiful apartment, Charlee," he told her, because he had to say something and he was nervous.

The young maid entered, carrying a silver bucket containing ice and a bottle of champagne. She had some trouble with the cork. "May I?" said David, taking it from her. The girl stepped back gratefully as he let it go with a gentle pop. A puff of condensation rose from the bottle.

"Thank you, Mairie. Why don't you bring a little something for us to nibble?" Charlee held two chilled glasses by their stems while David poured. "She's new—experienced maids are hard to find these days. Our butler left for a war job. Good riddance, as far as I'm concerned. He was an old sour puss, but Bruce liked him."

"How is Bruce?" David asked.

She smiled archly. "Same as ever, except he loves playing soldier. I've hardly seen him. He seldom comes to New York and I don't care for Washington, with all those cigar-smoking schemers trying to see what they can get out of this war."

"What do you do with your time?"

She fitted a cigarette into a gold holder and leaned forward for him to light it. "Oh, the usual—Red Cross, USO, bond drives—but the cause that interests me most is a committee for Jewish war orphans. We raise money and find homes for children whose parents have been killed or put in concentration camps. We always keep sisters and brothers together, if we can."

"How many have you placed?"

"Only a few hundred so far. We have more sponsors than children. I wanted to take a child, actually, but Bruce won't hear of it." She flicked the ash of her cigarette impatiently. "It's so heartlessly frustrating! There were thousands and thousands of children left behind in France when their parents were taken away. Very few got out, and not all that many are being let *in*. To the United States, that is."

"Really? I hadn't thought that. I was under the impression we've accepted a great many."

"That's what they *want* you to think! The fact is, David, lots of people in this country don't like Jews, even the children. If a refugee doesn't have American relatives, there's almost no hope for a visa. There are very strict quotas, but our State Department hasn't even begun to fill them."

She discussed the agencies and Jewish leaders who had tried to influence Washington to take in more refugees; and the lobbyists who continued to fight against Jewish immigration, even after the United States had entered the war.

"They give all kinds of sanctimonious reasons, but they're all anti-Semites," she said, anger narrowing her eyes. "Jewish refugees have merely trickled in since we've been in the war, even though hundreds of thousands have applied. George Stearns, who's the chairman of our group, told me only twelve thousand refugees came in last year. I don't know where he gets his information, but he assures me it's reliable."

"Suppose the children did get U.S. visas, how would it be handled? Who in France could organize it, with the occupation?"

"Well, *now* it's quite hopeless. A number of agencies were active in Vichy France until it was occupied at the end of last year: Quaker groups and the Jewish agencies—mainly the American Friends Service Committee and the

Joint Distribution Committee. But, I'm surprised you don't know all this, David!"

He felt ashamed. "I'm not active in any Jewish organizations. We go to services in Durham on the High Holidays, and that's about it. I guess we're going to have to do something about the children when they're older—Sunday School . . ." It was a lame, inadequate response. "I know the situation is desperate for the Jews, of course, but I'm not as well-informed as you are. Our newspapers at home don't cover international events as thoroughly as the New York *Times* and the *Herald Tribune.*"

"Hah! Don't kid yourself. There's a conspiracy of silence in the press. The *Times* buries any article about masses of Jews being murdered—they're afraid of being labeled the Jewish newspaper. George Stearns says there's documented evidence coming through Switzerland that the Nazis intend to exterminate the European Jews, but our government ignores the subject. It certainly hasn't made the slightest impact on our immigration policy!"

David regarded her with amazement. This was a different Charlotte from the one he had known, or thought he'd known. He rather liked her.

"Charlee . . . I think I've done you an injustice all these years."

"I didn't mean to depress you," she said lightly. "More bubbly?" She refilled their glasses.

Taking his champagne, David walked over to the piano and fingered a few notes with one hand.

"I'd forgotten. You play, don't you?"

"Used to. I haven't touched it for a while."

"Please, won't you now, for me?"

He stared at her for a moment, then put his glass aside and sat down, letting his hands wander over the keyboard, finding their way into one of his old medleys. He was acutely aware when Charlotte came across the room and stood behind him.

The maid brought in a tray of canapés. Charlee took it from her, helping herself and feeding one to David. As her fingers brushed his lips, he tried to ignore the thrill of excitement that shot through him. She leaned over the piano and began to sing in a low, pleasing voice. He found it easy to transpose to her register, improvising as she sang tunes from the latest Broadway shows.

From the fireplace the flames cast a rosy glow over the bookshelves and the comfortable couches and club chairs. Now that he was warmed up, David played well. They harmonized, laughing together as they sipped champagne between songs. He unwound, listening to Charlee's rich contralto, surprised at how easy they were with each other.

Suddenly the mellow mood was broken by the sound of laughter from the front of the apartment. In answer to David's questioning glance, Charlee said, "I forgot to mention I've invited some friends." She leaned forward, her face an inch away from his, "You play a mean, sexy piano, Captain Bernard." She touched the bars on his shoulder before hurrying into the gallery to greet her guests.

David remained seated at the piano. He could not deny his disappointment. He should have been relieved that other people were present, but instead—he realized, to his dismay—he felt a keen regret. Lowering his head in his hands, he groaned, "David . . . you should not have come here."

Charlotte returned with Audrey and Steve Burns, a lean, dark couple from Scarsdale with an air of complete satisfaction. It must be wonderful to feel that pleased with yourself, thought David.

A tall, distinguished looking man with deep-set dark eyes and just the right amount of silvery gray at his temples followed them into the library. At his side was a short, enormously overweight woman dressed in a tight-fitting black velvet suit. Her bosom was covered by a mass of pearls clasped with a showy diamond brooch. Above the several folds of her chin, you could see she had once been a beauty.

". . . and these are some old friends of Laurie's, David—Norma and George Stearns."

"So *this* is the man who managed to sweep the beautiful Lauren Jacobson off her feet," said George heartily, as they shook hands.

Behind his back, Charlee rolled her eyes comically at David. "Who wants champagne?" she called.

"I'll fix some martinis, if I may," said Steve Burns, going to the bar.

"What do you hear from Blanche and Jules?" Norma asked Charlotte when they were all seated with drinks.

"Jules is at the Great Lakes Naval Station in the Supply Corps. Blanche is *enceinte* again—she lost the first at three months."

"Then, it wasn't meant to be," said Norma. "Isn't that so, Capt. Bernard?"

"Please, call me David."

"Very well, David—isn't it so, that when a woman has a miscarriage, the baby would have been a monster?"

"Well, that's a bit extreme, but if something interferes with the process of a normal pregnancy, it could result in damage to the fetus."

"Lots of women are put to bed in order to keep a baby when they threaten to miscarry," said Charlee, her tone intensely earnest. "Those babies aren't damaged."

David nodded. "Generally, if the woman carries to term, the child will be normal, even if she has experienced some difficulty. There's a lot we don't know about birth defects. It's an interesting field."

"What is *your* specialty?" asked Audrey Burns, who had been wandering around the room examining the framed prints and sculptures.

"I'm an orthopedic surgeon."

"David's here to learn the latest techniques in bone grafting and artificial joints," Charlee added proudly.

"You'll be going overseas, no doubt, after that," said George Stearns.

David shrugged. "I suppose so, although I really don't know my orders. I could be here until summer, and I expect to rejoin my unit at Fort Bragg after that."

"You shouldn't ask him to give away military secrets, George," chided Audrey.

"Nothing's classified in the Medical Corps," said her husband Steve in a denigrating tone, and David found it rankled him. What was Mr. Burns doing for the war effort, in his pin-striped suit and custom-made shirt? The man was typical of everything David disliked in Northern Jews—brash, materialistic, overly self-confident, hard-driving, and nervy as hell. As Aunt Ethel would have said, "lacking in refinement."

"Time for one more drink," announced Charlotte briskly. "Cook will have conniptions if we don't go into dinner soon! I wouldn't want her to quit. Where would I ever find someone these days?"

The other Charlotte had returned. David watched her play hostess to these sharp-witted, influential people with an enviable skill, but he preferred the woman he had seen for that brief interlude before her guests had arrived.

At dinner he was seated at the foot of the table, with Norma and Audrey on either hand. "Tell me, how is dear Lauren?" asked Norma. Despite her roundness, there was a pinched, hungry look about her, like a stealthy beast.

"Lauren is fine. Working hard on her doctorate at the university."

"She always *was* a serious little thing." Norma looked over at Charlee who was engaged in conversation with George. "How *nice* that you two are keeping up the family tie . . ." Her eyes gleamed wetly beneath the bulge of her brow.

David noticed how Norma studied everyone at the table with avid attention while gulping wine. She seemed to be collecting impressions and tucking them away for future use. That is one dangerous woman, he concluded. Charlee ought to watch out for her.

From Audrey Burns he learned that her husband was in the Fields firm. "Steve flunked his physical, thank God—flat feet. I shouldn't say that to an officer, but someone has to stay home and practice law. He's working too hard, though. I keep telling him he needs to take a little vacation. After all, normal life does go on, doesn't it?"

"I'm not really sure what's normal," he replied. "Except for these past few weeks, I worked longer hours before I went into the Army."

After dessert, the women retired to an upstairs sitting room, while the men had brandy and cigars. They treated him with polite deference because he was a surgeon and an army officer about to go overseas. It was almost enough to overcome the fact that he was not one of them, and a Southerner at that.

"I went down to see Bruce in Washington the other day," Burns told them in a confidential manner. "He's traveling around the country, doing something hush-hush. I imagine that's why Charlee hasn't gone to stay with him."

"She's better off at home," said Stearns with a note of authority. "The housing shortage is even worse in D.C. than it is in New York."

When the women returned, their makeup freshened, they all went into the library. George put some records on the phonograph and danced with Charlee. Norma, in conversation on the other side of the room, kept her eyes on them, ever watchful. "Doesn't anyone play the piano?" she called. "We could sing."

David studied his brandy, not saying anything. Would Charlee ask him to play? Somehow the time together before dinner had seemed special, for just the two of them. When he looked up, her smoky eyes were on him, and with satisfaction he thought, *She feels it too.*

The Burnses were saying good night because they had to drive to Scarsdale. "Can we give you a lift, David? It's not out of the way," offered Steve. David had hoped for a moment with Charlee, but it would not look right for him to stay on when the others were leaving.

"That's *so* dear of you, Steve, but David promised to advise me on some family matters," Charlee said before he could reply. The elevator door closed on Norma's speculative smile.

"You didn't want to get stuck with them, did you?" said Charlee.

"Not really. But I should be going, it's late."

"Not yet. Come sit for a minute." She led him back to the library and poured two brandies, kicking off her backless velvet slippers and sitting cross-legged on a couch. "What did you think of Norma?"

"I wouldn't trust her from here to the corner."

She laughed. "I don't. But then, she doesn't trust me either. She's afraid her husband is having an affair with me."

He was shocked. "She can't be serious!"

"Oh, David, you're very sweet. I keep forgetting what men are like down home."

"Was that meant to put me in my place?"

"Not at all. Right now, I would say there is nothing so appealing as a handsome, gentlemanly captain from North Carolina."

He studied his hands, wondering whether she was toying with him. They were seated across from each other on plump, downy sofas. Charlee was all silk and shimmer . . . her hair, her eyes, her skin, her clothes and her expensive, exotic scent. He shut out the vision he had of her in George Stearns's arms. He would not ask her to deny it, but the idea was unthinkable.

"Why do you suppose Norma is jealous of you?"

"Once I would have said it was because they lost everything, and we didn't. They had a difficult time during the Thirties. Gave up their town house and winters in the South, brought an end to the fabulous entertaining. I have to admire Norma, she's the one who kept George afloat during those years." Fitting another cigarette into her holder, Charlotte leaned across the cocktail table toward David, who half stood to light it. "Now, George is in the heavy equipment business, selling to the armed services—construction, tractors, tanks. He's making a bloody fortune on this war."

"He's a profiteer, in other words?"

She nodded, reluctantly, he thought. "You and my father-in-law! He detests George Stearns, thinks he's unscrupulous, and therefore 'not a gentleman.' That's the worst indictment Malcolm Fields can make against a man."

"Norma drinks rather a lot," said David.

"Yes, it's gotten to be a problem for George. Well, they're not perfect, but they're old friends." She stubbed out her cigarette and took another, as David frowned. "And I smoke too much . . . don't tell me, I know it."

"Don't worry, I won't be your conscience, Charlee," he replied, rising. "I really must go now."

In the foyer, he put on his overcoat. "Thanks for the dinner."

He leaned down and placed a kiss on her cheek. As the elevator doors closed, she blew him another.

Chapter 26

Spring 1943

DIAMONDS OF LIGHT danced across the moving train, patterning Lauren's arms. She stared out the window with unseeing eyes, taking no pleasure in the passing landscape. A soft afternoon sun bathed the sloping mountain sides, dappling neat rows of tobacco plants, curing sheds, and weathered houses.

The coach was filled with young service families journeying to army camps, or returning home after their men had been shipped overseas. They traveled like gypsies, encumbered by the paraphernalia of infant care. The mothers seemed barely out of their teens, as they bolstered one another, drawing courage and comfort from trading stories. With weary resignation, Lauren closed her eyes, lulled by the drone of their voices and the monotonous sound of the wheels on the track.

It did not surprise her that her life had become so suddenly altered. She had been reared on a philosophy of doom: This was too good to be true; that wouldn't happen because she so wanted it. When she was young she had been certain she would not live beyond twenty; then, that she would never find someone to love. Now that she was David's wife and had children of her own, she could never quite believe it would last. Not believing in happiness made it difficult to accept.

I'll never have what I want, she thought. *Every time I think I've found it, it turns out not to be enough.*

No sooner had David left for New York, than she regretted her decision to remain in Chapel Hill. Consumed with loneliness, she had missed him dreadfully, reaching out for him in the night, needing his touch. Sick with the knowledge that he wasn't lying there next to her in the morning—and that she had herself to blame. If she had gone with him when he asked, she would have missed a semester. *One lousy semester!* Whatever had been going through her head when she refused him?

After two weeks alone, she called to say she had changed her mind. "David, I was thinking we should come up, after all. I can't believe I was so selfish."

"No, honey, you were right, as usual. Finding a decent apartment would be impossible. The kids would have hated it here, and I'm never home for dinner." It wasn't worth the trouble for her to move the family to New York for a few months, he told her.

"But you said you'll probably go overseas after that . . . and I miss you so. I wish you could get home for a couple of days."

"I miss you, too, sweetheart. I'm not due for a furlough for a while, but why don't you come up in the beginning of March during your spring break?"

Longing to see him, she had so looked forward to the trip, but the week before the vacation, both children had come down with chicken pox, and Amanda, as well. Chicken pox in adults was not a simple childhood disease; by the time Mandy had recovered, classes had resumed and it was too close to midterms for Lauren to leave.

David's assignment in New York had been extended, and Lauren planned ahead for the summer. Term papers and finals would come in May, and as soon as they were behind her, no matter what, she had been determined to go up North for as long as he was stationed there.

Then, it had all come apart.

Two nights ago the children ran to her for kisses when she walked in the kitchen door after work. "Sorry I'm so late, Mandy. How was everything today?"

"Just fine, Mrs. Bernard. Your brother Philip phoned from Randolph Springs. He said to tell you he would call back tonight because he has something important to discuss with you.''

She sighed. ''That can only be about my mother.'' The last time she had spoken to Phil, he told her Miriam was becoming more disoriented.

Lauren had just put the children to bed when the telephone rang. She would never have guessed why Philip was calling. ''I've joined the Army, Laurie. They're sending me to Fort Lee to Officers' Candidate School.''

''You've *joined the Army!*'' cried Lauren, aghast. Somehow she had never thought of Philip as a soldier. This was not going to be his war—her family had given one son to a European war.

''Do you think your husband is the only one who's patriotic in this family?'' he asked, stung that she implied he was not army material.

''No, of course not. I just thought you were needed on the home front . . .'' Philip had been exempt from the draft because he was running an essential industry. ''How will the plant manage without you?''

''Lionel can handle the business alone. He's over forty and he has a heart murmur, so he won't be called up. We've got some excellent foreladies who can take over as department managers.''

''What does Jeanette have to say about this?''

''She's behind it a hundred percent. As soon as school's out, she'll come to Virginia to be near me.''

But of course, Jeanette would go with Philip, even if it meant giving up her teaching job! Only Lauren Bernard was fool enough to let her husband go away without her.

''And what about Mama?''

''That's why I'm calling you, Laurie. I haven't told her yet. She's—well, she shouldn't be left on her own and she refuses to live with Joanna. Pansy can't stay at night, so Jeanette and I look in on Mama every evening. Moving in with Lionel wouldn't work, either, because Mama doesn't get along that well with Fay. It's all part of her condition, I guess. She's kind of difficult these days, but she *is* our mother . . .'' Philip was beating around the bush, leading up to something that Lauren did not want to hear. ''I was wondering—since David's in New York and you're alone, I thought maybe you might have her come there for a while. I know it's an imposition . . ."

There it was. She should have known her plans for joining David were not going to work out. "Do you think she'll be willing to leave Randolph?" she asked, all the time thinking, *I want to go to New York to be with my husband!*

"I suppose you could move here with the children for the duration, if I can't talk her into it."

"Philip, *no!* I have a *job.* And I've just begun my Ph.D. I couldn't possibly do that. Please don't make me feel guilty."

"Okay! Don't get excited, it was just a suggestion. I really hate for her to stay in her house alone. Maybe if you came to Randolph, you could convince her to go back with you for a couple of months—just temporarily, until she gets used to me being away."

As the train rounded a bend, the faint outline of Shadow Mountain came into view, the first distant sighting of Randolph Springs. Inexorably Lauren felt the walls closing in on her.

Philip met her at the station. "How's Mama?" she asked. "Have you told her she's going to be living with me for a while?"

"Not really. It's better if she thinks it's just a short visit. Her sense of passing time is off." When he saw the expression of dismay on Lauren's face, he reassured her. "Don't worry, she'll be fine. You'll soon get to know her limitations."

Miriam cried when Philip reminded her he was leaving for the Army. She had no recollection of discussing it the previous day. He sat down and took her hand, "Look, Mama, I know how unhappy you are about this, but it's something I *have* to do. Don't worry about me. They're not going to put me up in the front lines at my age. As long as I'm in Virginia, I'll come to see you often."

Miriam agreed to "a visit" in Chapel Hill. For the first few days she was docile, contented to watch the children and putter in the kitchen with Amanda, but Lauren was afraid that would not hold her attention for long. A chance meeting with Selma Rosenbloom in Foister's camera store, where Lauren stopped to pick up some prints for the bookshop, resulted in many happy hours for Miriam.

Selma had aged considerably in the six years Lauren had known her. A good-hearted woman, she wanted to hear the details of Miriam's failing health and Philip going into the Army. The result was that she came over that same afternoon to visit with Miriam and invited her to join her sewing circle. Soon Lauren's mother had made friends with a dozen aging ladies and was embarked on a slew of needlework projects.

That was the happier side of their arrangement. But there were long periods each day when her mother would sit with a vacant expression, taking no interest in what went on around her, or accusing Lauren of keeping her a prisoner, locked in the house. Which was true, in a sense, for Miriam had disconcerting habits—wandering out of the house in her nightgown, or collecting objects from everyone's bedroom and putting them in unexpected places. It was like having a gremlin in the house, Lauren thought with wry humor, when she discovered the egg beater in the bottom of Miriam's knitting basket. Her mother's memory of events long past was amazing in its detail, but she often forgot where she was that instant.

Lauren made an appointment with the chief neurologist at the Russell Clinic, who referred her to a Duke internist with an interest in geriatric patients. After additional consultations and another battery of tests, the doctors were confirmed in their opinion that Miriam was indeed suffering from *Alzheimer's dementia,* which they described as a presenile mental deterioration.

Just the sound of it was alarming. Little was known about the disease, which first had been described by a German neurologist in 1907. There were no laboratory tests to confirm the diagnosis. The condition would grow progressively worse, the doctors told Lauren, at a rate no one could predict, and there was nothing to be done, other than keeping Miriam as stimulated as possible.

The one bright moment that spring was David's unexpected weekend furlough at the end of April. He flew down to Bragg on an Air Force plane and they had two days together. "If it's not a good time, Laurie, I mean with your exams being next week . . ." he said, when he called to tell her.

A flood of tenderness and guilt swept through her at the hesitation in his voice. "To hell with my exams! I can't *wait* to see you, darling." She was so excited, she was unable to do any studying that night, and she didn't care.

But the weekend was disappointing. David looked pale and had circles under his eyes, and he seemed restless and unusually reticent with her. He enjoyed playing with the children, and talked for hours with Miriam, whose spirits lifted to see the son-in-law she favored.

"It's surprising, your mother can still carry on a normal conversation," he remarked after the first day at home. "It could go on like this for years, or there could be a sudden decline." He patted her shoulder. "I know how tough this is on you, dear."

They talked about Lauren's work, David complimented her on how well she was managing on his army pay, and although she did not like to burden him on his leave, there were a few problems they had to discuss—like Mark's recurring strep throats that seemed not to respond to sulfa drugs. Their regular pediatrician had gone into the Army, and Lauren did not have the same confidence in the older man who had taken over. "Dr. Dodds is always so absent-minded, half the time, I think he's not listening to me," she told David.

"I know Dodds. Not much personality, but I think he's a pretty solid man." David examined Mark's throat, nose, and ears and declared him in perfect health, which greatly relieved her mind. She thought how reassuring it was to have a doctor for a husband.

But it wasn't the way it had always been between them and she wondered whether she was the one at fault. When they were alone, she had to think of something to say, almost as if they were strangers. David made love to her, but it was a rather automatic exercise, and in the dark, she felt that she could have been any woman.

He must have felt the strain, too. Before leaving on Sunday afternoon, he suggested she come to New York in the beginning of June for their fifth anniversary. Lauren was counting on those few days together, with just the two of them. Uncomplicated by children or her mother's presence, it would be like a second honeymoon.

By late May it was already oppressively hot in Chapel Hill. Lauren took Miriam to the air-cooled Carolina Theatre on the Saturday afternoon before her planned trip to New York, to see "Reveille with Beverly," a rather foolish movie with the popular singer, Frank Sinatra.

In the middle of the film, Miriam suddenly exclaimed, "Will you look at that disgraceful behavior!" She pointed to a couple in the next row. The young man, sitting with his arm around his date, would occasionally turn to kiss her. The boy was in uniform, probably one of the naval cadets stationed at the university. "You ought to be ashamed of yourselves," Miriam scolded in a clear, audible voice, leaning forward to address them.

The couple hastily changed their seats while a titter ran through the audience. When Miriam continued commenting aloud, there was a chorus of complaints and whistles in the theater. Horribly embarrassed, Lauren exited with her protesting mother and took her home. It was a terrible moment. Miriam became greatly agitated and even with Amanda's help, Lauren could not quiet her. They had to call the doctor, and for the first time, he prescribed a sedative.

"I really am a bother to you, Laurie," Miriam said that night, when she was herself again and comfortably settled in bed. "It's not right that the baby has to take care of the mother."

"You're not a bother, Mama," she protested. "It's wonderful having you here."

At least tonight her mother knew who she was—half the time lately, she called her Joanna. Lauren kissed her good night and Miriam clung to her for a long moment. "I really do love you, Laurie, I always have."

Lauren smiled, thinking how sad and how late it was

for her mother to be telling her that now, but she said, "I know you do, Mama, and I love you, too."

David telephoned that evening from Charlee's apartment. They certainly did seem to be spending a lot of time together, she thought uneasily. Every time I've talked to Charlee lately, she mentions seeing David . . . Now, if that isn't *ridiculous* of me! When he *wouldn't* get in touch with her, I wasn't satisfied—and now that they've become pals, I'm looking for something *else* to complain about!

"We're going out to dinner and theater with some of Charlee's friends," David explained. "They're so insistent, I have a hard time saying no."

Charlotte was in high spirits when she got on the extension to speak. "I can't wait to see you next week, Laurie. Of course, you'll come here and David can sleep over with you. That is, if they let him out of that monastery up on Riverside Drive!"

Charlotte hadn't lost that teasing, seductive manner that everyone had always found so charming. "That's really sweet of you, Charlee . . ." Lauren would have preferred to stay in a hotel so that she and David could spend more time alone. Not that it mattered now, for how could she go away and leave Miriam?

"How's your mother doing?" David asked when Charlotte had relinquished the phone.

"Not at all well, darling." She related the episode in the theater. "I'm so discouraged, I don't see how I can come up to New York next week for our anniversary. Mandy can't manage the children and keep an eye on her, too. If she should have another episode like today, it would be a disaster."

"Why don't you get a nurse to come in for a few days?"

"I'm afraid that would only frighten her. She doesn't understand what's happening."

"Gosh, Laurie, if it isn't grad school, it's your mother! Do you know how long it's been since we've spent any time together, just the two of us?"

Did she know? For all these four months she had been miserable without him! At least *he* was in New York, doing what he loved best, orthopedic surgery. He was always being invited to parties with Charlee's crowd—not that he particularly enjoyed them. Or so he claimed. Who knew what he really felt? Charlee said David was much admired and "an attractive man was a scarce commodity." Tears of self-pity welled in her eyes. She took a deep breath, trying to calm herself.

Suddenly, for no particular reason she could conceive of, Lauren had a premonition that her marriage was actually in danger. That she could be losing her husband. She *had* to go up there to see him. *She simply had to!*

"Oh, David, I'm sorry—" Her voice caught and she swallowed. All she needed was to break down on the phone! Poor David, she was practically driving him away, with her moods. "I don't know what's got into me. I've had such a rotten day."

"I know you have, honey," he said, all solicitude and concern. "Believe me, I wish I were there to help. I do understand if you can't leave your mother."

"Don't worry, darling, I'll find a way. I promise I'll come to New York next week."

It was Amanda who saved the day.

"Now honey, you just go right ahead up there to Dr. Bernard," she insisted. "My neighbor used to be a practical nurse before she retired, and I'll get her to look after my father. That way, my sister can help me here during the daytime. I'll manage the nights just fine, when the children are asleep, and I can keep an eye on your mama."

"Oh, Mandy! Are you sure?" cried Lauren, hugging the black woman who was becoming more a friend than an employee.

"Just as sure as there's a God in Heaven."

"Laurie!" The moment the elevator doors opened, Charlotte practically knocked her over with her exuberant greeting.

"I'm thrilled to see you, Charlee," cried Lauren, as she hugged her cousin. "It's been so *long.*"

"Honey, how wonderful to have you here." She held Lauren at arm's length. "I'm glad to say you don't *look* scholarly, at any rate. You positively *intimidate* me with all your achievements, you know."

Lauren laughed, thinking that her tailored navy blue linen suit, crumpled from the long train trip, was probably a little staid and country-come-to-town for Charlotte's chic set. She looked around expectantly. "Where's David?"

"I forgot . . ." Charlotte answered somewhat distractedly. "He's still operating, he said to tell you he'll be along as soon as he's finished." She directed a maid to take Lauren's luggage up to the guest room. "Come have a drink."

"Not a 'drink' drink," said Lauren. "Perhaps some tea?"

As they entered the gallery, Lauren stood stock still in wonder. The apartment had vastly changed since her previous visit. Gone were the heavy period pieces, the dark tapestries, and rococo landscapes. In their place, an expanse of airiness and light stretched before her. Oyster colored walls hung with huge, exciting modern paintings; deep, square, loungy white couches and starkly sculptural chairs in leather and steel; exotic woods and complicated fabrics in the palest earth colors. The wall-to-wall carpeting had been torn up in the living room, baring superb parquet floors, which glowed with the muted, jeweled tones of rare antique Oriental carpets.

"Charlee, you've created a masterpiece! It's positively the most glorious room I've ever seen."

Clearly delighted, Charlotte said, "You like it, then? I'm so glad. Come see the rest . . ." She led the way through the Art Deco dining room, which seemed a trifle cold to Lauren, and on into the library, snugger and more homey, now dominated by a nineteenth-century Kazak area rug with a persimmon field and a border of bright navy, palest lemon and teal green in a geometric pattern.

Admiring a pair of bronze fauns, Lauren again marveled at the changed decor. "Yes," she said, "this is much more your style. You do have the best taste, Charlee." With a sigh of relief, she sank into a club chair and put her legs up on the ottoman.

"You must be exhausted," Charlotte said sympathetically.

Lauren nodded with her eyes closed. "I had to sit up all night, couldn't get a berth."

Her train had been three hours late, arriving at Penn Station during Friday afternoon rush hour. After standing in line for half an hour, she had shared a taxi with a naval ensign and his girl, who couldn't keep their hands off each other in the back seat. What a letdown that David wasn't here waiting for her . . .

"How's Bruce?" she asked.

"Having himself a ball down there in Washington, hobnobbing with all the brass."

"Why don't you go to stay with him?"

Charlotte gave her an arch look. "What—and cramp his style?"

"Oh, Charlee . . . whatever do you mean by that?" Was she implying that Bruce was seeing other women?

Charlotte shrugged. "Nothing, darling. It's just that Bruce and I have different ideas about what's fun. I *detest* the Washington scene. Much better to wait for him to come up to New York for a weekend. Actually, I was expecting he'd be here today, but he disappointed me."

"That's too bad," said Lauren, thinking that it sounded like Charlee and Bruce, like so many other couples, were growing apart. It was this damn war!

"You and David are my guests at a benefit dinner for the USO tonight," said Charlotte, as she poured tea from the tray served by a uniformed maid. "It's at the Starlight Roof of the Waldorf."

"But I didn't bring a long dress to New York," Lauren protested, "and I'm really too tired."

"It makes no difference what one wears to these things." Charlee gave one of her mischievous little smiles. "You'll change your mind when David gets here. I bet a bath and some bedroom time with your husband will fix you up just fine."

Lauren laughed, shaking her head. "You'll never grow up, will you?"

"I certainly hope not!" said Charlee. "Come on, I'll

take you to your room so you can get out of your travel clothes." Lauren followed her up the stairs to the guest suite, tastefully redecorated in a blue and white Chinese motif.

"This black silk will do just fine, Laurie," announced Charlotte, after she had examined the few garments the maid had hung in the closet. "I'll lend you a wrap and some jewelry to dress it up. With your handsome husband on your arm, you'll be smashing!" Charlee made a last inspection to be certain Lauren had everything she would need. "I'll let you get some rest now. See you in a bit, love."

An hour later, just as Lauren had finished bathing, David walked into the bedroom. Wearing a robe, with her freshly shampooed hair wrapped in a towel, she rushed across the room and flung herself into his arms.

"I'm so glad you're here, Laurie," he murmured, kissing her deeply.

As she felt his arms around her, Lauren thought that coming to New York for this visit had been the wisest decision she could have made. An entire four days ahead to be alone with him! She sat on his lap in a chair, answering his questions about the children and Chapel Hill, thinking he had never looked so well—much better than the last time she had seen him. Charlee was right, he was absolutely handsome in his uniform.

"It's wonderful to hold you, darling," he whispered, kissing her neck, and sliding his hands down her back. As she closed her eyes, nestling closer in his embrace, he glanced at his watch. "I guess I'd better let you get ready. Charlee says we're going to a benefit."

"We don't have to go, if you don't want to. I'd just as soon be alone with you tonight."

He made a regretful gesture. "I sort of promised we would. Bruce isn't coming and Charlee has a table full of guests to play hostess to. You won't mind, will you?"

"No, of course not," she answered quickly.

"Tomorrow will be ours alone, our anniversary," he assured her. "Get dressed. I'll wait for you downstairs."

Lauren dried her hair, grateful that its natural wave

meant she didn't have to fuss with it. She considered pinning it up in front in a pompadour, but on second thought, David had never seen her in the new style and he might not like it. She finished dressing slowly, wishing they had been able to make their own plans, and trying to muster up some enthusiasm for the evening ahead.

As Lauren came down the stairs, she heard piano music coming from the library and she recognized David's playing. He often used to sit down at the keyboard during a party, with their friends gathered around to sing. And when they were courting, he had played for her alone—love songs that seemed to have been written exclusively for them. But how long had it been since he had played for her?

She stopped at the threshold, her footsteps silenced by the thick carpet. Charlotte was leaning over the piano, resting an arm on top, with one hip slung out in a languid manner. David's hands moved lightly over the keys. Gazing directly into each other's eyes and smiling, they seemed completely at ease, singing together, as if this was an old habit with them.

A harsh, bitter tightness permeated Lauren's throat as she stood watching. David saw her first, springing up, with a wide smile on his face. "Here she is! You look beautiful, darling." He strode across the room and took her in his arms to kiss her.

Charlotte stayed near the piano, lighting a cigarette. Then she turned. "Open the champagne, David. We might just as well begin celebrating your anniversary tonight."

I don't think I can get through this, thought Lauren, as she accepted the champagne he poured. I don't think I can manage to share David with Charlee all during this visit. I know there's a war on, and I know her husband is away. But I'm just not . . . that . . . generous.

For the entire evening, her face was frozen in a set smile. She greeted the Burnses, Audrey and Steve, whom she remembered from her first visit. She made polite conversation during dinner, and sat through the speeches, which were endless and boring. She danced with Steve and the other men and she watched David dance with

Charlotte and the other wives, and finally he danced with her.

Around eleven, when the party was at its height, she told David she was exhausted. He made their excuses and they went back to the apartment alone. Lauren knew she had had too much to drink. She wasn't drunk, and she didn't feel sick. The alcohol gave her the courage she needed to seduce her husband.

And she did need courage.

On the morning of their fifth anniversary, David found himself unable to make love to his wife. Just at the critical moment, he lost his erection. That had never happened to him before. What the hell was wrong with him? He was only thirty-two years old, for Christ's sake!

"I'm sorry, Laurie," he apologized, his lips against her throat.

"Why?" she asked, after a few moments.

"I don't know why. Maybe too much partying last night . . . that happens to men sometimes."

Lauren was very quiet in his arms. "David, do you still love me?"

"Of course I love you!" he said, sounding angry. "This has very little to do with love. Let's not make a big deal out of it."

"I'm not." She smiled at him with an attempt at good humor. "I guess women aren't the only ones who have problems with sex."

That made him angry, too. I don't have problems! he wanted to say, then thought better of it. "Why don't we get dressed and I'll take you to Rumpelmeyer's for breakfast."

"Oh, wonderful," she cried, springing out of bed.

When they came downstairs the maid, Mairie, handed them a note from Charlotte: "Dearest Lovebirds, I've gone off to Southampton until tomorrow. I'm sure you'll find something worth doing without me! As they say, south of the border, *Mi casa es su casa.* Happy Anniversary! Ta, Charlee." Enclosed was a pair of third row center orchestra seats for *Oklahoma!*, the new Rodgers and Hammerstein musical hit.

"Isn't she special?" said Lauren, feeling terribly remorseful for the uncharitable feelings she had been harboring against Charlotte. Jealousy could make you blind to reality.

"It certainly is generous of her," David agreed. He put his arm around Lauren's waist, giving her a playful squeeze. "And tactful! We'll have to see that we put the time alone to good use."

She smiled up at him, feeling as if an oppressive weight had been lifted from her heart. "I never even wished you a Happy Anniversary, darling."

They were kissing when Mairie came back to say, "Cook has prepared breakfast for you, madam."

Lauren blushed and David laughed. "Well, there goes Rumpelmeyer's," he said.

The weather was hot and muggy and they got caught in a sudden thunderstorm as they were exploring a charming little mews David wanted to show her. Lauren's new beige pongee dress was soaked by the time they reached the garden restaurant he had chosen for lunch. She dried off in the ladies' room and returned to their corner table to find him waiting with a chilled bottle of white wine and a gift-wrapped anniversary present. When she opened the box, she saw a beautiful gold bracelet watch with a circle of tiny sapphires around the face.

"I've never had anything like this before. It's absolutely beautiful, darling! I love it."

"I knew you'd like it. Charlee helped me pick it out."

Why did he have to tell her that? And why did it matter?

Somehow after that, everything was forced. By dinner time, they were both grateful that they had tickets to the play, because that meant they would not have to make conversation all evening long.

That night in bed, in the dark, it was better.

On Monday morning, David left for the hospital very early. "I'll see you tonight," he said, sitting on the edge of the bed to kiss Lauren.

She snuggled into his arms. "Mmm, that sounds so wonderful. I'll never again take for granted saying good-bye in the morning and knowing you'll come home at night," she murmured, her voice groggy with sleep. "Shall I come down to have breakfast with you?"

"No, honey. It's only six o'clock. I'll grab something at the hospital."

She slept late and had breakfast on a tray in her room, a luxury unimagined in Chapel Hill, unless she was sick. After dressing in casual clothes, she went looking for Charlee. Unable to find her, Lauren was about to ask Mairie where she was, when she heard a strange sound from down the hall.

The study door was ajar when Lauren pushed it open to discover Charlotte sobbing into her hands. It had been decades since she had seen her cousin weep. Even when her father died, Charlee had managed to express her grief in a dignified, contained fashion, almost as a protest against her mother's hysteria.

"Charlee! Darling, what is it?" Lauren rushed in and put her arms around her.

Charlotte clung to her for a moment, continuing to cry. Then she pulled herself erect and took out a handkerchief, wiping her eyes and blowing her nose.

"My Lord, Laurie—" Her voice was tremulous as she forced some of her customary bite into it. "I don't believe I've ever done this in all my life! Forgive me, darling. It was that, or break all the Baccarat vases."

"Charlee, what's wrong?"

"Oh . . . never mind. It's really a lot of nonsense."

"You can tell me."

For a moment she stared at Lauren. "It's Bruce . . ." she said, looking frightened. "We just had a terrible row. The worst ever. He hung up on me." She lit a cigarette with shaking hands and inhaled deeply. "Things are terrible . . . *Dammit!* I've *got* to go down there, Laurie. If I don't, I don't know what will happen to us—Will you forgive me if I leave you here?"

"*Forgive* you? Don't even ask. You absolutely *have* to go. What can I do to help?"

"I doubt there's anything you or anyone else can do." She smiled sadly. "Come in with me while I get ready, will you?"

Charlotte flung an assortment of clothing on the bed for Mairie to pack. While she dressed, she chattered aimlessly with Lauren, as if she had already said too much on the subject of her husband. Less than an hour later, she was ready to leave and the doorman announced the car was downstairs waiting to take her to the station.

"Do me a favor, Laurie, please don't say anything to David about—you know, about before, when I was carrying on. Every marriage has these little episodes, I suppose, and—well, I wouldn't want anyone else to know that Bruce and I . . ."

"I promise I won't say a word. I'll tell him you suddenly decided to go to Washington for a while after speaking to Bruce. How's that?"

"Perfect. I knew I could count on you. Now, you just pretend this is your home and enjoy the rest of your stay. I'll call you in a week or two." The elevator arrived, and Charlotte hugged Lauren. "I don't know what I'd do without my Laurie! Good-bye, love."

When she was gone, Lauren sat in the study, brooding about Charlee's unhappiness. Was it a momentary problem this time, something new and unexpected that had risen between her and Bruce? Or was it deeper and more basic than that, part of the trouble she had observed on previous occasions? They had always had a volatile relationship, but the present state of affairs seemed more serious than ever. She had never seen Charlee so upset before. But after the first burst of emotion, it was obvious she did not care to talk about it, even to her.

Thoroughly depressed, Lauren decided to spend the afternoon at the Metropolitan Museum before meeting David for dinner in Greenwich Village. But first, she was going to call the housing office at Columbia University . . .

"Just like that, she went to Washington?" David said that night when she told him. "Wasn't it kind of sudden?"

"She spoke to Bruce and I guess they decided she should come down. She was in such a rush to leave, we didn't really discuss it." Lauren hated lying to him, but she couldn't betray Charlee's confidence.

They were having dinner at Monte's, a family-style Italian restaurant on MacDougall Street. "Are you sure everything is all right?" David said, after the antipasto was served.

"What?"

"I mean, with Charlee—or, with Bruce."

"I don't know. Why do you ask?"

"It seems strange for her to leave without warning when you're here. She's been looking forward to seeing you."

"Well, David, I guess she thought it was more important to be with Bruce." If only *I* had felt that way about being with my husband, she thought, we might not be sitting here like strangers.

What was happening to them? All through the dinner, David seemed distracted. Their conversation was stilted, with long silences. Afterward, they went to a little café for pastry and European espresso, and listened to poetry readings. Except for the Bohemian atmosphere, it was very much like the departmental workshops in Chapel Hill.

On Wednesday afternoon, David was able to get away from the hospital to take her to the train. "I hope you enjoyed yourself, honey. I know it was hard for you to leave your mother."

"I'm so glad I came, David. We need to see as much of each other as possible," she said, looking at him honestly.

"Yes," he agreed, but his eyes dropped.

They kissed good-bye, and she held onto him. Was it her imagination, or did he seem *relieved* to see her go? How could that be, even if the visit hadn't been the great success she had been counting on? After all, he had begged her to come up. It was the artificiality of it, that was the problem! She felt like an intruder in the life he had made for himself in New York.

As the train gathered speed, Lauren opened her purse and again went over the listings she had obtained yesterday afternoon from the information office at Columbia University. A number of faculty apartments were available for sublet for the month of August. She was convinced that the only way to preserve their marriage was for them to live a normal home life again, before David went overseas.

The children were ecstatic at her return. Summer, without classes, gave her more free time to be with them and she found them developing in the most rewarding way. Babs was such a bright child, she hungered for conversation with her mother, and Mark was at that adorable, cuddly age between two and three. Although he loved splashing in the swimming pool with other children, he was a little trooper, not even crying when she kept him out of the water because of his persistent red throat. Barbara still resembled David, while Mark looked like a Jacobson, with blond hair and vivid blue eyes. Lauren would like to have stayed home with them all day during the summer, but she continued to work two afternoons a week, more to get away from the increasing stress of being with her mother than anything else. Miriam wasn't nearly as demanding with Amanda.

Gretchen was still her best friend in Chapel Hill. They had become more dependent on each other since the war, working at the Bull's Head Bookshop, running errands together to save gasoline, taking their children swimming and on picnics, and confiding in each other—or rather, Gretchen confiding in Lauren, telling her personal details of her life with Ralph that she would just as soon not have heard.

Gretch was finally pulling out of her depression. She regularly heard from Ralph, who was in Algiers with the U.S. Command. He wrote long letters, assuring her he was out of danger, claiming his affair with Carol had all been a terrible mistake, and that he wanted to start over again when he came home. "I don't know whether to believe him or not, but for the moment, I'm happier thinking he means it."

"I'm sure he does," Lauren told her, but she had her

doubts. She wondered how Gretchen could still want a husband who had been unfaithful.

"I expected when I married a nice Jewish boy, he wouldn't play around like my father did—or does."

"I've always thought that was a myth, Gretch, about Jewish men. Why would they be any different?"

Gretchen smiled knowingly. "They're different, all right, Lauren. Take it from one who knows."

Lauren giggled. "I'm not sure I understand what you mean by that."

"Well, they're just better lovers, that's all. More romantic and passionate."

Was that true, Lauren wondered. David used to be passionate when they were first married, but she would hardly call their most recent times in bed *romantic.* Maybe that wasn't fair. It was tough on him, being away from home, and she had been worn out from the trip . . . living in Charlee's apartment had put both of them under a strain.

"You're daydreaming, Laurie . . . I wonder what about!"

Lauren blushed. To cover her embarrassment, she said, "It does sound like Ralph regrets the way he acted, Gretchen. Aren't you glad now that you didn't go home to your parents?"

"I guess so. I'll reserve judgment until after the war. Meanwhile, I'm managing better on Ralph's army pay than I did on his university salary. And they can't put me out of this house—it would be unpatriotic!"

Lauren studied her friend, reflecting that Gretchen was a woman who had taken herself in hand. She had lost weight, cut her hair, and looked younger and prettier than ever. Ralph would find a remarkable change in his wife when he returned from the war.

Philip called in the third week of June to say that he and Jeanette would drive down to Chapel Hill from Fort Lee over the July Fourth weekend to visit Miriam, Lauren, and the children. He had completed OCS and would be commissioned as a First Lieutenant. "A ninety-day wonder!" he joked, using the regular army term for the products of the accelerated Officers' Training Corps. "I've got my orders, Laurie. They're sending me to the Army Language School at Berkeley. I took a whole bunch of tests and it seems I have a gift for languages." Philip sounded as excited as she'd ever heard him.

"That's so far away, Phil. Jeanette must be disappointed."

"Jeanette's coming with me! I'll be there for at least a year."

"Oh . . . that's great."

"Yeah, we loved it out in California on our honeymoon. It's really terrific."

"*Terrific*, is it?" she exclaimed aloud after hanging up. Pacing the floor of her room, she was in the grip of an incendiary rage.

Philip and Jeanette had made their plans without a by-your-leave, showing not the slightest concern for how it affected *her* life. What had happened to the so-called "temporary arrangement" of having their mother live with her in Chapel Hill until he completed OCS? No one in the family had suggested that it was time to think about another arrangement. Did they expect she was going to care for Miriam indefinitely? Had it ever occurred to them that she might want to spend some time with her husband before he went overseas?

Something was happening to her and David. Something terrible. But she seemed powerless to prevent it.

Lauren cried that night, for the first time since her husband had gone away. David . . . *David!* He was slipping away from her. Each time she spoke to him, she could feel it more and more. She dared not even consider the reasons why.

Well, dammit, she wasn't going to just sit here and take it. For too much of her life she had gone about the business of pleasing other people. No more. It was time for Lauren Jacobson Bernard to assert herself. She knew exactly how she was going to begin.

Chapter 27

WATER WAS SEEPING into the corridor when David reached his apartment on the tenth floor of the building at 163rd Street and Riverside Drive. He did not need any problems tonight; the humid summer weather was enough to cope with. Afraid of what he would find, he turned the key in the lock.

"Ahh, *shit!*"

His bed and desk were littered with fallen plaster and debris from the sagging corner of the ceiling. Water covered the floor and had soaked his canvas overseas bag, the shoes he had set out to be polished, his papers, and four books from the medical school library. He called maintenance to report the damage and began salvaging whatever he could from the sodden mess on the desk.

The superintendent arrived, shrugging helplessly, followed by a stooped janitor, who scurried around with a mop and bucket. "Why don't you try stopping the leak?" said David, pointing to the dripping ceiling.

"Plumber gone home," the old man answered calmly, continuing to mop.

This was Friday, which meant no plumber until after the weekend. It was clear he could not be sleeping in this room tonight, or for many nights to come.

Downstairs in the lobby, David learned that four officers had been moved to other apartments that afternoon when a water pipe burst, but no one had bothered to check his floor. The major next door, a captain across the hall, and David were issued expense vouchers with a list of hotels, and told to find their own living accommodations—an impossible task in wartime New York.

After dialing a dozen numbers without locating a vacancy, David found himself in the residence office arguing with a secretary who was eager to leave for the weekend. "There's absolutely nothing available in university housing, Captain Bernard, but let me see what I can do."

The best she could come up with was a filthy room without a private bath in a rundown hotel on Broadway at 178th Street. It was almost dinner time when he threw his bags on the sagging bed, tired and aggravated at the thought of spending two weeks in this dismal cell. He called to break his appointment with Charlotte, who had invited him to another one of her endless benefits that evening.

"You're welcome to stay here, David. There's plenty of room."

"No thanks."

She chuckled. "No, I didn't think you would. Are you worried about *my* reputation, or yours?"

"Charlee, I am in no mood to joke with you. If I don't want to sleep in this fleabag tonight, I have to find another room."

"Don't be such a grouch. Come on down and bring your luggage. I'll make some calls, and by the time you get here, I guarantee you'll have a decent place to rest your weary head."

Less than an hour later, Charlotte, dressed casually in mulberry linen slacks and a silk shirt, was waiting for him in the foyer of her apartment. "Done!" she exclaimed, the moment he stepped off the elevator.

"I don't believe it." He regarded her skeptically from the corner of his eye.

"It's true. You have a suite at the Ambassador. No charge."

He shook his head, "No you don't, Charlee. The Army pays."

"The Army couldn't *afford* it! Anyway, it belongs to my in-laws. They sold their apartment last year and they keep rooms at the Ambassador for when they stay in the city, but they're in California now. I called Malcolm—he's an old dear, really—they are positively *delighted* to have Cousin David stay there as long as he likes. He said to tell you it's an honor to help one of our gallant officers."

"I don't know, Charlee . . . I'm not sure I want to be in their debt."

"Don't be a fool. The suite is empty and they won't be back in New York until Labor Day." She nudged him playfully with her elbow. "You really are a stick-in-the-mud, aren't you? Poor Laurie!"

The remark irked him. He kept returning to it while he showered and shaved upstairs in Charlotte's well-appointed guest room—the same room where he had stayed with his wife just last weekend. What had Charlee meant by that? Was he dull and lacking in imagination, was that what she thought? *Poor Laurie,* she had said. Had Lauren told her something about their marriage?

He supposed he *had* become more serious lately. Medicine did that to you. Dealing with illness and death every day tended to get to you after a while. Much that had happened to him in recent years was sobering . . . marriage and the responsibility of children, sickness in the family and death. And now the war with its uncertainties . . . knowing he would soon be going overseas and having no idea when he would be home again. And Lauren.

With a sigh, he considered their growing distance. The anniversary visit had not been a success. He had to admit he had been glad when it came to an end. It was too difficult pretending, trying not to show feelings that would be hurtful to Lauren. They seemed to have so little to say to each other, and although they never really argued, he had the impression that she was angry a good part of the time. And he had been angry, too.

In April, when he had gone home on leave, he had hung around for hours waiting to hitch a flight down to Bragg on a military transport, borrowed a car and driven to Chapel Hill that night, aching to see his wife and children. He would never understand what went wrong. They had been awkward with each other from the start, even in bed. Especially in bed. That was to be expected, he supposed, after the long separation, and in addition, there had been a considerable loss of privacy with her mother living in the house. During that weekend, when they planned Lauren's trip to New York, he had thought they would benefit from being alone together away from home.

Well, it hadn't worked. If anything, the visit had made things worse. What happened to the idea of Lauren and the children spending the summer with him? Not once had she mentioned it. He wondered why her mother couldn't have gone to stay with Joanna for a while, but truthfully, it no longer mattered to him as much.

David finished shaving and put on his summer dress uniform, which fortunately had not been hanging near the leak. When he came out in the hall carrying his musette bag, Charlotte was talking on the telephone in the upstairs study. She beckoned him to come in and take a chair.

He observed her as she held the receiver with her chin in the crook of her neck. With those wickedly flashing, smoky eyes, the sensuous, tantalizing mouth, and the cleft chin that was a common feature in her mother's family, she was as beguiling as she had been the first time he had seen her. Her hair was becomingly arranged in a pompadour with a loose shoulder-length pageboy, the currently popular style. She had changed to a simple navy silk dress and matching jacket, and with it she wore a single strand of opera-length pearls. The look of annoyance on her face did not detract from her beauty.

"Yes, Bruce, I heard you," she was saying impatiently, biting one side of her lower lip and puffing nervously on a cigarette. "I repeat—let me know when Nick is gone, and I'll be there."

David could hear Bruce's angry voice coming through the receiver. He started to leave the room, but Charlotte indicated he should stay. "I've got to go now. We'll discuss this another time." She rang off without saying goodbye.

Embarrassed, David said, "I didn't mean to intrude."

"Don't worry, I was glad to have an excuse to hang up. Let him find someone else to be his hostess!"

He could see she was extremely angry and upset.

"Charlee . . . it's none of my business, but when a man's away from home, he's lonely and vulnerable. It's not a good idea to say things you might regret."

She threw her head back with a harsh laugh. "Oh, David, if only you knew—what I *really* regret are the things I *haven't* said!"

As she stubbed out her cigarette, he saw tears glittering in her eyes. He would like to have offered some comfort, but she picked up her purse and gloves, forcing a smile. "We'd better hurry or we'll be late."

David had been living in the Fields suite at the Ambassador for a week when Charlotte dragged him up to Harlem with two couples who wanted to hear jazz. "You're so quiet tonight," she remarked on the way home in the cab. "Will you come up for a drink?"

"Not tonight, thanks. Surgery in the morning." Pretending not to see the hurt in her eyes, he got back in the cab without the usual kiss on her cheek. "Good night."

Out on Park, he paid the taxi driver, preferring to walk the twenty-five blocks to the hotel. If he was tired enough, he would fall asleep more easily. And he wanted to sleep, to prevent himself from lying awake and thinking. Too often these days, his late-night thoughts dwelled on Charlotte—or more specifically, on a troubled blend of Lauren and Charlotte . . .

Let me show you the city, she had said in the winter when he was new to New York. It had become their habit to see each other on the weekends. She invited him to opening nights, U.S.O. benefits, the symphony, private showings at the Metropolitan Museum of Art, previews at Madison Avenue galleries . . . Manhattan was crawling with army and navy brass, government procurement agents, and foreign diplomats. Theater tickets were scarce, the good restaurants completely booked, but for Charlotte Fields there were orchestra seats to the latest hit shows and the best table at the Colony or 21.

Her friends had grown accustomed to seeing him at her side. With Bruce away, she needed an escort, and what better man than her cousin's husband? He didn't even have the excuse that his wife might object, for Lauren had always urged him to keep in touch with Charlee. Everyone accepted it without question, but it was time to ease off.

Once he had walked up a mountain and found her among the clouds and the birds. At the time he thought it had been a chance encounter, but now he suspected she had been waiting there for him. Since that day he had never fully trusted himself with her, he saw that now. For all these years, he had pretended not to like her, purposely not going to Randolph Springs when she came down for her annual visits, discouraging Lauren from inviting her to Chapel Hill—and in the process causing Laurie pain at his lack of feeling for her favorite cousin.

He had never known anyone remotely like Charlee. Ever changing, she enchanted him. He was captivated by her creamy-skinned beauty, the flashing amber eyes, and the glistening chestnut hair—a weather vane of her moods, swept on top of her head in a careless mass, hanging glamorously long and silky about her shoulders, or pulled back in a severely stylish chignon.

Clinging to his loyalty, he had been loathe to discuss Lauren with her, afraid to reveal his discontent. And since the evening he had heard her arguing with Bruce on the telephone, they had avoided talking about her husband.

After her sudden trip to Washington in early June, she had told him, "It was a mistake. I won't go down again." He had not asked why, not wanting to hear about her marriage, but she persisted. "All we did was fight! There's this simply adorable refugee baby—the sponsors changed their minds. I want to take him, but Bruce says he couldn't love a child that wasn't his own."

"A lot of people feel that way before they adopt, Charlee, but they find themselves very attached to the baby afterward."

"Bruce might get to love him if he lived with him, but you can't very well take a baby on approval, like a puppy. I *do* want children, as many as possible, but I don't think Bruce and I—well, thus far, we haven't had any luck."

His natural instinct had been to help. "Have you consulted someone, a specialist?"

Her laugh was harsh and explosive. "David, do you mean to sit there and tell me that doctors can do anything about *that?* The ones I've spoken to are the most bumbling idiots I've ever come across."

"We don't know nearly enough about infertility, Charlee, but there's a lot of research going on. Some excellent men are in that field. It takes time and patience on the part of the couple, as well as the physician."

"Isn't that just like the medical profession—defend your brothers, at all costs!"

"You're being unfair. Doctors aren't God. They don't know everything."

"The trouble is, *they* don't seem to be aware of that." Her eyes had flared and she reared her head like a highly bred pony.

That was *some* temper she had. He would hate to really tangle with her. Charlee would be hard to live with, he imagined. Not like Laurie, who was easy on the nerves. Even now, when he thought of Lauren, he missed her dreadfully . . . When he rejoined his unit at Fort Bragg, if they weren't immediately sent overseas, he would be able to get home on the weekends. And then they would surely work out their problems. It wouldn't be long now, just another two months.

Meanwhile, it might be better if he did not see Charlee for a spell.

As with many things about Charlotte, he was never certain whether they met by design that summer evening at the exit to the Lexington Avenue subway. It was the end of a sultry Friday, and he had the weekend off for the Fourth of July.

As he emerged from the underground, he heard a woman calling his name. It was Charlee, looking young and fresh in a tailored pink sharkskin dress with a pleated skirt. Her hair was pulled back behind her ears, fastened with a large bow.

"Don't tell me you take the subway!" she exclaimed, smiling radiantly and leaning up to kiss his cheek.

Hiding his pleasure at seeing her after the self-imposed

respite, he replied, "It's the most efficient and cheapest way for me to get back and forth to work." God, how he had missed her.

"It's beastly hot. Come buy me a drink—unless you have a better offer."

"What offer could be better than that, Charlee?" He tucked her arm in his and headed for the back entrance to the Waldorf.

The lobby was teeming with high-ranking officers, alone or in groups, some with glamorous women who were obviously not their wives. There was a charge of excitement in the atmosphere, for the tide of the war was changing since Axis resistance had been crushed in Africa. The news from Germany was that women and children were being evacuated from Berlin in anticipation of stepped-up Allied air attacks against the Fatherland. In the Pacific, too, the Japanese were on the defensive.

Peacock Alley was alive with young officers and their dates dancing to the string orchestra's society beat. Miraculously, a pair of naval lieutenants vacated their table as David and Charlotte stood waiting to be seated.

"I've missed you," she said, when their order had been taken.

He looked at her honestly. "I thought it was better if we didn't see so much of each other."

Nodding, she made a regretful moue and looked down, tracing patterns on the table with her finger. David was relieved when the waiter brought their drinks.

"So," said Charlee, saluting him with her cocktail and smiling brightly, "how are your rooms, still comfortable?"

"Pure luxury. I'm sure it's illegal for a mere captain to be living this well. I just had the bad news that my old garret will be ready for occupancy next week."

She laughed. "You might as well stay on at the Ambassador, David. Malcolm and Adele have decided to remain out West until the end of September."

"I won't be here that long, Charlee," he reminded her. "I should be returning to Bragg by the end of August."

"So soon . . ." She stared at him and a tremulous sigh

escaped her parted lips. There was an awkward silence and then she said, "Dance with me." Silently he stood up and followed her onto the dance floor.

They had danced before during these months and he liked the way Charlotte's tall, slender body moved with his. "You dance marvelously, you know," she murmured, as the music changed to a slow love ballad. She moved closer and he caught a hint of the gardenia scent she used.

As she pressed against him, he was suddenly consumed with wanting her, and afraid she would know. "Let's sit down," he said.

"No . . ." she answered, locking eyes with him. "Let's go to your room."

He drew in a sharp breath. "Are you sure?" His arms were still encircling her.

Closing her eyes, she said in that low, breathless voice, "Oh yes, darling. Please . . . let's just *go!*"

He threw some bills on the table and followed her through the lobby and out onto Park Avenue. As they walked north toward the entrance to the Ambassador apartments, he told himself, *I am crossing this street with the intention of committing adultery.* As they took the elevator to the sixteenth floor, he thought, *I am going to have an affair with my wife's cousin.* Amazed at how calm he was, his hand did not even tremble when he inserted the key in the lock.

Inside, he hesitated, overwhelmed by the enormity of what they were doing, "Charlee . . . I don't know if we should—"

She put a finger against his lips, "Shhh . . . don't talk, darling. Not now. I think I couldn't bear it, if you don't take me to bed."

When they kissed, he knew it had been fated from the moment he first set eyes on her in front of her parents' house on Shadow Mountain. "I've always wanted you," she murmured.

They left a trail of clothes across the living room. The covers had been turned down and Charlotte sat on the edge of the bed in a brief and fragile lacy garment of a kind he had never seen, holding her arms out to him. When he removed the last of his clothing and turned, he heard her strangled gasp and then she pulled him against her, covering him with her mouth, sending shivers of ecstasy through him.

Her kisses were wild and demanding; the touch of her hands, magical. Her lips, her tongue tantalizing every part of him. Where on earth had she learned these things?

She was wondrous . . . This was the sublime love he had dreamed about. *Do this,* she whispered frantically, *do that! Kiss me there, and there . . . yes, yes . . . like that!*

He paid not a thought to Lauren as he gave himself completely to Charlotte. She was all he had imagined, in all his untold fantasies . . . unbridled, seductive, funny, romantic, passionate. He loved her, loved her, *loved her!*

When it was over, and they lay damp and sated in each other's arms, David stared at the ceiling with a sinking heart. In all his life, he had never felt so full of bliss . . . or so utterly wretched.

Chapter 28

LAUREN WAITED FOR David's call, but he did not phone on Friday evening, as he usually did. When she tried to reach him at the Ambassador Hotel on Saturday, he either had never returned to his room, or failed to pick up his messages. Would he have gone away for the weekend, she wondered.

Perhaps Charlee knew where he was. She was tempted to call her, but hesitated. If she spoke to her cousin, something in her voice would give her away, would reveal that she was afraid of losing David. Wasn't that her real fear? Lauren closed her eyes in an effort to rid herself of these thoughts. Living with her mother was making her neurotic!

Philip and Jeanette had arrived late Friday night, intending to stay until Sunday evening. On the way, they had visited Jeanette's family in Rocky Mount, planning to stop in Randolph Springs before traveling west to California. On Saturday morning, Lauren asked Philip to go for a walk, and they had a frank discussion in which he agreed to help her carry out her plan for their mother, promising to talk to Reba and the rest of the family when he reached Randolph. She should have realized her brother was unaware of her feelings, rather than selfish. Discussing it with Philip helped to reassure her that she was doing the right thing.

She decided not to say anything to David until all the arrangements had been made. And then, she would call him with the good news.

* * *

They had driven to Charlotte's country retreat in Westport that same night.

She slipped out of the Ambassador alone to pick up her car, calling him from her apartment. "Meet me on the corner of 52nd and Lex in ten minutes," she said, sounding like a schoolgirl about to go off for a night of camping in the woods.

David was waiting on the dark, silent, summer-weekend street when she pulled up in a racy little red Jaguar, with a red and white scarf tied around her head, wearing a blue one-piece pants outfit like the women who worked in airplane factories. They shot out of the city and up through Westchester to Connecticut, breathing in the free country air.

Charlotte had telephoned the caretakers from the hotel while still lying in his embrace. Everything was prepared for their arrival—beds freshly made, refrigerator stocked with wines and food enough to feed a crowd, including a delectable seafood casserole that Charlee reheated for dinner the following evening.

No one disturbed them. Not the middle-aged couple who maintained the property and lived in a cottage far from the house, nor the neighbors secluded on private fenced-in acreages of their own. They swam in the small pond fed by a dammed-up brook, picnicked under ancient shade trees, walked through fields of high grass and wildflowers, and romped with a pair of golden retrievers owned by the caretakers, but they never saw another soul for the entire weekend.

The spread-out old farmhouse had been reconstructed into a perfect country hideaway, breezy and cool in the afternoon heat, snug and intimate at night. As soon as they arrived they made love, before falling asleep in Charlotte's four-poster bed. And again, first thing in the morning, taking a chilling dip in the pond afterward.

Charlee made an enormous breakfast of Virginia ham and blueberry hotcakes with melted butter and Vermont maple syrup, and he was surprised that she could cook. "I can't find grits up here," she apologized, and David told her he hated grits, and she said that meant he wasn't a true Southerner. Then they went upstairs and made love again, and once more after lunch, on the living room floor—he could not imagine Lauren making love anywhere but in bed with the door securely closed—and then Charlee, her long, graceful body natural and boyish, ran nude over the lawn to dive into the pond, and after a startled moment of disbelief, he joined her.

Late Sunday afternoon when it was time to leave, they walked out and closed the door, after rumpling the beds in the guest room for the benefit of the staff. It all proceeded in such an uncomplicated fashion that if David wondered how often she had taken a lover to her bower in Connecticut, it would not have been surprising.

But as Charlee had observed, he was a Southern gentleman and the thought never crossed his mind.

There was an urgency to their affair. They met on weekday evenings at the Ambassador, even though David had moved back uptown. They took risks. Charlotte would often dismiss the servants so they could be alone in her apartment. And whenever he had a free day on the weekend, they would drive up to the farm in Westport. The need for secrecy made it even more delicious for Charlee, who adored intrigue.

David was learning about Charlotte, things he would never have suspected. Perhaps knowing their time together was coming to an end, she revealed hidden parts of herself, although her real essence remained ever elusive.

She and Bruce did not share a bedroom, either in New York or in the Connecticut house. "Bruce craves privacy, he has peculiar sleeping habits," she explained in an offhand way, but by now, David was aware they had a troubled marriage.

She was full of anxieties. He remembered Lauren telling him how Charlotte used to tempt fate with her daredevil antics on horseback, and yet, she had a multitude of fears. The things that haunted Charlee were factors she could not control—death, the elements, the unknown. She was superstitious, and she hated being alone, she was afraid of dying, she was terrified of lightning. But most of all, she dreaded growing old and losing her appeal to men. "Why do you look so astonished, darling?"

"You, of all women—you'll be beautiful when you're old."

They were in her bedroom on Park Avenue; like Charlee, the most glamorous room David had ever known, all beige and cream, with rosy-shaded Swedish crystal lamps and an enormous soft, shimmering Impressionist landscape above the bed. He watched her shimmy out of her dress, stirred by her slim, small-breasted figure. She wasn't wearing a brassiere, just one of her handmade French teddies, in a pale lilac with intricate floral edging.

She turned to face him, smiling mischievously. Over each breast a blossom was appliquéd, with a sheer cut-out center through which her nipples pointed. Immediately he became aroused. She scrunched up her shoulders. "Do you like it? I bought it in Paris just before the war, at a shop they say all the legendary courtesans favor."

"Good Lord, Charlotte, you *do* have an imagination."

"Lucky for you I do!" she whispered, reaching for him.

He never knew what to expect from her, except always she was fresh and alluring, like a rare work of art, meant for rapt appreciation, and tender, worshipful handling. Now she was always in his mind. During the day, he found himself wondering where she was, what she was doing, and with whom. When they were together, he was intoxicated, obsessed with her, wanting all of her attention.

She never said she loved him, and he didn't seem to notice.

In the wake of the Allied landing on Sicily, seven medical officers in the battle casualties course at Columbia had been suddenly transferred to hospital units bound for North Africa. David was informed he would not be returning to Fort Bragg. With the invasion of Italy imminent, the 65th General Hospital would soon be coming North to a staging area for transport overseas.

He agonized over what he would do about Lauren. Torn

between his guilt and a need to be honest, he wanted to confess to her, yet he was sensitive to the timing and how cruel it would be on the eve of his departure. He was uneasy whenever they spoke, for surely she would intuitively divine the truth from his tone of voice. She had always been perceptive, especially attuned to his moods. In fact, Lauren, better than anyone else, understood him. Near the end of July his orders came through, and he called to tell her.

Lauren sounded breathless on the phone. "Where have you *been,* David? I've been trying to reach you all week."

"We had a rush of cases, Laurie. They were short-staffed because of the holiday, so I stayed in one of the residents' rooms at the hospital."

How smoothly he lied to his wife. Like all adulterers.

"Well, anyway, I've got wonderful news. Aunt Reba is coming to take Mama to live with her permanently. She insists, and Mama is eager to go."

"That *is* good news, Laurie. I wasn't too pleased with you shouldering that burden alone."

"It's been hard at times, but I'm glad I did it. Mama is so appreciative when her mind is clear, and I'll always feel I did what I could for her. I know she'll be much happier in Randolph, though."

"What made Reba come round all of a sudden?"

Lauren did not bother explaining her role, or Philip's. "You know Aunt Reba—she always has her reasons. Basically, she's lonely and wants someone living in the house with her. But I think it's an ideal arrangement, especially with Phil and Jeanette going to California."

"California?"

"Yes, darling, I'm *sure* I told you about that last week. Philip is being sent to Army Language School. Oh—and Jeanette's expecting. Isn't that lovely?"

"Great! That's really terrific." Had she mentioned that? He'd been so nervous, trying to cover up his weekend absences, he probably hadn't paid attention. It looked like Philip had gotten over his sexual hang-up, whatever it was. "You sure are a harbinger of glad tidings today, Laurie."

"Yes, and I have something else to tell you . . ." She laughed, in that delightful thrilling way, and it made his heart clench. Oh, Lord, what was he doing? How could he abandon her?

". . . so that means we can come up next week."

Next week! What was she talking about. "I'm sorry, I didn't hear you, Laurie."

"I said that as soon as Aunt Reba comes to fetch Mama—early next week at the latest—we'll get the first train to New York. And we'll be there to stay, as long as you are, darling. I think this time, it really will come to pass."

Christ! he couldn't let her come. It would be a *disaster!* "Uh—Laurie, by next week, it'll be sort of too late. I've got new orders."

There was a long silence. "You have?"

"Yes, that's what I was calling to tell you. The 65th is coming up to Camp Shanks—that's a staging area just across the Hudson. I'm getting ready to move over there now." He was talking fast, saying anything to prevent her from coming to New York. "You'd better stay put. I'll get a furlough before—"

"Oh, David! I really do think I should come up alone, then. Just for us to be together, even for a few extra days."

"Honey, I'll be so busy, I'll hardly have a chance to see you. You can't stay in my quarters. It's 'bach' officers."

"That's not a problem. I'll go to Charlee's. We can stay there together."

"*No!* I mean, I can't do that."

Now she was angry. "What *is* it with you and Charlee? You've always had an attitude about her. And after all she's done for you!"

"I *haven't* had an attitude—Laurie, please, listen to me. I'll try to finish my processing early and get some extra leave. It's better if I come home, really it is. We'll have a chance to talk, and I'll see the kids."

"All right," she sighed, sounding so dejected that he

felt like a cad. "I was kind of looking forward to getting away, truthfully."

"I know you were, but New York isn't the right place for us. It'll be much better for me to come there."

That was how they left it. But it was time for him to confront Charlotte with some hard questions.

Chapter 29

CHARLOTTE LEE MORTIMER Fields decided she did not like herself very much. What had started as a flirtation, a typical Charlee thing of seeing whether she could attract a man, had become a rather *heavy* affair. And with David, of all people. She had never meant it to get out of hand. The trouble was, she had been so *bored* without a man—and even when Bruce was around, he wasn't that much of a husband.

For a long time, she had thought she could make it work. Bruce, even more than she, had wanted to keep the marriage going for appearances' sake. And she really had tried. Until quite recently, Bruce claimed he was still in love with her, and in his own way, she supposed he was. But whatever deep feelings she once held for him had long since dissipated.

She should never have gone back to him in France. When Nick had appeared in Monte Carlo on their honeymoon, she should have known it was hopeless. What a simpleton she had been in those days! Completely naive, she had gone to pieces when she finally understood what was going on—becoming quite hysterical, crying and carrying on so. Nicholas had fled Monaco, not showing up again until the next year in New York.

Bruce could be enormously persuasive . . . following her to Paris after she had left him, swearing it would never happen again. Like a fool, she had believed him!

Of course, now she realized he had been scared out of his wits. He had blamed the episode on opium: "Nicky brought this crazy stuff and we were smoking pipes, just for the hell of it. I can't even remember what happened,'' he had claimed, when he caught up with her at the George V. "I love you, darling, no one could ever come between us!''

He had bought her those gorgeous pieces from Cartier—a delicate diamond-encrusted watch and the triple-strand choker of Oriental pearls with the ruby and diamond clasp. The first of many such exquisite gifts of conscience. As if jewels could take the place of his love! As if anything could make up for his depriving her of happiness and children. She had been so young at the time, so easily taken in. Dreading the shame of facing her family and friends, of having to admit to the world that her fabulous marriage was a mistake, she had agreed to return to New York with him.

In many ways, she and Bruce were well-suited to each other. Despite it all, she had still been in love with him for years. It might have been all right, if Nicholas had stayed away. But whenever her hopes were raised, he would appear. The idea that she was unable to hold Bruce's love had undone her. Of other women, she had no fear. But this? She could never come to terms with it.

After three years of broken promises, she had finally confronted Bruce in the fall of 1939, a month before Max's last visit to New York. She knew she could count on her father's support. "I want a divorce, Bruce,'' she announced, when he came home late one night from whatever lair he had been holed up in.

"I don't think so, darling,'' he calmly replied.

"You don't have to agree, Bruce! You can make it easy or difficult. Either way, I'll get what I want. My father will see to that.''

"No, I don't think so,'' he repeated, smiling.

They were in the study that connected to their bedrooms. Bruce had gone to his desk and unlocked the drawer. Taking out a leatherbound calendar, he leafed through its pages. "Let's see, now. Oh yes, here we go . . . *March 10th, 5:30 P.M.: Entered office of George Stearns; departed 6:45. March 17th, 4:45 P.M.: Entered same, departed 5:30.* That must have been what is known as a quickie.'' He smiled at her, but she remained stone-faced. He continued turning pages and reading the notations there . . . ''Lately, you seem to be going in for some variety. There's a small brownstone on East 36th Street just off Park where my good friend and colleague, Steve Burns, keeps a pied-à-terre, I believe . . .''

A cold dread had taken hold of her. Not for herself would she care about a scandal, but it would have killed her parents!

She did not speak to him for weeks after. They no longer shared a bedroom, so there were actually days at a time that went by without their seeing each other. And then they had called a truce.

''Look, Charlee. I need you. I need a wife, and you could do worse in a husband. I don't abuse you, I don't embarrass you, and I think I keep you in grand enough style to suit even you. So, let's say we have an arrangement, shall we? You're free to live your own life, as long as you're discreet.''

''Just keep that faggot away from me, do you hear?'' she had screamed.

But what did it matter now? She had long since passed the point of caring what other people thought. Her father was dead, her poor mother had practically retired from life down in Randolph, taking care of Aunt Mimi. With the world at war, there were more important matters to worry about.

The affair with George had ended long ago, although they remained good friends. And Steve had been a momentary fling, never repeated. She did like men, though, and so, she had let herself get involved with David. Seeing him so often, she could not deny the physical attraction between them. That he was Laurie's, in a strange way, made him all the more desirable . . . There was a reserve about him that intrigued her, and it fascinated her to think of him aroused, losing control, getting carried away having sex. She had thought about it a great deal during the months before their first time, until she realized it was on his mind, too. And then, it had happened—with a little encouragement from her.

David had turned out to be more of a lover than she bargained for. She told him as much last weekend when they were up at the farm. Ridiculous, wasn't it, to call that manicured compound with its few acres of vegetables, no more than a glorified victory garden, a *farm.* But that's what people did in Fairfield County. They had been going at it rather strenuously and David was practically comatose, the way he became after sex. She, on the other hand, was usually immediately ready for another go-around. But she had been feeling quite satisfied and mellow on that particular night.

"Ummmm, Davey, you're *good* . . ." she said, as she stretched cat-like on the bed. Then her lips lifted at the corners in a teasing little Charlee smile. "You weren't always, you know."

His eyes had flown open. "I wasn't?"

Sometimes she found it useful to revert to her Southern speech patterns. "No, honey. You were quite inhibited at first, really. But, I declare, you sure learned fast."

Glancing at the Cartier watch, she wondered what was keeping him. He was usually so punctual. In a hurry when he spoke to her, he had sounded abrupt, saying his unit had received new orders. Did that mean they were shipping out? She would miss him when he was gone, but it was probably just as well he was leaving. If this went on much longer, someone was bound to find out.

There was only one thing she regretted. If only she had thought of it sooner. But perhaps it wasn't too late.

The minute he came in, she could see he was perturbed. "What you need is a drink," she said.

"Not now." He threw his cap on the table. "Another switch—the 65th is going to Massachusetts next week, for more training at Devens. I swear, I don't understand who makes these decisions! I hope we're not fighting the war in this disorganized, chaotic manner."

"How long will you be in Massachusetts?"

"*I* won't be there at all! I have a furlough at the end of next week, and then I go with an advance party."

"Oh, David, then it's come." She walked over, putting her arms around him.

He kissed her gently and gave her a sad smile. "Charlee, we have to talk."

"About what, darling?"

"About us."

She pouted and brushed the hair back from his forehead. "You look so *serious*, David."

He held her away from him. "I know no other way to be about this. I hope you're not playing games, Charlotte."

He was sweet, really, and vulnerable. She hated to give him up, but there were too many other people involved.

"It's time we were honest with each other. I despise sneaking around, deceiving everyone."

Oh *dear*, she did not like the direction in which this was going. She had to put a damper on it before he began to get dangerous ideas! "Listen to me, darling," she said quickly. "You're going away and we won't be seeing each other for Lord knows how long. It's all so complicated. Your marriage, and mine—we're all involved with family and children—"

"You have no children."

"No, but *you* do . . . and there's Laurie."

He sighed deeply. "Yes, don't think that isn't always on my mind. She's still very dear to me, and I feel I owe it to her to be truthful. I intend to have a talk with her when I go home—"

"You *wouldn't!*" she cried in alarm. "Oh, please, *please* promise me you won't! She'd be *devastated* and you're going so far away. It's the wrong time now, believe me. We *must* wait until you return." She was practically hysterical. "Promise, *promise* you won't tell her!"

"All right, all right," he soothed her, seeing how agitated she had become. "I guess I just can't stand the deception. I've never lied to Lauren about anything until now." And then he said the words she had been dreading. "Have you thought about a future for us, Charlotte?"

Her eyes were large and frightened as she shook her head. "I—I can't . . ."

He stared at her and she had no idea what he was thinking. "Sometimes I wonder if you really love me," he finally said.

She wound her arms around his neck. "Of course I love you," she whispered in that low, caressing voice that always stirred him. "Do please kiss me now."

With relief, she felt David's arms tighten around her. She had managed not to promise anything. There was just one thing more she needed from him, and they were running out of time . . .

On the following Thursday evening, Charlotte stared moodily into space. She had been feeling exhausted all week. Sending David away tonight, she had told him she felt one of her headaches coming on, and would see him tomorrow. He would be leaving for Chapel Hill on Monday, his last furlough before going overseas. Neither of them mentioned that if he were not spending the weekend with her, he could have had a longer stay at home with his family.

She decided to retire early, asking for a tray in her room. "No calls, Mairie," she ordered.

"Yes, ma'am," Mairie bobbed a curtsy and left, after setting the tray on a small table in front of the sofa.

Charlotte regarded the meal with distaste. What passed for coq au vin again, and brussels sprouts—a terrible combination. Really, she must tell Cook to use more imagination. Why couldn't the woman prepare simple food—a poached or broiled breast of chicken and some cheerful looking vegetables? The rich sauce turned her stomach, the aftertaste lingering, and she took a spoonful of fruit compote to get rid of it, but that disagreed with her, too. Pouring tea from a small pot, she pushed the table away, holding the cup in her hands.

So . . . David was going home to Lauren on Monday. And then he would be on his way. Would he make love to Laurie, she couldn't help but wonder. But of course he would! A man about to go overseas couldn't very well not sleep with his wife. Anyway, that's how men were. Hadn't her father had a mistress? And he was a good husband.

David would be coming back to New York and they were to see each other once more, for one last, glorious night together before he embarked. And then what! He could be gone for years, and who knew what would happen in his absence. He was convinced he was in love with her, but despite her strong attraction to him, she could not see herself as a doctor's wife—a faculty wife at that. Academics intimidated her; they were some of the few people who did. Lord, but her visits to Chapel Hill had been dreary! She remembered how out of place she felt with the Bernards' friends. She'd been completely over her head during the more intellectual discussions. And bored silly.

There was a knock on the door and Mairie entered to take away the dinner tray. "Didn't you like it, Mrs. Fields? Cook will want to know."

"It was fine. Tell her I'm not feeling very well tonight. It must be something I had at lunch."

Charlotte lay back against the bed pillows, feeling slightly queasy. Breathing deeply to conquer the nausea, her thoughts turned to Lauren. Ever since she had started the thing with David, she had avoided talking to her cousin. She was in the habit of phoning her often, and she'd missed their long chats. And then one afternoon a week ago, out of the blue, Laurie had called.

They had a long, rambling conversation without much point. Charlee had asked about Miriam and how she was getting along in Randolph Springs with Reba. Lauren had told her about submitting a topic for her thesis proposal. Charlotte could detect a hesitant note in her voice. Something was bothering Lauren. Oddly enough, she had not mentioned David. Could she possibly *suspect?* A chill had come over Charlee. She decided it would be better if she were the first to refer to him. "I hear your husband's coming down there soon."

"Yes." There was definitely a hesitation, a soberness in her manner. "He goes overseas after that."

That was it, of course! Lauren was just worried about

him, afraid he would be in danger. Charlee breathed a sigh of relief. She had practically been in a cold sweat, wondering if Laurie had guessed about them.

Suddenly Lauren was speaking in a rush of words. "I'm so nervous, Charlee. There's something amiss with David. I have no idea what it is, but I can sense it. I know him so well, and he's been completely different since he went into the Army. Usually I understand what's in his mind, but this time I'm at a loss. I don't know how to act with him anymore. Whatever I do or say seems to be just the opposite of what he needs—and I *so* want him to go away feeling it's right between us and knowing how much I love him . . ."

Lauren's voice broke and Charlotte thought she would like to die. This was *Laurie,* her *dearest Laurie,* the person she had been *closest* to for all her life! At that moment, she had hated herself more than anything in the world. There had been a long silence, as Charlotte tried to think of what to say.

"What shall I do, Charlee? There's no one else I can talk to. You're the only one I can trust. You've always known so much about men—and you've seen David recently. Can you tell me what's troubling him?"

She tried to make her voice sound normal. "I don't know nearly as much about men as you suppose, Laurie. At least, not these days. Bruce has been acting strangely, too—"

"He *has?*" Lauren seemed to grasp at it, looking for reassurance that this was normal behavior.

"Yes . . . I think it's the war and being in the service. You know how men don't want to let on when they're afraid or lonely. I'm sure that's behind whatever you sense in David's manner. He misses you and the children, and—and he's probably worried about what lies ahead—I mean, it's a new job, a bigger responsibility he's going to. When they're all geared up for sailing and all the other groups go and not theirs, it's bound to keep them on edge. I'll bet all the wives are feeling the same as you, wondering what's wrong with their men."

"You're right, of course. Oh, Charlee, I'm just so *glad*

I called you. You've made me feel a million times better. Now I can be more relaxed with David, understanding what's in his mind. You really are a comfort to me . . ."

The memory of Lauren's words cut into her like a knife. This was the worst thing she had ever done. In all her life, through all her wiles and deceptions and manipulative scheming, she had never wrought serious harm to anyone, let alone the one person in the world who would never hurt her. She *adored* Laurie, who had always been her trusting confidant. How could she have even *thought* of taking away Lauren's man? How could she ever explain it to her family, or to the Fields family? Despite everything, she still had a loyalty and affection for Bruce, and Blanche was one of her best friends . . . No, it was quite impossible, out of the question.

But she could not bring herself to tell David now. Not before he went overseas. Later, after he was gone, there would be time.

Charlee was awakened early on Saturday morning by a soft knock on her bedroom door.

Damn, she thought, reaching for her silk kimono. She should have insisted Mairie leave the apartment yesterday before David arrived, but the poor girl had nowhere else to go. They had been so cautious all these weeks; however, now that the end was coming, they'd grown a little careless.

She walked barefoot to the door, opening it a crack. "What in the world do you want, Mairie?" she whispered. "I told you I'm not feeling well and was not to be disturbed."

"Forgive me, ma'am, but there's a telephone call for you. It's . . . it's . . ." Her eyes involuntarily shifted sideways, as if she could see through the door to where David was asleep in the bedroom.

Charlotte let out an exasperated sigh. "Well, for heaven's sake, tell me who's calling!"

The maid drew herself up, her eyes downcast. "Mrs. Bernard is calling you from Chapel Hill. I told her you were sleeping, but she said it's important and she *must* speak to you."

Laurie! Charlotte was swept by a wave of panic. Why on earth would her cousin be phoning her now, at this early hour? Her instinct was not to take the call—if only Mairie had told her she wasn't at home. What would she say to Lauren? How would she keep from sounding guilty, with David lying right there in her bed? Thank goodness, she had unplugged the telephone in the bedroom, so it hadn't wakened him . . .

The maid was waiting. "Will you speak to her, ma'am?"

"Uhh—yes, Mairie. I'll take it in the study."

As she tiptoed across the darkened bedroom, David stretched, raising his head. "Where are you going?" he asked.

"It's just the telephone. Go back to sleep, darling."

She closed the connecting doors, and with her heart beating nervously, picked up the receiver. "Laurie, honey, is that really you? Heavens, it's practically the crack of dawn . . ."

At first she was guarded, despite Lauren's offhand manner when she asked whether Charlotte had talked to David. "No, honey, I haven't heard from him in ages . . ." *Did Laurie suspect he was here?* There was a dryness in Charlotte's throat, as she sank into a club chair. "How are those adorable children?" she asked automatically.

"Well actually, Mark's been running a temp and I can't get the pediatrician to make a house call . . ."

"I suppose it's always something with children." As if *she* knew anything about children! She hardly paid attention to the rest of the conversation, wanting only to get Laurie off the line. Should she tell David? He could always say he just happened to call Charlotte to say good-bye and heard that Lauren had been trying to reach him. But then, that meant he would probably leave for Chapel Hill immediately, and she had counted on this weekend. It was very important to her.

Was Mark really ill, or was that Laurie's usual apprehensive nature? She'd always been a worrier, got it from her mother. By the end of the conversation she sounded fine, insisting that Charlee not try to find David. Oh, it was probably nothing—one of those countless illnesses that children were forever having . . .

It was almost midnight when David put down the war novel he was reading and turned out the lamp next to the four-poster bed.

The drumming of rain on the farmhouse roof had a soporific effect. Charlotte had fallen asleep next to him as soon as they finished making love—or having sex, as she usually referred to it, the term jarring somehow, coming from a woman. Lauren would never call it "having sex," for that would rob it of its romance and meaning. In many ways, Lauren was more refined than Charlotte. Funny, he'd never thought about that before, but she was. Deeper, too. Charlotte was sophisticated and witty—she had a smattering of knowledge on a broad range of subjects, none of it bearing scrutiny, whereas Lauren was intellectually curious and if interested in something, eager to learn all she could about it. Lauren was the better company of the two, truthfully. Not that Charlotte was boring—never that! It was just that they had to always be *doing* something.

Take this weekend, for example. It had been raining since Friday night and they had decided not to come to Connecticut, when Charlotte had suddenly changed her mind early this morning. But once here, she had become restless and moody being stuck indoors. They had spent all day reading in front of the fire, not even having proper meals because Charlee was feeling rotten, claiming she was coming down with something. Oddly unresponsive, she had been in a strange mood tonight, their last night. In fact, it occurred to him she had been behaving in a very peculiar manner all week.

Was Charlotte as guilt-ridden as he, he wondered, now that he was about to go home to his family? Repeatedly, she insisted he should not tell Lauren anything about their affair. He had agreed, but the dishonesty weighed as heavily on him as his unfaithfulness. All week long, he had slept fitfully, worrying about how he would act with Lauren. Hoping for a decent night's rest, he closed his eyes and immediately fell into a deep slumber.

When the telephone rang, the sudden shrill sound shocked him, and for a moment David did not know where he was, thinking he was back home and it was a night call. In all the weeks they had been coming to the farm, no one had ever phoned. Charlotte stirred in the bed beside him, but neither one of them reacted at first.

"Ohhh," he groaned, reaching for her, "don't answer it."

"I have to, darling," she whispered. "It's probably the caretaker. No one else knows we're here."

"Let him wait 'til morning."

"It must be important, why else would he call at this hour?" She groped for the receiver, picking it up after the third ring, and David tightened his arm around her. He buried his face against her neck, inhaling the lingering aroma of their love.

"Yes . . . Where? . . . What time was that? . . . What did you tell her?" Charlotte reached over to turn on the light, both of them blinking in the sudden brightness. She raised herself on one elbow, looking worried and running her hand back through her hair. "You did the right thing," she said. "I don't know where he is, but I'll try to find him." She hung up slowly and waited for a moment before turning to look at him. There was an expression of anguish on her face.

"What is it?" he asked. She opened her mouth, but had trouble getting the words out. He took her in his arms, but she stiffened. "Charlee, who was that?"

"Mairie."

"Mairie? You mean, your maid?"

She nodded.

"What did she want?"

"Laurie called a couple of hours ago. Mairie said she was very upset. She's been trying to reach you at the base and no one knew where you were. They told her you had gone on leave."

"Oh, no! What did Mairie say? What did she tell her?"

"Nothing. She has strict orders not to disturb me or give out this number. But she thought I should know and so she finally decided to ring me here."

"Why was Laurie calling, did she say?" Charlee nodded. "Well, *tell* me!"

He saw the tears spring to her eyes, and his heart turned over with a sickening thud at her words.

"Mark's in the hospital, David. They think he has infantile paralysis."

Chapter 30

At midnight Lauren was standing next to the hospital crib, her heart aching as she kept watch over her sleeping son. She almost wept as he stirred restlessly. Poor darling, he had been such a brave little man, only crying when they inserted the needle for the intravenous solutions, or took blood samples.

The nurses had objected to her spending the night, but she stubbornly insisted. They put Mark in a private room in the isolation wing and required her to wear a mask and gown, which was patently ridiculous. If he did have polio, it was too late to prevent her from being exposed, since she had been with him constantly for the past forty-eight hours.

His eyelids trembled and opened. She pulled the mask down so he would not be frightened. But Mark seemed beyond fear, looking at her with large, suffering eyes, his forehead wrinkled with pain. "Hurts, Mommy," he whimpered.

"I know, darling. Show me where it hurts."

He pointed to the hip and leg and foot, and then to his head and neck, and finally both elbows and wrists, and she was terrified because there was nothing the doctors could do for him. She rubbed his arm until his lids drooped and he drifted off into slumber again.

She tried not to give in to her fear. *Where was David?* If only he was here! The sooner he reached home, the better. Time was important. If Mark's condition should get any worse—*Oh, God, I'm so afraid!* No, I have to keep my head, I must stay calm so I can think clearly.

She sat in the reclining leather arm chair, lowering the back and raising her feet on an ottoman. Her anxiety was too deep to permit sleep, but she closed her eyes to get whatever rest she could. A nurse looked in and changed the compresses, then nodded at Lauren and tiptoed out.

After speaking to Charlee's maid, she had given up trying to reach David, hoping against hope that he was on his way to Chapel Hill . . . Mark had been drowsy all day and she had mistaken his stupor for fatigue until she took his temperature in the late afternoon. Alarmed when she saw the fever had spiked to 104.6, she had bundled him into the car and driven to Strickland.

I should have brought him over on Thursday, the moment he said his head hurt!

All day Friday and Saturday she had given Mark aspirin and kept him quiet, forcing fluids, while Mandy took Babs away, just in case it wasn't the flu . . . Lauren hadn't wanted to even think about her worst fear, polio. Tony and Grace Strouds' four-year-old daughter had the bulbar type, and had been rushed to Duke Hospital last week, where she was in an iron lung.

Driving at top speed along the Raleigh Road, she thought: I should never have let him go in the swimming pool last week, but it was such a hot day, and all the children were there . . . *I'll never forgive myself if he has polio.* All the time thinking it wasn't possible.

The new pediatrician had a terrible manner with children. He wasn't unkind, but he was so matter-of-fact and he inspired no confidence in her. "I'm going to admit him, Mrs. Bernard. We'll keep him here in isolation until we know, but it looks like polio."

She'd had a hard time keeping her voice steady. "I was afraid it might be. He had that persistent strep throat, you remember, and I think it lowered his resistance. I did try to reach you yesterday."

"I'm sorry I wasn't able to return your call. If I'd known it was Dr. Bernard's wife . . ." Annoyed, she wondered why on earth that should make a difference. "We'll do a blood count and urinalysis, which is routine. He's pretty dehydrated, so I'm going to start an IV." Lauren looked distressed at that and he said, "We won't hurt him, don't worry."

"It's just that he'll be frightened. May I stay with him?"

"It might be better if you weren't there. Sometimes children are braver when their parents aren't around."

She did not believe that for a minute. She couldn't wait for David to get there.

It was the resident who picked up on the leg. His name was Jeff Greenberg, he spoke with a New York accent, exuded self-confidence, and remembered David, who had been chief resident in surgery when Jeff had first come down to Duke. "Mark has substantial pain in the right leg radiating to the joint," he told her when he had made his examination. "There's a synovitis of the knee and a small contusion on the lateral surface along the tibia—"

"I forgot, he fell from a jungle gym the week before last and hurt himself. I put ice on it and the pain subsided after a few minutes. He's been complaining about the leg, but to tell you the truth, I never connected it with the fall."

"I've ordered some more blood levels, a Schilling index, hemoglobin, and cultures," he said, rereading the chart. "This could be acute anterior poliomyelitis, as Dr. Dodds suggests. But the picture isn't that clear. You mentioned he's had strep throats?"

"Yes." She repeated the history.

"I'm putting him on sulfadiazine and we'll keep the infusions going," he spoke to himself as he made notes on the chart. "I want to get an X-ray of that leg in the morning."

"Does polio show up on an X-ray?"

He smiled cryptically. "No, Mrs. Bernard, it doesn't. But I'm not convinced this is polio."

"Oh, that would be so wonderful!"

"We can't rule it out until we get all the tests," he cautioned. "I'm really sticking my neck out, but Mark seems to have a systemic infection. His white count is elevated and there are white blood cells in the urine. As soon as we get a blood culture, we'll have a better idea. Meanwhile, I think it wouldn't hurt to splint that leg and keep hot compresses going." He winked at her. "And since it's Saturday night, we needn't disturb Dr. Dodds with that bit of information."

Somehow Lauren had confidence in this brash young man's judgment. Dr. Greenberg looked down at his small patient, thinking that his diagnosis, if it was correct, wasn't exactly comforting. Mark was a very sick little boy.

As she tried to fall asleep, Lauren worried about the contradiction in the diagnosis. If the resident disagreed with Dr. Dodds, what then? She was afraid the pediatrician was touchy and would be offended if she asked for a consultation. She wondered what David would do. And suddenly she knew. First thing in the morning, even though it was Sunday, she would call Tom Sayles and ask him for another opinion.

The steady rumble of the DC-3's propellers reverberated in David's ears. They seemed to be mocking him. *You pay for your sins,* they droned. *Youpayforyoursins . . . youpayforyoursins . . . youpayforyoursins . . .*

Was God punishing him? That was ridiculous, of course. His son was the one who was ill. Mark! His wonderful boy, sweetly trusting, with the unshakable belief that his daddy would protect him from anything bad. His daddy, the soldier-doctor, who could do no wrong, who healed sickness and was fighting the war. For, what would a tousled little tike know about a soldier-daddy who fornicated in the bed of a velvet-thighed siren, while his wife kept vigil over their child and tried in vain to summon him home?

God, please, *please* . . . don't make Mark pay for my failings! He pressed his face into his hands as tears burned behind his closed eyelids. In the dim interior of the big lumbering military transport plane, the nightmare of the last six hours replayed in his mind.

He flinched as he remembered Charlotte's reaction when he grabbed the telephone to call Lauren. "What are you doing?" she had cried frantically. "Are you *crazy?* You can't call her from here—you *can't!*"

"What the hell difference does it make, Charlee? She

won't know or care where the call is coming from. Don't be such a selfish fool." As she stalked out of the room, he heard the telephone ringing in his house.

It was Amanda, not Lauren, who answered, sounding groggy and anxious at being awakened so late at night. He explained that Lauren had been trying to reach him.

"She stayed at the hospital with Mark, Dr. Bernard."

"Did they go to Strickland, Mandy?"

"Yes, to the Russell Clinic."

"What time?"

"Around five o'clock. Mark was so sick, and the doctor couldn't make a house call."

He was filled with remorse. Lauren must have been trying to reach him all evening. "Have you heard anything from her?"

"Not since about nine-thirty. She said they were doing tests. The pediatrician thought it was infantile paralysis, but Mrs. Bernard said another doctor wasn't sure."

There was no phone in Mark's room in the isolation wing, so David asked to speak to the resident. "I know you, Dr. Bernard, I did a rotation under you in '42," Greenberg told him. David could vaguely recall a short, dark, smart-ass kid from Brooklyn. He had been good.

"What can you tell me about my son, doctor?"

Jeff outlined Mark's condition in detail, including Dr. Dodds's diagnosis. At the end, he paused. "What's your opinion, Dr. Bernard?"

David's voice was heavy with sorrow as he uttered one word. *"Osteo."*

"Yeah," was the soft reply.

Osteomyelitis as a severe infection of the bone. In its acute form, when septicemia was present—that is, infection in the bloodstream—it had a seventy percent mortality rate. The younger the patient, the higher the likelihood it would be fatal.

It took David several minutes to gain control of his emotions after saying good-bye to the resident. He steeled himself to think as a physician and not a parent. Only a second was necessary for him to decide on the next move. He immediately called Tom Sayles at home.

"David! How the hell are you, boy? It's good to hear your voice."

"At this hour, Tom, it's not good to hear anyone's voice. I wouldn't have called you unless it was urgent." He explained what had happened. "I hate to impose, but I would really appreciate it if you'd look in on Mark's case."

"Sure enough, Dave. I'll get right on it. It does sound like osteo to me. Where can I reach you?"

"I'm going to try to get on an Air Force plane down to Bragg, and I should be at Strickland sometime tomorrow—" he glanced at his watch, "make that today."

"Maybe he'll be lucky, David," Tom said gently. "The sulfas are powerful, and with drainage and transfusions . . ."

"What about penicillin?"

He heard Tom's frustrated expression of disgust, "Hell, we can't get any, Dave. There's a limited supply and it's all going to the military."

Science had given them a new wonder drug that could save his son's life, and they were unable to get hold of it! David knew Mark could be dead by the time he reached home. His mind was so clouded, he couldn't seem to think straight.

"Don't worry, Dave. We'll take good care of your boy."

"I'm very grateful to you, Tom," he said hoarsely. "Poor Laurie, having to go through this alone."

"That's what women are doing these days, David. And frankly, they're doing a darn sight better than the men."

Lauren couldn't have been more surprised when Tom Sayles walked into Mark's room with Jeff Greenberg at two in the morning. "Lauren, there you are. I had a call from David less than an hour ago. He'll soon be on his way home."

Her hand flew to her mouth. "Thank God! Oh, Tom, you'll never know how relieved I am to hear that—and I'm *so glad* to see you. I was going to call you as soon as the sun came up."

"I wish you had done that when you brought your boy in, Lauren. Some things are too difficult to manage alone.

You must remember we care a great deal about all of you." He had such a warm and reassuring way about him, she immediately felt better.

"Of course, I'll give Dr. Dodds a call and inform him that David asked me to step in—no reason why you should have to worry about that." He patted her arm, then directed his attention to Mark, who was pushing fitfully against the straps that restrained him from dislodging the IV. "Now let's see to this young man. Why don't you stroll down the hall for a while, Lauren, while Dr. Greenberg briefs me. I'll call you when we're finished."

She fell asleep in a quiet lounge at the end of the main corridor, confident about Mark's care, now that Tom was there. An hour later when Dr. Sayles looked in on her, she was half-reclining on the couch with her arms folded against the chill of the night. He asked a nurse to place a pillow under her head and cover her with a blanket. She looked exhausted from worry and lack of sleep, and he knew she would need all her strength in the days ahead.

Lauren awoke to the bustling early-morning hospital noises, as nurses gave out medications and bed pans, took temperatures and blood pressures, and hastened to finish up charts before turning their charges over to the next shift. There was a methodical, practiced pattern to the heightened activity.

A flurry of motion in the hall caught Lauren's attention. Something was out of synchrony with the regular heartbeat of the pediatric floor. It had the frantic, jarred rhythm of crisis. An orderly went speeding around a corner wheeling a cart, while nurses hurried in and out of the isolation wing. All of her senses became alert as she instinctively knew the commotion was focused on Mark's room. She raced down the hall, turning a corner and almost colliding with Dr. Dodds, who came out just as she reached the doors to the isolation section.

The first thing she noticed in Mark's room was an oxygen tank that had not been there before. White-coated figures were swarming around the crib. Alarm coursed through her as she saw that her son was bathed in perspiration and shivering uncontrollably. A nurse was sponging him in an effort to bring down the fever, while a resident pumped up the pressure apparatus and pressed a stethoscope to the rapidly heaving little chest. Dr. Dodds returned, and with an annoyed glance in her direction, hurried to join the group of doctors and nurses surrounding Mark.

Things happened swiftly after that. Horrified, Lauren watched the small sturdy body go rigid and the eyes roll back as Mark convulsed. She saw an oxygen mask being placed over his face and she couldn't help crying out.

"Get the mother out of here, for God's sake," she heard Dodds shout, and someone wrapped arms around her and removed her from the room.

"My baby, what's happening to him?" she pleaded through her panic, and they said soothing things to her as they took her into an empty room.

"Where's Dr. Sayles—call Dr. Sayles," she kept repeating.

"He's with your son, Mrs. Bernard. Don't worry." And Tom *was* there, stopping in briefly to tell her they were taking Mark to surgery in order to drain the infection from the leg bone.

"I don't understand," she said, bewildered. "It's not polio, then?"

"I'm sorry, I should have explained earlier, but you were sleeping soundly. The X-rays show an infection in the right tibia. Mark has osteomyelitis." He gripped her arm reassuringly as a gurney passed bearing her son to the operating room. "I have to go now, Lauren. I promise I'll do my best for him."

Suffocated by apprehension, she returned to Mark's empty room. The sides of the crib were down and the covers thrown back. There was something so eloquent about the vacated bed of her son who had been taken away to surgery. She touched the rumpled sheets. They were still damply warm from him.

She knew what osteomyelitis could mean. David had done a rotation at the Crippled Children's Hospital and often enough he had spoken about the tragic case histories.

Mark could die from the infection. He could lose his leg. Or, he could be crippled for life.

She looked out the open window at the rolling green meadows and surrounding woods. It was a sparkling, sunny day, and she could hear churchbells in the distance calling the faithful to Sunday services. How deceptively beautiful and serene their world appeared.

A nurse rapped on the doorframe and entered the room with the cushioned, starchy rustle that accompanies nurse movements. She was carrying a small tray with a medication cup and water. "Dr. Sayles ordered a sedative for you, Mrs. Bernard."

Shaking her head, she said, "I don't need a sedative."

"This won't put you to sleep. It will just calm you down."

"I'm quite calm, thank you."

The nurse made a grimace of disapproval. "Well, then, will you have some breakfast? They're coming around with the trays."

Lauren smiled gratefully. "Perhaps just some coffee, if it's not too much trouble."

Soon an aide brought a tray with juice, coffee, and toast. Lauren drank the juice and nibbled a wedge of soggy buttered toast, and then sat in the armchair, cradling the cup of coffee in her hands. She constantly looked at her wrist watch while the seconds dragged by . . . eight-twenty . . . eight twenty-three . . . eight twenty-seven. She went into the bathroom, rinsed her mouth and washed her face, then searched through her handbag for a comb to run through her tangled hair.

When would David get here? What was happening to Mark? She wished David were in the operating room with him. He must have been terrified when they gave him anesthesia. She wanted to be with him, to hold his hand and tell him Mommy was there. If he should die . . . She hadn't even held him in her arms or kissed him this morning, she hadn't even told him good-bye before they wheeled him away!

For more than an hour, she paced back and forth in the hallway with her private agony, attracting curious and sympathetic glances through the glass partition from technicians and house staff. Her watch had stopped and she lost track of time.

Back in the room, she leaned her head against the wall, thinking she could not bear another minute of not knowing, when she heard the door open. She turned, and David was standing there in surgical garb, looking haggard and unshaven . . . and as if he had lost everything in the world.

Try as she might, Lauren could not keep her tears from flowing. She buried her face in David's chest, sobbing as he enveloped her in his embrace, and David was crying, too.

"You don't have to tell me," she wept, her voice muffled against him. "I can see it in your eyes. He's dead, isn't he?"

Chapter 31

THOMAS SAYLES WOULD never understand what had prompted him to call the switchboard that morning before drilling into the infected bone of Mark Bernard's leg.

"I'll be in the OR, in case Captain Bernard comes in," he told the operator. "We've got his son up here."

"He's just calling, Dr. Sayles. I was about to page you," she answered.

"Good—Let me talk to him."

"Tom, I'm at Bragg," David sounded breathless.

"How soon will you be here, David?"

"If I can get hold of a car right away, about an hour and a half, maybe two. How's Mark?"

Should he tell him then or wait until he arrived. Tom thought he deserved to know. "It's osteo, David, and it's broken loose. We get staph and strep in the cultures. I believe it's confined below the knee. I've decided to go in and try to clean it out. They're prepping him now."

"*Jesus,* Tom, listen . . . I—I've got a supply of penicillin from the base hospital here. It was waiting for me when we landed—I called the 65th General and they arranged it. How long can he hold out?"

Sayles paused before answering. "I don't want to wait for two hours, Dave. Little fellow like that, you know, if it gets near the hip . . ." The closer the infection came to a hip or shoulder, the greater the danger—on the other hand, going in surgically was extremely hazardous at this acute stage of infection.

"I'll try to get a light plane to fly me to Chapel Hill.

Give it a chance, Tom,'' he begged, his voice breaking. ''I don't want my son to be crippled!''

It was a stroke of good fortune that a pilot about to take off for a training run in a single-engine plane had agreed to fly David to the small municipal airstrip outside of Chapel Hill. Less than an hour after he had spoken to Sayles, David was racing up the front steps of Strickland, clutching the dry ice pack containing penicillin compound.

Dr. Sayles was waiting on the surgical floor. He had aspirated some fluid from Mark's leg at the site of the infection and he injected the antibiotic preparation directly into the affected area. If the penicillin did its job, they would be able to avoid operating.

For the next three days, Mark remained seriously ill, while he was given intravenous penicillin and sulfadiazine and constant applications of hot moist poultices. His blood levels, urine, and vital signs were carefully monitored and his parents knew that he was at grave risk, and any moment could bring another crisis. Although Mark had special nurses around the clock, Lauren spent every night at the hospital, and after the third day, she was at the point of total exhaustion. ''Let me stay with him tonight,'' David urged. ''You're going to be sick if you don't get a decent night's sleep.''

''But, what if he wakes up and cries for me?''

''Don't you think he'd settle for me?'' he asked gently.

Of course he would, Lauren assured him. Mark always perked up when his daddy walked in. David was so tentative with her, almost as if he was begging her to forgive him for not being there when Mark became ill. It wasn't *his* fault. If anyone was to blame, it was she, for not taking Mark to the doctor at the first sign of illness, and for dismissing his injured leg as just one more bump in the childhood of an energetic boy who was in perpetual motion. She hoped this would make her overprotective of him in the future. Thanks to David's quick thinking, Mark would have a future.

They took turns on night duty, and by the end of the

week, it was clear that Mark was responding well to the treatment. His infection subsided without forming an abscess and no further drainage was necessary. They fully understood how lucky they had been. Osteomyelitis often became a chronic or recurring condition, requiring repeated, invasive surgery. Until the advent of penicillin, sterile maggots were often inserted in the open wounds of stubborn chronic infections—and in fact, that treatment was sometimes still used when the new drug was not available.

With the acute phase of osteo behind, Mark's leg was encased in a plaster cast up to the hip to protect the weakened bone. They could bring him home in a few days, but the cast would remain on for at least two months, and he would have to be taken to Dr. Sayles's office daily for tests and penicillin injections until there was no sign of infection. David's commanding officer had given him three days of extra compassionate leave, and now they would all be able to spend it at home.

Amanda and Babs hung the house with streamers and welcome home signs, and Mandy baked a layer cake with fudge icing to celebrate Mark's homecoming. They were a family again, all of them together for the first time in four months—since that brief unsatisfactory weekend in April.

Whatever it was that had come over him when he was home on leave, thought David, it had started him on a downward spiral, continuing on Lauren's visit to New York in June—and leaving him vulnerable to Charlotte's attractions. Or so he believed. The truth was, he wanted to find a *reason* for his actions. What would make a perfectly sane man go crazy and risk losing his wonderful family? It haunted him. Now that the crisis with Mark had passed, he was in a state of confusion about his love for Lauren and whatever it was he felt for Charlotte. Was it possible for a man to be in love with two women at once? Regardless, he felt unworthy of Lauren and would have confessed everything to her, if he did not know it would break her heart.

She regarded him through eyes filled with love. His

family, especially the children, treated him with an adulation he did not deserve. Mark's piping voice constantly prattled about "My Daddy!" as if he were a god. Babs clung to him, climbing on his lap and laying her head against his chest. For three days he was bathed in love, surrounded by a blissful normality.

"Daddy?" Babs asked at dinner on their first evening home.

"Yes, sweetheart?"

"Are you going to get killed in the war?" Her voice sounded so innocent, it caused a lump in his throat.

He saw a shadow pass over Lauren's face, and quickly replied, "No, Babs! I'm a doctor in the war, same as I am at home. I won't be near the fighting."

"But they drop bombs on people."

He was shocked at her precociousness and the terrible things she knew. Four years old, and she was talking about bombs. "They don't drop bombs on hospitals, honey."

"I got my own liberry card!"

Laughing at the non sequitur, he realized how much he had to learn about children, not least of all, their giant conversational leaps.

That night in their room, after the children had been put to bed, Lauren said, "Darling, I'm so grateful you were here. We almost lost our little boy. You saved Mark's life."

"It was fate, Laurie, a series of lucky breaks. My CO ordered them to release the penicillin, the pilot got me to Chapel Hill, Jeff Greenberg made a shrewd diagnosis, and Tom took over from Dodds in time."

"None of it would have happened, if it weren't for you," she insisted. "Dr. Dodds was pretty nice about it, after all, wasn't he?"

"He's a decent man. I'm sure he tried to do his best for Mark, but he was in over his head. Lots of second-rate men are stepping in when other doctors go into the service."

David slid under the covers, and she realized it was the first time they had shared their bed since he had come home. The first time since New York. It was different now, because she felt united in their love and by the ordeal they had shared for the past week. She held out her arms to him. Was it her imagination, or did he hesitate before kissing her? But she was immediately overcome with the joy of having him in her embrace, and feeling his lips on hers. There was a rising fire within, and she knew this time it would be right—

"Mommy! *Mo-om-my . . .*" Mark's screams suddenly pierced the night.

Lauren stiffened and immediately drew away from David, jumping out of bed and racing into Mark's bedroom. David followed, worry wrinkling his brow.

"What is it, Mark, what happened?" cried Lauren, holding him and rocking him back and forth in her arms.

His body was rigid with fear. He could hardly speak, for crying so hard, telling her about the bad men and knives and terrible threats he had encountered. *Nightmares,* she mouthed to David, who was sitting on the other side of the bed rubbing Mark's back. "It's all right, darling, it was just a bad dream. Mommy and Daddy are here and no one is going to harm you."

Lovemaking was forgotten. They took Mark into their bed, and he slept between them for the rest of the night.

They had one last day together. David would be flying to New York the next morning, and although he was not permitted to tell her where, Lauren knew he would be going overseas. Again that night, Mark awakened with nightmares, but this time they did not take him into their bed. "He could form a habit very quickly," David told Lauren, "and it would be difficult to break."

Lauren stayed in Mark's room until he dropped off. When she returned to their room, David was sleeping, his breathing deep and regular. She lay next to him, longing to reach out and waken him, yearning to run her hands over his long, hard body, to devour him with kisses, and to feel him take her in passion. They had not made love once while he was at home.

In the morning, they said good-bye to the children

and she drove him to Fort Bragg. "Take care of the kids, honey," he said kissing her tenderly. "I'll miss you."

"Be careful, David. Come back to us safely." She could hardly hold back the tears. "I love you, darling . . ."

And he was gone.

Chapter 32

ON ROSH HASHANAH morning Lauren went to temple in Durham with the Rosenblooms. She and David had always joined a group of Jewish students and faculty couples from Duke and Carolina for the High Holidays, but this year, all the men were away in the service.

The rabbi's sermon was ominous and heartbreaking. Gradually the chilling stories had filtered to the free world. During the past year—5703 in the Jewish calendar—all across the European continent in conquered lands, the Germans had rounded up, imprisoned, and put to death untold numbers of men, women, and children, for no reason except that they were Jews. And no nation seemed capable of stopping them.

A heaviness, a pall of desolation hung over the congregation. At the end of the service, there were an unusual number of mourners. Middle-aged couples grieved for sons lost in the war, while young women rose to recite the *Kaddish* for their dead husbands. Watching them, Lauren had an attack of anxiety and an overwhelming desire to flee from the crowded synagogue. To overcome her feelings of panic, she closed her eyes and breathed deeply, concentrating her thoughts on David, somewhere in England, trying to imagine where he was and what he was doing.

Was he in danger? The Germans bombed English cities; they attacked indiscriminately, not caring whether they hit civilian targets or hospitals. *Oh God, I feel so alone without him! If anything happens to him, I'll never forgive myself for not having spent those months in New York with him.* If God would bring David safely home to her, she vowed she would be a better wife to him. Never again would she put her own interests ahead of his.

As the final portion of the service began, the minor melodies and melancholy chanting of the cantor brought tears to her eyes. She was relieved when the closing prayer was recited and they all filed out of the synagogue.

"We're having some boys from the Navy Preflight School for dinner this afternoon, Lauren," Selma told her on the way back to Chapel Hill. "We called Commander Kessing's office at the university to arrange it."

"What a wonderful idea, Selma. Mark will be in seventh heaven, having dinner with the cadets!"

"When is the Navy coming, Mommy?" Mark kept asking, until Babs, who had been kneeling on the couch and looking out the front window of the Rosenblooms' living room cried, "They're here! Here they come!"

There was a furry of excitement as the children rushed to the door, Mark hopping along on his cast, his eyes shining in anticipation. "Please be careful, Mark," Lauren called, fearing he would fall. She had discovered it was virtually impossible to keep an irrepressible three-year-old from running around, even with his leg immobilized in plaster. Oscar Rosenbloom, a grandfatherly man, scooped him up in his arms and carried him out on the porch to greet "the Navy."

Five midshipmen and a handsome lieutenant shook hands with Oscar, making a fuss over a suddenly shy Mark. From the hallway, where Babs clung to her and stared wide-eyed at the uniformed young men, Lauren heard the officer introducing the cadets. "Midshipman Robert Berger, sir . . . Norman Lang, sir . . ." It was the voice of a cultured Northerner. A familiar-sounding voice.

Oscar ushered his guests through the front door. "Lauren, may I present Lieutenant Wise, and I'm afraid you other men will have to repeat your names to Mrs. Bernard."

Lauren could hardly believe her eyes.

"Hello, Lauren, it's nice to see you again," said Peter Wise, removing the billed officer's hat that had obscured his features.

"You know each other!" exclaimed Selma, taking it as a sign this would be a hugely successful occasion.

"We're old friends," said Peter, looking composed and grinning broadly as he kissed Lauren's cheek.

She could feel the color rise in her face and she thought the cadets were enjoying her discomfiture. After Babs had been coaxed to come out from behind her skirts, she was able to have a word with Peter. "This is such a surprise, meeting you here! Don't tell me you're learning to fly."

"Not with *my* eyes. They've got me teaching school. I'm giving the course on Naval and Aviation History." Still charming, he was even more attractive in uniform. She noted that he wasn't wearing his glasses. Or smoking a pipe.

"How long have you been in Chapel Hill?"

"A while." He looked down for a moment, then met her eyes. "I knew you lived here, and I suppose I would have called eventually." Lauren suddenly felt very married. She looked over at Mark and Babs, who were each seated on a cadet's lap, loving the attention. "Your children are adorable," said Peter.

"They're on their best behavior today, overawed by the Navy." She was immensely curious about him. "Are you married, Peter?"

He shook his head. "I guess I keep chasing the impossible dream," he said, with an imponderable expression.

Before she could answer, the maid appeared in the doorway and nodded at the hostess. "Dinner is served, everyone," Selma announced, leading them to the dining room. "Lauren, I'll put you right here next to Lieutenant Wise, and we'll set Mark's chair on your other side."

Before they sat down, Oscar said the blessing over the wine: *"Boruch attoh adonoi, elohenu melech ho'olom, bo're p'ri haggofen.* Blessed are Thou, O Lord our God, Ruler of the universe, Who hast created the fruit of the vine." He then asked if one of the midshipmen would recite the blessing over the bread, afterward distributing pieces of the round *challah,* especially made for the holiday.

"Before we begin our Rosh Hashanah meal," said Oscar, his voice sincere with feeling, "let's just pause for a moment to remember our servicemen overseas and our brethren who are imprisoned under the Nazis. And let us thank God that we are fortunate enough to be Americans."

They were silent, and even the children seemed to sense the solemnity of the moment. Oscar then told them, in his gracious way, how privileged he felt to have them as guests in his home. There was a sense of kinship around the table, and Lauren noticed several of the cadets were visibly affected by Oscar's words. Everyone present except for the children knew these young men, who would soon be Navy fighter pilots, had only a forty percent chance of surviving the war.

It was Babs and Mark who invited "the Navy" to go home with them when dinner was over. All the men squeezed into Lauren's automobile, taking the children on their laps, and she drove to her house, wondering what she would do with them when they reached there. The cadets immediately removed jackets and ties, rolled up their sleeves, and started a game of basketball in the garden, with one of them holding Mark on his shoulders so that he could toss the ball. As the daylight faded, the delighted shrieks of the children sounded over the lawn to the screened porch where Lauren sat with Peter.

"What nice boys. Surely they'd rather be somewhere more exciting than this."

"They're a little homesick today, Lauren. Being here makes them feel less lonely. And I think they sense this is where I want to be." He was looking directly at her.

"You really ought not to say that, Peter," she said quietly.

"Yes, I know, but I've already said it. So there!" She laughed. "Your husband's overseas, this is a small town where you're known to everyone. I understand all of that. But I hope we can be friends."

A great sense of affection came over her. "Thank you, Peter. I can use a friend."

Chapter 33

SUNDAY AFTERNOONS WERE the worst, when the children were getting cranky and she faced the long empty evenings. During the week, when she was busy with classes, library research, and her job, when she rushed across campus, stopping at the dry cleaners or grocery store on her way home, keeping so busy there was no time to think, then the loneliness was bearable.

Standing in line at the butcher shop to redeem her ration coupons, she would make a list of what to tell David in the next letter. She wrote to him often, messages that were long, warm and loving. She could keep from giving in to despair if she pretended there had been nothing wrong between them. She blamed herself. If she had acted like a normal wife, David would have no cause to doubt her love. And she was convinced he did, for why else would he have been so guarded, almost apologetic, with her before he left for overseas? His letters revealed nothing, but he was hardly apt to write about intimate matters, knowing they would be read by a censor.

She called Randolph Springs every Sunday to speak to her mother, even though Miriam often did not realize who she was. Reba assured her there was plenty of assistance in caring for Miriam, with both Lady and Bertram, as well as Pansy and an extra maid to clean and do laundry. But Reba raised a disturbing question one Sunday: "I do think you should get rid of Mimi's house, Laurie. Why don't you let Lionel put it up for sale? She's never going back there to live."

"I'm afraid it would upset her, Aunt Reba. Why don't

we wait 'til Phil gets home on leave, then we'll talk about it."

The family seemed to be scattered at such great distances . . . Jeanette wrote regularly, reporting that she and Philip adored California living. Their baby was due in January and she was feeling wonderful. It had been much too long since Lauren had spoken to Charlee. Whatever had happened between her and Bruce in June, after that terrible argument, she wondered. Charlotte had never referred to it again, and Lauren was hesitant to pry. In October, when she phoned to say happy birthday, Charlee was away and never returned the call. Which was odd—not at all like her. And then Reba mentioned that Bruce was soon going overseas, which explained it, for she said Charlee was spending all her time with him in Washington.

"Do you know where Bruce is going?" Lauren asked Reba. The men weren't supposed to say, but the families usually had some idea.

"I think Charlotte Lee mentioned England, Laurie," she answered, in her usual distracted manner. "Wouldn't it be wonderful if he and David can see each other!" Lauren thought Bruce might have as little interest in such a meeting as David, however she could hardly tell that to Reba.

At the end of each day, she was terribly tired. Her eyes were bothering her, and she went to an ophthalmologist who prescribed reading glasses. It troubled her that her work was not going as well as she had hoped. She had begun the weekly conferences with her new advisor; the man with whom she had planned her thesis had been drafted. The first session had produced very little in the way of guidance, and was marked by a singular lack of enthusiasm on his part for the courses she had chosen for the semester. She did not like him at all.

His name was Donal Sullivan. They skirted around first names, however, one had to be civil, and it seemed foolish to address someone no more than three years her senior as "Mr. Sullivan." His area of interest was modern poetry and he was teaching undergraduate courses in creative writing. Which was precisely why she felt he was the wrong advisor for her, since he was concentrating on the Elizabethans. She would see how it went in today's meeting, she thought, as she approached his office.

"I worked out my schedule and the topic for my dissertation with my former advisor, Jim Bartlett, at the end of last term, but he's gone—"

"To the Army," Donal Sullivan finished, flipping through her transcript without looking up.

That's right, she thought, and why aren't *you* in the Army or some other service? He appeared to be around thirty and perfectly fit, if a little thin, in his heather brown tweed jacket and gray pants. Earnest looking, with an angular face, his unruly russet hair and horn-rimmed glasses gave him an owlish sort of intellectualism. In his left hand he held an unlit pipe—crutch of the academic—that he periodically put between his lips, then removed without lighting.

"It's going to take you forever to get your degree at this rate, Miss Bernard."

"*Mrs.* Bernard. It was the only way I can do it because I work three afternoons a week, and I have two children."

He was busily engaged in lighting his pipe, adding tobacco from a pouch, tamping it and holding a match to the bowl while he puffed, exuding streams of aromatic smoke. He raised his eyes at her over the pipe until his brows knit together. "Well, let's see what you intend to contribute to the world of scholarly research," he said, with weary resignation.

Reluctantly, Lauren handed him the typed précis that was the preliminary outline from which her formal thesis proposal would stem. The topic, which Bartlett had suggested, was an analysis of male-female conflict in Shakespeare. "I hadn't gotten very far with this when Jim left."

Puffing on his pipe, Sullivan studied the paper without comment, then put it down. "I think we should explore some other ideas."

"What's wrong with that one?"

"It's been done and done. Is it a problem that will really grip you enough to devote two years of your life to it?"

"Well . . . I find it interesting."

"For a term paper, yes. But you'd be bored as hell by the time you hit page forty."

"Have you got a better suggestion?"

"Actually, yes I do . . ." If he didn't stop fiddling with that damn pipe! "I was thinking of your exploring the portrayal of the Jewish character from Marlowe to Fry."

She was silent, feeling her rising anger. "Is that supposed to be funny?"

"Not at all," he answered, in a cloud of blue smoke. "I think it'd be a fascinating topic, and I'm not aware it's ever been done."

"Well, it sure as hell *won't* be done! Not by me, anyway." She snatched the paper from him and ran out of the room.

"Hey!" she heard him call, "don't go away mad."

She reached an exit door and hurried down the darkened stairway, holding back tears of vexation. Of all the colossal nerve, how *dare* he! This was her life's work and he was making a bigoted joke of it. She had nearly reached the ground floor when she heard Sullivan's voice above her in the stairwell. "Mrs. Bernard—Lauren—wait for me. I can't keep up."

"Not on your life!" she shouted.

"I'm sorry," he called. "Let me explain."

He had nearly gained on her, reaching the top of the last short flight of stairs, but as he started down, he tripped and stumbled, catching himself on the banister. Hearing him cry out, Lauren turned and saw his face contort in pain. After a moment's hesitation, she ran up to assist him. Holding onto her, he carefully lowered himself to the stoop and rocked forward, biting his lower lip. As he massaged his thigh, his trousers hiked up, revealing an artificial limb.

He heard her gasp and looked up, the pain still etching his face. "Thanks," he said, his voice hoarse with strain. "Afraid I'm not quite used to it yet."

"It's my fault you fell! Forgive me—I had no idea."

He smiled weakly. "If I didn't know better, I'd say you were Irish, such a temper you've got."

She laughed. "Now you're adding insult to injury."

Donal winced, "I suppose I deserve that." He started to rise.

"Can you walk?" she asked, taking his arm.

"If I could just lean on you a little, until I get down the stairs." He draped his arm over her shoulders and let her help him.

"Come sit over here for awhile," said Lauren, when they were outside. She led him to a bench. "Is . . . is it fairly recent?"

"I lost the lower part in May of '42 in the Coral Sea. I was on the *Lexington* when she got it. Couldn't seem to shake the infection, so they had to remove more in Boston. That was in March . . ." He looked away. "I used to teach at Boston University before the war, but I decided to try something different, since I've outlived my usefulness to the Navy."

"I'm feeling really terrible, you know. Behaving that way to a war hero—and making you chase me."

"Chasing you is a rare pleasure, Mrs. Bernard," he drawled, taking his pipe out of his pocket and beginning the process of lighting it. "I take it there is a . . . Mr. Bernard?"

"My husband is a doctor and he's with the Army in England. During peacetime, he was at the Russell Clinic."

Donal continued to rub his thigh, as he puffed on the pipe. Now she could see the signs of suffering beneath his fading summer tan. There were lines in the forehead and on either side of the prominent, high-bridged nose, with faint blueish depressions, like brush stokes, under his eyes. They were deepset, thoughtful eyes, a warm honey color with large dark pupils. The full head of crisp reddish brown curls seemed too heavy for his drawn, sensitive, oddly attractive face.

"Does the leg still hurt?" she asked.

"Much better now," he smiled. "I have to learn not to make sudden pivoting movements." He gazed across the campus for a few seconds, then nodded at her. "I'm okay now. Let's go get a cup of coffee. My treat."

He wasn't nearly as gruff or unpleasant as she had

thought. In fact, he was quite agreeable and extremely bright, with a droll sense of humor. Within an hour, Lauren decided she was quite satisfied to have him as her advisor. Her topic *did* seem a little pedestrian, now that she considered it—however she was *not* interested in exploring the Jewish character in Elizabethan drama and she told him so.

"I didn't think you would take offense at that," he said. "I did my dissertation on the Irish poets. It seemed like a natural."

"I guess I'm too sensitive, and maybe a little defensive."

He smiled. "You're a pretty sight when you get your dander up, Lauren Bernard." It made her self-conscious, the way he regarded her with that knowing half-smile.

She pushed her coffee cup away. "I'm afraid I have to get home. My children will be waiting for me."

"How old are they?"

"My daughter is four-and-a-half, and my little boy is three."

"That's close, all right. Are you sure you're not a Catholic?"

She laughed at his gentle ribbing. "I wasn't exactly thrilled at the time, but it's nice to have them near the same age. They keep each other company."

"I'd like to meet them sometime. Do you suppose I could?"

"Well—I—sure—that is, sometime, yes."

He threw his head back and laughed. "I wasn't suggesting anything indecent, you know." But they both knew he had been putting out a feeler. He walked her to the car, refusing her offer to give him a lift. As he continued on his way, his limp was so pronounced that if she had seen him walking before, she would certainly have known he had an artificial leg. That night, Peter Wise telephoned. She had been expecting to hear from him, in fact, had been surprised when he hadn't called. "I've been in St. Petersberg," he told her. "They sent me down for a training drill, even though I'm not eligible for flying. Can you believe that?"

"After what my husband has told me about the Army, I'll believe anything." Should she invite him over, she wondered. He must long for some home-cooked meals.

"Well, I—uh—thought I'd just call to say hello . . ."

"Peter, would you like to come for dinner next Saturday?"

"I'd like that very much, Lauren. I was hoping you'd ask."

When they hung up, Lauren pressed her hands to her cheeks. What she had done was only the polite, decent thing, extending a bit of famed Southern hospitality to a serviceman and old friend. So why did she feel nervous? She knew David would not object. Having spent so much time with Charlee when he was in New York, he would understand, and of course she would tell him in her next letter. There were people in the village who might think it odd, but none of her friends would. It might be better to invite one or two other guests, though, just for appearances. Yes, that was an excellent idea. It would remove any doubts and make it more comfortable for both Peter and herself. Besides, it had been ages since she had given a party.

Satisfied with her decision, she asked Amanda if she would stay to serve dinner on Saturday night, then she considered who else should be invited. Gretchen, of course, and Tom Sayles and his wife Helen, and perhaps the new pediatric surgeon who had been following Mark's progress. Surprisingly, they all accepted her invitation. Poor Peter, the conversation would easily turn medical. She might ask someone from the English department, but she hadn't become part of that crowd socially. Maybe she should invite Donal Sullivan—he was new in town and probably didn't know many people, and now that they were on more amicable terms, it would be sort of a peace offering. She would have time to think about it. They had another conference on Thursday and if he was cordial, she would offer a casual invitation.

On Saturday evening, Lauren checked the dining room table, counting ten places. There were two more women coming. Helen Sayles had a sister who was visiting from Charleston and Donal Sullivan called at the last minute to ask if he could bring a date. Lauren was pleased when it turned out to be Mary Callabrizzi, one of her favorite English professors.

Peter was the first to arrive, carrying a large bunch of flowers and a ring-toss game for the children. Babs and Mark, in pajamas, ran to him immediately and he set the game up on the screened porch to play with them. If he was surprised at the arrival of other guests, he concealed it well, taking a place on the sofa next to Tom's sister-in-law, a delicate, blown-away looking young woman with fine brown hair and a sprinkling of freckles across her ivory complexion. She spoke in a lyrical voice, with the distinct low country accent peculiar to aristocratic Charlestonians, and lost no time in telling Peter about her life's work, a historical novel based on her family's long association with Charleston.

Donal Sullivan quickly discovered Gretchen and, reinforced with a double shot of Jack Daniels, devoted himself to her during the cocktail hour, while Tom came to help Lauren with the drinks. "How do I make a martini?" she asked in a stage whisper. Tom expertly mixed the gin with a splash of vermouth for Peter's cocktail. "Thanks, Tom, I'm afraid I'm not great at this—David has always taken care of the bar."

"I admire the way you're managing without him, Lauren," said Tom. "David would be proud of you. Many women go around griping about rationing and having to get along without their menfolk. I've noticed how uncomplaining you are."

"I do have my moments of feeling sorry for myself. I never realized how much I depended on David."

"You and I have a lot in common, then—so do I. The division is just not the same with him away. David is that rarity, a compassionate healer, and a born surgeon."

She smiled and kissed him on the cheek. "You're so nice to say that, Tom. I'll be sure to mention it to him in my next letter." Lauren knew that Tom, like many of the other senior faculty at Duke, had volunteered for the Army, but the Surgeon General said they contributed more to the war effort by staying at their posts and training new young doctors.

When they were going in to dinner, Gretchen sidled up to Lauren and whispered, "Beware of Donny-boy, Laurie. He has the gift of the silver tongue, but it's another one of his organs I'd worry about."

"Gretch! You're outrageous!"

"Observe," Gretchen said in an undertone, her eyes twinkling as Sullivan moved in on the Charleston authoress, who quickly turned her attention from Peter to him. "I know whereof I speak, Laurie. The ladykiller is a species I have had the opportunity to observe at close range. That Boston Irishman can't resist snowing anything in skirts. Never say I didn't warn you." Gretchen smirked in the direction of the buffet where Donal was generously helping himself to Mandy's fried chicken, while complimenting her on the tempting food platters. Amanda loved it, laughing delightedly as she heaped mashed potatoes and gravy on his plate.

Lauren placed Tom on her right, Mark's doctor on her left, and distributed Peter and Donal among the women. She had wanted a menu that was less homestyle, but Amanda held out for the fried chicken, which she considered her specialty. From the looks of the men, who all took second helpings of everything and double portions of deep dish apple pie with ice cream, Mandy was right. They fairly groaned when they left the table to have coffee in the living room.

"What a delicious dinner, Lauren," remarked Peter, coming to sit next to her.

"Thank you, Peter. It's David's favorite meal." Without warning, her voice faltered, and she had to look away. Peter reached out to touch her arm, and after a minute, she regained control of herself.

The conversation, which went on for another hour, was witty and spirited, her guests were having a wonderful time, but suddenly, Lauren could not wait for everyone to leave. She detested being a woman alone, playing the hostess without David. Eventually Peter sensed what was going through her mind. It was not long before he stood up and started the process of saying good-bye, and the others followed his lead.

When they were finally gone, she went up to her room and reread all of David's letters. Long into the night, she lay awake with her troubled thoughts.

Chapter 34

December 1943

DAVID HAD A recurring nightmare.

He was tearing through the blacked-out streets of London toward a house at the end of a cul-de-sac. Exploding bombs fell on all sides, blowing deep craters in the earth where moments before there had been buildings. Laurie and the children were in the house! He had to get to them. His chest was bursting, he was unable to breathe. The faster he ran, the farther he had to go, and he knew his strength would give out before he could reach them. He covered his ears, trying to block out the screeching sirens—

The telephone awakened him. David sat up and held his head in his hands, taking deep breaths to still the frantic beating of his heart. He reached for the receiver.

"Fucking bloody awful, Major—ten dead and nineteen wounded!" Shaking off his leaden fatigue, David listened intently to the flight surgeon's report: One bomber down, six hit, and one crash landed at the base, erupting in flames. That meant burns and head injuries, and God knows what else. Every day brought a flood of casualties from the U.S. Eighth Air Force heavy bomber units at the Suffolk airbase. Today there had been another strike against industrial targets in Germany—this time, aircraft plants in Schweinfurt and Leipzeig.

David shivered as he pulled his trousers over his long woolen underwear he habitually slept in. It was itchy as hell, but it sure beat freezing your ass off. Moments later he was jogging through a cold rain across the compound toward the cluster of Nissen huts that housed the working guts of the hospital complex. The first ambulances had drawn up to the shock ward where fresh battle casualties were received. With plasma bags held high, orderlies rushed the wounded into the hospital. Most of the men were in shock, for their wounds were grave and it had been hours since they were hit.

As David came into the shock ward, shedding his trenchcoat, nurses and orderlies were attending to the patients, elevating the heads of the chest and cranial cases, lowering the others. The medics worked as a team with practiced efficiency. In rapid order, pulse and blood pressures were recorded, blood typed, and transfusions of whole blood begun. They spread blankets over the shocked men, while the triage nurse moved among the cots, inspecting wounds, issuing orders, deciding which cases needed immediate surgery and which could wait. And all too often, which had no chance.

"Bad one, Major!"

They were placing a wounded crewman on a cot, unstrapping the cocoon-like Neil Robertson litter that immobilized him from head to foot. As David approached, the patient's face—so *very* young and pale from shock—stabbed at him as the medics cut off clothing and removed temporary dressings to reveal the wounds. "Whew!" whistled an orderly.

David grunted in reply. Pressure bandages covered the mangled thighs. Heavily sedated and lying in a pool of blood, the boy was moaning softly. Quickly David scanned the flight surgeon's chart on the eighteen-year-old waist gunner. He was in shock, but there was no time to lose. "Get him X-rayed and into surgery fast," he ordered.

By the time David had scrubbed, the injured man was prepped for surgery, and endotracheal ether anesthesia started. The nurse-anesthetist signaled them to begin.

David reviewed aloud each step as he went along. The habit of teaching was hard to break and it seemed to help him in the procedure. His assistant, a young lieutenant who had recently finished an internship at Hopkins, irrigated and sponged the periphery while David began the painstaking process of debriding the wounds surrounding the fractured femurs. Layer by layer, he cut away traumatized tissue, following the path made by the flak particles, devoting considerable time to removing specks of fragmented bone. There were bits of foreign matter in the wounds and a scrap of clothing had wrapped itself around a shell fragment. Background noises faded as David concentrated on his task, hardly aware when a nurse stepped forward to wipe perspiration from his brow. "Signs?" he asked at one point, and the anesthetist gave him respiration, pulse and blood pressure readings.

Hours later, after the fractures were reduced, there was considerable bone loss in the right leg. "The boy's youth is in his favor, but in the future, he's going to need some reconstructive surgery," David commented to his assistant, as the patient was wheeled away to the plaster room. For the first time since he had entered the OR, David looked at the young face and permitted himself to think of the boy as someone's son or brother or sweetheart, whose body would always bear the scars of war.

Twenty minutes to scrub and a complete change of cap, gown, and mask, and David was back in the surgery. The patient was a navigator this time, with multiple trauma to the legs . . .

It was night before the surgeons were finished with the fresh casualties. By the time they conducted secondary closures—the suturing of wounds that had been left open to drain—David had been on his feet operating for fourteen hours. There were not enough general surgeons and he was doing every sort of emergency procedure imaginable. It was as bad as his first year of residency, except that he was eight years older now. And he felt it. By midnight he had finished with the last patient, and after stopping at the mess for a bowl of soup and some bread, he returned to the barracks, where he fell into bed in his underwear, too exhausted to even brush his teeth.

He awakened in the black hours before dawn as a wave of bombers taken off thundered overhead. Unable to go back to sleep, he turned on his light and reached for Lauren's latest letter, which he had given only a cursory reading before going to the surgery two days ago. Her letters were beautiful, so real that each time he received one, he felt touched by her spirit. Loving and warm, tender and amusing, they restored him and he had saved every one, rereading them so often, they were in danger of coming apart at the folds.

As he studied her words, he closed his eyes for a moment, picturing Lauren in their house. The hideous war and the tragedies he witnessed every day in the hospital faded and seemed not to exist on the same planet. This letter had been mailed two weeks before Thanksgiving, and had reached him fairly quickly by sea mail. "Bruce is probably in England by now," she had written. "You may already have heard from him. Please be nice if he calls you, darling. For me!" The thought of seeing Bruce Fields made David more than a little uncomfortable, but with their family ties, if Bruce did get in touch with him, a meeting would be difficult to avoid.

David's thoughts were constantly of his family now—of Lauren and Barbara and Mark. At night, he often lay awake agonizing over his betrayal of them. Sometimes he groaned aloud or wept in his sleep, and his dreams were filled with haunting visions of his wife and children in jeopardy, and his helplessness to rescue them.

Over and over he attempted to write an explanation to Lauren. "My Darling," he would begin, "In the months since I've been in England, I have been consumed with guilt. My love for you is all that has kept me from—" He would tear up the sheet of stationery and start again: "My Only Love, Sometimes, no matter how much a man loves his wife, he may commit a dreadful—"

It was not good. Unlike Lauren, he had never been able to express his feelings in writing. As many times as he tried, the words he wrote looked false and melodramatic, and he always ended by destroying them and composing sentences that sounded perfunctory and impersonal by comparison. If only it were possible for him to spend one day, one hour, with Lauren to prove to her how much he loved her and needed her, then perhaps he could forget his torment and the madness of those few months in New York.

It seemed insane to him now, his affair with Charlotte . . . What had possessed him? How could he have thought he was in love with her? In *love!* What they had wasn't love. It was more like a sickness, a terrible malady that had almost killed him, and he would give anything to obliterate it from his past. At times he hated Charlee, but no more than he despised himself. He had considered seeking the counsel of a Jewish chaplain, but coward that he was, he lacked even the courage to bare his weaknesses to a stranger. He was left with his remorse, and for the rest of his life, he would do battle with it and try to make amends.

Before leaving the States, he had wanted to tell Charlee it was over, needing to impress on her their shared guilt. But she had been away when he came through New York in September, before sailing on the *Queen Elizabeth.* Or so the maid had told him. He half suspected she was there and would not answer his calls. All the way across the Atlantic, as the ship zig-zagged for five days to avoid German submarines, he had brooded about their affair. Until he came to the realization that it had been *sex,* and not love, that had entrapped him.

Lauren watched a platoon of V-12s march smartly across the campus on their way to class. There was such verve and purpose in their steps. Officers training afforded them action and clamor, both essentially male needs. In a little boy like Mark you could see it, enthralled as he was by military parades and martial music.

Sometimes Lauren felt a sentiment remarkably like resentment at being a woman in a world of men primed for war. Alone in the evenings or on weekends, the children were often difficult for her to handle, especially Mark. "I want my daddy!" he had screamed last night when she spanked him. Later, he had looked so angelic falling asleep with his finger in his mouth, that she was ridden with guilt for venting her anger on her small son. It was the war, she told herself.

Lauren knew that she had been greatly changed by the circumstances of war. She had less patience, it was true; but at the same time, she was stronger and more in harmony with herself. Most of all, she had become a self-reliant woman. Over the past year, she had grown to relish her privacy and independence, taking a certain satisfaction in not having to count on men.

But she had to admit they were useful! On a crisp Sunday in November, Peter Wise had appeared suddenly at her door wearing casual clothes. "I've come to rake your leaves, ma'am."

"Mandy and I can manage," she protested, "I've been trying to find a high school boy . . ."

"And take all my fun away? Not on your life! C'mon kids, grab a rake."

With whoops of delight, Babs and Mark followed him outdoors and were soon having a marvelous rollick, jumping in mountains of dry leaves. Afterward, Peter stayed for an impromptu supper and read stories to the children before Lauren put them to bed.

"Will you come again?" asked Babs, hugging him good-night.

"Yes, yes," begged Mark, "Please say yes!"

Peter began dropping by on Sundays on the pretext of some minor task or repair that needed doing around the house. The children were always thrilled to see him, and to Lauren it was like having a big brother or a comfortable old friend around. It soon became their habit to linger after dinner over coffee.

Reba had coaxed her to bring the children to Randolph Springs for Thanksgiving, but Lauren could muster no enthusiasm for the trip. Mark's cast had just recently come off, and his leg was weak, so she used that as an excuse, promising Reba a long visit at Christmas. Instead, she invited Gretchen with her three children for Thanksgiving dinner, and Peter, as well as the cadets they had met at the Rosenblooms'. Thanks to "the Navy," it was a festive holiday, and it was only at the end of the evening when she was preparing the children for bed, that Lauren realized this was her first Thanksgiving in six years without David.

He wrote often, and gradually his letters had become more expansive and affectionate, giving her hope that the loving phrases she composed for him were drawing a response. She kept the letters all together in the small drawer of her night table, and frequently she would take out three or four to read, always searching for more meaning than his words conveyed. Something about his life away from her escaped her, some essential truth to which there must be clues, if only she could detect them. Each night before turning out the light, she would gaze at his photograph, then lie awake for hours yearning for him.

The weeks between Thanksgiving and Christmas were spotted with faculty parties and official, if austere, university receptions. Occasionally she invited Peter to come along, and they always took Gretchen or another friend. "Going steady, are we?" Donal Sullivan inquired on the second occasion he met them together.

Before Lauren could get out an annoyed retort, Peter answered with the most equable good humor. "Don't pay any attention to me, I'm just the official escort of the war wives," and he deliberately walked away with Gretchen and another woman whose husband was overseas, leaving Lauren with Sullivan.

If Peter had any romantic interest in her, it was imperceptible. Until one night, when she looked up and found him gazing at her in an unguarded moment. He immediately looked away, but not before she became aware of his deep sigh. She pretended not to notice, however it greatly troubled her. Peter deserved better than to languish after something he could never have. With all the women complaining about the scarcity of men, it seemed ridiculous for this desirable specimen to waste his time dreaming of her, if indeed that was what he was doing.

"I just met a terrific new assistant in the history department, Peter," she ventured to say. "I think you two would really like each other . . ."

It was the first time she had ever seen him angry. "I can arrange my own dates, thank you, Lauren," he replied, picking up his papers. He left, and did not visit the house that weekend, nor the following week. She wondered whether he would ever come back. Perhaps she had been mistaken in thinking they could remain just friends.

She left with the children for Randolph Springs the Wednesday before Christmas. Babs and Mark had never been on a train before, so the trip was a grand adventure. Bertram met them at the station, looking grayer and somewhat frail. After a solid night's sleep at Shadow Mountain, with the children in the former nursery across the hall, Lauren felt completely relaxed for the first time in months. As she sat talking with Reba over a cup of freshly brewed coffee the following morning, the sunny breakfast room brought back memories of happier days.

Across the table, her mother sat staring out the window at the mountains with a wistful smile on her face. "It's pretty here, isn't it, dear," she said, to no one in particular.

"Yes, Mama, it is," answered Lauren, moving her chair closer and taking her hand. Miriam had become sweet and childlike, oblivious to the activity around her. The children did not bother her, but neither did she take any delight in them.

"Are you going to the station to meet Charlotte Lee, Laurie?" asked her aunt.

"Yes, Aunt Reba, don't worry, we'll leave in plenty of time."

Reba gave a self-conscious laugh. "I'd go with you, dear, except I'm a little nervous. It's near a year since she's seen me, and—well, I'm not at my best these days."

"You look just fine," Lauren assured her, but it was true that Reba was tremendously overweight, and appeared years older than fifty-two.

Lauren took the children along to meet Charlotte's train. How many times had they clasped each other in greeting or farewell at this station, thought Lauren, as her cousin stepped down from the Pullman car into her embrace. It was only six months since Lauren's anniversary visit to New York in June, but it seemed so much longer. The familiar scent of gardenias and furs, that crisp winter, high-life-elegance that was Charlee's signature, swept over Lauren, pungent with memories.

Charlotte made a big fuss over Babs and Mark. "Look how *gigantic* you both are!" she exclaimed, giving them hugs and taking Mark on her lap in the car. They both giggled and clung to her, but in a few minutes, she tired of playing auntie, putting Mark on the jump seat so she could light a cigarette.

"So wonderful to see you, Laurie. You're absolutely *blooming!*"

"You, too," echoed Lauren, but actually, she thought he cousin looked a little peaked—Charlotte mentioned that she'd had the flu. Restless as a fly on a griddle, she smoked constantly. When they reached her mother's house, she retired to her old room, taking a long time bathing and changing and redoing her face before joining them at the lunch table.

"Have you heard from Bruce?" Lauren asked, as Charlotte picked at her food.

"Just a couple of short notes from London."

"I wrote you David's been promoted, didn't I? He's a major now, and Group Consultant in surgery." Some perverse impulse prompted Lauren to persist, despite Charlotte's obvious lack of interest. "Did you tell Bruce how to contact David?"

"I'm sure I must have, Laurie. I can't seem to remember, I've been so busy." Lauren couldn't help feeling irritated at the indifferent reply. Charlotte certainly did display an interest in the children, though. "Mark won't have a permanent limp, will he?" she asked, watching through the glass doors as the children played on the terrace.

"No, it's just that he became accustomed to keeping that leg stiff. When he's absorbed, he walks normally."

"Babs looks a lot like David, Laurie. Has she always been so bright?"

"She has an unusually high I.Q. She was selected as one of the children at nursery school whose development some psychologists from the university are tracking." Charlee couldn't stop staring at Barbara, but fortunately, the child didn't seem to notice. Babs did have fetching mannerisms, with her father's reserve and his staggering smile that made you feel rewarded when it was directed your way.

Despite Lauren's attempts to rekindle the intimacy of the past, Charlotte was unusually quiet and withdrawn a good part of the time. The two cousins spent the days in relaxation, walking for miles along the old bridal paths, but avoiding the back road on Shadow Mountain where Max had met his death. The old house embraced them in a world of peaceful order. Enclosed in the tranquility of the estate, they could almost forget the nation was at war.

On Christmas Eve, they gathered around the radio to listen to the President's address. Mr. Roosevelt assured the nation that although a long and costly struggle lay ahead, he could promise them certain victory and lasting peace when it was over.

The day after Christmas, a Sunday, was cold and clear. When Charlee suggested a round of golf, Lauren agreed, even though she no longer kept up her game. They wore woolen slacks and heavy Shetland sweaters, taking hats and gloves in case a wind came up. In slacks, Lauren noticed, Charlotte seemed to have lost that spare leanness she had always admired.

The course was almost deserted, with just a few older men putting around. They played through a foursome of women, and Charlee was winded as they climbed the steep slope to the seventh hole. As she teed up, she staggered for a moment, and might have fallen if Lauren hadn't caught her. She sank gratefully onto a bench on the side of the teeing ground. "I think I'm going to be sick to my stomach," she said in a shaky voice, but after a few minutes she felt well enough to walk back to the clubhouse. In the massage room she lay on a cot with a cold cloth on her head until the wave of nausea passed, as quickly as it had come.

"Whew! glad that's over," she said, sitting up.

"You look absolutely green. I'd better take you to a doctor."

"Don't be silly, a doctor can't do anything."

"We have to find out what's wrong with you, Charlee. How long have you felt like this?"

"I'm not sure—a few weeks."

"Flu doesn't hang on that long. It has to be something else."

Charlotte was looking at her in the oddest way. "Oh, Laurie, you might as well know . . . I'm going to have a baby."

Lauren's mouth flew open and her eyes misted. "Oh, Charlee, that's the most *wonderful* news!" she exclaimed, as she threw her arms around her cousin. "You *ninny*, making me think something was wrong with you! Why I was so worried, I didn't know what to do."

Now Charlee was grinning, too, and looking flushed and pleased with herself. "I haven't known for long, and I didn't want to tell Mother for a while. You know how she fusses."

"Bruce must be absolutely thrilled."

"He doesn't know yet. He was already gone when I found out, and I think it's just as well to wait, since he's so far away. He'd just have it on his mind all the time."

"But it's such happy news, I'm sure he'll be overjoyed. David was always more excited about my pregnancies than I was."

"I'll tell him soon. There's plenty of time."

That seemed rather strange. They'd hoped so long for children, you'd think Charlee couldn't wait to tell him. Of course, Bruce could be peculiar at times—was it possible she was afraid he wouldn't be pleased to hear he was going to be a father? It was easy enough to imagine Charlotte in the role of mother, but truthfully, Bruce was not the sort of man who made a fuss over children . . .

Now that she knew, Lauren realized Charlee *looked* pregnant. She had been wearing loose-fitting dresses, but in slacks her condition was obvious. "When are you due?"

"In June, I think. I'm not absolutely certain of the date because my periods have been irregular, but it must have happened in September, when we heard Bruce was going overseas. I spent most of that month with him in Washington, and he was home on leave in New York before he left."

"You're not going to be able to keep it secret too much longer, Char. You're beginning to show."

"That's because for once in my life, I've been eating to my heart's content—that is, when I haven't felt sick to my stomach." She fished in her handbag for a cigarette. "You won't say anything to Mother, will you, Laurie?"

"No, of course not. But you better tell her soon, or I won't have to." She watched Charlotte light a cigarette and take a deep drag, inhaling. "You know, you really should try not to smoke so much during your pregnancy, Charlee. David says it's not good for the baby."

"David says, does he? I thought he was just an old *sawbones.* Now all of a sudden, he's an expert on obstetrics!"

Lauren felt a stab of hurt at the venom she heard in Charlotte's voice. There really was an animosity between them! Whatever could have caused it? Charlotte may not have been David's favorite person, but he was always a gentleman, and Lauren was certain he would not have done anything to offend her. Funny, they had seemed to be getting along so well in New York . . .

To think she had actually worried that they might be attracted to each other.

That same night, in London, David met Bruce Fields at a private club, where they were guests of Sir Richard Benedek-Cohen. A longstanding friendship with Malcolm Fields had prompted the British financier to invite Malcolm's son and cousin-in-law to a party he was hosting for members of the General Staff. David accepted because he wanted to get away from the base and there was little else to do over the Christmas holiday weekend.

Bruce came along rather late, and it was apparent he had gotten a head start on the drinking. "Great to see you," he greeted David jovially, apologizing for not having contacted him earlier. "I promised my mother-in-law I'd get in touch, but a month went by and then when I called, they said . . ." Bruce seemed to have picked up an annoying British inflection in his few months in England.

"That's all right, Bruce. We're all busy, and I don't get down to London often. What do they have you doing?"

"Staff stuff, mostly. I can't really talk about it."

David knew Bruce was in intelligence work, but somehow he did not look like the espionage type. "Everything all right at home?" he asked, trying to sound casual.

"Not much news. Charlee's down visiting her mother for the hols. I understand Laurie's going too, with the children."

"Yes, she wrote about her plans."

A handsome captain came over to Bruce, and David left them talking, but joined Bruce again for supper. After a final glass of port, he excused himself, "I don't want to miss my ride back to Redgrave Park. Otherwise, I'll have a long wait for the train."

"Let's get together sometime," said Bruce, in a manner of Wall Street.

A few weeks later, David was having a drink at an officers' club in London when a noisy crew came in and took a table near the bar, attracting irritable glances from others around them. "Bunch of fags from the Cloak and Dagger Corps," muttered a man at David's table, indicating the group. David listened without interest as the men at his table discussed the jealous rivalries and backbiting amongst the secret intelligence services.

Later, as he was passing by the raucous party on his way to the door, one of them stood up and draped an arm over his shoulder. "Well, if it isn't my old buddy, David!" It was Bruce Fields and he was very drunk.

Bruce called him after that, and from time to time on David's infrequent trips to London, they would meet. On one such evening, they were at Bruce's club—a guest membership he had managed, thanks to the good offices of Sir Richard Benedek-Cohen. Sipping his third Scotch in front of the fire, Bruce said, "Invasion fever is hitting everyone."

David thought about the Allied offensive pinned down

on the beach near Anzio. "I would imagine it won't come for months. Our armies are preoccupied in Italy."

"We're making regular drops into France these days."

"Are you in touch with the French underground?"

Bruce's Top Secret mask dropped over his face as he gave David his you-should-know-better smile. For someone who's supposed to be carrying military secrets around in his head, he drinks too much, mused David. He knew Bruce worked on Grosvenor Street in the section of London where most of the foreign intelligence community kept offices. They had a connection with the SOE, the British Special Operations Executive that conducted clandestine warfare, and Bruce seemed to relish the covert nature of his assignment—often dropping hints at the importance of what he was doing, then clamming up if David showed any curiosity.

The family tie had endowed them with a strange sort of bond. As reluctant as he was to admit it, David found Bruce rather good company. On the other hand, the better he knew him, the more he wondered why Charlotte had ever married him. Probably because of his outstanding good looks and his wealth—both meant a lot to Charlee. In retrospect, David saw her as a shallow and pampered woman, despite her concern for war orphans. That too, he suspected, had a selfish motive, for Charlee had been hoping to adopt one of the children.

Even in wartime, London appeared to be Bruce's natural milieu. He reveled in upperclass privilege and had a reverence for the traditional English institutions. When David once mentioned that his olive drabs were rather more stylishly fitted than normal U.S. Army attire, Bruce admitted to having his dress uniforms tailored in Savile Row.

David recalled the remark he had overheard in the officers' club . . . *bunch of fags*. Was it true about Bruce, he wondered. If so, was it really that surprising? It would explain a great deal about Charlotte and her marriage. You couldn't tell by appearances, of course, but there were certain signs. That group of friends he hung around with, for example . . . the handsome American captain who had been at the Christmas party, and Brent, the young English intelligence liaison officer with a dissolute air about him. David had met them together on several occasions. And then there was that White Russian emigrée, Nicholas, who spoke five or six languages and seemed to be a man without a country. An odd fellow, he was involved in some way with Bruce in the intelligence operations.

One evening in late February David met Bruce for a drink. He was already half loaded. "I'm going for curry with friends. Will you join us?"

"I don't think so, Bruce. I'm not particularly fond of curry."

"You'll like this, it's special." He grasped David by the arm and propelled him toward the door.

Bruce had not mentioned what friends would be there, but David wasn't surprised when they reached the restaurant and it was the English major and the Russian. "You've met Nicholas and Brent."

"Yes, good evening."

"You're Charlee's cousin," said Nicholas.

"By marriage."

"David's married to Lauren. You remember her, Nick. The little blonde with the Southern accent."

David did not like the way he said it. And he did not at all care for the currents going back and forth among them, either. They traded *bons mots* that went over his head, and he wondered if they weren't at his expense. Why should he give a damn, anyway?

"Brent will order," announced Bruce, his words slurring. "He's our expert on curries. Did a tour in India, you know."

"Is that right?" said David. "I've always wanted to go there."

"Bloody hot," Brent replied, "full of flies and niggers."

"Well, it *is* their country, isn't it?"

"David's from our South," explained Bruce. "He's rather touchy on the subject of races."

"I thought it was you chaps who whipped niggers," said Brent.

David did not bother to hide his dislike. "The War Between the States ended all that, if you know your American history."

"Come along, fellows, quit the nasty stuff," Bruce interrupted, raising his hand and snapping his fingers for the turbaned waiter, who came running. "Bring us a bottle of your best champagne," he ordered.

"What are we celebrating?" asked Nicholas.

"Patience, dear boy." When their glasses were filled, Bruce raised his and said, "We are toasting . . . my paternity."

"I beg your pardon?" said Brent, while Nicholas smirked and David wondered how he could manage to slip away before dinner without being rude.

"You heard me right, Brent, old chap. This man you see before you, sitting here in this chair, is going to leave posterity."

Nicholas threw his head back and let out a guffaw, which was more animation than he had displayed in the several times David had met him. Bruce was drunker than he had suspected—in fact, he was acting downright foolish.

"You mean . . . ?" Brent asked hesitantly.

"That's *just* what I mean." Bruce exploded with laughter, spilling his champagne.

"Congratulations," Nicholas said in a quiet voice. He glanced across at David expectantly.

David finally spoke. "I'm afraid you've lost me, Bruce."

"I'm going to be a *father,* David. Char-r-lee is preggers, old boy!"

Bruce should have been born English, was his first thought. And then it hit him, a strange feeling in the pit of his stomach.

Charlotte was going to have a baby . . .

Could it be his child? He knew it could. What if it was? *No! Please, no,* he prayed. *It can't be!* But if the baby isn't mine . . . it certainly hadn't taken her long to get over him, had it?

Cold sweat was running down his back beneath his uniform. He realized they were all three staring at him expectantly. "Congratulations," he said, not recognizing his own voice. "When is the happy event?"

"In June," said Bruce. "It seems I did my duty just before shipping out."

Not long at all.

Chapter 35

Spring 1944

PETER WISE DROPPED by to say good-bye. He ended up playing blindman's buff with the children and their friends, letting the kids tie a kerchief around his eyes and making a big show of not being able to catch anyone. They screamed in giddy mock terror whenever he approached, dancing beyond his reach. He was a natural with children and Lauren hoped he would marry soon and have some of his own.

"The children have missed you," she told him when he finally came in the house to talk with her.

He was honest. "It was time for me to stop fooling myself. When I began fantasizing about your husband not coming home, I knew I was going round the bend."

"Peter, I never—I hope you didn't think—"

"Hell no, it had nothing to do with you. It was all in my mind, and it was crazy." He sat as far away from her as possible in the living room, drinking Scotch and soda water. "I've put in a request for sea duty. I was getting pretty damn bored with this assignment, anyway. I thought I would write my Navy novel in Chapel Hill, but it's not working."

In two more days, Peter would be transferring to a destroyer. A most unlikely warrior, thought Lauren, as she watched him being pummeled by six young girls and boys. She would be glad when he was gone, though. He was too easily available, and being an attractive man, he made her think about sex and the more she tried not to think of it, the less she was able to blot it from her thoughts. Sometimes she was consumed with visions of the act of love, but always her fantasies were about David.

His letters arrived in bunches, and she would sort them out chronologically, sitting down to pore over them again at the end of each day until the next batch arrived. He made an effort to write in a cheerful vein, but reading between the censors' blacked-out markings, it sounded like their hospital beds were full of depressing cases.

He often spoke of love now, as if his closeness to the war had given him a greater appreciation of love's meaning and its importance. In every letter, he told her how dreadfully he missed her, how much he desired her, and that she was in his thoughts every night when he was falling asleep. She treasured his words, holding them close to her heart and hanging onto them as a lifeline stretching across the ocean between them.

Sometimes when her own longing for him was intense, she wondered whether being so far away from her, David ever succumbed to the temptation of other women. After all, it had been so long, and he was surrounded with American nurses in the hospital, as well as English women, who were reputedly very beautiful. Now and then she would hear stories about men they knew who had written their wives, telling them they had fallen in love with someone else while overseas. She could not imagine David with another woman—and yet, the fear was undeniably there.

The men may have been fighting the war, but there was the battle of the home front, too. An insidious, demoralizing, lengthy struggle, full of treacherous doubts and uncertainties. Gretchen was constantly worried about Ralph, stationed in Cairo. "He's probably taken up with a belly dancer," she moaned, when she had received no letters for a month.

"Don't be silly. Egyptian women aren't permitted out of their houses alone long enough to become acquainted with foreign men," she replied, not at all convinced that Ralph had reformed, but wanting to raise her friend's spirits.

Lauren had given up her job in the bookstore. Thanks to Donal Sullivan, she had been awarded a teaching fellowship, which meant she would get some academic experience. But the best part was that she could now take a full course load, and would complete all her credits by the end of the next academic year. Half done with the research for her thesis, ''Paganism in Elizabethan Literature,'' she would have her Ph.D. by June 1945.

''I would never have been able to do this without your help, Donal,'' she told her advisor late one afternoon, after a seminar at his apartment.

''Sure you could, Bernard. You need to have more self-confidence. Christ, you're better qualified for that fellowship than most of the grad students in the whole fucking university.''

''If you say so!'' she laughed.

Donal had gradually found his niche in Chapel Hill. Some of his essays had been published in the *Chapel Hill Weekly* and Lauren knew he was accepted by the group of writers centered around Paul Green and Betty Smith. He lived in two book-lined rooms on the second floor of an old frame house on McCauley Street. It was shabby, but attractive and homey, with colorful woven spreads thrown over the dull brown upholstered pieces. Like many of his colleagues, Donal liked to hold spring classes outdoors under the trees; however, it had been raining all week, and while not strictly according to university rules for a seminar to meet in a professor's apartment, it was a convenient location not far from the campus.

''Mind sticking around a bit, Lauren?'' he asked, as she prepared to leave with the others. ''We might as well have our conference today.''

She would have preferred meeting in his office, but she agreed. ''I can't stay too long, though, I like to have dinner with the children.''

''No problem.'' Sullivan looked at his watch. ''It's that time of day when if there were a sun, it would be over the yardarm. Join me in a drink?''

''No, thank you,'' she said primly.

He gave a silent laugh, half closing his eyes. "Suit yourself. I hope you won't mind if I have one."

"Go right ahead."

In the small alcove kitchenette, he plopped ice cubes in a glass, and splashed a generous amount of Jack Daniels over them. Lauren took out the draft of the chapter she had begun, a gentle reminder that she was there for a purpose. "Let's have a look at it," he said, coming to stand in front of her and reaching for her work.

His shirt was open at the neck, and the cuffs turned up casually. She noticed he had nice hands with clean, well-shaped nails. There was something about his wrists that had a masculine appeal, with the band of untanned skin left by his watch and the curling golden red hairs. She stared at his hands as he held the folder, at his long and tapered fingers. He wore faded khaki slacks, navy issue. They settled low on his slim hips, anchored there by a web belt. She had a sudden vision of herself putting her hands on his waist and pulling him against her. The image brought a hot flush to her cheeks. At just that moment he looked up, his glance penetrating and knowing.

Lauren turned her head away. Deliberately Donal put down the glass and sat next to her on the sofa. He took hold of her chin, making her look at him. "You needn't be ashamed."

"Ashamed?"

"You know what I mean. Ashamed of wanting me."

"I don't . . . I'm not . . ."

He nodded. "Oh, yes you do, Lauren. And I want you. There's nothing wrong with that. We're two normal people, a man and a woman, and we're attracted to each other."

"Stop it!" She was on the verge of tears, mortified, yet feeling an intense exhilaration.

"I won't push it, but I think you should know what I feel." He stroked her hair gently. "You're so beautiful, Lauren." He caressed her neck and a rush of feeling went through her. "Let me make love to you."

She held her breath for the briefest moment, then let it

go, shaking her head. "I can't. Please don't make it awkward for me—"

"Because of your husband?"

"Well, of course. What better reason?"

"Is he a good lover?" She was caught by surprise. He saw the doubt in her eyes before they avoided his. Taking her in his arms, he kissed her, gently at first, then with growing fervor. "Let me love you," he murmured, lips against her hair."

"No," she whispered. "Donal, *don't do this,*" she managed to say. He saw that she was starting to cry and let her go. She ran into the bathroom and splashed her eyes with cold water. Looking in the mirror, she saw her agitation and wondered whether Donal had seen a need in her that she herself had not recognized. Had she sent out some sort of signal that had made him behave as he did? If so, it must not happen again. She smoothed her hair back, then opened the door and returned to the living room.

He was seated in an old, sagging club chair, reading her draft and sipping whiskey, acting as if nothing out of the ordinary had happened. "I poured you a drink," he said without looking up.

"I think I'd better go now. You can return that to me tomorrow."

"You're angry."

"No, Donal, I'm not. I should have left when everyone else did. What happened just now proves that the conventions have a purpose and should be followed."

"Well, la-de-dah! Spoken like a true flower of the South."

"You never miss an opportunity to insult me, do you?"

"I didn't think you'd consider that insulting."

"You *hate* the South! You look down on us."

"Now we're getting off the track. I was referring to your attitude about men. There's this preoccupation with the purity of womanhood down here that really gets to me at times."

"And there's a preoccupation with *sex* among men like you that really *offends* me!"

"Oh? Women don't think about sex?"

"We keep it in its proper perspective."

"Do you mean to say you haven't been with another man in all the time your husband's been away?"

"*No,* I have not, if that's any of your business! Not everyone is so oversexed they have to go to bed with the first attractive person they see!"

"What about that naval officer, Peter whatshisname? Haven't you slept with him?"

"Of course not! Peter would *never*—He respects me, and my marriage."

"Sure he does! I almost forgot—he's *Jewish,* for Chrissake. Only a coarse, lowdown mick like me would try to seduce a married woman when her husband is off preserving our freedom."

"I never said—"

He laughed harshly. "Ah, Lauren, you didn't have to. It sticks out all over you, that precious, nurtured upbringing. Mother's little rose, daddy's little pearl."

"You really enjoy making people feel rotten, don't you, Sullivan?" Despite all her efforts, her voice began to sound wobbly. She *couldn't* cry—that's all he needed to hold over her. She closed her eyes.

Donal was there suddenly, enveloping her in his arms, kissing her tear-wet lashes and murmuring soft love sounds. Locked in his embrace, she stood straining against him, unable to free herself. Nothing could prevent the glow of desire that coursed through her, beginning in her loins and spreading until it reached her extremities and flushed her cheeks. She shook her head in denial, but his mouth covered hers with deep, searing kisses and she was unable to keep from responding. Her kisses were as wild and needful as his, and they couldn't seem to stop, drawing breath only to begin again. Stumbling a little on his good leg, he lowered her to the couch. He touched her face with such tenderness, such delicate wonder, like an angel's wing. He kissed her eyelids and throat, and then he bent his head to press his lips against her breast.

"No, Donal, no," she gasped. "Please, don't." And now the tears flowed and her breath came in gulping sobs.

"God, Lauren, I want you so!" His voice had a musical lilt, like the language of love, and his hands were stroking her back and running through her hair, sending waves of disturbing, yet soothing comfort. "Ah, little girl, you're starved for love, I can feel it! Let me love you . . ." She shook her head and wept all the harder.

He held her against him then, while she cried. Finally, when she could get the words out, she gasped, "I love David *so much,* and he's so far away. It's been too long since he left. What if something should happen to him—what if he—"

"Sshh . . . sshh, darling, don't be harboring such thoughts in your head. He's coming back to you . . . one day, soon."

Donal kept his arms around her, but without passion now, and she knew she had nothing to fear from him. "I could show you what making love really means, Lauren, but I'll never try again, unless you ask . . ."

By the beginning of May, Lauren was finished with her final papers and exams. She intended to work on her thesis all summer, but first, she took the children to Randolph Springs to visit her mother and Reba. She was also delighted to see Jeanette, who had recently arrived home from California with little Sharon. Philip was on his way to the China-Burma-India theater, where presumably his language skills would be employed when the Allies invaded the Japanese homeland.

Two days after Lauren arrived in Randolph, Malcolm Fields called from New York to announce that Charlotte had given birth to a son. Reba went into a tailspin when she heard that her first grandchild had arrived. "But the baby wasn't due until next month!" she cried in alarm. "What's wrong? What has happened to Charlotte Lee?"

"Nothing, Reba. Charlotte is fine, and the baby couldn't be healthier—weighed over seven pounds and he's perfect. If he'd gone full term, he would have been enormous!" Malcolm sounded absolutely ecstatic. This was his third grandchild—Blanche had given birth to a second girl three months ago, while Jules was in the Pacific—but this was a boy, and he fully expected he would be named Malcolm Bruce Fields III.

Reba left for New York the following morning. They had to pull all sorts of strings to get her a compartment on the sleeping car, but after half a dozen telephone calls to Malcolm, it had been arranged.

By that time, Mr. Fields sounded a little less exuberant. Charlotte had named the baby John Maxwell Mortimer Fields, after her father.

Chapter 36

DAVID'S INSTINCT LATELY had been to avoid Bruce Fields, but he went to his flat when invited, drawn by curiosity. "It's important that I see you. There's something I have to say," Bruce had told him on the telephone. "I'd appreciate it if you would come by next time you're in London."

As he approached the neat brass-knockered door at the end of a charming little brick-paved cul de sac, David worried that Bruce had somehow found out about him and Charlotte. They had been discreet, but someone was bound to have seen them together and guessed. It was naive to think otherwise.

Thus, his nerves went into alarm when they were settled with drinks and Bruce said, "Are you ever bothered by conscience?"

Now. Now he would pursue it, cornering him with the accusation.

"Who isn't?" David answered guardedly, holding his breath for what was coming next.

But Bruce had other concerns. "What kind of father will I make?" he asked in some agitation. "I never wanted children. I'm afraid of the responsibility for a life. To have the future of a child in your hands—how do you manage it?"

"It comes quite naturally, you'll be surprised."

"My father and I, we didn't get along well. I never measured up. Whatever he expected of me, I failed him."

"You followed in his footsteps. You went to his schools, were a decent student."

"Mediocre. I never made anything above a gentleman's C at either Princeton or the Law School."

"You made it through, though, and joined his firm."

"But with absolutely no distinction. I always wanted Dad's approval, but I was a constant disappointment to him."

"Your mother—"

"My mother only made it worse. Women will suck your life's blood if you let them." It was harshly said and David decided not to pursue that avenue.

"Now that there's a child, I'm sure your parents will forget about any past disappointments."

Bruce brightened. "My father's been dying for a grandson. This might be the first good thing I've done."

There was a sadness about him when he dropped the habitual supercilious veneer. David actually found himself liking Bruce, despite his weaknesses. "You're too hard on yourself," he said. "You'll make a fine father, at least no worse than anyone else." When he left Bruce, he thought he had helped to relieve his anxieties.

But what if that baby is my son? Can I *bear* the idea of Bruce Fields being father to a child of mine?

It was too coincidental. The timing . . . Charlotte's "flu" during that last week in August before he had left for Chapel Hill. Supposedly, the baby had been born a month early. An incompetent cervix, they said, nothing to do with the development of the child. But David wasn't having any of it. For he knew the child could be his. Knew it with an ever-deepening conviction.

He had tried writing to Charlotte, but how was he to commit his thoughts to paper? Words, once written, could never be retracted.

Anger, regret, and guilt were raging within him, for he had no illusions that she had been in love with him. She had *used* him! Used his masculinity to father a child. How he despised her. And yet he remembered being in the grip of her fascination. His own weakness continued to appall him. But whatever had been between them, surely it should not resolve itself in hatred. Especially now.

He thought they had escaped any consequences. All his

life he would have carried the burden of guilt, but he would have born it alone, with no visible damage to anyone else. But no, it was not to be that way. Now there was a child . . . and forever after, their lives would be tangled up with that boy.

In the dark before morning David heard the bombers. Wave after wave, passing overhead on their flight across the Channel to France. Accustomed to the regular raids from the nearby bases of the Eighth Air Force, he sensed that this was different, and knew the invasion had begun.

In the wards he saw the men's faces, both exultant and fearful, half wishing they were part of it, half thankful they had endured the worst and survived. This was the day. At last it had come. Yet they were oddly restrained as they raised their heads to listen, many of them with tear tracks on their cheeks.

A group of medical officers had been assigned to the invasion force going in on landing crafts, or at receiving stations on the docks at Southampton and Portsmouth. David wished he were among them, but the OR was where he was needed. In the hospital, they were on alert for the maximum number of cases. Detachments of enlisted men were on special duty in the shipping depots and railroad yards to handle the first casualties from the beachheads at Normandy.

What conflicting emotions must be raging in the generals' hearts today, thought David. He did not envy them the horror of sending hundreds of thousands of young men to be killed or maimed. The insanity of war preyed on his mind. All the following week they waited and imagined what it was to be there on the coast of France. And then, with the first trainloads from the front, there was little time for thought.

London was under assault again. The Germans had devised a new type of weapon, a flying bomb. You heard a high, screeching sound, and when it stopped, the rocket hit, obliterating an entire building. As they had all during the blitz, Londoners persevered and dug out.

In the middle of July, Bruce telephoned David, insisting he had to see him. David sensed a new and alarming urgency in his voice. "Please, I *must* talk to you," he pleaded. "I'm in trouble, David."

"What kind of trouble?"

"I've been ordered back to the States. Don't you see, I can't go home! Nick is still missing and—" Nicholas de Georgenov had been wounded and was presumed captured, when he was dropped behind German lines in France in the days preceding the invasion. "There's more. I need advice, David, and—well, I think you're the best person—the only one, really. Can you possibly meet me?"

"Of course," he answered, "I'm coming down for a meeting next week."

David had an appointment in London to submit his report on air combat casualties to the Air Surgeon's office. Finished with his meeting in the late afternoon, he called to tell Bruce he would be there shortly to have a drink with him. The line was out of order, and since it was still early on a pleasant summer evening, he decided to walk.

By now, David was aware that Bruce had many problems. Aside from his marital difficulties, he was a truly troubled man, fraught with guilt and anxieties. Bruce was brooding over the disappearance of Nicholas, holding himself responsible, since he had recruited his friend for intelligence missions. Then there was the drinking, which was getting worse each time David saw him . . . And the other. David would like to have offered help, but what did he know about homosexuality? Unlike many people, he was not repelled by it, but it was not something he understood.

When he rounded the corner near Bruce's flat, the street was roped off. Ambulances and fire trucks crowded the end of the court. David began running, oblivious of the shouts of police guards. As he sprinted down the block, he was in the grip of déjà vu, for it was the terror of his recurrent nightmare he was experiencing. This time he was able to reach the house at the end of the cul de sac. What was left of it.

Bruce was dead, killed by a buzz bomb. A direct hit on

the row of buildings where he had been sleeping in his flat with Brent, his English lover. It was a lovely, green twilight in late July—much too beautiful an evening for death.

"Coupla nancy boys," remarked the cockney warden who allowed David to search through the debris for any personal objects to send home to the family. Or any incriminating mementos. There was nothing, but the evidence was damaging enough. The two bodies had been crushed by an overhead beam, and it had taken hours to remove them.

David did what he could to cover it up. "Can't this remain confidential?" he asked.

"I should hope so, sir! A disgrace to the service, if y'ask me."

"Perhaps we shouldn't judge," David replied gently.

The man gave him an odd look. "I suppose they'll be judged by a 'igher Authority now."

David remembered something Bruce had said during their last conversation. "Sometimes I think it might be better if I didn't survive the war. If I were to die in combat, for instance, the baby would have a hero for a father, and never become disillusioned."

As he sifted through the broken furniture and plaster of the flat, he wondered whether Bruce had courted death. That was impossible, of course. A V-1 rocket landed at random, wherever it fell to earth. It had been Bruce's bad luck to have been there in its path.

David wrote a letter to Charlotte, and in a remarkably short time, it was returned to him unopened. All through the remaining year he spent in England, his thoughts would dwell on the child in New York who could be his son. And the mother. If she thought she could avoid him, she was wrong. For they had unfinished business between them.

Chapter 37

August 1945

THE WHOLENESS OF New York came as a shock to David. Despite the throngs of men in uniform returning from overseas, here was a country untouched by the war. Shoppers strolled on Fifth Avenue, office workers streamed in and out of subways. Taxis and buses honked noisily and hurtled along a Broadway gay with lights and activity.

It all seemed foreign. He thought of the bombed out streets of London, the mountains of rubble from leveled buildings, the children evacuated to the counties. Did Americans realize what they had escaped? To have been in the war, but not to suffer the civilian casualties, the nightly bombings, the fear of invasion.

For the first few hours after docking, he was disoriented, trying to get his bearings. Later in the afternoon he would call home, after reporting to sign the application for his discharge. Lauren would be surprised. She did not expect him for another two weeks, when the remnant of the 65th General Hospital would arrive on the next crossing of the *Elizabeth*.

Afterward, he could not remember whether he had a plan, just that he had been walking on Madison Avenue and seen a window full of teddy bears and toy soldiers. He stopped, thinking that he should buy something for Mark and Babs, but he had brought gifts for his family from England.

A string of tiny bells danced merrily as he entered the shop. He stood for a moment, then picked up a floppy-eared spaniel from a basket of stuffed animals. A pleasant middle-aged woman wearing the kind of tweed skirt and brown sweater set women wore in England, laid her needlepoint down on the seat of a rocker and came forward.

"That's one of my favorite dogs," she said. "A lady from North Carolina makes these for me."

It seemed an unusual coincidence. "I come from North Carolina," he answered, wondering why he would tell her.

"Then you know how talented the mountain people are. Our quilts are made down there, too. In the Carolinas, Georgia, and Tennessee. Everything has been thoroughly sterilized, of course."

"I suppose that would be important." Why was he chattering on, clutching this soft toy animal?

"They put everything in their mouths."

"I beg your pardon?"

"Babies. The little ones, when they cut their teeth, tend to chew on everything. That's why we used only washable materials and sterilize—"

"Yes, yes," he was suddenly impatient to get out of there. "I'll take the dog."

Out on the avenue, David hailed a cab and told the driver to travel north. As the streets flew by, he panicked, wanting to stop the taxi and get out. And finally he did, walking the last ten blocks on Park Avenue. Self-consciously he carried the gift-wrapped parcel, and wondered how he would get into the building. It was rather like approaching a Norman castle, impossible to gain entrance without being challenged.

At the entrance to the familiar courtyard, he faltered and would have turned away, but a doorman stepped out of the gate house and ran ahead of him to open the door. "Afternoon, Colonel," he said, giving it a military snap as he eyed the new silver leaves on David's shoulders.

Miraculously, the lobby was empty, the attendant having been called away from his post. Without pausing, David headed for the elevator in the right wing, and was taken up to the penthouse. He hesitated at the door until the elevator closed, then rang the bell.

His heart was racing and he had no idea what he would

say. What if she refused to see him? He should not have come, but *he had to know.*

It was taking so long, perhaps no one was there. Again he had an urge to flee, and was about to press the button for the elevator when the apartment door opened. It was the maid, Mairie, who stared at him with disbelieving eyes.

"Oh! It's *you,* Captain, isn't it? I didn't know she was expecting you." She looked so nervous, he knew she must have been told at some time in the past not to admit him. "I see you're not a captain any more."

"Hello, Mairie. Is Mrs. Fields in?"

"I don't . . . she's up with the baby."

He walked in, forcing her to step back and open the door wider. "Which is the baby's room?"

"Oh, but I can't let you go up without telling 'er first!"

"It's all right, Mairie. I'll take full responsibility. Which bedroom?"

"The . . . the blue one, sir. Used to be."

He was almost at the top of the stairs when Charlotte came into the hall, quietly closing a door behind her. She looked up just as he reached the landing. She didn't move, her hand still on the doorknob. He noticed she was thinner and her cheekbones stood out prominently. She was more beautiful than ever.

"I brought a toy for him. The baby."

"That was thoughtful of you."

"I arrived this morning on the *Queen Elizabeth.* Not first class, by a long shot." He stopped and shook his head. "This is ridiculous, but I don't know what to say."

"There is nothing to say."

"You should have told me, Charlotte."

"Told you what?"

"About the baby."

"What was there to tell? It wasn't really your affair."

He stepped closer to her and she let her hand fall to her side, squaring her shoulders. He noticed there were fine lines in her face, at the corners of the eyes and mouth. There shouldn't have been, at twenty-nine.

"I saw Bruce before he died. We became friends, of a sort."

She nodded. "He told me. When you haven't actually seen someone dead, it's hard to believe. I mean, it's as if he's just gone away."

"Maybe that's a good way to think of it."

"His family will never get over it. None of them, even Blanche."

"I'm sure they won't."

They were as formal as strangers. You would never know they had been lovers, and in fact, he found it difficult to believe. It occurred to him she might have the wrong impression about why he had come.

"I'd like to see him."

"Who?"

"The baby, of course. That's why I'm here."

He thought she blanched, he couldn't be sure. "He's asleep now. I've just put him down for his nap."

"I'm surprised you don't have a nurse for him." He hadn't meant to be unkind, but it sounded that way, as if he thought she was too pampered to be responsible for her own child.

She smiled for the first time. "You're not wrong. It's the nurse's day off. I rather enjoy taking care of him, as long as I know Nanny will return."

"I'd like to see him anyway, Charlee, even if he's sleeping." Her head moved vaguely from side to side. "You can't refuse me."

She closed her eyes and let out a sigh of exasperation. "All right, but please don't wake him." Opening the door, she led him into the former guest room, transformed into a nursery, with colorful Mother Goose wallpaper and curtains, and shelf after shelf of toys against one wall.

David held his breath as he approached the crib. John was lying on his stomach with his knees drawn up and his rounded backside poking in the air in that sweet, appealing position babies assume. He looked like a cereal box child, sucking his thumb in his sleep. David saw the curve of a rosy cheek, one dimpled little hand against the mouth, while the other was entwined in silken baby hair, so blond it was almost white, like Bruce's must have been. Or like

David's when he was an infant, so Aunt Ethel had told him.

Charlotte was watching him with a dark expression. The baby stirred and wriggled his body, burrowing deeper into the mattress. Suddenly David had an irresistible desire to hold him in his arms, and before Charlotte could stop him, he reached into the crib and lifted John against his shoulder.

The sweetness of it! The softness and warmth, the need! He closed his eyes against the sting of tears. Could you tell by the feel if it was your own flesh, or would any fifteen-month-old snuggling against his neck cause him to react this way?

Charlee's face had gone soft, and she looked away as David kissed the chubby cheek and sniffed the clean baby smell. John's eyes opened and he raised his head sleepily to look at David and smile, revealing small, perfect teeth. His eyes were a dark blue, brilliant and intense.

David's breath caught. "Hey, big fella," he whispered, stroking the baby's cheek with his finger. "What a handsome boy you are."

John patted David's face, saying, "Da, da, da . . ."

"God!" He looked at Charlotte in panic.

"He does that to every man," she hastened to say. "It's because I taught him to say da-da by pointing to Bruce's picture."

John put his head down on David's shoulder, stuck his thumb in his mouth again, and was asleep in a minute. David kissed him and gently laid him back in the crib. Following Charlotte down to the library, his head was bursting with anguish and confusion.

"Whose child is John?" he demanded, when they were in the library.

She put her face in her hands, shuddering. "I don't know," she cried, "and that's the honest truth."

A sickness rose in him. "Oh, God!" Miserable, he turned away from her. "He's my son," he said, when he had gained some control of his emotions.

"No, David, he's Bruce's son. He will always be Bruce's son."

"You know what Bruce was! And I know, too."

He saw her eyes widen. He thought, in fear. "That doesn't mean he couldn't be John's father."

"What was he to you? Was he ever your husband?"

"Yes! He really was. He was a *normal* man. It was only one person who . . . who he—"

"Nicholas?"

She nodded.

"There were others, Charlee," he said as gently as he could. "I don't want to hurt you, and I have no wish to tarnish Bruce's memory, but there's something more important at stake. Is John mine?"

She shook her head defiantly. *"No!"*

"How can you be sure?"

"Because he *can't* be yours! Don't you see that? Even if I thought he was—which I don't. He *mustn't* be!"

They sat staring at each other.

"Think of it, David! Think of what it would mean. My mother, Bruce's parents—*Laurie!* You do see, don't you?" she pleaded.

"What will become of him?" he cried.

"I'll be with him. He'll be fine."

Somewhere he heard a chime, and a minute later a tall man came striding into the room and embraced Charlee. It was George Stearns, one of that group she and Bruce used to run around with before the war. David had never cared much for George the few times they had met. An older businessman who put on airs. He recalled hearing there had been a rather messy divorce from—what was her name?—that obese woman with the vicious tongue. Laurie had written that Stearns was very helpful to Charlotte after Bruce died.

"You remember my cousin, David Bernard, don't you? He's just returned from overseas."

They shook hands, George saying with a hearty smile, "Of course, of course! Welcome back. And what's that insignia I see? Lieutenant Colonel! Very impressive."

"I didn't do much to earn it. It came with the job."

George kept an arm around Charlee's waist. "Am I interrupting?" he asked.

"Not at all," she replied, "David was just leaving."

"Oh, too bad. Has she told you?"

"Told me what?"

There was a certain smile on Charlotte's face that David recognized. Not one of her better expressions. She looked at him from under her lashes.

"Can you keep a secret, David? George and I are going to be married."

Chapter 38

THE DOORBELL CHIMED, startling Lauren, even though she was expecting him. She jumped out of the chair, almost knocking over an end table in her haste to reach the front hall. David had let himself in. He dropped his bags, and her heart contracted as she saw the weariness in him when he threw his hat on the bench and turned to face her.

"David! Oh, my darling," she rushed to him and took him in her arms. His tentative embrace tightened and when they kissed, it was both strange and familiar. And then they held each other, taking and giving comfort from their nearness.

"Let me look at you." She drew back and smoothed his brow with an old remembered gesture. "I've missed you so," she said with a catch in her voice.

He kissed her again, and for the first time smiled, a weary, defeated smile. "Just to see you, Laurie," and he could say no more, for his tears overwhelmed him. Over her shoulder, his eyes fell on the photographs of his children on the piano and he thought, *Oh my God, how could I have ever thought of betraying them, of betraying her?*

"You look so tired. I'll get you something to eat."

He eased himself into a chair. "No food, just a drink," he said, looking around the living room for remembered objects.

She fixed him a bourbon and branch water, and sat on the ottoman at his feet, holding his hand and regarding him with a radiant smile.

"How are the children?" he asked.

"Wonderful! They wanted to wait up for you, but I didn't know when you would arrive."

"I didn't either. A space cleared at the last minute and there was no time to call." He sipped his highball. "You look beautiful, Lauren." He met her eyes for the first time. "I am *so glad* to be home."

They climbed the stairs and he stood for several minutes in each of his children's rooms gazing at them, with his arm around Lauren. A fleeting picture of that other small boy lying in his crib passed through his mind, and he drove it away. *He can't be, he mustn't be!*

When David had showered, he came to their bed and made slow, tender love to her in a way she did not remember. This was how it was supposed to be, should always have been. So beautiful, this love she had never before experienced. On and on, this wonderful melding together, never ending, ever, ever.

At last he fell away from her and into an exhausted sleep. Something had happened to him, Lauren knew. Something beyond the war and the years away. Whatever it was, it made her feel more well-loved than ever.

The children came running into their room at dawn, tumbling into bed with them, then drawing back shyly as they realized this stranger, their father, was sharing the bed with their mother. David kissed them over and over, and hugged their wiry bodies to him, and Lauren slipped out of bed, leaving Babs and Mark there talking excitedly with him while she quickly showered and dressed, then went down to prepare breakfast.

They had finished the buckwheat cakes and Lauren made another pot of coffee. The children were playing outside on the swings after showing David all of their schoolwork and drawings and toys.

"Let's go away for a few days before you go back to the hospital, just the two of us," she said.

They rented a small cottage on the Outer Banks near Cape Lookout, where they had gone on their wedding trip. It was the first time they had been to the ocean together since then, and they spent a week riding the waves, lying on the dunes, and walking for miles on the deserted beach. At night they fell asleep to the pounding of the surf, and it was more of a honeymoon than they had ever known.

Their newness with each other in this isolated spot altered them both. David made love to her with that same slow tenderness as on the night of his return. Each time he claimed her body, he brought her a pleasure that rose and waned, then mounted again, until one night it crested overwhelmingly, and Lauren knew for the first time, the bliss of complete satisfaction.

"Darling . . . my darling!" she cried in exultation. "Oh, David, my love . . ." In the dark, her hands stroked his face and she felt the wetness on his cheeks. "Why are you crying?" she whispered.

"Because I love you so . . . and because I wish the last three years had never happened."

It was true the years had been taken from them, but Lauren knew they had gained something in the separation. She would never be the same immature woman she had been before the war. But in an indefinable way, David was different, too. Why, how, was hard to explain, but he had changed. The way he made love . . . so much more sensitive and tender, he made her feel not just loved, but cherished.

In the morning, she woke first and lay beside him, watching his face, so dearly familiar, yet still unaccustomed to seeing him there. He looked younger and untroubled in sleep. She felt the wonderful mystery of him and the depth of her love, and she knew there was a part of him that would always elude her, despite her understanding of him. She vowed she would never again take him for granted. Now that he was home, she would fill his heart as he filled hers, and her work would receive whatever of her was left.

The peace and balm of home enveloped David's spirit and the vitality of the area energized him. He was eager to return to work. Three and a half years was a long time, and he wondered whether there would still be a place for him in the Russell Clinic's surgical group. He made an appointment to see Thomas Sayles on the following Monday morning. The medical complex at Strickland had grown during the war, when it was used for hospitalized servicemen.

"Great to see you, Dave," Dr. Sayles greeted him, throwing a comradely arm around his shoulders as he led him to his private office.

David noticed that Tom had turned gray over the past few years. "It must have been difficult running the department without a full staff," he said.

"Let's just say I'm glad to have you back," Sayles replied. "I want to hear all about the work you were doing over there."

David described the military hospital, telling Tom about some of the surgical techniques they had used, many of them developed in desperation when a flyer was so badly damaged, they were willing to risk anything to save a limb. Sayles listened carefully to everything David said.

"When do you plan to come back to work?" he finally asked.

David grinned. "As soon as you want me. I wasn't sure there'd still be a place for me."

"The appointments committee hasn't made it official yet, but you're going to be offered a full-time post here and a joint appointment as an associate professor of orthopedics at Duke. I hope you'll accept."

"*Accept?* Wait 'til I tell Lauren!"

"Hail the conquering hero, so I hear," said Donal when Lauren appeared in the English office after a week's absence.

She smiled and answered lightly, "That's right, Sullivan. David's home."

"You have the look of a woman who has been well and frequently bedded."

She stared back at him. "Married people go to bed together, in case it has escaped your attention."

His eyes dropped. "Sorry. That was just my jealous nature getting the better of me."

They had become good friends as well as colleagues

over the past two years. It was Sullivan who helped to secure Lauren's appointment as an assistant professor for the coming academic year, and she impulsively invited him to the party she was planning to celebrate David's return.

As she walked across campus that afternoon, Lauren reminded herself to call Charlee after dinner. They had been together in Randolph Springs last summer, just after Bruce was killed. Charlotte had been brave, and still so beautiful, and Lauren was glad she had been there to comfort her.

"I really did love Bruce, you know, despite all our wrangling," her cousin had said one evening when they were alone.

"Charlee, darling, I never doubted it!"

"Bruce never saw his son, Laurie. That's the hardest part to bear," she wept, breaking down for the first time.

Charlee obviously took great comfort in John, who was a dream of a baby. She had cut short her visit to Randolph Springs in order to take him out to the West Coast to visit Blanche. Even before Jules was discharged from the Navy, the Taylors had bought a home in Pasadena, intending to settle there after the war.

Before leaving for California, Charlotte had remarked, "David won't be coming home to the same little wife he married."

"I was never that little wife, Charlee. He just didn't realize it, and maybe I didn't either. David worked nearly all the time when we were first married, and the children came along so soon. There was no time for us together. He went off to war before we really knew who we were."

Charlee had looked thoughtful. "Nevertheless, you've changed a great deal."

"I'm sure he's changed, too."

All the way back to Chapel Hill, Lauren had brooded about the conversation, sadly aware that Charlotte would not have a husband coming home to her . . .

As soon as the children were in bed, she screwed up her courage and called New York. "David's home, Charlee. He came last week."

"Splendid, darling! How is the old dear? Does he have a thousand war stories to tell?"

"Not a one. He doesn't seem to want to talk about it, so I've stopped asking."

"You always were the understanding sort. He's a lucky man, our David. Give him a hug."

"Don't you want to say hello to him?"

"Uh—I'm in rather a hurry, love, but all right, I'll say hello."

"David . . . David, darling," she called to him down in the basement where he was putting up shelves in the playroom. "Charlee's on the phone. Can you pick up?"

There was a long silence. "Another time, honey. I'm busy now."

She shrugged philosophically. "He can't come to the phone, Charlee. We'll call again. How's Johnny?"

"Terrific! Getting to be the spitting image of Bruce."

"What a love! Kiss him for me, and please come down to visit. We'll never get to New York, now that they've made David an associate."

Later she said, "Darling, I know you were busy before, but I think Charlee may have been offended when you didn't talk to her. I'm sure she'd like to hear about your last meeting with Bruce. It's very hard for her, knowing you and so many other men have come home to their wives, and Bruce never will."

"Yes, I imagine it is," he answered. "Maybe Charlotte will marry again."

"I hope so. But despite their stormy marriage, she adored Bruce, and I don't see how she'll ever find someone else."

The guests began to arrive at seven, on time, as they always were in Chapel Hill. Gretchen and Ralph were the first to come, Gretch looking wonderfully happy and Ralph a little sheepish, Lauren thought. His thin, fine sandy hair had receded considerably in the three years he had been overseas.

Next came the Strouds, Tony just back from the Pacific. "Tony, how marvelous to see you!" she kissed their friends and passed them on to David, turning to greet the Sayleses and the Kramers—he was an internist who had gone to Duke with David and his wife taught in the elementary school Babs attended.

The children were permitted to stay for the cocktail hour. Babs passed a tray of canapés and Mark hung around David while he mixed drinks and talked with Tony, almost as if they had never been away. Lauren was filled with contentment, as the conviviality made it real that the war was over and the men were home to stay.

''There's the bell,'' called Mark, but before he could move, Sullivan had entered with a marvelous looking woman.

''Here's Donal Sullivan, David, my colleague from the English department.'' Donal had brought Maureen O'Shaughnessy, equipped with glorious red hair, freckles, green eyes, gamin grin, and a genuine brogue. Maureen groomed horses at the veterinary school, she told Lauren, and was an honest-to-God Irish lass, born in Dublin. It was too much.

''Sullivan, you old devil, you've done it on purpose!''

''Like unto like,'' he answered. ''Straight from the ould sod.''

''Oh, God spare us!''

They were all here. She surveyed the room happily. I love being a faculty wife, she thought. *Wait a minute . . .* I love being *faculty*—and don't you forget it, Lauren Bernard!

''Dinner is served,'' announced Amanda.

The dining room looked lovely with candlelight and roses from the garden. Amanda had prepared an overabundant buffet of David's favorite foods. Spicy shrimp creole, fried chicken, corn pudding, spoon bread, her special tomato chow-chow, and a variety of desserts including the hot rum apple and pecan pie with whipped cream that she had refused to make all during the war, as long as he was away.

When everyone was seated, Lauren tapped her glass with a spoon. ''I want to make a toast. Welcome home to David, Tony, Ralph, and to all of the husbands who have returned safely . . . And let's please remember those who haven't."

Her eyes met David's across the length of the table and she was suffused with love for him. They had weathered the worst, and surely their future would be bright and wonderful.

Book IV

BINDING TIES

1947—1948

Chapter 39

Randolph Springs, Summer 1947

"CHARLEE, I *DO* wish you'd come back to Chapel Hill with me," Lauren urged her cousin. The two women were lingering over coffee on a sunny July morning, in the breakfast room of Reba's house. "Johnny would have such fun with Babs and Mark."

"Maybe some other time, Laurie, but I have to get on home."

Charlotte had her froggy morning voice and that dry cough Lauren had noticed over the telephone. It was no wonder, smoking the way she did; she reached for a cigarette even before she drank her morning juice.

"Why not come for just a few days? Our children don't even know each other!"

"I can't, Laurie. George is being a real pain as it is about my staying away for two weeks."

"You only visit Randolph once a year. Why doesn't George come with you?"

"He says coming down here brings back bad memories of his days with Norma, when she was 'spending him out of house and home.' Now he's trying to do the same to me!" Her bitter laugh ended in a paroxysm of coughing.

Lauren couldn't hide her surprise. "Why should he be spending *your* money? I thought he made a fortune—" (she just caught herself from saying 'during the war') "—in heavy equipment."

"A relative fortune. He has a little problem with what he calls 'cash flow.' Norma got a huge divorce settlement, and all his remaining capital is tied up in long-term investments. Thank heaven, my father-in-law left everything in trust for Johnny when he died. George would just love to get his hands on some of that money.''

Lauren was shocked, but no more than she had been when Charlotte had called them two years ago, on Thanksgiving night, to announce that she and George Stearns had been married that afternoon . . .

She and David always made a big fuss over Thanksgiving, inviting medical students, interns, and junior faculty who had no family nearby. There had been twenty-two of them for dinner, and afterward, gathered in the living room in front of a fire, everyone enjoyed singing while David played the piano. After the last guests had departed and the children were in bed, Lauren had been sitting with David watching the glowing embers in the fireplace, in that pleasant aftermath of a successful party, when the telephone rang and it was Charlotte.

''Ta-*da*-da-dumm . . .'' sang Charlee, to the tune of The Wedding March.

Of course, Lauren had said all the correct things, but her heart sank at the idea of Charlee married to George Stearns. Why, he was old enough to be her—well, not exactly her father, but fairly close to it.

''Good old David,'' chuckled Charlotte, just before hanging up. ''He didn't spill the beans!''

''You mean you went to see Charlee in New York when you came back from England?'' said Lauren afterward. ''You never told me that, David!''

''Charlotte swore me to secrecy, so I didn't say anything at all, because I was afraid I'd slip. You know I'm not very good at keeping things from you, Laurie.''

''I'm rather surprised she would tell *you* and not me,'' she said peevishly. She had thought her old uneasiness about them was something she had put aside forever.

''Charlotte didn't tell me. George did. He was there at the apartment.''

''Oh, I see. Well—that does explain it,'' she replied, feeling a vast and unexplainable sense of relief.

David sat down at the piano, idly playing a few bars

from one of her favorite Gershwin songs . . . *For you, for me, forever more* . . . Unbidden, the image came to her of that moment in New York during the war, when she had entered the library to find him and Charlee singing and looking into each other's eyes.

Her gaze remained on his bent head and his fine surgeon's hands, running over the keyboard in that easy, melodic cabaret style. "Then, you must have seen Johnny when you were there."

For a moment he stopped playing. "Briefly. He was taking a nap."

"Isn't he adorable?" she said, to fill the uncomfortable silence. "Charlee says he's getting to look more and more like Bruce."

David hadn't replied immediately. He began another piece, and then he said, "All babies look pretty much alike when they're not your own . . ."

Lauren always timed a trip to Randolph Springs with her children during Charlee's annual summer visit home. This year, both Barbara and Mark had preferred to stay at day camp in Chapel Hill with their friends, and now that their grandmother Miriam was in the Mission Home and could not really recognize anyone, Lauren had not insisted they accompany her.

Johnny, at three, was getting old enough to be fun, and she did want their children to grow up being friends. But Charlee never accepted her invitations to bring John to Chapel Hill, always finding some excuse not to come. Of course, it was because she and David didn't get along! There was no explaining that alienation.

Lauren was not ordinarily one to make a fuss over children, but Johnny had completely captivated her. "I could just eat you up!" she cried, giving him a hug, when he came over to the breakfast table and leaned against her affectionately.

"Lions eat boys," answered John solemnly.

"Well, then, aren't we lucky there are no lions around here?"

"There's lions in the zoo," he said.

"Um-hmm, but they're all locked up in cages."

"They're near my 'partment."

She had forgotten. Was three years an especially fearful age? Maybe John had anxieties about lions. "A lion can't possibly get out of his cage, Johnny. And even if he could, he wouldn't know how to take the elevator up to your apartment."

He giggled at the idea of a lion taking an elevator, and as his face broke into that heart-stopping smile, Lauren's thoughts were of Bruce. Not to ever have laid eyes on his precious little son! It was too heartbreaking for words. Malcolm Fields had grieved himself to death over it.

And no doubt, Charlotte's marriage to George Stearns had been another bitter blow for Bruce's father. Lauren remembered Charlee once telling her years ago that Mr. Fields had no regard for Stearns, whom he considered an unethical businessman. After their marriage, George had moved right into Charlee's duplex and taken over, and—according to Reba—Malcolm had rarely entered it after that, except to visit the grandson he adored. It must have been a constant aggravation for Malcolm, to see a man he despised usurping his son's place, living in his son's home, and being a father to his son's boy.

Charlee's coughing brought her back to the present. "You've had that all week, Char."

Shrugging, Charlotte lit another cigarette. "It's nothing. I had my usual allergic bronchitis in the spring, and I'm always left with an irritated throat afterward." She lovingly stroked John, who was half lying with his head in her lap.

"It's time for me to pack up and get home to Chapel Hill," said Lauren. "A week is long enough for me to be away from David and the children. I guess I'll go out to the Mission Home to see Mama once more before I leave. Not that she'll know. I've finally accepted what the doctor said, that her mind isn't functioning. But I can't convince myself she's not suffering."

"You have to believe she isn't, Laurie. She doesn't look unhappy or in pain."

"She doesn't look *anything!*" Lauren pushed her chair

away from the table. "Aunt Reba said she wanted to go with me this morning, but she gets so emotional, I'm not sure it's good for her."

"I think you're right. Mother's still asleep, anyway, so why don't you go without her? If she insists, I'll take her out there later."

Reba had become distraught six months ago when they had been forced to move Miriam into the nursing home. She had seen it as her duty to take care of her sister for the rest of her life. "Mimi *needs* me," she had lamented. "She'll give up and *die* if I'm not there every morning to hold her hand and talk to her."

That might prove to be so, but it had become impossible to maintain Miriam at home, even with twenty-four hour nurses. She had bedsores, had lost control of her bowel and bladder, and was unable to eat properly. You couldn't blame Reba for going to pieces, though, thought Lauren. Perhaps she imagined herself in her sister's place at some future date.

Each time Lauren went to the nursing home, she had to prepare herself, for the woman in the bed bore no resemblance to her mother. If this should ever happen to me, I would want them to let me die, she thought. But you couldn't say that to the nuns who took such good care of Miriam.

Driving back to Shadow Mountain after leaving her mother, Lauren felt her usual remorse for not sharing the burden of Miriam's last days. The responsibility had fallen on her brothers, her sister, and Reba, and knowing it wasn't her fault that she lived in Chapel Hill did nothing to relieve her conscience.

It was almost noon when she got back to the house. Charlotte was on the telephone with her lawyer in New York, and Pansy was playing with John out on the back lawn. Lauren heard her call, "That's enough baseball, Johnny. It's time for your lunch and nap."

"Oh, phooey," said John.

Pansy laughed, and Lauren fondly reflected that the black women who had cared for the children in her family had never lost their patience with "their babies." They smothered them with love and enforced rules with gentle persuasion.

"Aren't you hungry?" Pansy asked.

"Yes, but I'm not sleepy," John lisped, with perfect logic.

"Well, we'll see how you feel after lunch. Maybe you can just play quietly in your room." She took him to wash his hands and put him at the kitchen table where Lady had set out his plate.

Lauren went in to ask Lady whether she could have a sandwich for the road. "Why don't y'all stay here and eat a good, proper lunch before you leave us, Miz Laurie?"

"I'm not hungry yet, and I want to get home before dark. It will take more than five hours driving to Chapel Hill today, with the weekend traffic."

"All right, child. I guess I just hate to see you go."

Lauren hugged Lady, feeling a sad heaviness at the frail bones and snowy hair. "Where's Aunt Reba?" she asked.

"Still sleeping, I reckon. She never did ring for her breakfast tray, and she don't like for us to disturb her 'fore she's ready to get up."

"It's noontime, Lady. Is she in the habit of sleeping this late?"

"No ma'am, she don't."

"I want to say good-bye before I leave. Maybe I better go peek in at her."

"I'll do it, Miz Laurie," said Pansy. "I has to go up there anyway to put fresh towels in her bathroom. Now, Johnny, you be a good boy and eat your lunch, hear?"

" 'Kay," said John, munching on the finger sandwiches Lady had prepared.

Lauren sat at the table with him. He had a white mustache from his milk and his eyes stayed on her as he drank from a mug. She reached out to brush his hair back from his forehead. As he grew older, it was turning a thick, luscious brown, and when he grinned at her, she was struck by how much he resembled Mark, especially around his intensely blue eyes. Mark, and perhaps . . . Babs? She had always thought Barbara looked more like David, but they all had Jacobson in them and you could certainly see it in Johnny. Not much Mortimer there. Nor Fields either, for that matter, despite what Charlee thought. She had been quite snappish when Lauren mentioned that Bruce's family weren't that vigorous in appearance, their coloring rather pallid and washed out, compared to John's vividness. Charlee *insisted* that John was the image of Bruce, but the truth was, there was no resemblance to his father that Lauren could see. Heredity was amazing—

Her thoughts were interrupted by a shriek from somewhere in the house, and then Pansy calling, *"Lady, Lady, come quick! Oh my Lord, Miz Charlotte! Sweet Jesus! Miz Reba, she's—"*

John scrambled down his chair, his eyes big with excitement, but Lauren quickly picked him up and despite her violently beating heart, said quietly, "Lady, will you go see what Pansy wants, please, while I take Johnny out in the garden?"

Her limbs were trembling, and she did not have to go upstairs to know what had happened. There was that shadow, that same sense of impending doom, hovering over them once again.

She walked with John among the flowers.

"You're a very tall man, Cousin David."

Sturdy and wide-eyed, the child stood resolutely looking up at him. The hard knot of bitterness inside David melted. It should not have been this way, he told himself. But would he have preferred that John had not been born?

He bent over and scooped him up in his arms. "And you're a fine big boy."

John smiled, such a smile of purity and love, his face radiated joy. "Do you like to read stories to little boys?"

"Oh, yes," he said softly, "I like that very much."

David was so full of emotion he thought his heart would burst, and he was sure his voice would give him away. They sat in a chair, John on his lap snuggling against him, while David read words that blurred before his eyes.

Charlotte passed through the room and for a moment paused, but she and David never looked at each other.

They had barely exchanged a word since he had arrived in Randolph Springs for her mother's funeral.

Lauren was still in a state of disbelief. That Miriam had outlived her baby sister! What was God thinking, to preserve the vegetative life in that room at the Mission Home, when Reba, who had just passed her fifty-fifth birthday in robust health, had been taken?

She had died in her sleep from a ruptured cerebral aneurysm and had been gone for hours when Pansy discovered her. For how many years, wondered Lauren, had that fatal weakness in the blood vessel been lurking? How tenuous was life, how fragile and vulnerable they were!

The funeral drew friends and relatives from all over the South, perhaps the last such gathering for many of the older generation. Reba's four brothers and their wives, all of them gray and suffering from one condition or another. Max's cousins from Atlanta and Baltimore, widowed and quite elderly. Certainly the Jacobson clan was well represented, with all the cousins, their children and grandchildren attending, a number of them traveling great distances at some inconvenience to reach Randolph Springs in time for the service.

George Stearns flew down from New York, putting on a display of bereavement, and a consuming interest in Reba's estate. Lauren noticed the coolness between him and Charlotte, but was nevertheless astounded the day after the funeral when George packed his bags to return to New York alone, after they had a bitter quarrel.

Poor darling Charlee—from a fairy-tale life of love, comfort, and promise, to this! She had been deprived first of her prince charming, then the parents who worshiped her, and now she had to endure a bad marriage. It was too much for any woman to bear alone.

Charlotte had met her mother's death stoically, taking care of the funeral arrangements herself, insisting on making many of the calls to notify relatives, and instructing Lady and Bertram to get extra help to handle the unending stream of visitors who came to pay their respects. The strain took its toll, however. By the second day after Reba's funeral, Charlee had a bad chest cold that quickly settled into bronchitis. When she went up to bed before dinner, Lauren knew she must really be ill.

"Let me feel your head," she said, placing her hand on Charlotte's brow. "You seem quite warm. Would you like David to look at your throat? He might prescribe something to get rid of it fast."

Charlee lay back against the pillows, coughing painfully and closing her eyes. "Yes, maybe that would be a good idea."

As Lauren came down the stairs, she could hear her brothers and cousins lingering in conversation around the dining table. David was in the little sun parlor, reading to Johnny. It was thoughtful of him to stay on in Randolph with her, especially since it was the middle of the week. He had been wonderful for John, keeping him entertained and taking him for walks. David had always been marvelous with children, and you could tell John responded to him. The child needed a man's influence, and it was obvious he did not get much fathering from George Stearns.

She waited until they had finished the story and John skipped out of the room. "Sorry to interrupt, darling. Would you mind taking a look at Charlee. She's not feeling at all well."

"I didn't bring my bag with me. Why don't you call Reba's family doctor?"

"There's a bag in the trunk of my car. You know, the old one you always keep there in case of emergency."

"I'm not an internist, Laurie."

"David, that's absurd! You certainly know how to use a stethoscope and look at a throat, for heaven's sake."

With a resigned look, he went to get the bag.

"I haven't been able to shake this rotten cough and it wears me out," Charlotte told David when he walked into her bedroom. "Every time I catch cold, it settles in my chest."

She noticed how remote and professional he was as he questioned her, yet pleasant enough to satisfy Lauren, who had come upstairs with him and was sitting across the room on the window seat. Making her presence unobtrusive, yet *there,* as if Charlee were a teenager on her first visit to a gynecologist.

With a deft touch, David looked in her throat and ears, felt her glands, then stuck a thermometer in her mouth while he took her pulse and blood pressure. That was one way of keeping her quiet, she thought with wry amusement.

There was a knock at the door. Laurie went to answer it and Charlotte heard Bertram's rumbling voice. ''It's Bruce's mother on the phone, Charlee,'' said Lauren.

''Adele's been calling me every day,'' Charlotte mumbled around the thermometer. ''She couldn't come to the funeral because of her arthritis.''

''I'll go talk to her and you can call her back later.''

There was less tension once Lauren had left the room. Even David seemed more at ease. She had noticed his jaws working before, when he wound that gadget for taking blood pressure around her arm.

He removed the thermometer. ''You have a low fever, a little over 100.''

''It was higher this afternoon. I took some aspirin.''

''I have to listen to your chest. Just undo your buttons, please.''

She gave him an ironic smile, but he looked severe as she unlooped the frogs on the front of the Mandarin style bed jacket of cream satin, letting it fall off her shoulders. Underneath she was wearing a matching gown, very simple, with a handmade corded edging that continued around the neckline to form thin straps. She was suddenly disconcerted and wondered whether her heartbeat would give her away.

David's eyes were on the wall behind her as he pressed the round contact against her chest. She saw him frown and lower his head, listening. The cold metal caused her nipples to harden and stand out against the thin fabric of the gown. A shoulder strap slipped down, half exposing one breast. Ridiculously, this embarrassed her, but he didn't seem to notice.

''Take a deep breath and let it out with your mouth

open.'' He had her repeat that several times while he moved the instrument around her chest and under her breasts.

''Now lean forward.'' He was intent as he listened to the muffled andantes and largos of her body through the stethoscope. ''Cough . . . Again.''

His head was very close to hers. She smelled his soap and shaving lotion, a clean, light scent. It dredged up all sorts of memories, of moments it was hard to believe had ever taken place. Remembering him, the way he was when they were lovers, so strong and passionate, she was swept with sadness. No regrets, considering. But many things should have been different. If only one could go back and do it over again.

''When did you last have a chest X-ray?'' asked David. He sat back and removed his stethoscope from his ears, letting it hang around his neck.

She adjusted her bed jacket. ''I seem to remember they took one last year, when the doctor thought I might have pneumonia.''

''I think you should come have a checkup at the Russell Clinic. You can do it on your way back to New York.''

''I don't have time, David. There are a million things to take care of here, and I have to be home by next week.''

''Surely nothing can be more important than this. You need to have a chest X-ray. At least do that much here in Randolph.''

''I promise to have one as soon as I get back to New York. Will you give me something for this bloody cough?''

He reached for the pack of cigarettes lying on the night table. ''First of all, stop using these. That's an order, and I mean it.''

She grabbed for them, but he was too fast. ''David! Give them to me. I promise not to smoke until I'm better.''

''Then you shouldn't mind if I take them away. You have to shake the habit, Charlotte.''

''I've tried. Don't you think my doctor has told me to quit? I get this uncontrollable craving for a cigarette.''

''You have a persistent cough, recurring bronchitis—

you're far too intelligent not to understand that you must stop smoking." Then he added quietly, "Your health is important, Charlee. You have a child to consider."

"Yes, you're right. I'll try, I really will. If only I weren't so *tense* all the time."

Life seemed to be closing in on her. She would like to confide in *someone*. Laurie just wasn't the right person, as willing as she would be to listen. Somehow, Charlotte had never been able to admit her failures to her cousin. She had always felt the need to appear happy and successful to Lauren. Her ridiculous pride! She couldn't help it, though—it made her feel so inadequate to see Laurie, with her life in such perfect order. Everything the way it should be—a handsome, devoted husband, two magnificent children, and a flourishing career of her own. And what did Charlotte have to show for her thirty-one years? Two rotten marriages and a pile of money—and Johnny. Oh yes . . . Johnny. That made it all worthwhile.

She really did need someone to talk to. If only her father were still alive. Or Malcolm. He had been fond of her in his way, and a tower of strength. She had such a need for a friend, and she had no one. Surrounded by nearly a hundred relatives all week long, she felt alone in the world. She wanted to confide in a *man*—she had always preferred men. But despite her large family, there was not a single male she could turn to. Except for David.

Had he always been this quiet? She didn't remember him that way, as such a private person. It made him somewhat unapproachable, but she trusted him.

"I've made up my mind I'm going to divorce George when I get back to New York."

"I'm sorry." He leaned down to replace his instruments in the black doctor's bag, so she was unable to read his face. "I'm sure you've considered the effect a divorce will have on your son."

"Oh yes, most of all him. If anything, it will be beneficial." She started to cough and he poured her a glass of water from a carafe. "When we were married, I thought George would be good for John. He put on quite a show of interest and concern after Bruce died. But he has no patience with children. Johnny keeps out of his way. I think he's a little afraid of him."

"George hasn't mistreated him, has he?" he was quick to ask.

"No, nothing like that. But then, they're never alone together. Either I or the nurse is always there. Soon John will be too old for Nanny. This is the first time he's been away from her for so long, but he doesn't seem to miss her."

"He's surrounded by love down here. Everyone in the family is crazy about him."

"Yes," she answered. "I notice he's really taken a shine to you."

She watched for his reaction, but he was inscrutable. "He's a wonderful boy. You're to be congratulated."

"Thank you. When they write my epitaph, producing Johnny may be the one good thing they can say about me. I seem to have made a bloody mess of everything else."

She wondered at his fleeting faraway expression. Thinking that Bruce had voiced almost exactly the same thought shortly before his death, David said, "You're too hard on yourself, Charlotte."

"Just realistic. I certainly can't claim to have made a success of my marriage with Bruce. And my current marriage is, to put it politely, a sham."

"If that's the case, then it's best that you should bring it to an end."

"Oh God, David, I don't know where I belong! Once I thought I would never leave New York, but now I wonder what keeps me there. It's a tough city. When you're on top, they adore you. But what can I do for them now? My marriage is over, Bruce's family has practically evaporated. All of my friends seem preoccupied with their lives, and many of them have dropped me."

"Then I wouldn't call them friends."

"I can't blame them. When George and Norma were divorced, most of the women sided with her. I feel inclined to come back to the South, but what is there in Randolph Springs? I could move into this house, I suppose. I see how happy John is here, playing on a green lawn, calmer and better adjusted, even with all the turmoil of Mother's death. I just don't know what to do."

"You must do what you want to do, what seems best for you. You have no financial worries, I'm sure, so that wouldn't stand in your way. Why not keep the apartment in New York and try Randolph for a while?"

"Yes, I could do that. I still have the farm in Westport, you know." That was almost too much. He looked really distressed. "I'm sorry. I probably shouldn't have mentioned that."

He shook his head sadly. "Oh, Charlee—"

"I understand. You'd like to forget all that."

"Yes."

"I hope you and Laurie are happy."

"We are. We really are." He seemed to be weighing his words. "There's just one question I wish—"

Whatever it was he was going to say, he never had a chance. There was a tap on the door and Lauren entered.

"Mrs. Fields sends her love, Charlee. I didn't tell her you were sick." Seeing that David was finished with his examination, she said brightly, "Well, doctor, how's the patient?"

"She should improve in a few days. There's no point in prescribing penicillin, since it doesn't look like a bacterial infection." Then he spoke directly to Charlotte. "I'll call the drugstore and order a strong cough suppressant so you can get some rest. *No smoking!* And I want your word of honor you'll go see your doctor and have a chest film when you get back to New York."

"Cross my heart."

They had not finished their conversation, thought Charlotte, but maybe it was just as well.

Chapter 40

Autumn 1947

CHARLOTTE CHOSE A chair in the corner of the waiting room. She was reminded of her fleeting glimpses through the windows of New York's distinguished men's clubs, where the members sat in pin-striped suits studying the *Wall Street Journal,* oblivious of the passing multitudes.

This was one exclusive club she would prefer not to join. No quantity of comfortable leather couches, tasteful etchings, or subdued lighting could diminish the tension and anxiety in the hushed lounge. Idly she studied a dull bronze plaque. The room had been given to the institution by Mr. and Mrs. Harvey Lowenthal in memory of their daughter Cecile, 1919-1936. Yes, one could die of cancer at seventeen.

That *word.* It was enough to strike terror in anyone. None of them ever used it, as if it were something to be ashamed of, as if you could catch it by uttering its name.

All of these pathetic souls were sitting here because of the unmentionable. The elderly man wearing an eye patch, accompanied by an earnest-looking young woman, probably his daughter. The handsome boy in his prep-school blazer, directing his fear and resentment toward his father, whose forced smile did not mask the torment in his eyes. The new mother cradling her boy baby in his blue bunting. The middle-aged woman in the neat black coat, like Charlotte, alone.

Across the room she noticed a couple with their young daughter, a painfully thin child of about eight with stringy blond hair, her skin so pale it looked unnatural. The father sat slightly with his overcoat folded across his lap, nervously rotating his hat in his hands, while his wife turned the pages of a book, pointing to a certain passage and laughing, trying to draw a smile from the girl. The child's face crumpled as she whispered a few words, and the mother gathered her into her arms, rocking her back and forth. Over her head, the man and wife's eyes met, and the hopelessness Charlotte saw there was terrifying. More frightening than the X-rays and blood tests and bone scans, and the countless probings and indignities that had made the last month a nightmare.

"Mrs. Stearns. Dr. Marcus will see you now."

It was like a clarion call echoing through the filled waiting room. A dozen pairs of eyes looked up briefly and went back to their magazines as Charlotte followed the nurse down the corridor to the office of one more famous specialist.

"Billy Quigley's father says you're a *conunist* and ought to go live in New York!"

David put his arm around Mark and drew him against his body. You didn't sit a boy who had just started the second grade on your lap, because that was kid stuff. But he could see the lower lip quivering and sense tears just below the surface.

"Communist, not conunist."

"Well, are you?"

"No, I'm not. I'm a registered Democrat, and a loyal American. A communist is someone who believes in a system of government that's different from ours. Russia is a communist country."

"Are they bad?"

"Only if they use force to impose their ideas on others. I suppose I can understand why some people become communists, but I don't agree with them."

"Then why did Mr. Quigley say you're one, Daddy?"

David sighed, knowing that Billy's father was the son of the powerful board chairman of Strickland Hospital. They always got you through your children!

"Well . . . I imagine it's because Billy's grandfather told him I had formed a committee at the hospital to convince them to admit Negro patients, and they don't like the idea. That's the simplest way to explain it."

"You mean colored people?"

"Yes."

"Oh." He seemed to be giving it serious thought. "Where do colored people go when they get their tonsils out?"

"If they're lucky, they can go to the colored wards at Duke. Or they can go to special hospitals just for black people. But those special hospitals aren't as modern or well-equipped as our hospital, and they're too far away for some of the Negroes who live near Strickland."

"People like Amanda?"

"Yes."

"Why are you doing it, Daddy?"

"Because I think it's wrong that a sick person can't be taken to the nearest or best hospital. I believe it's wrong when people are prevented from doing *anything* important because of what they are—the color of their skin or their religion."

Mark was puzzling over his father's words. "Do you think the movie theater is wrong not to allow colored people?"

"Yes, I think they're wrong."

"Daddy," he said, considering the idea for the first time, "do you think it's wrong that colored children don't go to school with us?"

David was choked with love for his son. He could not escape the clear-eyed scrutiny of his gaze. It was a moment for complete honesty.

"Yes, Mark, I do."

Despite his exuberance and unruliness, there was a gentle sensitivity about Mark. He had Lauren's cleft chin and wavy blond hair, and a shining intelligence that emanated from his blue eyes.

"Well, Dad, I guess if you think it's wrong, then I do, too."

* * *

It was at the end of October, two weeks after Mark's seventh birthday, when Lauren answered a late evening phone call from Charlee. They always talked for ages, so David was surprised when after a few minutes of chatting, she handed the telephone to him.

He no longer dreaded an encounter with Charlotte. Since July at Reba's funeral in Randolph Springs, he had made his peace with the idea that they would be forced to see each other from time to time. They could never escape the family tie and in fact, he looked forward to being with John again. He would probably never know for sure whose son he was, but did that matter? There was an affinity between them, a strong attraction that drew him to the boy.

"How's John?" he asked.

"Getting terribly big. I hate to see him lose his baby ways. This is such a sweet age, and I *do* enjoy it."

"There are wonderful stages ahead, too. You'll have plenty of pleasure from him."

For a long moment there was silence. "I finally went to the doctor and got that chest X-ray."

"You mean you waited all this time? I hope it was normal."

"I want to talk to you, but don't say anything in front of Laurie."

He glanced over to where Lauren was grading papers for one of her classes. "That may be a little difficult."

"Is she right there?"

"Yes."

"Can't you go to another room?"

"All right. Let me call you back. What's the number?"

She gave a little laugh as she repeated her private telephone number, the one he had once known by heart. Lauren looked up as he left the room. "What's the secret? Why are you calling her back?"

"She wants to discuss something personal—medical, I guess. You don't mind, do you?"

"No, of course not." But he could see she was curious.

Charlee picked up on the first ring. "That's what I like, immediate attention!" Then her voice became controlled, and he realized she was frightened. "They've decided there's a shadow in my left lung. I'm going in for bronchoscopy. What does that mean?"

He tried to ignore the alarm that flashed through him. "It's a safe procedure. You'll be sedated and—"

"David, I *know* what a bronchoscope does! What I'm asking is, what are they looking for?"

"If they knew, Charlee, they wouldn't be doing this," he said guardedly. "They have to find out what the shadow is. What has your doctor told you?"

"Just that they have to be sure it isn't a tumor."

There was a squeezing in his chest, a sort of breathless sensation. "How have you been feeling?"

"So-so. It's been pretty unpleasant with George. He's fighting me on the divorce."

"You don't need that aggravation."

"No."

He knew she expected him to say something encouraging, something wise and supportive, but he felt helpless. "What made you go for the X-ray now, all of a sudden?"

"The cough never really went away." As if to underline her words, she coughed briefly, a tight, dry rasp. "Could it be cancer, Davey?"

He closed his eyes. She used to call him that when . . . "I don't know, Charlee," he said gently. "It's always a possibility."

"Oh, God, I feel like the odds are against me. Do you know what I mean? For so many years I was known for my good fortune—although, now that I think about it, I wonder why!" She laughed, that low, delicious laugh, and for a moment he was transported back in time. "I think my luck began to run out the day I was born."

"You mustn't say that—don't even think it!" He felt so damned sorry for her, despite everything. Life had dealt her a rotten hand, certainly from the day she had married Bruce Fields. "Now listen, I'll call your doctor tomorrow morning and find out what's going on."

"Oh *would* you? I'd like that."

"Where is he?"

"At Memorial. His name is Chester Woods. Wait, I'll get his number."

That night, David was unable to sleep. He kept tossing and turning, and was up and dressed before dawn. At the clinic, he waited until eight o'clock before calling Dr. Woods in New York. Not surprisingly, Woods was in his office, even though his nurse and secretary had not yet arrived.

"Charlotte Stearns is my wife's cousin, doctor. I called to discuss her case with you."

At the other end of the connection, the specialist let out a long sigh. "We haven't completed our tests, so we don't have the full report," he said cautiously, "but, I'm afraid she came to me too late."

And when they had concluded their conversation, David knew that Charlee was going to die.

Chapter 41

CHARLOTTE WANTED TO come to the Russell Clinic for her surgery. "I've encountered enough hardboiled, big city nurses to last me a lifetime," she told them. "If I'm going to be sick, I want to hear soft Southern voices."

Ordinarily David would have advised her to stay in New York at Memorial. There was no better hospital in the world for the treatment of cancer, but what would it matter? The Russell was in the forefront of modern medicine, its chief thoracic surgeon was one of the country's best, and having family with her would be a comfort to Charlee. She would need whatever comfort they could give her.

"Oh, Charlee," cried Lauren, "get right on down here and let us take care of you. Do you want me to come up and travel with you?"

"Don't be silly, Lauren. I'm no different than I was yesterday. I can manage just fine."

"But what about Johnny?"

"He'll be at home with Nanny, I guess. I—I haven't thought it through. George has been around a lot lately—seems he was here every time I checked into a hospital. Maybe he'll come stay again."

"Are you *crazy?* You're about to divorce him!"

"I know. The thing is, he's been rather decent since all this illness began."

"Does that mean you're not going through with it?"

"No, it's just that everything's more or less in a state of confusion right now. My attorneys are going ahead with the divorce, but—I just don't know how it will all turn out."

''What she means is, she thinks she's not going to live through this,'' Lauren said to David in dismay.

''She may not, honey,'' he answered softly, and he had to comfort her for a long time while she wept.

''Poor Johnny,'' she said, wiping her eyes. ''Charlee's going to leave him home with George.''

''She shouldn't do that! George doesn't even *like* the child. When we were in Randolph Springs for her mother's funeral, Charlotte told me that John's afraid of him.''

''What can we do? Legally he's still her husband.''

''But they're separated, and he never adopted John.''

''No, but Charlee said he's stayed at the apartment with him when she's gone in for tests.''

''Doesn't it jeopardize the divorce if George moves back into her home?''

''I don't know that much about it, darling—luckily.'' She shrugged. ''If that's the arrangement Charlee wants, what do you care?''

''I'm thinking of the child, Laurie. Charlotte will be sick a long time. There will be weeks, perhaps months of treatment after her surgery. If she's down here, then John should come, too. Can't he stay with us?''

''Well! I'm completely *flabbergasted.* That was what I wanted to suggest, but I was afraid you'd object.''

''Why would I object?'' He seemed genuinely puzzled.

''You know, David, how you've always been about Charlee. I just naturally assumed . . .''

''Laurie, just because Charlotte and I used to get under each other's skin now and then, doesn't mean I'm not fond of her. I'm very concerned about her and I certainly have nothing but affection for that little boy. I can't stand the idea of him being left up there alone for all those weeks with his nurse and a man who—''

''Is only interested in his trust fund.''

''Yes, I think that's the crux of it.''

''Here they come!'' cried Barbara. ''I recognize Cousin Charlee.'' She and Mark jumped up and down on the tarmac at the Raleigh-Durham airport, while Lauren restrained them from running toward the plane.

How can someone appear so beautiful and healthy, yet be as sick as she is, Lauren wondered. Charlotte came down the steps of the airplane holding John's hand. She looked radiant, although a little thin, in a hunter green and lavender tweed suit. They embraced, and Lauren couldn't hold back her tears.

''Don't weep over me yet, Laurie,'' Charlotte said drily. ''I intend to lick this thing.''

''I'm awfully silly,'' said Lauren, choking on the words, ''I'm just so glad to see you.'' She bent over to hug John. ''How are you, darling?''

Charlotte threw her arms around Babs and Mark, who were suddenly tongue-tied, as was John. ''Don't be shy with each other,'' Charlee teased them. ''Johnny couldn't wait to get here to see you two!'' Babs grinned and took John by the hand.

''David apologizes for not coming to the airport. He operates on Mondays.''

''He's forgiven. You both are so *wonderful* to do this, darling.''

''Oh, honey . . . what is family for? We're just happy we can help, even a little bit.'' God, if she didn't stop crying, she'd drive Charlee into a fit of despair!

Glad for an excuse to get away, she rushed off to get the car while the luggage was being unloaded. The three children sat in back, with John between Babs and Mark. Lauren noticed Babs was being very tender with him. Let's hope it keeps up, she thought. Suddenly bringing another child into the house for an extended period of time was not without its hazards.

She should have guessed Amanda would know what to do. Mandy was standing on the side porch waiting for them when they pulled into the driveway. ''Welcome, Mrs. Stearns,'' she exclaimed, helping Charlee out of the car and spontaneously embracing her. ''We're so glad you're here and we're going to get you fixed up good as new in no time at all.''

''I feel better already, Mandy. I've been dreaming of your fried chicken all the way down on the airplane.''

John was staring at Amanda with a shy smile. ''And

you must be Johnny. What a handsome big boy! Why don't you and Mark help me bring all these valises in the house?"

In no time, Amanda had John settled in Mark's room, with drawers and shelves and part of the closet assigned to him for his clothes. It was a new experience for both boys, sharing a room, and Mandy made it a great adventure. They had taken out a carton of Mark's outgrown toys, and Lauren had asked Gretchen to select some of the newer books for young children from the bookshop.

"You'd think he never had any toys before," laughed Charlee, when she saw how excited her son was. "You're terrific, Laurie. You've thought of everything."

After lunch, Lauren said, "I have to run over to the English department for a meeting. We'll have an early dinner this evening, since you can't eat anything after eight o'clock."

Charlotte was reporting to the Russell Clinic first thing the next morning. They would probably admit her immediately and repeat the diagnostics.

"I dread going through all those tests again."

"Maybe they won't be as bad this time," Lauren replied sympathetically. "You look tired, Charlee. Why don't you lie down for a little while?"

"I *am* feeling a little tuckered out," she admitted. "It's so good not having to pretend with you."

How quickly her verve had faded! From the time she had come rushing into Lauren's embrace at the airport until this moment, wearily climbing the stairs, she seemed to have lost all her energy. After driving away from the house, Lauren pulled over on Gimghoul Road for several minutes, until she felt composed enough to face her colleagues at the faculty meeting.

"How did you like Dr. Livermore?" asked David, standing at the foot of the hospital bed.

"An absolute stick, darling. Positively devoid of charm."

"He's a top man, Charlotte. Surgeons are not paid to be charming."

"Does that mean you're not a top surgeon, Davey?" She raised an eyebrow and chuckled. "You still blush, don't you?"

He shook his head, sighing, "Will you never learn to be serious?"

"Lord, I hope not! When my sense of humor fails me, I'm a goner."

He made a moue of regret. "You're right." Then he became professional. "I thought maybe you'd want to ask some questions. Sometimes doctors don't explain enough to their patients."

"He didn't, but then he didn't have to. I keep waiting for my body to develop some subtle new imperfection, some alarming failure of function. It never disappoints me."

David swallowed. "He told you about the scans?"

She nodded. "At least I'll be spared the horror of growing old. I couldn't bear that!"

"You mustn't take a defeatist attitude. You're going to have the latest treatment, and there are some new drugs they're experimenting with—"

"I refuse to be lied to, David, so don't you dare try to con me."

He walked around the bed and took her hand. "Oh, Charlee, I am so sorry. So damned sorry!"

He saw her eyes grow moist and she squeezed his hand. "Thank you. I believe you."

With her face scrubbed of makeup, she looked fragile and girlish in the dimly lit room. Far too young, at thirty-one, to be facing death from an incurable illness. "They're going to give you radiation after the surgery. It will help to contain the—uh—disease."

She smiled wryly. "Why don't you call it what it is, Dave? *Cancer.* I'm not afraid to hear the word."

"Okay," he whispered. The silence in the room was deafening.

"I have something to ask you, David." She cleared her throat, then lifted her chin in a characteristic manner. "I'd like you and Laurie to be Johnny's guardians if—when it happens."

He stared at her without speaking for the longest moment. "That's premature, Charlee."

"I know, but I've always been superstitious. I felt I had to finalize it before I 'went under the knife.' Now that I'm divorcing George, I wouldn't want *him* to have John." She smiled cynically. "Even if I weren't divorcing him. But if you don't want to—"

"Well, of course we want to! You must know how much we love him."

"I put it in my will. It can be changed, of course—I guess I should've asked you first, but time got away from me. The papers weren't quite ready when I left, so they had to send a young man down here from New York. I just signed the damn thing today—talk about *macabre.*" Her smile was wan as she wearily leaned her head back against the pillows. "Steve Burns is my lawyer. You remember him, don't you, from the old crowd during the war?" She looked at him questioningly. "Well, for heavens sakes, Dave, don't act like none of it ever *happened!*"

He couldn't believe what she was saying!" I thought *you* were the one who wanted to pretend it never happened."

"Did I? I hadn't meant to. Anyway, Steve knows everything about my affairs if you have any questions. You have no idea how complicated it is to have money."

"No, I'm afraid I don't, and I probably never will."

"George will get something as a consolation prize. I made you and Laurie trustees along with the bank. Johnny will be well provided for." She gave a cynical laugh. "That is a gross understatement! You're going to have to work hard to keep him from knowing what a rich young man he'll be someday. Rest assured, he won't be a financial burden on you."

His heart was thundering. "*Burden!* Do you suppose I would regard it as a burden?"

"Dave, don't, please . . . I can manage all right if I don't have to deal with too much emotion."

"I just want to *know*, Charlee! I want to hear it once, from your lips."

She shook her head and closed her eyes. "I'm really very tired now. It's strange, I've been sleeping rather well.

I always hated the nights. All my life, even as a child, I was an insomniac. What I liked best about being married, was having someone there with me to share the dark.''

Two days later, at eight o'clock, David was on hand when Charlotte was wheeled into the operating room, where Dr. Livermore and a team of surgeons prepared to remove her left lung. It was a spectacular fall morning. A Charlee day.

Chapter 42

NINETEEN FORTY-EIGHT BEGAN as a dark and hopeless year. The winter was upon them, damp and dreary, when Charlotte decided she would go to New York, against all medical advice. The course of therapy had ended with encouraging results, but in the colder climate with her lowered resistance, her doctors were afraid she would develop pneumonia in her remaining lung.

"I won't stay up North long," Charlee assured Lauren and David. "There are things I must do."

Later they learned she had settled her affairs, arranging for the sale of the farm and her apartment. And then she returned one last time to her home on Shadow Mountain, where she spent an exhausting few days making arrangements for a future she would not be witness to. Only Philip knew she was there, and what she was doing.

John stayed behind in Chapel Hill. Charlotte did not say, but Lauren and David realized she was preparing him for the day when he would live with them permanently.

When they put her on the plane for New York, Lauren whispered to David, "She looks so happy!"

Waving gaily and blowing kisses to the children, she flashed the old, dauntless Charlee smile. "Wait until spring," she told them just that morning, "then Johnny and I will move into Mother's house in Randolph."

But long before springtime, Charlotte was back in the hospital in Oakland Hills with metastatic cancer of the bone. If they had known all along, why did it come as a fresh shock? Hope . . . always hope.

In constant pain now, Charlotte at first refused morphine. "They're not going to make an addict out of me!" she shot back when David or Lauren begged her to accept narcotics. "I might as well give up and die if I'm in a stupor all the time."

Her rapid deterioration was terrifying. They could see her growing weaker each time they walked into her room. One day she asked them to bring John to visit. When they arrived, Johnny clutching Lauren's hand as they silently rode up in the elevator, Charlotte was sitting up in a chair, wearing makeup, her hair neatly combed and tied with a pink ribbon.

"Hello, my darling boy," she called, holding out her arms to him. He ran to her and started to climb into her lap, but when she bit her lower lip, David quickly picked him up and pulled a chair next to hers, sitting John on his lap.

"When are you coming home, Mommy?" the child asked, looking at her with large, saucer eyes.

"Not for a while, love. I have to stay in the hospital until the doctor makes me a little better." She stroked his arm and gazed into his face with such love and longing that Lauren, unable to contain her emotions, had to leave the room.

"Isn't he going to make you *all* better?" John asked, on the verge of tears.

"Probably not," she said softly. "Sometimes things get so broken, they can't be fixed."

It wasn't long before the pain medication that she had taken for the occasion, was wearing off and the effort became too great. "I guess maybe you'd better take him home now," she gasped to Lauren, who had returned. She kissed John good-bye, running her hand through his hair. "You be a very good boy for Laurie and David, darling. They're your make-believe mommy and daddy now."

"I don't want a make-believe mommy," he said in a trembly voice. "I want *you.*"

She laid her cheek against his head and whispered, "Mommy loves you so much, Johnny!" He smiled up at her, his sun-breaking-through-the-clouds smile, then obediently scampered out of the room with Lauren.

The moment they were gone, Charlotte put her face in her hands and broke into wracking sobs. It was all the sorrows of a lifetime, welling up in her heart and spilling over.

Awkwardly David put an arm around her shoulders and she leaned against him. He had never felt so sorry for anyone in all his life. "Don't cry, Charlee."

"Haven't I the right to a few tears?" she wept.

"Oh yes," he said. "Oh yes . . . you have every right."

His pity, like her sorrow, was a bottomless well. What had her life been, after all? Years of unfulfilled promise and dashed expectations, shattered dreams of the joy to which any beautiful young woman is entitled.

David wet a face cloth and brought it to her. Her hands were trembling, and she was completely drained of strength. "Would you call the nurse, please," she whispered.

"Of course. I'll be around for a while if you need me."

David was standing at the station when her nurse came out in the hall, carrying a syringe. "Mrs. Stearns asked to see you again, Dr. Bernard. I gave her another injection, so don't keep her talking too long."

It was dark in the room. Outside, the February afternoon had given way to a storm-threatening dusk. Charlotte seemed to be asleep, but she opened her eyes when he moved.

"Is that you, Dave? Come a little closer. Sit here near me."

He pulled a chair next to the bed.

"I want . . . to tell you something."

"Shhh, don't talk, Charlee. Rest, let the medication take effect."

"I'll have long enough to rest." The words were slurred, but there was a hint of irony. "You . . . you wanted to hear it . . . from my lips."

"Never mind, dear, it's all right."

"No-o-o. You have to know, before I . . ." She drifted off for a moment under the influence of the powerful narcotic, but then her eyelids fluttered open again.

"Go to sleep, Charlee," he whispered.

She gazed at him with pain-limned eyes, and two large tear drops formed, spilling over and slowly trailing down her cheeks. "He's yours, Dave . . . your son."

The shock ran through him like a needle. "Don't!" He stroked her hand, his heart bursting. "I'll love him anyway, no matter whose—"

"But he is! Johnny . . . you're his father."

He was reeling, stunned at her words. He felt unable to breathe. "Please, don't say it, Charlee. Not unless it's true."

"It *is* true, I swear. I knew . . . before you left for overseas. That's why . . . why I wouldn't see you. I was afraid . . ."

"What about Bruce? You told me—"

"Bruce . . . poor Bruce. We never had much of a marriage . . . only for a while in the beginning. I went to be with him in Washington . . . after you were gone. One night . . . he passed out. I told him . . . told him we made love . . . Don't know if he believed me."

David remembered a night in London, Bruce's fear of failing as a father, and his genuine pride in his son. "I think he did. In fact I know it. Bruce was thrilled about the baby." And now David was filled with a strange mixture of elation and panic. "God, Charlee, is it true? Is it really true?"

"Yes," she whispered, reaching out to touch his hand. "Can't you see yourself . . . in him? I can . . ." Her brow wrinkled and she caught her breath with pain. She grasped David's hand tightly. "You mustn't tell Laurie! She would never forgive me. *Promise you won't.*"

His thoughts were so disordered, he could hardly imagine what to say. "I—I'm not certain that's a promise I can keep. I'll try, Charlee, but I might *have* to tell her sometime." His head was spinning. "I swear I'll try not to. Is that good enough?"

Her lips formed a suggestion of a smile. "I guess it will have to be . . . hardly in any . . . position to object."

The morphine grabbed hold and she gave into it, closing her eyes and gradually relaxing in sleep. David watched until her breathing became deep and even. His mind was in turmoil, but at the same time there was a questing place inside where he felt at peace.

With compassion, he looked on the face of the sleeping woman. So. It was settled now between them. He didn't hate her anymore—that was long over. But he didn't love her, either. He felt a deep affection for her. And sorrow. So much sorrow. Charlotte was the mother of his son, and he would grieve for her and honor her memory.

There was a subtle difference that afternoon. Lauren felt it from the first moment, when Charlotte greeted her with a soft, contented smile, reaching out to touch her. She took the hand in hers, and bent to kiss her sunken cheek, fighting her revulsion at the odor of decay that rose from the sick bed. *Charlee* . . . of the embroidered linens and scent of gardenias! She stayed next to the bed, stroking the emaciated hand.

It had been a hectic morning. Lauren had given two review lectures to prepare her students for midterm exams, then hurried to pick up Johnny at nursery school. He had cried when she left him at home with Amanda, saying he wanted to go with her to see his mother. It was going to be harder than they had anticipated, helping him to adjust to Charlee's death.

Charlee's death. She had learned to say it, but she couldn't believe it, couldn't accept that some miracle would not occur. A remission, a cure. A last minute rescue of the heroine from the onrushing train.

"You seem better today, Charlee."

"I had a good night. Only needed one shot." She sighed deeply, almost pleasurably. "I'd like to talk to you now, Laurie, while my mind is fairly clear."

"All right, dear, but you mustn't tire yourself."

"There are so many things I want to say . . . If you only knew what you've meant to me, Laurie. All my life I've been able to count on you."

"We've counted on each other, Charlee," she murmured, stroking her forehead.

"You've always been there for me. And now I want to ask, will you be there for Johnny?"

"You know I will. I'll always love him as if he were my own child." Thank heavens, she was able to hold back her tears.

"Will you make me a promise?"

"Of course, dear. What is it?"

"When all this is over and things have settled down, I want you to go back to Shadow Mountain. I've left various items there—everything's in my old room—and it's very important to me that *you* be the one to look through them and preserve whatever you think is worth keeping. I tried to do it myself, but I just wasn't up to it."

Lauren started to speak, but Charlotte stopped her with an importunate gesture.

"Phil's one of my executors, and I would ask him, but I have a horror of anyone going through my personal things—anyone except you. Isn't it strange, Laurie—all our lives, I was always afraid to show you my weaknesses, but now you're the one person I can count on."

"Charlee, darling . . ."

"Don't go crying on me, honey. That won't help. There's a great pile of junk there. You're absolutely going to hate me when you see it! I would have destroyed it all, but some of it might be valuable . . . There are things, Laurie—things that no one should ever see. I kept *looking*, but my strength gave out. I just know there must be *something!* You're the only one I can count on, Laurie. The only one who would understand. So remember—only you, Laurie, no one else. Will you do that for me?"

"Oh, Charlee . . ." Her eyes were flooded with tears. "I can't even think of having to! Let's hope it won't be necessary."

Charlotte gave one of her old valiant Charlee chuckles, a poor replica, yet recognizable. "You make me see I can still laugh. My dear, darling Laurie . . . I no longer have time to pretend. This is something that means a lot to me, so please say you'll go, Laurie. Promise me . . . *promise!*"

"I promise," whispered Lauren, her voice choked with tears.

* * *

Now Charlotte was fully occupied with the task of dying. Lauren sat for hours at a time in the hospital room, saying little, pretending to read or correct papers, surreptitiously watching the rise and fall of Charlee's chest as her remaining lung labored for air.

Periodically, the nurse hovered around, checking vital signs and adjusting IVs. Hooked up to tubes and catheters and oxygen, Charlee was half her former size. Because the pain was excruciating, she was usually heavily sedated, now and again emerging to murmur a few words, or simply to smile.

"She's become so *sweet,*" Lauren sadly told David. "I long to hear her say something nasty."

"They say a person's true nature emerges under stress," he answered. "Perhaps all that caustic bite was a cover-up."

Lauren appreciated David's endless patience during these long, torturous months. She was neglecting her family, but he never complained, and in fact, he was filling the gap of her absence with the children. With John, as well as Barbara and Mark.

"You're my tower of strength," she told him after a particularly draining day. "I could never endure this without you. I know you're going through a bad time with the hospital board, and I'm sorry I haven't been there for you."

"Don't apologize. You're where you have to be, where you belong," he answered.

And Lauren swore to herself she would make it up to him. Soon.

Charlotte was moaning. She tossed her head, mumbling unintelligible words.

Lauren moved to her bedside. "Do you want something, Charlee? What is it, darling? Are you in pain?"

"Sorry, so sorry . . . cause trouble. Selfish . . . heartless."

Sorry? What had she to be sorry for, except losing her life? "Don't say that. You're no trouble for anyone."

"You, Laurie . . . I envied you so. What I always wanted . . . to be loved the way you were."

"That's not true! It was *you* everyone loved and wanted to be like. You were my *idol,* Charlee."

"Ah, no . . . if you only knew. I was jealous . . . always wanted whatever you had. Please, please . . . forgive me, Laurie. What I did . . . the closest I could come to being you." Tears were streaming down Charlee's face.

"Sssh, darling, don't cry."

"Have to—have to explain—before it's too late. When I knew Bruce—Nicky always there—no time for us to—to . . . Children . . . Wanted . . . wanted so . . . desperately . . ." She strained to sit up, but fell back sobbing, her tears choking her. "Why didn't I—Bruce would never agree to—what else could I *do,* Laurie?"

"*Charlee!* Charlee, please stop talking. You're just getting yourself worked up over nothing. Whatever it is, it's long over and you mustn't let it upset you now."

But Charlotte clutched her arm with a clawlike hand. "Can you forgive me . . . *ever?*"

"There's nothing to forgive, honey."

"Oh, yes there is! For Johnny's sake. Please . . . *tell me you forgive me!*" With a wrenching effort she lifted herself, reaching toward Lauren. Suddenly she screamed with pain, clutching her shoulder in agony.

"Charlee, what is it?" Lauren cried in alarm.

But Charlotte was unable to answer, gasping for breath, rocking in torment and screaming, "*Oh God—oh please, do something—do something!*"

Terrified, Lauren ran down the hall, yelling for a doctor, oblivious to the other patients and visitors. Charlotte's private nurse, who usually sat outside when Lauren was in the room, hurried in to see what had happened. A resident arrived, followed shortly by the internist, Gerald Kramer. Lauren put in a call to David, but he was in surgery. She lingered outside the door, hearing Charlee's tortured moans and fighting back panic.

"I'm afraid she's had a spontaneous fracture of the clavicle, just from the stress of changing positions," Dr. Kramer told her. Oh, the horror of this dreadful disease!

They gave her a stronger dose of pain medication and applied a padded splint, but the ordeal was not ended until late at night. David arrived in a scrub suit, having come straight down when he finished operating. They stayed until midnight, when at last, Charlotte seemed to be resting more easily.

Lauren leaned over to kiss her good night. Charlotte was barely conscious from the medication, but she smiled. "I haven't . . . had much luck, have I?" she whispered.

That was the last time Lauren saw Charlee alive.

They buried her in Randolph Springs on a green and peaceful knoll. To the west, you could just see the outline of Shadow Mountain. It was March, and there was still snow in the Smokies, but next to Charlotte's grave, a single dogwood was beginning to bud.

Chapter 43

"WHERE'S MOMMY?"

"Mommy's gone away, Johnny. She was very sick and she had to—she had to go to heaven, with God."

Heaven made it easier to explain.

"But, I want to see her! When is she coming home?"

Lauren took him in her arms, wiping his tears. "She can't come home, darling. God wants her to stay with Him, but she'll always love you, and you'll always love her."

"I want my mommy . . ." He sat in her lap, sobbing as if his heart would break.

They let him sleep with them those first few nights, and it was mostly to David that he clung, creeping into his arms, and falling asleep against his chest. What a wonderfully comforting and patient man he was, thought Lauren, the way he held the little boy, stroking his head and telling him everything was going to be all right because he would always live with Cousin Laurie and Cousin David, who would be his mommy and daddy now.

John had not understood the finality of the funeral in Randolph Springs. Bewildered by all the relatives and strangers who dissolved in tears when they saw him, he had become truly upset only once. Lauren had been seated in the front of the chapel with Johnny on her lap, when she was appalled to see George Stearns walk down the aisle and take a seat across from them in the second row. When David, who had been assisting some of the elderly aunts, joined her, she whispered, "How can George have the nerve to come here?"

"It's pretty insensitive," David agreed, glancing over at Stearns. "Maybe he thinks he has an obligation to attend."

"I can't imagine why. I can't bear to look at him, knowing he made Charlee unhappy."

After the burial at the cemetery, Stearns came over to them. "Lauren . . . David," he nodded gravely, shaking hands. "A terribly sad day."

Then he glanced down at John, who shrank against Lauren's skirts. "Well, Johnny, aren't you going to say hello to Daddy?"

A look of fear and loathing came into John's eyes. "No! You're not my daddy!"

David had picked him up then and John cried against his shoulder. "You've upset the boy, George. I think it would be better if you leave now."

But George had actually gone back to the house, where the mourners gathered for a buffet luncheon, prepared by Lady, Bertram, and Pansy, who had been caring for the property in anticipation of Charlotte's return. He hadn't stayed long, but he behaved as if he were still Charlotte's husband, pacing around the rooms with a proprietary air and accepting condolences from people who did not know he had been separated from Charlotte.

"We'll no doubt be in touch about the arrangements," he remarked to David, as the taxi arrived to take him to the airport.

"Now what do you suppose he meant by that?" demanded Lauren.

"Damned if I know. George may not be aware of it, but he'll have absolutely no contact with us in the future."

As the weeks passed, Lauren was ever more grateful to David for the time he devoted to John. He read to him and played games in the evening, got up with him at night when he cried, took him for walks and pony rides on the weekend. It was dear to see the little boy holding the big man's hand, skipping along beside him. The child grew increasingly better adjusted and when he lapsed into occasional periods of melancholy, David could always bring him out of them.

If the other children resented the attention paid to John, they were sufficiently ashamed to conceal it. This young cousin personified their worst fears of being orphaned, and they brooded about it, especially Babs. "Where would we live if you and Daddy died?" she asked.

"Daddy and I are in perfect health, and we plan to stay that way, so don't you even think about us getting sick or dying," Lauren answered. But still, she knew they worried.

Only when the children were not around could Lauren give vent to her own sorrow. One breezy April afternoon at the peak of the azaleas and dogwoods, she walked under a canopy of greenery broken by showers of sunlight from a crystal blue sky. It was a *Charlee day,* when it felt good to be alive! She had an irresistible urge to pick up a telephone and call her cousin. There came the realization that it was exactly one month since Charlotte had died . . . and she would never hear her voice again.

And then a certified letter arrived on a Saturday morning when Lauren was at the library. David had come home early from work, planning to take all three children to a baseball game. He was in the study when she came rushing in. "Sorry to be late. It took longer than I expected. Lunch is all ready—" She stopped, seeing how stricken he looked. "Darling, what's wrong?"

In his hand, he held a sheaf of papers, some sort of legal correspondence. "The *bastard!* That slimy, stinking, rotten, lowdown, conniving scum—"

"David! What on earth are you talking about?"

"George Stearns." He struggled for words, then thrust the pages into her hands. "Here, read it."

It was a long and wordy document, typed on the impressive letterhead stationery of a well-known New York law firm, and there was a summons enclosed. She could not digest it, except to grasp that amongst a profusion of *whereases* and *parties-of-the-first-parts* and *aforesaids,* George was contesting John's trustees and guardians, and the estate of the late Charlotte Lee Mortimer Fields Stearns.

"What exactly does it mean?" she asked, with a sinking heart.

"It means," he struggled to control himself, "it means that George is petitioning the court to remove us as John's guardians."

"No! How can he *do* that?"

"By claiming that he's still Charlotte's legal husband and John's guardian—that the will she wrote before she died is not binding, since it was signed under duress." Lauren had never seen David so furious. "George is accusing us of bringing undue influence on her."

"He *knows* that's not true! Charlee rewrote her will in New York right after Aunt Reba died. She had already filed for divorce. There was a long delay in preparing the will, and then she got sick."

"I know, and you know, but . . ." He sighed in exasperation. "Unfortunately, Charlotte died before their divorce became final. I suspected George was up to something that time he moved back into the apartment."

"All George cares about is the *money!* Charlee knew that." Lauren burst into tears, pressing her face against his chest. "David—oh, God, we must do something to stop him."

He was in a cold fury, as his arms tightened around her. "You bet we're going to stop him!"

"George was always fond of me," Lauren said hesitantly. "Maybe—maybe if I spoke to him, he would listen to reason."

David thought about it for a minute and shook his head. "No, sweetheart. I think it's better if we let the lawyers handle this. After seeing him in Randolph Springs, I believe it could get rather nasty."

David placed a call to Charlotte's lawyer, Steve Burns, at his home in Scarsdale. A copy of the letter had already been sent to Steve at Fields, Fields & Burns.

"Stearns always was unscrupulous, David," he immediately responded. "Malcolm Fields had his number."

"What's your opinion of this, Steve?"

''His claim is outlandish, but it's more than a nuisance suit. The will is perfectly valid—however, wills can be broken. Since their divorce wasn't final when Charlotte passed away, the court will probably rule that George is entitled to a share of her estate. I wouldn't be too worried about that, though. So much of it can be touched because it's in trust.''

''That is not my worry!'' said David impatiently. ''What about her son's guardianship?''

''Naturally, our first concern is for the child. My guess is George's lawyers will try to get the court to appoint a guardian *ad litum* until the case is settled. The boy could temporarily be taken away and made a ward of the court.''

''That's unacceptable! We promised John he would live with us always. He believes in us. He's just coming out of his depression. This would absolutely destroy him, leave psychological wounds for life.''

''I'll try to get a stay before they take action, and move to have you appointed interim guardians.''

''But that's a temporary measure,'' protested David.

''Right. The real threat is, they might succeed in having the will thrown out because of a technicality.'' At that, Burns adopted a defensive tone. ''I warned Charlotte not to leave New York before signing. Her will should have been properly notarized and witnessed in our offices.''

David wasn't going to let him get away with that. ''If you people hadn't dragged your feet, the will would have been ready in ample time for her to sign there! She told me you sat on it for months.''

Steel crept into Burns's voice, and David remembered he hadn't much liked the man on the few occasions when they'd met. ''A complicated document like Charlotte's will cannot be prepared overnight. Her mother's estate, which affected us, hadn't even been settled at the time.'' And then he softened. ''We did the best we could, David. I had an associate and two secretaries working overtime.''

Somewhat mollified, David realized he had better learn to like Burns, or at least have confidence in him. He was, as they said in New York, the only game in town. ''Charlotte's health was the first priority, Steve. If she hadn't delayed getting medical attention for so long a time, she might still be with us."

"Yes, of course, David. I'm not implying she's to blame for this."

"Were you suggesting before that her will wasn't properly witnessed and notarized?"

"Not at all. But if they're looking for technicalities, they'll jump on anything irregular. Signing in a hospital a few days before undergoing cancer surgery—I'd just feel more comfortable if it had been done up here."

"We want to adopt John," said David suddenly, looking over at Lauren who grinned, despite her anxiety. She had been waiting for the right moment to discuss adoption with him.

"You can't begin that process until this matter is settled," Burns replied. "The burden is on them to prove the will is not legitimate. Charlotte's previous will was written immediately after her second marriage, when the glow was still on them. Against my advice, I must tell you, she appointed George as John's guardian, and a co-trustee. George stands to gain control of a considerable amount of money, as well as a sizable personal bequest, if the new will is thrown out—not to mention complete governance of John's person."

"We don't give a damn about the money. All we want is custody," David asserted. "George Stearns doesn't care a fig for the child, and in fact, John is afraid of him."

"I'll start working on this right away, David. I can talk to the other attorney, see if they won't consider a settlement. I'll also get in touch with Bruce's mother and sister. I'm sure they'll want the boy to remain with you and your wife. The courts take those things into consideration, and they always favor blood relatives. You'll hear from me in a few days."

After the conversation with the lawyer, they were too agitated to each lunch, but they went to the baseball game in order not to disappoint the children. Johnny looked so happy, mimicking everything Mark did, jumping up and down and cheering when the Chapel Hill team scored. As Lauren watched the delight on his face, she was filled with a tender love for him. It was more, much more, than just having promised his mother she would take care of him. She *adored* this little boy and knew she could not give him up. It would truly break her heart. Surely fate wouldn't be that cruel to them.

Now the threat of a court order to surrender John was constantly with them. Not wanting to rely solely on Steve Burns, they called Stanley Eisen who handled their legal affairs. He referred them to a man in Raleigh renowned for family law, but the lawyer confirmed that no judge would grant an adoption decree with the matter of prior guardianship unresolved.

"Since Mrs. Bernard is a blood relative," the attorney advised, nodding in Lauren's direction, "it's likely that your cousin's son will eventually be given into her custody. Especially if his paternal grandmother agrees. A judge would always rule in favor of a blood relationship."

Lauren was moved to tears one night to hear Johnny ask after a bedtime story. "Will I live happily ever after with you?"

"Absolutely!" David responded, giving him a fierce hug.

Soon it would be John's fourth birthday. They were determined to make it a happy celebration; but what if he was gone by then?

After she had kissed the children good night, Lauren found David sitting alone in the study. "I feel so helpless," she told him. "I *swore* to Charlee just a few days before she died that we'd always take care of Johnny. How can George be so cruel? Doesn't he have any compassion, any respect for her memory or her wishes?"

"It appears he has more feeling for her money," he answered bitterly.

"Oh David, there must be *something* we can do! I can't just sit here and wait any longer. Don't you know anyone with influence? Maybe we can appeal to our congressman—or—or, the governor!"

David's brow was furrowed with concern. "You're making yourself sick over this, Laurie."

"I'm just so afraid we're going to lose him. I don't know what I'll do if they take him away from us, David. I love him just as if he were my own son!"

She did not see the torment in David's eyes as he took her in his arms. "It might be a long haul, darling, but I'm sure we'll win in the end. Remember what that lawyer told us—they always favor blood relatives."

Lauren hung onto his words like a talisman, remembering them in the still hours of the night when she was unable to sleep.

Chapter 44

LAUREN PICKED UP John's teddy bear from the floor and tucked it under the covers with the sleeping child. She bent to kiss him, thinking that she had come to regard him as one of her own children. She found herself becoming obsessed with the need to bring him up in the bosom of her family.

The fear of Charlee's son being torn from them was never far from her mind. She tried to keep busy in order not to dwell on it, for she thought of nothing else when she wasn't occupied. It helped to know that David felt as strongly as she did about keeping Johnny with them. Not every husband would.

Poor David, he had so many worries these days. Not only the lawsuit with George Stearns, but his struggle with the Strickland Hospital board, which would be meeting in a few weeks to hand down a decision on his proposals for admitting black patients to the Russell-Strickland complex. He knew better than to expect them to agree to everything, but he was hoping they would come back with a reasonable compromise.

For a surgeon at the threshold of his career to risk alienating his hospital's trustees was a rash move. Lauren knew he had incurred the wrath of many powerful people who had heard about the petition. For a while there, she had some doubts herself—especially when a delegation of Jewish men from Oakland Hills, fearing a wave of anti-Semitism, had asked him to cease his efforts on behalf of blacks. She admired David's principles and fully supported him in what he was doing, but she couldn't help worrying about possible repercussions.

Those anonymous phone calls were not contributing to their peace of mind either. And the letters! Calling David a "nigger-loving Jew bastard," and threatening to "get" his family. It was unnerving; but thank goodness, it would soon be over.

She found David in the study, sitting on the couch looking utterly dejected. A chill of apprehension went through her. "Oh, darling, bad news from the board?"

"No, no, it's not that. It's just . . ." He closed his eyes, shaking his head in despair. "Laurie, I—I must talk to you." He drew her down next to him and stared at her with the most fearful expression. "Laurie . . . darling, do you believe that I love you with all my heart?"

She smiled, caressing his cheek. "Of course I do, David."

"Nothing could ever destroy my love for you, Lauren. No matter what you did, I would still love you."

"I know that, dear. Just as I would love you."

His eyes lit. "Well then, if I—Laurie, there's something—"

"Yes, go on."

But then David shook his head and sighed. "It's nothing. I'm very tired, that's all."

She thought he looked especially drawn tonight, with dark circles under his eyes. "Come to bed now, honey. Soon everything will be settled and then we'll take a vacation with the children, maybe at the beach. They'd love that."

After the lights were out, Lauren was unable to fall asleep. David had behaved so peculiarly, it was worrisome. A coldness ran down her spine as she remembered his haggard appearance. Was David ill? She couldn't possibly bear it if something was wrong with him! Lying in bed, she listened to his steady breathing and tried to calm the rapid beating of her heart. He *was* under enormous pressure these days, it was true. That must be the answer. But in his profession, there was always tension . . . No, it had to be something else.

Lauren recalled how all during the months when Charlee was dying, she had felt guilty for neglecting her husband. And now she was allowing the threat of John being taken from them to preoccupy her. David should be her first priority! It wasn't fair to him. From this moment on, she promised herself she would pay more attention to his needs.

Again and again, Lauren turned restlessly, and did not close her eyes until the sky was lightening in the east.

"Mine used to be the only May birthday," Babs remarked as she watched Amanda icing the cake for John.

Lauren met Amanda's questioning glance. After a consultation, they had headed off a potential conflict by scheduling John's party two weeks before Barbara's. Not that her daughter appeared jealous of Johnny, but they were all new at this three-child family arrangement, and it showed up in strange ways. Or was she just looking for signs of a problem?

John was so excited, you'd think he had never had a birthday before. All the children in his nursery school class were invited, and by three o'clock on Saturday afternoon, when David arrived home from the hospital, the house was jumping with four-year-olds.

"I'll do snapshots and games, Laurie," David volunteered, and for the next two-and-a-half hours, he kept the party going at a lively pace.

When the last little guest had departed, Amanda called the children for an early supper. "Not that they'll eat anything, after all that ice cream and cake," she chuckled, with her usual good humor.

"Thank you, for helping, David," Lauren said gratefully. "Children's parties have never been my finest hour. I like planning them—but I like it even more when they're over."

"It was fun. John really got a bang out of everything, didn't he?"

"It's about time he had some joy in his life, poor darling."

They could hear John's excited chatter from the

kitchen. "Listen to him, talking a mile a minute in there," laughed David, as they went upstairs to dress for the evening.

Lauren kept glancing at her husband as he shaved, relieved that he seemed more relaxed over the past few days. Perhaps her fears about his health had been unfounded. David might have had a down moment last week. Everyone was entitled to moods now and then.

Amanda was sleeping over that night because they were going to a dinner party in Durham. "We'll be home late, Mandy. You have the number if you need to reach us."

When they returned to the house after midnight, there was a note from Amanda on the front hall table: "A special delivery letter came. I put it in Dr. Bernard's study."

Lauren smiled at Amanda's insistence that the new addition to the house was David's, when it was Lauren who really used it as a study, especially now that they had given the extra bedroom to John. "You go see what it is, David. I'll look in on the children."

By the time Lauren was ready for bed, David had not come upstairs. She slipped on a dressing gown and went down to the study. He was seated at the desk facing away from her, with his head in his hands. An open letter lay in front of him.

His long back had a wounded look and when he looked up, she saw misery in his eyes. "What is it, David?"

"From Steve Burns." He picked up the letter and in a voice like old leaves, began to read: "The judge now feels that it would be in the best interests of the child to live with his closest blood relative. In that case, he will most likely decide to award custody to Blanche Fields Taylor, since she is the sister of John's father. The Taylors have indicated their readiness to assume the responsibility. I'm not recommending that we give up your claim to guardianship, but this should allay your misgivings about the possibility of George Stearns serving as John's guardian."

Involuntarily Lauren put her hand to her heart, thinking foolishly that it was a theatrical gesture. "Well—that's kind of a surprise, isn't it? I mean, Blanche. She has never before been mentioned as a possible guardian. I suppose it would be the natural thing in the judge's eyes, since she was his father's sister . . ." She was struggling to hold back her tears. "I truly can understand his point of view, David. And yet . . . it . . . it wasn't Charlee's wish, was it?"

"It isn't at all what Charlee had in mind," he said softly, putting his arms around her.

Lauren took his handkerchief to wipe her eyes. "I didn't realize Blanche even wanted Johnny. Why do you think this has come up all of a sudden?"

David scanned the letter. "It's a concession. According to Steve, George's lawyer is now willing to discuss terms, but he still refuses to agree to anything in the contested will for fear it would weaken their case."

She felt an intense, choking pain in the back of her throat. "Is it settled, then?"

"No, not at all. Not for weeks. Steve just wanted us to be prepared to . . . to surrender John."

To surrender John. With those words came the realization that Charlee's son was going to be taken from her. Very soon, in a matter of weeks, she would have to hand John over to Blanche and Jules Taylor! All of her senses seemed to have gone numb.

She reached behind and slowly sank into a chair. *"No!"* she cried. "They're *wrong* for him! Really, David, it's not just because *I* want him, but they're the coldest, most self-centered people. I can't imagine them giving Johnny the kind of love and devotion he needs. They'd just park him with a nanny, the way—"

He smiled sadly. "The way Charlotte did?"

"Oh, but Charlee did love him, and she was a good mother!"

"Maybe Blanche is a good mother, too, Laurie. Let's not be unfair to her. It might not be so bad for John." There was little conviction in his voice. Again he referred to the letter. "Steve says the Taylors have two little girls of their own and are anxious for a son."

"But Johnny would have to live in California! How often would we get to see him?" And then she remembered her resolution not to let her concern about John take precedence over David. "Oh, I don't know what I'm saying, I'm just upset. I suppose as long as Johnny isn't given to George Stearns, I ought to be relieved that he'll be living with Bruce's sister. You're right, David—they would give him a good home. And Blanche idolized her brother, so she would certainly love Bruce's son . . ." She knew she was rattling on in order to convince herself.

"Bruce's son!" he said bitterly. "Bruce never set eyes on that boy. He was Charlotte's son, and she wanted him to live with us."

At David's vehemence, Lauren's control melted away. "He's so happy here with us, and with Babs and Mark." She began to cry, leaning her head against his shoulder. "Oh David, isn't there *something* we can do? We mean more to him than Blanche—even if I'm not his closest blood relative!"

David's anguish at the prospect of losing John was compounded a thousandfold by Lauren's unhappiness. After the months of tension and worry she had endured throughout Charlotte's long illness, he could see the strain of waiting was telling on her. What wouldn't he do to ease her pain! He felt such tender concern for her. And guilt. So much guilt. It preyed on his conscience. He thought it had long been put to rest, but now it was there with him, a constant, terrible, suffocating reminder.

He longed to unburden himself, and yet when he had tried to tell her, he found it impossible to utter the words. If it came to a choice between Laurie or John, as painful as it might be to give up the little boy, he would. And yet, for Lauren's sake, he had to find another solution, for she no more could bear to be parted from his son than he could.

His closest blood relative.

The words haunted David. He believed he had one last option that would enable him to solve this dilemma. There was a way he could protect this child he had grown to love, while at the same time give Lauren her wish and make John theirs forever. By going to the judge and revealing that he was John's father, he had no doubt he would be granted custody.

David met Stanley Eisen at a quiet restaurant halfway between Greensboro and Durham.

Over drinks, they exchanged pleasantries, until David at last said, "I need some legal information, Stan. It's a rather delicate matter. May I speak freely?"

"Attorney-client privilege, David. I assure you it will go no further."

"How does one go about establishing paternity of a child?"

"I should think you'd know that better than I. Are there any medical tests?"

"Nothing conclusive. Blood type can often rule it out, but there's no scientific way to prove a man fathered a particular child. I was hoping there was a legal means—that is, if this man were to swear before a judge that he was the father, would that suffice?"

"This isn't my area of the law, but offhand, I'd say a judge would require hard evidence." Stanley cocked an eyebrow. "It's a bit unusual, isn't it? Ordinarily, in a paternity suit, it's just the opposite; the man trying to prove he's *not* the father."

There was no joy in David's smile. "This is not a paternity suit. In this case, the man wishes to prove he *is* the father."

"Where's the mother?" Stanley asked. "She would have to corroborate it, I would think."

"The mother is dead."

"I see." He fiddled with a swizzle stick. "Were the parents ever married?"

"Not to each other."

Stanley seemed to be considering his next question.

"What is the reason for the father wishing to be recognized, after the fact?"

Another silence. "He wants to gain custody of the child."

Stanley stared at David. Then, astonishingly he said, "David . . . are we talking about Charlotte Mortimer's son?"

For a moment David rested his forehead on his folded hands. Then he raised his head and looked directly into Stanley's eyes. "We are." He was rather glad Stan had guessed. It shouldn't have surprised him, considering that his friend was aware of the circumstances of Charlotte's will. "Are you shocked?"

"Nothing shocks me," Stanley replied, which David realized was not an answer at all. "In the practice of law, we see every variation of human behavior—and we learn not to judge. Just as I imagine you do in medicine."

"Ah, Stan . . ." He looked down at his hands, as if he could find some reassurance there.

"Do you want to tell me about it?"

"God, yes." He had to talk to someone, and he knew he could trust Stanley, who had always been a faithful friend.

"It happened during the war. One of those crazy, inexplicable affairs. Short, wild—and a dreadful mistake. I have no excuse, none whatsoever. Except that it was a difficult time for Laurie and me." He turned away. "The child was something I never expected."

"May I ask how you know he's yours? He doesn't particularly look like you. At least not to me, the few times I've seen him. But then, neither does Mark."

"Charlotte told me before she died."

"And you believed her, absolutely?"

"Yes, I believed her. She and her first husband were not living together. I have no doubt that John is mine."

"As your lawyer, I hope you'll forgive me for asking about other men."

"There were no other men," he answered firmly. "Certainly not at the critical time."

After a moment's hesitation, Stanley said, ''Laurie doesn't know, I presume.''

David shook his head. ''No! she hasn't the slightest suspicion. I've wanted to explain, and yet I'm afraid— Well, I just can't predict what the consequences would be. But she's so distraught over the possibility of losing John . . .''

He brought Stanley up to date on George Stearns, the contested will, and the judge's inclination to name Blanche as the permanent guardian. ''We can't let John go, Stan! I wish there were a way I could get custody of him without hurting Laurie. My intentions are to go to the judge and explain the circumstances—''

Stanley held up his hand. ''Wait a minute. That would not be advisable at this point.''

''Why not?''

''This is going to be hard for you to accept, David. In the eyes of the law, John is considered the son of his mother's legal husband at the time of his birth. The putative father is not recognized and has no rights— just as John would have no entitlement to a share in your estate.''

David gripped his glass. ''That's absurd! I'm his only living parent, Stanley,'' he protested. ''Surely a judge would take that into consideration.''

''We live in a conservative society, David. As long as there are other relatives who want him, the chances are that a judge would rule against you.''

''Even though it was the mother's wish?''

''If Charlotte's final will is upheld, there will be no problem. But if it's thrown out, then Stearns would be the guardian.''

''He's bad for the child! You should see how disturbed John becomes in his presence.''

''Nevertheless, if he is the appointed guardian, you would have to prove him unfit. Now, a stepfather can't be forced to serve, and from what you tell me, it doesn't sound as if he really wants to—''

''I'm sure of it. What he's after is the money, not the boy.''

"The laws on custody are inexact and highly interpretive. Guardianship of a person is largely at the discretion of the court," Stanley said, taking a lawyerly attitude. "If he's willing to give the child over to the custody of another person, then it becomes the court's duty to determine what's in the child's best interest, the legal father's sister or the deceased mother's cousin—that is, Lauren."

"I told you, we've already heard that the judge prefers to give John to his closest living relative," said David. "But that's *me!* Regardless of the legal circumstances, I am his father. Couldn't I take it before the judge in confidence? Especially if, as you say, it's discretionary."

"You could. But you'd be throwing yourself on the mercy of the court." Stanley looked skeptical. "It might get messy. You'd have to offer proof—witnesses, affidavits, going back through Charlotte's life, obtaining records of her first husband's blood type and activities, such as other women."

"I thought records could be sealed," David interrupted.

"It would still mean a trial, David. Not necessarily public; but even *in camera,* the details may slip out. Anyone who testified that he saw you and Charlotte together might later talk. There would be speculation. Are you prepared to put Lauren and your family through all that? Dragging your good name through the mud? It would hardly be in the boy's best interest, to say nothing of Babs and Mark."

David's spirits sank as he realized there was going to be no such thing as an easy solution for him. "What in hell am I going to do?"

"They may yet settle. If Stearns and Charlotte were not divorced, he's entitled to a share of her estate. Unless he's consumed with greed, he can take that share without breaking the will—in which case, you and Lauren would remain the guardians."

David's eyes were bleak. "I've never lied to Laurie about anything else, Stanley. Only this."

* * *

Lauren finished cleaning out her desk in the English office after grading final papers, relieved that the academic year had come to an end. If she had made it through this dark period in her life, she was convinced she would be able to handle anything.

Life was so tenuous. When she remembered her high hopes last fall, it seemed impossible that the year would hold Charlee's death, or that John would now be theirs; for despite what they had heard about the judge favoring Blanche as his guardian, she still found it impossible to accept that they would have to give him up.

David was sitting in the deep armchair in the study when she reached home. "Hello, my darling!" She leaned down and wrapped her arms around him.

"I've been waiting for you," he said, gently disengaging himself. He led her to the sofa. "Come sit with me, Laurie. I have something to say to you."

Afterward, she remembered thinking he sounded severe, and she made a quick mental assessment. Had she forgotten the insurance bill, or the mortgage payment? Had she failed to balance the checkbook properly, so that they were overdrawn?

If only it had been that!

He began hesitantly. "Every time I look at John . . ." he began, "He's more than you know to me, Laurie."

"Darling, you don't have to convince me of that. You've been so wonderful with him. No one could be a better guardian, not even his own father."

For a long moment, David stared at her without speaking. "I am his father," he said quietly, letting out a long, shaky breath.

A rush of love went through her, of gratitude for his generosity. "Johnny feels that way, too. Why, he's almost forgotten we're not his real parents, calling us Mommy and Daddy half the time!"

David's skin had turned ashen. "Laurie, listen to me. What I'm trying to tell you is—I *am* his real father."

And still his words made no sense, for she was so concerned about his appearance. She had never seen David like this. He was breathing hard, and she realized he was trying not to weep.

"David, darling, get hold of yourself . . ."

"I'm trying to," he gasped, and she almost wept for him. "In all my life, I've never had to say anything as difficult as this."

She stroked his arm soothingly. "You're overwrought, honey."

He grasped her by the shoulders. "I love you, Laurie. Oh God, I love you so!" As he clasped her against his body, she could feel him tremble, and she knew something terrible was happening to them. "I don't want to hurt you! Please try to understand," he begged.

Alarmed by his agitation, she wondered if she shouldn't call someone. Kneeling in front of him, she thought she had to reason with him, the way she had with her mother when she had first become ill. "Of course, dear. I do want to understand—"

She gazed at him with frightened eyes. He was David, strong and handsome, and she loved him so. He seized her hands. "Laurie, my love—don't you realize what I'm telling you?"

A sudden terror went through her and she closed her eyes. All she could think was she didn't want him to say it, didn't want to know, for it was something evil, something she had always feared in the deepest recesses of her consciousness. "Don't," she pleaded. "Don't do this!"

At that moment, she had a sudden overwhelming desire to get up, to leave the study, before they went any further. It was her favorite place in the house, this room that they had designed together. They had planned every detail of its fieldstone chimney wall and raised hearth, the natural oak beamed ceiling and paneling, the shelves and cabinets filled with all their books and records. On the first wintery evening after its completion, they had made love on the rug in front of a leaping fire, with the flames casting orange and gold reflections on their bodies, and she had thought it the most romantic and glorious experience she had ever known.

Nothing—*nothing!* must be permitted to intrude into this safe haven where they had been happy and loved each other.

"Didn't you hear me?" David was gently repeating. "John is my son."

"No!" She shook her head in denial. "You don't know what you're saying—"

"Laurie, darling, I would do anything not to hurt you this way, but you have to know. I can't keep it from you any longer. I . . . am . . . his real father."

She sat back on her heels staring at him. In the silence, she was conscious of the erratic beating of her heart, the trembling in her limbs.

"You're serious, aren't you?" she whispered, incredulous.

He nodded and she was swept with a wave of dizziness. *It couldn't be true, it couldn't!* Such things happened to other people, not them! The room seemed to tip and grow dim. David reached for her, but she shrank away from him, unable to catch her breath. She heard someone crying out from a distance, and realized it was her own voice.

"You! You and Charlee?"

"Quiet, Laurie! Calm yourself . . ." He had hold of her arms.

"Don't touch me!" She shook him off, hating him. She wanted to scream, she wanted to beat at him, tear at his hair and eyes, rip the clothes from his body. Clenching her hands until the nails dug into her palms, she fought to maintain her composure. "You—you—*How?"*

He threw up his hands helplessly. "It happened. It just happened."

"Nothing like that just happens! You have to *will* it."

"I didn't want it to, I swear. I tried to prevent it."

Lauren drew herself up disdainfully. "She seduced you!"

"No, not exactly."

"Did you love her?" David closed his eyes. "Well, *did you?"*

He sighed. "I thought so at the time. For a very short

time. But I was wrong, dreadfully wrong. Oh, Lauren, I have no excuse, except that I was lonely and felt unloved."

"Unloved?" How could he have believed that, for even a second? She had always adored him, practically worshipped him! Her mind cleared, and she remembered. "When you were stationed in New York and I wouldn't move up there. That's when it was. So you're implying it was *my* fault!"

He shook his head, looking down at his clasped hands. "No, the fault was all mine. It should never have happened."

She stared at him as if he were a stranger. He didn't look any different to her than he had a few minutes ago. The dark waving hair, the firm jaw, and the deep blue of the troubled eyes were the same. And yet he was a person she had never known.

Anger, sick and deep, poisoned her. "Charlee always said she loved sex! What whore's tricks did she use on you?" she hissed. "She could get any man she wanted—did she have to take my husband?"

"Please, Laurie . . ."

"Please *Laurie?* I think I'm entitled to know why, David."

"There's no explaining it. It was so long ago."

"A mere five years." She was shouting again, but she didn't care. "I want to know how my cousin, who claimed to be my dearest friend, got my husband to fuck her!"

"Ah, Laurie, no . . . don't."

"I'll say whatever I damn please! *Tell* me. Was she so much better in bed than I am? What exotic things did she do to you?"

"The children!" he cried, looking horrified. "This doesn't become you, Lauren."

"That's just the kind of sanctimonious, hypocritical remark I'd expect from you, David. You were such a *paragon!* I was always afraid you'd think I was oversexed if I indicated I wanted more than you gave me."

Lauren saw the shock on his face and heard herself laugh, knowing there was an edge of hysteria to it.

"Was I *insane*—to throw the two of you together!" she cried. "I thought I was *imagining* you were attracted to Charlee! I actually felt ashamed of myself, because I was jealous of her in New York! You must have been extremely amused by my naiveté." And then the tears were streaming down her cheeks. "So, Charlee had everything that was mine, after all," she sobbed. "Isn't it ironic?"

Lauren struggled to her feet, feeling the gorge rise in her throat. David moved to help her, taking her by the arms. "God, Laurie, I'm so sorry," he said.

"Please . . ." She broke away, running out of the study and racing up the stairs to her room.

In the bathroom, she leaned over the bowl and was violently sick. Waves of heat and cold swirled through her until she thought she might faint. Oblivion, she thought, panting—how she would have welcomed it. Gasping for breath, she looked up to see David holding a glass and a wet towel.

"Here, drink this," he said, sponging her face and brushing back her hair. "Come lie down. You'll feel better after you've slept."

All of her strength had deserted her. Like a child, she allowed him to guide her to the bed. After covering her with an afghan, he turned out all but one corner lamp and sat in the slipper chair.

Glancing at the bedside clock, Lauren was amazed to see that it was only half past ten. How was that possible? It should have been the blackest hours of night, she thought, as she closed her eyes.

She awakened at midnight to the sound of a window being lowered. The curtains billowed in the breeze and outside a soft summer rain was falling. Her head ached, her eyes felt puffy from crying. For a moment it was all unreal. Then she remembered, and wished she had died.

David stood looking down at her. He was still dressed,

although he had pulled off his tie and opened the neck of his shirt. She thought he had been weeping.

"Laurie, can we talk now?"

She pushed back the throw and sat up. "What is there to say?"

"A great deal!" He sat on the bed next to her. "If I explain to you how I feel—"

"How *you* feel! What about my feelings? To think, all these years I've been deceived."

David tried to put his arms around her, but she pushed him away. "Oh God, Laurie," he groaned. "I can never tell you how sorry I am. I'm begging your forgiveness. Is there nothing I can do?"

"Why Charlee, David? If it had to be someone, why her?"

"Those were crazy days, I regret them so. I was such a country boy. I seemed to be . . . I don't know . . . bewitched by her."

"Charlee bewitched everyone, including me. What *was* she, anyway?" she cried angrily. "I thought, at least, that she loved me."

"She did. And so did I."

"Please—spare me that!"

"It's true, whether you want to believe it, or not."

He took her hand and kissed it. She let it lie limp in his. "I loved you so much, David. I couldn't believe my luck when you fell in love with me. It was a dream come true. I found you on my own, and you were the only person, the only one who was ever all mine, completely mine."

"I still am all yours."

Lauren stood up, wiping her eyes with the back of her hand. "Oh, no. No more."

"What are you going to do?"

"I don't know. Maybe go away for a while."

"No! Laurie, please listen to me." She had never heard that kind of fear in his voice. "I'll spend the rest of my life making it up to you, I swear."

"You can never make it up to me." Her tears had

stopped. She felt drained of strength and feeling. "I wish you hadn't told me. Why did you?"

"Because if there's no other way we can keep John, I would want to take it before the judge. It would be difficult—and it might be in vain. But I would need your support." He took her hand again. "I couldn't go on any longer, living a lie, Laurie. I've never lied to you about anything except this. Do you believe me?"

She nodded.

"Then, can't you believe me when I tell you that you have all of my love? Can't you find it in your heart to forgive me?"

She wanted to—oh, how she wanted to.

If only she could go back to that moment earlier tonight when she had parked in the driveway and carried her briefcase to the side door. If only it were possible to erase the last four hours, as if they had never taken place.

Nothing would ever be the same again.

Chapter 45

ON THE LAST day of school Mark Bernard walked home from the bus stop, clutching his report card. He was a third grader now. In the sunshine, he squinted up the hill toward their house. Usually Johnny would be sitting on the bank at the side of the yard, looking out for him.

He was cutting across a vacant lot that had been cleared for a new house, when he saw them. Billy Quigley and two older boys, waiting for him. They were fifth graders, and one was a real tough kid, a contractor's son from out on the highway near the last stop before Oakland Hills. Mark had a sick feeling inside, but he kept on walking.

Billy and one of the boys jumped him, while the biggest one started hitting him like he was a punching bag. The blows were short and sharp, aimed at his face, and with the other two hanging onto him, he couldn't even get his hands up to defend himself. They were calling him names, and the fists kept coming. *Nigger-lover!* Punch. *Dirty Jew!* Punch. He kicked out and got some small satisfaction when his chief tormentor yelped and grabbed himself. After a minute, the boy lit into him again, and by this time, Mark was crying and choking, and bleeding a lot—

Dimly in the background, he heard screaming, "Get off Mark! Let him go! Let him go!"

He could see John sliding down the rock hillside from their back yard. It was too steep on that side, more like a cliff, where they'd cut into the hill for a retaining wall. Mark tried to shout a warning, but the boys knocked him down and one of them picked up a rock. He felt something in his nose crack and give way, and he knew he would pass out.

Later, Mark was told that if the woman hadn't come to see the lot where she was going to build her house, they could have fractured his skull. She shouted at them to stop beating him and they ran away. Then she put him in her car and drove him to Strickland Hospital.

By some good fortune, Gerald Kramer happened to be in the emergency room when Mark was brought in. He was more than surprised to learn that the battered urchin was none other than Lauren and David Bernard's son. Mark's nose was broken, both eyes were swollen shut, and he had a split lip, which required stitches. Dr. Kramer ordered X-rays and a range of tests to rule out other injuries.

After making sure that Mark was being properly tended to, Gerry put in a call for David, who was over at Duke. No doubt he was trying to pick up the pieces after last night's massacre, Kramer thought, for Dr. Bernard had been the one to take the full brunt of the trustees' displeasure.

"Are you sure you're not coming down with something, Mrs. Bernard?" Amanda asked, seeing how listless her employer acted when they were making out the shopping list for tomorrow's company dinner.

"I'll be all right," Lauren answered. Mandy knew more about her and David than anyone else, she realized, and yet, how shocked the housekeeper would have been if she were to learn the truth about them.

Lauren felt so alone. The fear of abandonment, she had always heard, was a terrifying state. She understood that now, for there was no one to talk to, no one in whom she could confide. Certainly, she wouldn't admit to any of her family or friends that David had carried on an affair with Charlotte and fathered her child!

She had been paralyzed with indecision since that awful night. After hours of trying to persuade her to forgive him, David had finally gone to bed because he had to operate the next morning. But Lauren had not shut her eyes until dawn. Ever since, she had been trying to decide what she would do.

She thought she would take the children and leave him, get a divorce . . . Wasn't it ridiculous, the things that kept her from ordering David out of the house? The people they had already invited for dinner on Saturday night; Barbara's first sleepover birthday party; the children's last week of school. How could she ruin those important childhood milestones, she asked herself. And then she would weep, as she reflected that the entire order of their lives was about to be disrupted.

The idea that David wanted to approach the judge, that it might become public knowledge, had *so* disturbed her. She could not bear the idea of a scandal! No doubt it was her Jacobson upbringing that accounted for her aversion to having the unsavory details of their lives become grist for the gossip mill. But there it was; she was a product of her upbringing—

"Mandy! Mandy—help!" John's high-pitched screams could be heard from the yard.

"Hmmm, sounds like trouble," Amanda said mildly. "I don't like him staying out there alone, but I thought Mark would be along by now."

As she followed Amanda to the back porch, Lauren could hear Johnny weeping and Amanda's soothing voice. "What is it, honey? Tell Mandy all about it. My, where did y'all get so dirty?"

When they were able to calm him down long enough to make some sense out of what he was saying, Amanda cleaned the scrapes on his legs while Lauren began making telephone calls. Soon she was speeding over to Strickland Hospital, to find David, hollow-eyed and haggard, waiting for her in the emergency room.

"Where's Mark? What's wrong with him?" she cried.

"They've already taken him upstairs. I'm on my way up there."

Lauren sat in the waiting room, numbed by shock, wondering what else could possibly go wrong. In the past five days the foundations of her marriage had crumbled, her lovely memories of Charlotte had been destroyed forever, and now her beloved Mark had been attacked by bullies because of David's insane crusade!

Oh, but Mark looked a *sight* when they allowed her to see him! A little boy with his nose swollen twice its size, blackened eyes, stitches, and bruises all over. If she could just get her hands on those boys, she'd like to break their necks, beat them within an inch of their lives. She was going to see a lawyer about this, and they would *sue* the Quigleys, those Bible-thumping bigots! Children learned hate from their parents—they surely weren't born hating.

They sent her down the hall while the neurologists finished examining Mark. If there were undisclosed head or spinal injuries, what then? Despite their differences, as long as David was there, she was reassured.

She was seated in the lounge, feeling miserable and trying to control her anxiety, when Gretchen arrived, breathless. "Laurie, I came the minute I knew."

"How did you ever hear so soon?"

"It's all over town. The woman who brought Mark to the hospital owns the new gift shop."

She was glad Gretch was there when David came out again. It made it easier for them to talk around each other, and Gretchen would assume their strangeness was because they were upset about Mark. Except for those few minutes when she arrived at the hospital, she hadn't spoken to him for days. David had stayed out very late last night. Not caring where he was, she had been asleep when he came in, and he had already left for the hospital when she woke up this morning.

After ten years of marriage, Lauren could read his moods just from the outline of his posture. The sadness in him reached into the frozen regions of her heart. "Mark's going to be all right," he said, and they were the sweetest words she had ever heard. "They want to keep him here for observation for a couple of days. I'll stay with him tonight."

There had been another time, five years ago, when they had kept a vigil over Mark in the hospital. She recalled on that occasion that David had been unreachable when their son was near death. Now she knew it was because he had been with Charlotte! She closed her eyes to shut out the sight of him and when she opened them, he had disappeared.

"I feel awful about David, Laurie," said Gretchen. "He looks just terrible. I guess he's really going through hell."

Lauren blanched. "Wha—what do you mean?" Had David actually told Ralph and Gretchen about them? Did he have so little sense of *decency?*

"You don't know?" Gretchen looked incredulous.

"I'm . . . not sure what you're talking about."

"The Strickland board, of course."

"The board?" She was in confusion. "I guess I haven't heard. What happened?"

"I can't believe you don't know. They turned him down! Flat. They held the meeting last night. It was in today's newspaper. You mean, he really hasn't told you?"

Too stunned to pretend, Lauren shook her head. "No—I—I'd forgotten about the meeting. I guess he didn't feel like talking about it."

"They asked for his resignation."

"Oh, my God."

"He must not have wanted to worry you. I'm really sorry, Laur. I wish I hadn't been the one to break the news."

Why did it hurt so? Why was her heart aching for him? Compared to everything else, it hardly seemed to matter. And yet, she knew how important it was to him, how dearly he loved this hospital and the Russell Clinic. Next to his family, this was his life—

His family! How much could we have meant to him, if he was willing to jeopardize everything we had together?

Her thoughts were going in circles. If only she could make up her mind what to do. To take the children and leave David? To order him to move out? To keep on living together, knowing he had been unfaithful to her?

"Are you all right, Laurie?" Gretchen was looking at her with concern.

"Ohh—I—yes, I'm fine. This has just been a terrible day. I'm still a little dazed."

"Maybe I should take you home. It's getting late. Won't Amanda be worried?"

"David called to reassure her. But, you're right, I should go home." She stood up and embraced Gretchen. "Don't worry, I'm perfectly all right to drive. Thanks so much for coming, Gretch. You're a wonderful friend."

Before she left the hospital, she went to say goodnight to Mark. They had given him a sedative to make him sleep and David was sitting at the bedside, holding his hand and looking down at his bruised face with stricken eyes.

"If he had been killed, it would have been my fault," he said in a low voice, when she came into the room.

"But he wasn't killed, and he'll soon be good as new."

"You're not even blaming me?"

She shook her head. "You're not responsible for the sick minds whose children would do this," she answered. "Gretchen told me about the board's decision. I'm really sorry."

He stood up then, and came to her, holding her by the shoulders. "I seem not to be able to do anything right. I don't mind for myself, Laurie, but when it brings harm to my wife and children, the people I love . . ." His voice broke, and she had all she could do to prevent herself from taking him in her arms.

"They had no right to ask for your resignation."

He shook his head. "I would have resigned anyway. I couldn't stay when they refused to budge."

"What about the other men?"

"They're fine. Quigley only wanted my head, fortunately. I've done enough damage by hurting my own family—but not any more!"

"What you did was *right,* David! Don't let them win by changing you."

For the first time since that awful night, there was hope in his eyes when he looked at her. "You're all I have, you and the children. I know I don't deserve your love, but if I don't have that, I don't care about the rest."

Lauren did not answer. She bent over to kiss Mark on top of his head. "Good night, David. If Mark wakes up, tell him I'll be here in the morning."

* * *

Barbara and John were in bed when she reached home. Amanda was staying over and had kept her dinner warm. "I'll just go kiss them good night first, Mandy."

"I let Johnny sleep in Mark's room tonight, Mrs. Bernard," said Amanda. "He seemed to be less upset in there."

Babs was asleep, but John was lying awake. "Where's Mark?"

"He's sleeping at the hospital tonight. Daddy's staying with him." Your daddy.

"Is Mark going to die?" he asked, on the verge of tears.

"No, Johnny! He's going to be just fine. I expect he'll be home day after tomorrow." Poor child, he probably thinks everyone who goes into a hospital dies, like his mother. "Mark just got a little banged up and they put some bandages on him."

"Those bad boys hurt him."

"That's right." She wished he hadn't been the one to see it. John had just about gotten over his night terrors. "But they'll be punished and they'll never do it again."

"I'm gonna beat them up!"

Lauren laughed, hugging him. "Okay, but why don't you wait until you're a little older." She kissed him and tucked the blanket around him. "Night-night, John. Sweet dreams."

"Night, Mommy Laurie."

He was the sweetest child! She couldn't help loving him. He was a little ray of sunshine in the house, and if he had never been born—if he hadn't been born, she would never have known.

What would happen now with John, she wondered, as she forced herself to eat the dinner Amanda had prepared. If she and David were divorced, who would get custody of him? Well, naturally Lauren would. That is, if he wasn't given to Blanche. They always gave the wife custody of the children, and in addition, Lauren was a blood relative . . . Ha! Blood relative! Wasn't that a laugh? David was his *father,* for God's sake!

David, the adulterer, had fathered that adorable child

who was sleeping upstairs in her son's bedroom. Fathered him in an act of love with her cousin Charlotte Lee. Her eyes closed as she tried to black out the picture of David making love to Charlee. A wave of nausea came over her and she pushed the plate away.

"You're not eating a thing, Mrs. Bernard," Amanda chided her.

"I'm sorry, Mandy. It's delicious, but I'm just too upset to eat any more."

"Your baby's going to be all right, Mrs. Bernard. Little boys get into fights now and then."

"Oh, I know he is, Mandy. It's just been a rather difficult time lately."

"I understand. Don't you worry, honey. Everything's going to be fine for Dr. Bernard, too. We're praying for him. The Lord always looks after good people."

Lauren realized that Amanda certainly would have heard about David's defeat by the board of Strickland Hospital. All of the blacks in town must know what he had tried to do and what had happened as a result of it. Amanda thought Lauren was upset about David being fired by the hospital.

"I'm not worried about Dr. Bernard. He can always go into private practice." She stood up. "I'm worn out. I think I'll take a bath now and go to bed. Thank you for everything, Mandy."

"Good night, Mrs. Bernard. God bless you."

Lauren bathed and got into bed, but her mind would not let her rest. Late into the night, she lay awake, wondering what would become of them.

Mark came home from the hospital looking like a wounded veteran, with his eyes still bruised and his nose splinted.

"He may have a permanent bump there," David told Lauren, and she lamented his chiseled nose. "Well, at least he isn't a girl," she said, not even minding her predictably Jacobson response.

There were two optimistic developments that week. Drs. Stroud, Kramer, Reynolds, and Greenberg resigned from the Strickland staff in protest and invited David to join them in a group practice. They would all keep their appointments at the Russell Clinic, which, Tom Sayles announced, would in the near future become attached to the proposed Memorial Hospital to be constructed in Chapel Hill. At long last, a four-year School of Medicine was about to become a reality at the University of North Carolina at Chapel Hill—and David would eventually be joining Tom in its Division of Orthopaedics. Meanwhile, he had been assured by the dean that he could continue as a faculty member at Duke . . .

Mark was enjoying his celebrity. Everyone they knew came to see him and brought presents. By the end of the week, his stitches had been removed, his nose splint replaced with a smaller dressing, and he was beginning to look normal again. John was his constant devoted slave, and Mark used him to full advantage. From a daybed on the screened porch, he directed Johnny to bring him an apple from the refrigerator, a cupcake from the pantry, his baseball cards from the bedroom, his catcher's mitt from the basement playroom, until Lauren had to put a stop to it, when she spied the short legs hurrying up the stairs for the tenth time.

She and David were living under a flag of truce, but it was a terrible strain. Therefore, by the following Friday she almost welcomed Philip's call asking when she would be coming to Randolph Springs to help him dispose of the contents of the house on Shadow Mountain.

"Jeanette will work with me on the inventory, Laurie, but Charlee left specific instructions that only you are entitled to go through her personal property."

"Are you sure we should go in there before the will is settled?" she asked, suddenly uneasy at the idea of touching Charlotte's possessions or of seeing the house again.

"Yes, because in any case, the property will be sold and the furnishings will have to be appraised. I've been in touch with the lawyers and they've given me permission to take an inventory."

"All right, Phil, I'll be there on Monday," she promised. Maybe if she got away from home, she would be able to come to some decisions.

* * *

She dreamed she was standing at the edge of a deep pit, surrounded by veiled figures in the black of mourning. Amid the sound of keening, clouds and darkness swirled around her. Wrapped in lengths of white linen, she struggled to bend her head forward, and found she was looking into her own grave.

Her convulsive sobs awakened her before the vision faded. David's arms were around her and his body pressed against hers in need. He smothered her with impassioned kisses, pushing her down with his greater strength and pulling off her nightgown. There was an alien roughness to his familiar touch and she was angry to find herself responding to being taken by force. She fought against him, trying to suppress the rising tide of erotic feeling that overcame her. David knew her body as a conductor knows the score of a symphony, and he used that knowledge now to bring her to a peak of excitement. Her feeble protests sank before a flood of desire. As he took possession of her, she ceased to struggle, yielding to the pure sensuality of him.

When their passion was spent, he tenderly kissed her cheeks where the tears had dried. "Don't you see, darling?" he whispered. "Nothing can destroy our love for each other."

Although her body knew satisfaction, her inner anguish persisted—for Charlee had been there in the bed with them. Lauren heaved a deep breath. "That was *sex,* David—not love!"

In the darkness, she sensed his shock. She knew she had deeply wounded him, but she was determined she would not give in. If he had won the physical contest, then she would defeat him with her coldness. Pushing him away, she abruptly rose and went into the bathroom. In the shower, she soaped herself thoroughly, then stood under the stream of water with closed eyes. After toweling herself dry, she put on a pair of slacks and a cotton shirt, and slipped into loafers.

That afternoon she had brought a suitcase down from

the attic in anticipation of her trip to Randolph Springs. Setting it on the bench, she began to pack.

"What are you doing?"

David was standing in the doorway watching her, looking dazed and miserable.

"I'm going to Randolph."

"*Tonight*—at this hour?"

"Why not? I couldn't possibly go back to sleep now."

"You can't do this, Laurie."

"I can do any damn thing I please!"

He watched her throw underwear and blouses into the case. "When are you planning to come home?"

"I honestly don't know, David. Perhaps not for a while."

"Laurie—please don't leave tonight. I don't understand what's come over you."

"What's come over *me!*" she cried. "You really think I'm just going to go on with our marriage as before, don't you? Forget everything, forget that you and Charlee both betrayed me!"

"I know you can't forget," he answered quietly. "But I hoped you might find it in your heart to understand, and to forgive."

"What is there to understand, David? If it had been anyone but Charlee, maybe I could forgive you. I realize that men in wartime, away from their wives, have physical needs. If it had been a girl in England, a nurse in the hospital, or even a prostitute—" She shook her head impatiently, not wanting to start crying again. "—but my *own cousin!*" Angrily, she pulled out a drawer, almost spilling its contents. "Why did she need *you*, anyway? She had Bruce—the handsomest man I ever saw! Wasn't he enough for her? Why couldn't she leave you alone?"

David looked away, struggling to hold back the words. And then he said, "The problem was, she did not have Bruce. They had a miserable marriage."

Her head jerked up. "A lot you know about it! Just because they fought, doesn't mean they weren't in love."

He shook his head. "She may have been in love with him, but—"

She snapped the suitcase shut, set it on the floor and turned to face him. "Are you trying to tell me Bruce Fields had another woman? I don't believe that."

"Not another woman . . ." He stopped. "Look, Laurie, this is something I don't want to talk about. They're both dead. What's done is done."

"It's *our lives* we're talking about, David! Our children's lives. If I couldn't trust Charlee—if I can't trust you—how can I believe in anything? I have to *understand*, if I'm going to know what to do."

David sighed with resignation. "Bruce and Charlotte did not have a normal marriage. Bruce had . . . other interests." He stopped. "Laurie, I feel I have no right to be telling you this."

"*Other* interests?" Her hand flew to her mouth. "You don't mean . . . men?"

Slowly David nodded.

Why was it such a shock to her? Certainly she knew about such things, even with her sheltered upbringing. Especially since coming to Chapel Hill. There were certain men on the campus who were not married and who were rumored to be 'unnatural.' But *Bruce!* Tall, athletic, masculine. Handsome and fawned over by women.

"Poor Charlee . . . but, if she knew that, why did they remain married?"

"I doubt that they would have, if he had come home from the war. Charlotte thought she could make it work—at least in the beginning of their marriage. I think it must have been very damaging to her ego when she realized her husband preferred a man to her—you see, she only felt threatened by one man in particular, a friend who was always with him."

Her brow wrinkled, remembering. "Oh, my God," she gasped. "Nick! Nicholas de Georgenov."

"Yes."

Lauren recalled Charlee mentioning that Nicholas had died in France during the war. "Charlee once told me that Bruce's family, especially Malcolm, disliked Nick, from the days the boys were at Princeton together." She shuddered. It was all so sordid, and yet—"I feel sorry for Bruce. It can't have been easy for him."

"Bruce was a terribly lonely and unhappy man," said David. "He wasn't a bad sort. I grew to like him in London during the few months we knew each other." His face contorted. "All this misery, Laurie! Please, darling, can't we try to get over this?"

"I feel so betrayed, David. It still doesn't explain Charlee. Was she in love with you?"

He threw back his head with a short, bitter laugh. "I was fool enough to think so for a few weeks. But no, not for a minute did she love me."

"Then it was just sex?"

"Partly, I suppose," he admitted. "She was bored, I was there. I don't pretend to understand it. But I believe Charlotte wanted a child. She had told Bruce she would like to adopt a war orphan, and he refused. So, she decided to become pregnant. If I hadn't been around, it would have been someone else."

I was jealous . . . always wanted whatever you had . . . forgive me, Laurie . . . the closest I could come to being you.

"No," she said. "It wouldn't have been anyone else. Charlee wanted *you* to father her child. For some unexplainable reason, the fact that you were my husband made you the one she wanted."

David came over to her and there were tears in his eyes. "Don't leave me, Laurie. Let me make it up to you." He pulled her into his arms. "Am I to pay all my life for a few weeks that I would give anything to undo? Whatever you want, I'll do it. I love that little boy, but I would even give up John if I thought it would make a difference."

"I'm so confused, I don't know what I want. I have to get away, David. Please let go of me."

There was a defeated slope to his shoulders. "It will seem strange to Amanda and everyone, when you're not here in the morning."

"You can explain that I left earlier than expected."

"The children—"

"They'll be all right with you. After all, you're their father." She picked up her suitcase. "All three of them."

"But what shall I tell them?"

"Tell them . . . Tell them that I love them."

She had never driven this far on a highway alone at night. Traveling through the dark, silent towns of the Piedmont to the foothills, she felt free. By the time she began the ascent into the mountains, there was a hint of morning in the eastern sky. Steadily she climbed along the serpentine road, locked in by forests on either side. It was a treacherous route, particularly in darkness, but instead of fear, Lauren experienced a sense of release.

After a series of tunnels, the road began to descend. As she started down the last decline to Randolph Springs, the soft glow of dawn broke through the morning mist over Shadow Mountain.

Chapter 46

June 1948

DRIVING THROUGH A patch of ground fog, Lauren almost missed the turn-off to Shadow Mountain Drive. When she came to the twin gateposts, she gripped the steering wheel, steeling herself against a fresh onslaught of sorrow.

As the automobile passed a profusion of dogwoods and crape myrtles, a cloud of quails startled from the underbrush. Silent and deserted, in the morning mist the house appeared to be floating on a sea of emerald green. With windows shuttered and doors locked against intruders, it projected an air of eternal autumn, like a monument to a lost civilization.

Here, in this leafy sanctuary, she had spent the happiest days of her girlhood, dreaming the moons of an impossible tomorrow. Under shaded verandas entrapped in sweet-smelling vines, she had learned the graciousness of the Southern way of life. And here had begun the treachery that had caused the brightness to shatter into a thousand dark realities.

From the terrace, Lauren gazed across the sloping lawns. Now that she had arrived, the house was working its charm on her. Closing her eyes, she allowed herself to imagine the gentle rhythms she had known there . . . Children's laughter ringing through the gardens . . . Charlee's quick footsteps clattering across the veranda on her way to the stables . . . Lifting her head expectantly, she inhaled the fragrance of magnolias and honeysuckles, longing for just one moment to recapture all that this place had meant to her.

Always she had loved it here, wishing the beautiful old mansion could be truly hers. During all the happy years, it had seemed an enchanted castle, safe and secluded. Certain she belonged, as surely a daughter of this house as Charlotte Lee, she had expected it would always be there as a refuge. But instead, it had become a symbol of her heartbreak and disillusion.

Lauren's eyes darkened at the remembrance of why she had come. She turned the key, pushing open the great front door. The interior was hushed and gloomy, the furniture draped in muslin, waiting to pass into other hands. Despite her bitterness, she rebelled at the thought of strangers claiming all this.

Climbing the graceful staircase, for a moment she imagined Charlee would be at the top to say, "It never happened, Laurie! There's been a dreadful misunderstanding." But silence greeted her in the upper hall, where sunlight filtered through the blinds, catching motes of dust in the stale air.

At the threshold of Charlotte's bedroom, Lauren paused with her hand on the knob, knowing she still had the right to walk away. Would it not be better to leave the past undisturbed and banished to these shrouded rooms? Let Philip dispose of it all without her.

She could hear Charlee's voice, begging, "Please say you'll go, Laurie . . . no one else, only you. Promise me . . . *promise!*" And she had promised. But that was before she had known the truth.

Slowly she opened the door and entered the dim chamber, throwing wide the curtains to let in daylight. Steamer trunks and boxes lined one wall, just as Charlee had left them.

"Some of it is family stuff, Laurie, but the bulk was shipped down from New York when Charlee thought she was coming back here to live," Philip had explained, handing her an envelope marked with Charlotte's familiar, flamboyant scrawl. "Her instructions—"

"Thank you, Phil. I'd rather go over there alone the

first time, if you don't mind.'' Philip had nodded, understanding how she would feel.

Helplessly, Lauren looked around her. It was a monstrous task. She had no idea where to begin.

Kneeling on the floor, she raised the lid of a satin-lined rosewood dress case. Tenderly, she pushed aside the layers of tissue, fingering the delicate skin and lace of the carefully preserved wedding gown that had graced two brides, and would never be worn again.

To think that ten years ago she had been married in this dress! If she had known then what lay ahead—but maybe it was better not to know, or else no one would ever take a chance on love. Overwhelmed with memories, Lauren buried her face in the billows of ivory silk.

She had finally finished sorting, labeling and discarding the amazing quantity of clothing, accessories, and trivia that Charlotte had accumulated. This pile for the Mission Home Thrift Shop, that for the Jewish Charities, another for the Salvation Army. An assortment of cashmere sweater sets with price tags still attached went to Joanna's daughters. Handbeaded evening bags, Victorian and Art Deco costume jewelry, silk scarves from France, Italian kid gloves still in their cellophane envelopes, had been distributed among the various young cousins.

Jeanette had been delighted with the tweed coat and suit ensembles, the many elegant cocktail dresses and evening gowns, and the furs. ''But why are you giving everything to me, Laurie? I'm sure you can have some of these altered to fit you.'' Let Jeanette think what she would, Lauren knew she could not possibly wear anything that had belonged to Charlotte.

A surprise had been awaiting her on the first morning. After allowing her to arrive alone, Philip had come over to Shadow Mountain Drive to show her the room where she used to stay. It was filled with a staggering number of files in cartons, all carefully labeled in Charlotte's hand.

''You're to go through everything, Laurie, and decide what to do with it.'' Noting her dismay, he said, ''I know it's an enormous assignment. I'd be happy to help, but . . .''

"I know, Phil," she sighed. "She told me before she died."

Death had caught Charlee mid-stride. She had planned for a more orderly departure, but her strength had given out before she was halfway through her blueprint of organization. As Lauren began to sort through the boxes, which were numbered in sequence, it became clear that her cousin had intended to leave a record of her life, beginning with her heritage. Her last act had been to assemble a storehouse of family relics in leatherbound albums.

The detritus of generations was there. Travel documents in Russian and German, immigration papers, marriage certificates, and worthless deeds to old properties. As the hours passed, despite her reluctance, Lauren was caught up in curiosity and nostalgia. She smiled fondly at the portraits of proud new Americans in dark vested suits and stiff bengaline dresses; arched an eyebrow in ironic salute to gallant Georgia grays, still tall and undefeated. They could only have been Max's kin.

There was an orderly, chronological progression to the page after page of family photographs. Lauren recognized most of them. Pictures of Charlee as a baby, Charlee with her parents, with her nurse, and with Lauren. There were countless snapshots of the two cousins growing up—one in particular that caught her eye, the occasion lost in memory, but they must have been riding, for they were wearing boots and britches. They had been closer than sisters then, totally dependent on each other for affection and friendship. When had it begun to go wrong, she wondered sadly. Surely there had been signs along the way.

More photo albums, and with each, Lauren relived a part of the past. Randolph Academy . . . the Great Road Show . . . the Alexander School. With tar-filled eyes she poured over poses of a vibrant and beautiful Charlotte, at dances and outings, surrounded by attentive beaux; Charlee on a yacht in Palm Beach; with Blanche at Fair Fields.

A lifetime . . . an entire lifetime in pictures.

And then prince charming entered the scene. Handsome Bruce, the perfect match. What irony! Now they were together in all the photos. Charlee and Bruce engaged, Charlee and Bruce at various prenuptial parties in Randolph Springs. Two entire books were devoted solely to photographs of the magnificent wedding.

The last album was incomplete. There were perhaps two or three dozen prints of Charlee and Bruce on their honeymoon: aboard the Normandie, at the Eiffel Tower, in Florence, and on the Riviera. And then the photographic record abruptly stopped, as if the archivist had suddenly been called away.

As Lauren turned the empty pages, she discovered one large print slipped in between the back leaves. Taken in front of the casino at Monte Carlo, it caught Charlee looking svelte in a white linen pants outfit, standing between Bruce and another dark, elegant young man whom Lauren recognized as Nicholas de Georgenov.

They must have seen him on their honeymoon, then—for the picture was dated August 1936. "Oh, Charlee . . . did it start even then? Is that when you found out?" she whispered softly.

After so many days, she was beginning to tire. By now she was able to enter the house in the morning and spend all day among the accoutrements of Charlotte's life without shedding tears. The files were of little consequence, and she was inclined to dump them in the rubbish. Who would know?

But Philip had cautioned her to examine everything thoroughly. "It's unlikely, but there could be stocks or valuable papers in there, Laurie. That's why Charlee didn't discard them in New York." And, in fact, in one folder Lauren found several war bonds. That gave her pause and she slowed down, realizing it was necessary to scrutinize everything.

This must be what comes of having a personal secretary, she thought. Endless papers. Social calendars, guest lists with menus, hundreds of invitations, all carefully arranged in folders. Bruce had been a saver. Meticulously, he had held on to every telephone bill, gas and electric statement, each record of servants' salaries. There were letters from his various boards and alumni associations, receipted statements from his clubs.

It struck Lauren that there was not a single picture or memento of George Stearns in the entire collection, as if Charlotte had wished any trace of him expunged from the record of her life. There were boxes and boxes of Bruce, though, and she wondered why Charlee had hung on to every reminder of the husband she no longer adored. It puzzled her.

Lauren had been staying with Philip and Jeanette, while spending most of each day at Shadow Mountain. "I had them connect the phone over there, Laurie," Philip told her at breakfast on Friday morning. "I didn't realize it wasn't working until I tried to call you yesterday. It's not safe for a woman to be alone in that big place without a telephone."

"You're a true Jacobson, Phil," she laughed. "I've been there all week and nothing has happened to me yet."

Lauren was nearing the end of her task. She had kept her promise to Charlee, but truthfully there was no item that could not have been seen by another person. Nothing so personal or revealing as to cause embarrassment to anyone, dead or alive. The files could be incinerated. As for the rest, she wanted none of it, except for the pictures, which Johnny would someday like to have.

She was leafing through a carton labeled #29 Bruce-Personal Files," when she came upon a cache of letters all addressed in the same hand and tied with silver cord. There were no return addresses on the envelopes, which bore postmarks from various cities—San Francisco, Boston, New Orleans . . . Paris, London, Geneva. In among them was a worn, folded card with a carelessly penned message, "Have a drink on me. N." It was engraved with the name of Nicholas Alexander P.F. de Georgenov.

Feeling like a trespasser, Lauren glanced through the first of the letters, dated 27 September 1936. It appeared to be a peculiarly intimate correspondence, and it was signed "Nick." With growing trepidation, she opened the next letter . . . and the next.

And by the time she had read all of them, Lauren at last understood the magnitude of Charlee's unhappiness.

* * *

Blinking back tears, Lauren closed the final storage carton and gathered the entire packet of papers. Gently she shut the bedroom door and descended the stairway. She walked past the closed paneled doors of the living room, the large dining room, and the library, past the music room and the sun parlors, to the rear hallway that led to Max's study. This had been her uncle's private domain and she had seldom had occasion to enter his retreat.

Seated in a burgundy leather chair, Lauren thought about the first time she had visited New York, recalling the strangeness of Nicholas and how Charlotte had objected to his presence. And yet, Lauren remembered, he was always around—often alone with Bruce whenever her cousin called home while visiting in Randolph Springs. After those calls, Charlee would be moody, passing cryptic comments—remarks that now made tragic sense to Lauren.

No wonder Bruce's father had hated his son's friend. For Lauren suddenly saw with utter clarity that Malcolm Fields had known what Nicholas was to his son, even before Bruce had married Charlotte. How cruel and cynical of Malcolm to have encouraged the wedding. And for Bruce to threaten to expose Charlee's affairs if she sued for divorce! For, judging by the contents of Nick's letters, Bruce had related everything to his lover: "Good going, buddy! Sounds like we have C. exactly where we want her, *in flagrante delicto . . .*" Nicholas had written in one correspondence.

It wasn't fair, it wasn't fair! Charlee had never had a chance at happiness. Whatever else she had done, she hadn't deserved to be denied the joys of marriage and children . . . Lauren's eyes grew moist with unshed tears and a hardness within her breast began to ease. *Oh, Charlee . . . I do understand what you went through.*

Max's study retained the aroma of wood and whiskey, leather and tobacco. Her glance swept the room, taking in the familiar framed family portraits, still in place. So many memories!

The telephone on the carved cherrywood desk seemed to beckon her. How she yearned to hear David's voice.

Last night when she had returned to Philip and Jeanette's house, another message from him awaited her. All week long, avoiding the question in their eyes, she had not answered any of his calls. Long into the nights since coming to Randolph Springs, Lauren had sat by the bedroom window, examining her innermost feelings, wondering what she would do.

At first, her pride had told her to divorce David for his betrayal. But she found it wasn't as simple as that. The thought of the empty years stretching ahead without him, left her feeling cold and abandoned. She didn't *want* to be a woman alone! Alone with her children.

And what about Johnny? They couldn't just wait for the court to come to a decision. What if she agreed for David to go to the judge and admit that he was John's father—better still, if they went together!

Through the French doors, she looked down the terraced steps to the rose garden. Beyond, in the grassy glen, she could see the twin magnolia trees that ten years ago had formed the canopy for her wedding ceremony. Her heart felt squeezed as she thought of David. How could she plan a future without him? Pressing a fist against her mouth, she tried to summon anger and outrage, but instead she was filled with longing. No matter what happened, she knew she still loved David. She was almost sick with love for him! Whether she left him or not, she would always love him.

Taking up the stack of letters from Bruce's file, Lauren turned them over and over. She could not believe a judge would take a child away from his real father. Especially with the evidence she held in her hands.

She lifted the telephone receiver.

David answered on the first ring. "I've been trying to reach you," he said in a distracted voice. In the background she could hear the children shouting. "You haven't returned any of my calls. I was worried about you."

"You would have heard if anything was wrong."

"I suppose so—quiet, Babs, I can't hear Mommy. Take that fork away from John before he hurts someone."

"David, I . . . How are the children?"

"Behaving like little monsters. I don't think I can hold out much longer without you."

"Where's Amanda?"

"She had to go to a funeral today." There was a commotion in the background and she heard a scream. "Hey, you kids, stop that!" shouted David. "Oh hell, John's crying—hold on a minute." He was back in a few seconds. "Laurie, will you say hello to him?"

"Mark took my mitt away," he wailed.

"Don't cry, Johnny. He'll give it back."

"Where did you go?" he asked, still sniffing.

"I had to come to Randolph Springs."

"Ohh . . . are you in heaven with my other mommy?"

There was a tightness in her chest. "No, darling. I'll be home soon, I promise you."

"She's coming home," she heard him say. Then David told the children to go into the other room.

"Laurie," he said, when it was quiet, "is it true? Are you really coming home?"

"Yes, it's true."

"Thank God. You'll never know how awful it's been without you."

She had to say it quickly before she lost her courage. "David, we have to go to the judge and explain to him—"

"Wait," he interrupted. "I have something to tell you."

"No, you must listen! We've got to inform the judge that you're John's father. I've found some letters that belonged to Bruce, and I'm sure that once he reads them, there won't be any question about custody."

There was a stunned silence at the other end, and when David spoke, his voice was choked. "Laurie, I—I was trying to tell you. Steve Burns is meeting with the other lawyer next week. He says they're going to drop the suit. Adele Fields has threatened to expose George for the scoundrel he is, and Norma, of all people, is supporting her."

"David, that's wonderful news! But what about Blanche?"

"Blanche is pregnant and she doesn't see how she can possibly handle four kids." He lowered his voice. "You really would have done that, Laurie? Let me put you and the children through—"

"Yes, if it was the only way we could have kept John."

His voice trembled as he said, "I don't deserve you, darling, but I love you. And I need you so much."

For a moment she held her breath. "I need you, too."

Lauren knelt at the fireplace to open the flue. She placed the letters on the grating and touched a match to them. Slowly the flames crept along the first envelope, with a flickering yellow light. Lines of brilliant orange formed where the edges curled and turned to ash, then the pyre blazed golden and bright with a brave blue center. She stared at the flames, warmed by the pain of love.

Yesterday at the Mission Home, she had sat at her mother's bedside, holding her hand, regarding with pity the wasted body and vacant, forever shadowed mind. This was the woman who had given her life . . . the woman who had taught her to withhold love. Too well she had learned that lesson, thought Lauren. If she had shown David the love he needed, perhaps he would not have sought it elsewhere. And if his love belonged to her now, did it matter that Charlee had once known his body?

The heavy door closed behind her. For the last time, she walked down the broad front steps. At the end of the driveway, she paused and turned toward the house, bidding a silent farewell. It had never really belonged to them. They were wayfarers, just passing through.

It was a short drive to the cemetery. She walked among the gravestones to the place where Charlotte lay. "I forgive you, Charlee," she whispered. A sad smile touched her lips. "You knew I would, didn't you? You meant for me to find those letters. It all worked out, just the way you planned . . .

"I promise we'll take care of John. We'll love him and

give him a happy home. And he'll never know your secret—at least, not until he's old enough to understand."

Somewhere a bird was singing. The sky was a clear, bright, startling blue. It was a Charlee day.

With one last look at Shadow Mountain, Lauren drove away from Randolph Springs.

Winner of the *Romantic Times* Lifetime
Achievement Award for Love and Laughter

CAUGHT IN THE ACT

75778-8/$4.50 US/$5.50 Can

In a Tudor England teeming with intrigues and absurdities, daring thief of hearts and an innocent, yet ingenious, youn beauty will be undone by rapturous, irresistible love.

BEHIND CLOSED DOORS

75779-6/$4.99 US/$5.99 Can

A sheltered English rose and virile "Viking" nobleman ar drawn together by reckless passion—surrendering to th forbidden ecstasy of soul-searing love.

And Coming Soon

MY WARRIOR'S HEART

76771-6/$4.99 US/$5.99 Can

Only by conquering the spirited woman whose breathtaking beauty haunts his dreams can Jorund win the respect of his people...and quench the searing flames of his desire.